Perfect Weddings

A romantic comedy by
Lynda Renham

About the Author

Lynda Renham writes romantic comedy novels. Lynda's novels are popular, refreshingly witty, fast paced and with a strong romantic theme. She lives in Oxford UK and when not writing Lynda can usually be found wasting her time on Facebook.

'Lynda Renham is right up there with chick-lit royalty! I'm not talking princess either, for me, the Queen of Chick-lit.' – Booketta Book Blog.

Lynda is author of the best-selling romantic comedy novels including *Croissants and Jam, Coconuts and Wonderbras, Confessions of a Chocoholic, Pink Wellies and Flat Caps, It Had To be You, Rory's Proposal, Fudge Berries and Frogs Knickers, Fifty Shades of Roxie Brown* and *The Dog's Bollocks*.

Lynda Renham

The right of Lynda Renham to be identified as the author of the work has been asserted by her in accordance with the Copyright, Designs and Patents Act 1988.

ISBN 978-0-9934026-2-3
first edition

Cover Illustration by Gracie Klumpp
www.gracieklumpp.com

Printed for Raucous Publishing in Great Britain by
4edge Limited

Chapter One

Don't you just hate wedding jitters? Maybe you don't. Perhaps your big day hasn't come yet but trust me, it will. If I, Amy Fisher, can get married then anyone can. I've waited one year, three months and twelve days for my big day; that's one year, three months and twelve days from the moment Greg proposed to me in the Little Chef. Yes I know, it isn't the most romantic of places, but it was Valentine's Day, so that makes everything all right. Although, to be strictly honest, it was me that proposed to him, but I am sure Greg would have done if I hadn't got in first. You know what men are like, they just need a little push sometimes don't they? We'd been on our way back from White Hart Lane and stopped at the Little Chef. Did I mention that Greg likes football? Does the Pope pray? Well, that's how obsessed Greg is with football. It's not just a game for him, it's a religion. I think if Greg could marry Tottenham Hotspur instead of me, he would. So, there we were, tucking into our all-day breakfast when Greg looked over his grilled tomato, gazed into my eyes, and said,

'You're the perfect girl for me.'

His words had sent a tingle down my spine. We'd been together for nine months and I just knew Greg was my Mr Right. I loved everything about him from his receding hairline to his bouncy walk. So, while still buzzing from our Tottenham Hotspur win, I asked him, right there, right then, in the Little Chef, to marry me. He looked so handsome in his Tottenham shirt that I just couldn't help myself. There was a heart-stopping moment when he hesitated, but then he said yes. That was one year, three months and twelve days ago. The time has flown by in a flurry of wedding magazines, dress fittings, reception venues, guest lists, seating plans, wedding cakes and of course football. And now the day is here. My stomach gurgles with excitement and Mum fumbles in her bag for the Windeze.

'Maybe pop a couple,' she suggests. 'Better safe than sorry, after all, we want a packed church don't we?'

I glance at a box of Thorntons chocolates that sit on the dressing table. One white chocolate truffle won't do any harm will it?

'I'm hungry,' I say. 'I didn't have breakfast.'

'How can you think about food today of all days?' scolds Mum.

I'm not thinking about food, I'm just thinking about chocolate. I've never been so nervous in my life and chocolate is the answer to all ills isn't it?

'Just one,' I say. 'One won't hurt, will it?'

She sighs and opens the box. I devour the white chocolate truffle and then feel myself drawn to the Hazelnut Heaven, but Mum slams the lid down and puts the box back on the dressing table.

'I'll straighten your veil,' she says nervously.

I look at my reflection in the wardrobe mirror. I can't believe I'm standing in my wedding dress. My hair hangs in a perfect short bob with a pretty slide clipping back one side so my diamante earrings can be seen. I'd gone for the natural look. There is nothing worse than an over made-up bride is there? I'd applied a small amount of blusher to my cheeks and a pink tint onto my lips with just a light brush of mascara to my lashes. I'm blessed with a clear, fair complexion and natural brown wavy hair. I'm not beautiful or anything but I think I'm reasonably attractive.

'You look stunning,' says Mum.

'You don't think I look a bit chubby?' I ask, swallowing the white chocolate truffle.

'Chubby?' says Mum, just a little too loudly. 'Of course not, you've lost loads of weight.'

That's true. I did lose a lot of weight. The only problem is I put it on again at the food tasting for the reception. At least that was the start; the diet went pear-shaped after that. Still, I can lose it again after the honeymoon can't I? After all, Greg loves me for who I am. Mum adjusts the veil while I fiddle with the pearls around my neck. The dress looks terrific. It had cost a fortune but it was worth every penny. I'd been dreaming of this since I was a child. It is the happiest day of my life and I want to savour every moment. I embrace a bouquet of lilies and sigh contentedly.

'You look like a princess,' says Mum.

'Not like Melissa McCarthy in *Bridesmaids*?' I ask worriedly.

'Don't be silly. Anyway she was the bridesmaid, not the bride, so you can't look like her.'

'You know what I mean.'

I reach for the Hazelnut Heaven before she can stop me. The chocolate hits my bloodstream sending a wave of temporary euphoria through me. I tick off an imaginary list in my head. *Something old, something new, something borrowed, something blue and a silver sixpence in her shoe.* The slide in my hair is the something old, borrowed from my grandmother. That's if borrowing something from someone dead actually counts, but I'm sure it does. She would have lent it to me had she been alive. The *something new* is the wedding dress. No way was I having a second-hand dress. I've got a garter which belongs to my mother, just in case borrowing from my grandmother doesn't count, and the something blue is the ribbon tied around my bouquet. The silver sixpence is pressed tightly against my little toe. I had forgotten nothing. There will be no bad luck on my special day. I'm marrying my Prince Charming, Greg Martin. Just the thought of him makes me quiver inside. Life is going to be magical from this day forth.

I walk carefully into the living room where Dad is waiting.

'Aw, you look a picture,' he says proudly.

'I'll see you at the church. Don't be on time,' laughs Mum. 'And don't get too nervous, you don't want to stutter through your vows.'

I'm going to be exactly three minutes late, no longer. I read in *Bride* magazine that it is unfair to make the groom stand at the altar for too long. I fidget as the garter cuts into my thigh. Those extra three minutes may be the difference between life and death the way this garter is constricting my blood flow.

'Ready?' asks Dad.

I nod. I'd better go before my leg turns purple. The neighbours stand at their gates and 'ooh' and 'ah' at me.

'Doesn't she look lovely,' says one as I climb into the Rolls-Royce.

There's nothing like a wedding is there, to cheer everyone up?

'Bring us back some cake,' shouts another.

We've got a three-tier wedding cake in blue and white icing. Blue and white are Tottenham's colours and Greg was insistent they should be the colours of the cake. Not my choice but you've got to have a bit of give and take haven't you? The photographer flashes pictures of me in the car making me feel like a celebrity, and then we're off. I wave in the manner of Kate Middleton, and feel very regal, aside from my numb leg. It takes ten minutes to reach the church. I glance at my wedding finger and tremble with excitement. Soon I will be travelling back as Mrs Greg Martin. It's better than winning the lottery.

'We should go in,' Dad says anxiously.

'Once more around the block,' I say. 'It's not time yet.'

I seriously can't feel my foot. After one more drive around the block we finally stop at the church and I can't say I'm not relieved. This garter is worse than a tourniquet. I'll have deep vein thrombosis if we wait any longer. So, here we are, or at least here I am, about to get married and I couldn't be happier. I limp from the car and Dad fiddles with the dress while managing to stand on my veil.

'Oh damn, I'm sorry love.'

'Not to worry, it could be worse.'

I'm more concerned about the pins and needles in my leg. At this rate I will be limping down the aisle like a zombie bride. It's then I see Rosie wiping tears from her eyes. At first I presume them to be tears of happiness but then I see my mother crying too and my stomach tenses. Then Jack, the best man, begins talking earnestly to my dad who this time steps on my wedding train. My stomach churns the half box of Thornton's chocolates that I had eaten this morning and for one awful moment I think I'm going to be sick down my three thousand pound dress. That would be the pits wouldn't it?

First my dad's foot and then my vomit. Not the best start to marital bliss. But something tells me that this wedding isn't going to start at all, that something had happened, something awful. Oh God, Greg has been fatally injured in a pile up or at the very least broken both legs.

'Greg isn't coming. I'm so sorry,' says Jack.

'Is he sick?' I ask stupidly.

'He said he can't go through with it. I'm so sorry.'

It takes me a few seconds to understand what he's saying. Obviously, I'm relieved that they haven't dragged Greg's battered body from a mangled car or amputated both his legs, but my relief turns to disappointment and then anger, and then I want to stab him to death myself.

'He's not coming?' I stutter, knowing I'm stating the bloody obvious.

Jack doesn't speak. My world reels around me. I try to cling onto Dad but I can't see him through my tears.

'Oh don't cry Amy, please don't cry.'

Everyone looks at me, watching my humiliation. The man I love is not coming. I suddenly feel fat, vulnerable and stupid.

'What a sod,' says Mum.

I couldn't have put it better myself, although I can think of more appropriate words for him. I, Amy Fisher, have been jilted by Greg Martin, and if there is anything worse than your dad standing on your veil, this has to be it.

Chapter Two

It's been three hours and fifteen minutes since Greg dumped me at the church gates. I've polished off the box of Thorntons. There's no bloody point dieting now is there? Who cares if I burst the seams of the dress? It's not like I'll be wearing it again is it? Rosie is sprawled on Mum's armchair, her lavender bridesmaid dress spread around her. My foot is totally numb. I don't think the blood has flowed to it in the past three hours. I've probably got gangrene. That will teach Greg. He'll be sorry when they amputate my foot won't he? I suppose I should remove the garter but I really can't be arsed.

The front door bangs and Auntie Val waltzes in with a plate of hors d'oeuvres.

'What on earth have you got there?' asks Mum.

'No one's eating them,' says Auntie Val. 'We might as well get something out of this wedding.'

She pulls off her pink feathered hat and tucks into a mini-salmon quiche, her false teeth slipping with each bite.

'I couldn't eat a thing,' says Rosie miserably.

'I just don't understand any of it,' says Mum, dabbing at her nose with a Kleenex. 'Why did he wait until the last minute? If he was going to do it why didn't he do it before today?'

'It has more impact,' sneers Auntie Val. 'Men like to catch you unawares.'

Well Greg certainly did that.

'Is it alright if I watch the wrestling?' asks Dad, his hand hovering over the TV remote.

'For goodness' sake Norman, your daughter's just been jilted at the altar, what's wrong with you?'

'There's no need to rub it in,' I sob.

'I don't see how watching the wrestling is going to make any difference now,' he grumbles, helping himself to a salmon and cream-cheese cracker.

I don't know how they can eat, especially my wedding food.

'What am I going to do?' I hiccup. 'What about our new flat and the carpets that were coming from Carpetright?'

'That's the last thing you should be worried about,' Rosie says.

'Have a Rich Tea biscuit,' suggests Mum. 'That will help.'

'Fiona McKay was jilted at the altar,' says Auntie Val, stuffing a cheese cube into her mouth. 'Mind you, he did it a few days before the wedding. I'll take my present back shall I? I mean, you won't need a salad tosser now, will you?'

'Salad spinner,' corrects Mum.

'Talking of tossers,' says Auntie Val, 'you should sell that engagement ring of his. That's what Fiona McKay did.'

I don't care if Fiona McKay threw herself under a train. It doesn't mean I have to do it too, does it? I twist the single solitaire around my finger and feel the tears flow again.

'Drink your tea,' says Mum, handing me another Kleenex. I'm drowning in tissues, Rich Tea biscuits and cups of sweet tea. All this fluid is playing havoc with my swollen foot. The doorbell rings and I sit up.

'What if it's Greg?' I say. 'I look terrible.'

'If he didn't turn up at the church, I can't see him turning up here,' scoffs Auntie Val.

Rosie rushes to the door and comes back with Jack.

'Hello everyone,' he says nervously and then his eyes feast on the food. 'Ooh, vol-au-vents.'

I stare at him with eager eyes as he dives towards the salmon quiches.

'Do you have news?' I ask, sounding like Scarlet O'Hara.

We all look at him expectantly.

'Your carnation's wilting,' says Auntie Val, offering around the hors d'oeuvres.

Jack pulls the wilting carnation from the lapel of his jacket and clears his throat.

'Greg says he's very sorry and that you can keep the ring ...'

Auntie Val scoffs.

'That's bloody big of him,' snaps Mum.

'What about the carpets?' chips in Auntie Val.

'I don't know anything about carpets,' replies Jack.

'They ordered them from Carpetright,' she explains.

I wish she would shut up about the carpets.

'It's because I'm fat isn't it? That's why he dumped me,' I say.

'Of course not,' says Auntie Val.

'Erm ...' mutters Jack.

'Don't be silly,' interrupts Mum.

'He's bald so he can't talk,' scoffs Rosie.

'I'm not bald,' says Jack.

'I meant Greg, not you.'

'I never liked him,' says Auntie Val. 'He's got shifty eyes.'

'He's got lovely eyes,' I argue.

'I'm so sorry,' falters Jack.

'It is because I'm fat,' I sob, dunking another Rich Tea biscuit.

There's silence. That says everything doesn't it? Greg jilted me at the church gates because I was fat and everyone else obviously thinks so too.

'He's not well,' says Jack.

'You're telling us he's not well,' says Auntie Val scathingly.

'It's a good job I didn't dump him because of his bald patch,' I say angrily.

'Quite right,' says Rosie. 'He's nothing but an arse.'

'Wait till your father gets his hands on the little sod,' says Mum.

'What's that?' asks Dad, looking up from the wrestling.

I look down at my Dior wedding dress. I knew I shouldn't have been so extravagant. Three thousand quid down the drain. What I could have bought with that money.

'Oh God,' exclaims Rosie, lifting up the hem of my dress.

'Your foot's all blue,' gasps Mum.

'It's the shock,' says Auntie Val.

'It's the bloody garter more like,' I say, 'it's too tight,' and then I burst into tears.

I so hate my fat legs.

Chapter Three

I don't know what I would have done without my best friend Rosie. She's kept me stocked up with doughnuts and booze since the day of the jilting. She's far cleverer than me, is Rosie, and works in accounting. She has one of those brilliant jobs where you can work from home occasionally, which is just as well, because I've been so demanding of her time since *the wedding that didn't happen*. For the first few days she'd burst into my dingy little flat calling, 'Has he rung yet?'

I was forever checking my voicemail even though I knew there were no messages. The only calls I get these days are from Vodafone, and I don't imagine I will get many more from them after telling them unceremoniously to stuff their upgrade and fuck off. I've got two weeks off work. I'm supposed to be on my honeymoon. I've not told anyone at work that the wedding didn't go ahead. They think I'm in Sardinia, bonking the brains out of my new husband. Not that there are many people to tell at work. There are more dead people there than living. Did I mention I was a mortician? Probably not, as it's not something you drop into the conversation is it?

'I must say you have lovely skin, ideal for embalming. Would you like me to do that for you when the time comes?'

No, it isn't something I advertise, and let's face it I don't need to drum up business do I? People think they have a higher risk of dying once they meet me. I don't know why. I'm an embalmer not a murderer. I like my job. It's peaceful. Dead people don't answer back, but it can be a bit lonely at times. What I really love are weddings.

Rosie bustles in with armfuls of carrier bags.

'Get the kettle on,' she gasps, 'those stairs kill me. I was so looking forward to your new flat ...' she trails off on seeing my raised eyebrows.

'Sorry,' she mutters.

I pull myself off the couch and fill the kettle.

'He still hasn't called,' I say miserably.

'It's only a matter of time,' says Rosie, although her voice lacks conviction. She stands in the doorway of the kitchen and pulls a face. I follow her glance and look at the dirty dishes and overflowing bin.

'I haven't had time,' I mumble.

'You're in denial, that's your problem. You really can't spend the next six months checking your voicemail to see if he's called. What do you do all day apart from look at that phone?' asks Rosie, pulling an enormous pizza from the bag. 'If you ask me, you should go back to work.'

'I can't face them,' I say.

'You've got to sometime. The sooner the better if you ask me. It will get your mind off things.'

I cannot face the thought of going to the funeral parlour unless it is as a corpse. Seriously, I feel *that* low. To make matters worse, I've got a humongous zit on my chin, which I'm sure is getting bigger by the day.

Rosie digs into the carrier and produces a bag of fun size Kit Kats, doughnuts and a bottle of red wine. I feel my spirits lift.

'I got chocolate fudge ice cream too,' she says gleefully. 'I thought we'd chill with *The Holiday* tonight and do some serious drooling over Jude Law.'

'Are you sure I shouldn't call Greg?' I ask, opening the fun bag.

'Absolutely not, do you want him to think you're desperate?'

'But I am desperate.'

'It's only been seven days. Anyway, where's your self-respect?'

'I don't have any,' I say, grabbing my BlackBerry.

Rosie sighs.

'Good job I bought the chocolate fudge ice cream,' she mutters.

I tap in Greg's number and wait. There is a painful few seconds before a mechanical voice tells me the number is no longer in service. With shaky hands I punch in the number again only to get the same irritating bloody voice.

'I don't believe it,' I say through a mouthful of Kit Kat. 'How can his number be out of service?'

Rosie shakes her head and puts the pizza in the oven.

'Surely he hasn't changed his number,' I say shocked.

'Maybe he lost his phone,' suggests Rosie.

'I'll phone his office tomorrow. Anything might have happened. Maybe he's been abducted by aliens. That would explain the jilting,' I say, feeling a temporary moment of euphoria, although that's probably the Kit Kat.

'They did put him under a lot of stress at work,' I add, helping myself to another fun bar. 'Maybe he's had a breakdown.'

'He's a shipping clerk,' scoffs Rosie. 'You don't have to be Einstein to do that job, do you? You keep making all these excuses for him.'

Because, frankly, I'm falling apart and can't bear to think that Greg dumped me because I'm fat. I keep having these horrible fantasies of him with some skinny blonde doing all kinds of disgusting things.

'Maybe I should see a therapist,' I say. 'I can't seem to stop eating.'

'That's because you're home all day. If you stay home much longer you'll be trapped in here and won't be able to squeeze through the door,' Rosie sighs.

'You've watched *Gilbert Grape* too many times. Anyway, I'll start dieting tomorrow,' I say, as the smell of the pizza wafts around us.

The problem is tomorrow never comes does it?

Chapter Four

'Ooh you're back,' says Lionel. 'I say, you've expanded. You're not pregnant already are you?'

Lionel is the kind of man that you could use as a blue print to build an idiot.

'Most people live and learn, Lionel. You just live,' I snap, pulling off my coat.

'What did I say?'

I sigh and walk into the staff room where Tracy squeals at the sight of me.

'Hey you're back. How was the wedding?' she asks.

'While you've been enjoying yourself in sunnier climates, we've been overrun with stiffs,' Lionel shudders. 'I nearly had to lay one out myself. Yuk, I don't know how you do it. So, how was the wedding and more to the point, how was the honeymoon? I say, you're not very tanned. Spent a lot of time in your hotel room I bet.'

Tell the truth Rosie had said. Don't drag out the agony longer than necessary. Just tell them right away. Of course, it's easy for Rosie to say, she wasn't the one dumped at the altar.

'Did you have bad weather?' asks Tracy. 'You don't have much of a sun tan.'

'They probably weren't lying in the sun,' sniggers Lionel.

'There wasn't a wedding and there wasn't a honeymoon,' I say flatly.

There's a deathly silence.

'What do you mean there wasn't a wedding? Where have you been the past two weeks?' asks Lionel, finally.

I swear he's worn that brown fisherman jumper every day since I started work here. I don't even want to imagine what his underpants look like.

'I don't understand,' says Tracy.

'The wedding never happened. Greg didn't turn up.'

There, I've said it. They stare at me and then I see pity cross their faces.

'Didn't turn up?' repeats Tracy. 'Was he ill?'

'No, and he didn't have an accident and have both his legs amputated, either.'

'Christ,' mutters Tracy.

'Holy shit, he dumped you at the altar didn't he?' exclaims Lionel. 'That's classic, I thought that only happened in films.'

I told you he was a blueprint for an idiot. Tracy nudges him in the ribs.

'What a ...' stutters Tracy.

'Bastard?' I suggest.

'All that money ...' begins Lionel before getting another nudge from Tracy.

I pull my gloves and overall from the cupboard while Lionel and Tracy stand transfixed.

'Is there anyone to prepare?' I ask.

'You mean a dead body,' stutters Lionel.

'I'm not going to lay out a live one am I?'

Lionel points nervously to the door of the morgue.

'There's Mrs Mutton. She always wanted to look glamourous apparently. Bit of a lost cause in my opinion.'

'Right, I'll get to work then,' I say briskly and walk through the door.

I close it behind me and let out a long sigh. It's then, right then, that I have my epiphany. I go to button up my overall but it won't meet in the middle. I check it's mine and try again but it's no good. It doesn't fit. Lionel was quite right. I've expanded. If I don't stop eating soon I'll explode.

'Do you want coffee and a doughnut?' calls Lionel.

I glance at Mrs Mutton and step around her to the work counter, except I can't squeeze through the gap between the table and the wall.

'Bugger,' I curse.

There is a light tap at the door and Lionel's head appears.

'Coffee and doughnut to cheer you up,' he smiles.

'Thanks Lionel.'

'I'll leave it out here shall I?'

'She won't bite Lionel,' I snap. 'Besides, I need you to help me move the table.'

'The table has always been there,' he says anxiously.

Yes, but I've not always been the size I am right now.

'Lionel, will you please come in. The dead can't hurt you. It's the living you have to worry about.'

Don't I know it?

'It's sodding cold in here,' he grumbles.

He lifts one end of the table and I lift the other. We're just about to move it across the room when Lionel screams and drops his end of the table. Mrs Mutton slides to the side and I just catch her before she tumbles to the floor.

'Her bloody foot moved. I saw it. I saw it with my own eyes,' he cries hysterically.

'For God's sake Lionel,' I sigh, struggling to lift her heavy body back onto the table. 'Can you please help me?'

He holds up trembling hands.

'I'm not touching her.'

There's nothing as heavy as a dead body I'm discovering.

'I'm going to give myself a hernia, Lionel.'

I take a deep breath, yank up the body and slam it back onto the table taking myself with it.

'Holy Jesus,' moans Lionel.

I lie panting across Mrs Mutton and feel a cold draft flicker across my breasts. I look down to see the buttons on my blouse have popped undone. Lionel stares in horror.

'There's no need to look like that,' I say irritably.

That's it. I really can't have my blouse popping undone in the mortuary can I? I'll get frozen nipples. I grab the doughnut and throw it in the bin. It's no good, it's time for me to go on a diet and who knows, perhaps I may even win Greg back.

Chapter Five

Three weeks later and several pounds heavier and I'm opening the doors of the church hall and hoping that I'm not the fattest person there.

'Are you looking for Strictly Come Slimming?' asks a woman.

That says it all doesn't it? She must think I'm so huge that there is only one place I could be going. Either that or she saw me stuffing the bag of mini doughnuts I'd bought from the garage on the way here. Well, I needed comfort food. It's very stressful going to a slimming club.

'Well ...'

'Straight through, you'll see the sign,' she says pointing.

I, Amy Fisher, have braved it to a slimming club. I'm twenty-eight years old and the heaviest I have ever been, and to top it all, I'm on the shelf. This is by choice you understand. There is no one other than Greg that I will want to marry because there is no one other than Greg that I will ever love. It is for love of Greg that I am here. I can and I will get slim and I can and I will get Greg back. So, here we are, or at least here I am at a slimming club and I've never been more nervous in my life.

There is something strangely comforting about a slimming club. I think it has something to do with the fact that there are always other women chubbier than you. So much so in fact that I almost leave, convincing myself that I'm not fat at all. It's all a big mistake. But I don't, of course, mainly because our leader, otherwise known as Madam Hitler, stops me before I can reach the exit doors.

'Welcome to Strictly Come Slimming,' she calls, love bombing me and blocking my path to the door. Her arms wrap around me and I'm pulled further in. There is no escape now.

'You're new aren't you?' she says. 'I'm Lilian, your leader, and what brings you here?'

It's like being at Guides again. Lilian is matchstick thin. In fact between you and me she looks like she could do with a good fry up. But, if this is what slimming clubs do for you, then bring it on. At least you can see her waist which is more than can be said for mine. I'm starting to wonder if I've still got one.

'I'm fat and need to lose weight,' I say bluntly.

Well, there's no point beating about the bush when your breasts are hanging down to your knees is there? Not that my breasts hang down to my knees you understand, but you get my drift.

She wags a finger and looks at me crossly.

'We don't use the 'F' word here. I tell my girls they are just a little overweight.'

Same thing isn't it? And, I hate to tell her this, but some of her girls are more than a *little* overweight.

'What I meant was how did you hear about us?'

'Everyone knows about you, don't they?'

All the fat people do anyway. Its common knowledge, like only fat people eat cottage cheese.

'At Strictly you will find that you can fill your boots and still lose weight. Come and join our other newbies. It's their first time too.'

Fill my boots? That sounds grand to me, just my kind of diet. I feast my eyes on the diet snacks that are piled up on a corner table. I only hope it isn't like Alcoholics Anonymous where we have to stand up, declare our weight and why we want to lose it. I really don't want to be saying,

'I'm Amy Fisher, twelve stone ten and counting. I've been overweight for the past four years and the reason I have come to Strictly Come Slimming Club is because my fiancé dumped me at the altar and it clearly had a lot to do with the fact that I'm fat. Forget the overweight. I'm fat. Plain fat and he obviously didn't want to marry a fat person. So I am determined to get slim and maybe get him to change his mind. Oh, and my last mini doughnut was forty-five minutes ago.'

Depressing when you say it like that isn't it? And there is nothing worse than being surrounded by lots of fat, sorry, overweight people. Not that I have anything against overweight people, after all, I am overweight myself. But, let's face it, no one wants to be overweight do they? Although, I was quite content the way I was. It just seems that Greg wasn't so content. Not that he ever said my weight was the reason for jilting me. Actually, the little sod never said anything at all. He just buggered off, never to be seen again. Like one of those husbands who pop out for a pint of milk and never come back. Except Greg wasn't my husband and he never popped out for milk. I wish I could stop thinking about Greg, the wedding and the jilting. It's been five weeks two days and a hundred and thirty-five mini doughnuts since Greg left me standing at the church, and I haven't got a clue where he is.

'Here's another newbie,' Lilian announces to the group of five who sit miserably in a circle. 'Isn't it nice to know you're not alone?'

I give a nervous little wave.

'Let's get you weighed, shall we Amy?' says the Führer.

'Oh there's no need,' I say, 'I know what I weigh.'

'But *we* don't,' she says firmly, pulling me towards the scales.

I step on them gingerly.

'Thirteen stone,' says the girl behind the weigh in.

I nearly pass out with shock. I can't read the scales because they are upside down, which seems spectacularly unfair considering it is my body they're weighing.

'That can't be right,' I say. 'Are you sure? I've never been thirteen stone.'

'It's never been wrong,' says Lilian.

There's always a first time. I sigh. Thirteen stone. Thirteen bloody stone, how did that happen?

'It's the doughnuts,' I say.

'That will do it every time,' says Lilian. 'Come and join us for some image therapy,' she smiles, pulling me into the circle with all the other overweight people. At least I don't look thirteen stone. At least I hope I don't. Thirteen stone, I can't believe it. I feel like a circus freak. I hope *image therapy* makes me feel better. How will I ever lose all this fat? I'll be ancient by the time I get this lot off.

'We're going to talk about breakfast,' Lilian tells the group.

I don't actually think talking about breakfast is going to make me feel any better. I study my booklets and feel like I've already lost weight just from being here. It's making the effort that counts isn't it? I'll show Greg. Well, I would if I knew where he was. The receptionist at his work won't tell me anything except that he has a new position in the company. That could be on the moon for all I know. The stupid thing is I still love him. Rosie thinks I'm totally mad but you can't help loving someone can you? I know if I lose weight he will come back to me.

'He's a pig,' said Rosie. 'Any man who dumps a woman at the church has to be.'

'I quite like being big,' says the lady sitting next to me. 'But I know it's not good for my health. What's your reason for losing weight?'

'I ... I ...' I begin but a lie isn't forthcoming. 'My fiancé dumped me on our wedding day. I feel sure it was because I was fat.'

And then I burst into tears. Everyone rallies around me and tells me what a fool Greg was. It's good to bond isn't it?

'How awful for you, it's not your fault that you're fat.'

Well, it is my fault really isn't it? It's not like someone else has been stuffing the doughnuts into my mouth.

'Did he actually say he couldn't marry you because you're fat?' asks another slimmer.

'Not exactly but ...'

'You just know though, don't you? What a bummer.'

A bummer indeed.

By the time I leave I have five new friends and my new bible, the *Strictly Come Slimming Club handbook*. Let's face it, if Pauline Quirke can do it then so can I. How hard can it be?

Chapter Six

Don't you just hate the gym? Maybe you don't. Perhaps you're super fit. Good for you. Rosie and I are far from that. We get our exercise from walking to the local. So, here we are, or at least here I am, at the gym and it's not at all what I had imagined. We stare in awe at men with wonderfully toned torsos and thighs like tree trunks.

'Good God,' mutters Rosie. 'Why haven't we done this before?'

'Because it's bloody hard work,' I whisper. 'And I want to live past thirty.'

All around us are fit people pumping iron. I feel exhausted just watching them. The place is packed with determined keep fitters. Loud music blares around us and I've never felt so uncomfortable in my life.

'Who's our instructor,' asks Rosie, her eyes sparkling. 'It's not that dreamboat by any chance, is it?'

I look to where she's nodding. A muscular blonde Adonis is walking our way. I pull my cardigan around my bulky body. I feel gigantic against the sculptured women on exercise bikes with not a bead of sweat between them.

'No, it's a woman called Monica.'

'Oh bugger,' says Rosie.

The cyclists look at us and I want to die. I can't wear Lycra and work out like this lot. Not without having a coronary anyway.

'I'm beginning to think this is a bad idea,' I say, turning to the door.

'Hello Amy, glad you made it,' says Monica, striding towards us, a towel draped casually around her neck. 'You've had your inductions haven't you?'

We nod dumbly.

'Brilliant, let's get you on the machines.'

'Shouldn't they check our blood pressure or something?' asks Rosie nervously.

'They've done that.'

'But that was last week. It could have changed in seven days.'

'Locker rooms are through there,' points Monica.

Please God, let them be empty. Ten minutes later Monica has me sitting on an exercise bike and Rosie on the treadmill. Once I get over the embarrassment of being dressed in Lycra I really get into it. I look the part and pump away at the pedals for at least two minutes. Then my lungs give up and sweat pours down my face. The Lycra sticks to my body like bloody superglue and my heart is fit to burst. What's more, I'm panting like an asthmatic. I don't even want to look at the display. It's most likely flashing *calorie burn overload*. I must have used a million calories in those two minutes

'Christ,' pants Rosie, 'are you okay? You look like you're about to drop dead.'

I struggle to climb off the damn thing, but my legs won't move.

'Steady at first,' instructs Monica as I collapse at her feet. 'Don't overdo it at the beginning. You must not forget that you are very unfit.'

Rub it in, why don't you?

'Once you've both warmed up we'll get on with some real exercise.'

'Warmed up?' I repeat. 'You mean we haven't even started exercising yet?'

'Blimey, I feel like I've already run a marathon,' groans Rosie.

'I can't do this,' I wheeze, walking like a geriatric to the changing room. 'Don't worry, I'll still pay. After all, I don't really need to exercise. It's not like I'm morbidly obese is it?'

Monica doesn't reply. I stop and wobble on my jelly legs.

'Is it?' I repeat, turning to her.

'You're quite close,' mutters Monica.

Six months membership I'd paid for, upfront. Am I a total idiot? Plus I'd paid extra for a personal trainer who tells me I'm morbidly obese.

'You can't just throw in the towel,' says Rosie making me sound like a female *Rocky*.

'She said I'm morbidly obese,' I complain.

'I know, what a cow,' says Rosie.

'Do you think I'm morbidly obese?'

She shrugs.

'Not morbidly.'

'What does that mean?' I demand.

'I don't know. I'm not an expert on morbidly obese people.'

'You think I'm obese?'

'I never said that. But I don't think you should throw your money away.'

She's quite right of course. I wobble back to the gym, my hair dripping sweat down my back.

'Okay, how long will it take you to get us into shape?' I ask Monica.

'Not long,' she assures me.

'Will we survive is what I want to know,' says Rosie before downing half a bottle of water.

'Oh yes,' smiles Monica.

'It's easy for you to say,' quips Rosie. 'You were probably kickboxing in the womb.'

'I was once fifteen stone,' says Monica, pulling her shoulders back.

'No way,' we say in unison.

'Combined with the Strictly Come Slimming Club, you'll lose the weight in no time.'

'Or die trying,' adds Rosie.

'Greg is worth it,' I say dreamily and climb back onto the exercise bike.

Chapter Seven

Six weeks later.

Always be suspicious of family members when you're free, single and available. It seems they can't bear it. Auntie Val has invited me for Sunday lunch. I should have known something was up. Auntie Val never invites me for Sunday lunch. The truth is I never see Auntie Val from one year to the next unless there is a wedding or a funeral, or in my case, an almost wedding. It seems that no one believes me when I say there is no one for me but Greg.

'It's not that dressy,' Mum had said on the phone. 'But try to look nice. After all we don't often get invited to Stamford Hill.'

The truth is I don't *ever* get invited to Stamford Hill. So, here we are or at least here I am, on a wet and windy Sunday morning, driving to Stamford Hill to Auntie Val's huge house. Uncle Malcolm made it big in fish. Unfortunately he also drank like one and dropped dead three years later. Auntie Val sold the business and has lived in luxury ever since.

'Darling, you're here, we've been waiting for you,' says Mum, greeting me at the front door. She teeters on high heels and balances a crystal wine glass in her hand.

This is ominous. Mum most certainly doesn't wear heels and pearls for Sunday lunch. Her wine-fuelled breath wafts over and I stare at her in disbelief.

'Why are you dressed up?' I ask worriedly.

'I'm not dressed up, silly,' she giggles, pulling me through to the living room.

'You said it wasn't dressy. You never wear pearls,' I say almost accusingly. 'And you're wearing your mother of the bride dress. Talk about rubbing it in. What's going on?'

Barry White drifts out from the living room. His music that is, not Barry White himself. That would be a bit surreal. Now I know something is going on. My family only play music when they have guests and I don't think Auntie Val considers me or my parents as guests. Mum pushes me in. The table is laid with Auntie Val's best china and my heart sinks.

'Here she is,' declares Mum and I almost expect a drum roll.

'We thought you weren't coming,' clucks Auntie Val pulling me into a hug.

I rather wish I hadn't. Then I spot him, standing by the fireplace.

'Val invited Malcolm's old business partner,' whispers Mum drunkenly. 'He's terribly rich. Has a house in Belgravia and all sorts.'

He also smells of kipper.

Before I can speak, Auntie Val has plonked him in front of me and I come face to face with a bespectacled man in corduroys and a green jacket. He's fifty if he's a day and so tall that I've got a crick in my neck from looking up at him. I wonder if he knows he smells of fish.

'How do you do?' he says, shooting out his hand. 'I'm very pleased to meet you. I've heard a lot about you.'

I hope he hasn't heard that I was dumped at the altar for being too fat. His hair flops across his eyes as he speaks and he swishes it back with a hand.

'This is Gerald Finn,' says Auntie Val when I give her a questioning look. 'Gerald runs the business now.'

Yes, I can smell that.

'Hello,' I say, taking his hand. Well I can't just ignore it, can I? 'Nice weather for a Sunday.'

What am I saying? What has the day got to do with the bloody weather? Good job I'm not out to make a good impression isn't it?

'Hello love,' says Dad, strolling in from the kitchen and stinking of Old Spice. 'Have you met Gerald?'

Yes, unfortunately. I don't believe this. They're only trying to set me up.

'Amy has lost tons of weight haven't you dear?' says Mum.

'Yes, I was really fat before,' I say, shooting her a filthy look.

'Well you look spiffing now,' he says, appraising me.

Spiffing? Has he time travelled from the nineteen twenties?

'Shall we check on the dinner, Val dear?' says Mum, wobbling on her shoes. 'Norman, show Gerald Val's new hi-fi unit.'

I dive through the door and follow behind them.

'Hi-fi unit?' I repeat as we stumble into the kitchen. 'No one has hi-fi units these days. And seriously, who plays Barry White? And what the hell is Gerald doing here?'

'I like him,' says Auntie Val defensively. 'He's very sexy.'

'You've got the worst taste in men if you think he's sexy,' I say.

'Lots of women think he's sexy,' argues Auntie Val.

'So, why didn't you invite one of them?'

'She's talking about Barry White, I think,' butts in Mum.

'Obviously,' says Auntie Val. 'Who do you think I'm talking about?'

Mum and I nod towards the living room.

'Heavens no, not him,' gasps Auntie Val. 'Barry White, you have to agree he is sexy and that husky voice of his,' she swoons.

'*Was* sexy, isn't he dead?' I say.

'Is he? Goodness I didn't know that,' says Mum groaning. 'These sodding shoes are crippling me.'

'Okay, what's going on?' I ask, helping myself to a glass of wine.

'What do you think of Gerald?' asks Auntie Val. 'He's rich, got a nice house in Belgravia. You won't get better than that and I don't think he'll care if you are overweight.'

Oh well, that's all that matters then isn't it? I gape at her.

'I'm not overweight,' I state firmly. 'And you can't be serious about me going out with him?'

'He is a bit old for her,' says Mum.

At last, Mum and I agree on something.

'And he stinks of fish,' I complain.

'There's no pleasing you,' huffs Auntie Val.

'He's a vegan, can you believe that?' says Mum. 'We had to Google it. I thought it was some kind of religion, and Val had already bought the joint. We didn't know what to cook. Do they eat sprouts do you think?'

'What are you on about?' I say, opening the oven door and peeking inside. Although all I can smell is Dad's Old Spice.

Auntie Val rushes to the hob and turns on the sprouts.

'I thought he'd be younger,' says Mum. 'Your dad says he's very comfortable. He's a widower. His wife died near Niagara Falls. I don't like to ask if she fell in. Well, you don't do you?'

I feel like I've entered some alternate reality. Auntie Val pulls a dish from the oven and looks at me over it, her face flushed.

'I've made a nut roast, what do you think? I've never made one in my life.'

I can tell. I look at the burnt offering and shrug. I really don't believe my auntie is setting me up with a bloody vegan.

'How much have you two had to drink?' I ask.

'Too much, I've been that nervous,' croaks Mum. 'I said to Val, Amy won't like this, and you don't do you?'

'I'm just trying to help,' sulks Auntie Val.

'Do they eat fruit?' asks Mum worriedly. 'Val made apple crumble but your dad said he might not eat that. So I bought strawberries on the way.'

'It's bleeding hard isn't it, feeding a vegan?' says Auntie Val.

'I wouldn't know. I've never fed one.'

You'd think we were talking about a newly purchased pet.

'I can't believe you're setting me up,' I groan.

'Your mum hates to think of you being alone.'

'It's not like your dad and I will be here forever,' says Mum tearfully.

God, I wish my mother wouldn't drink.

'You're not going anywhere yet,' I sigh.

'We've always wanted to go to the Caribbean.'

'Presumably you'll be coming back?'

She sighs and pulls a joint of beef from the oven.

'You don't think he'll mind us eating meat do you?'

I shake my head in exasperation.

'Oh God,' she moans, carving manically at the roast. 'I told you this was a bad idea, Val.'

My mother and alcohol just do not go together. I gently remove the carving knife from her hand and take over.

'If you don't want me to be alone, why on earth are you setting me up with someone old enough to be my father?'

'Oh no dear, he's much younger than your dad,' says Auntie Val, pulling roast potatoes from the oven. 'He's only fifty-three.'

God, he's older than I thought.

'*That* old?' I say. 'He'll be dead before I hit my prime.'

'You need to think about getting married soon,' says Auntie Val, downing half a glass of wine. 'You do realise time is running out don't you?'

'I'm not dead yet.'

'Your ovaries aren't far off it,' she says, following it up with a belch.

'My ovaries are in ...' I begin.

'Sorry to interrupt,' Gerald says as he opens the kitchen door. 'I wonder if I can put a vegan sausage in the oven.'

'Well, erm ...' stutters Auntie Val, looking at me.

'Val's had beef in there,' says Mum, blushing profusely.

'They've made you a nut roast. It looks lovely,' I say.

It looks gross in fact.

'Great, I'll have it with my sausage.'

Seriously, who goes out with a man that carries his own sausage?

'Have you brought your own dessert too?' I ask.

'Well ... I ...' he mumbles.

'I have strawberries,' says Mum, her voice strained.

'And double cream,' chips in Auntie Val.

'I don't eat cream,' he says sternly.

Mum splutters something incoherent.

'More sherry Gerald?' says Dad, strolling into the kitchen clutching a bottle of Bristol Cream.

Auntie Val is setting me up with a sherry drinker. She must think I'm desperate.

'Amy works out,' says Mum. 'She's very health conscious. She only eats healthy food.'

I roll my eyes. One glass too many and she loses the plot.

'I'll put your sausage in shall I?' I say.

It's very uncomfortable chatting to a man who holds his sausage in his hand. I'm starting to feel like I'm in a cheap porno movie.

'That's grand. Thank you,' he smiles before dropping his sausage into a dish. I glance at Mum, who glances at Auntie Val, who bows her head in shame. Gerald strolls back into the living room and I turn to Mum.

'How can you do this to me? I can't even drink to deaden the pain.'

'Yes you can,' she sighs. 'You can stay the night at ours.'

Well, that helps. But honestly, do I seem that desperate that I'd saddle myself with a 53-year-old vegan who smells of fish, drinks Bristol Cream sherry and carries a sausage? Still, it's nice to get a good roast. Make the best of a bad job, that's my motto.

Four glasses of wine later and Gerald isn't looking half as bad. He still looks old and smells like a fishmonger, but let's face it, after enough alcohol even Hannibal Lecter looks appealing.

'Terrible about your wife,' slurs Mum, throwing an arm around his shoulders.

'One copes,' he says bravely. 'It must have been just as painful being jilted.'

I don't know about that. Even being jilted doesn't compare to popping your clogs does it?

'Has it put you off weddings for life?' he asks.

'Oh no, not at all,' interjects Auntie Val.

I don't know why she is being so hopeful. There is no way I am going to become Mrs Gerald Finn, wife of fish man extraordinaire.

'I love weddings actually. I really enjoyed organising mine.'

'She did a wonderful job too,' Mum points out. 'Just a shame the groom didn't turn up.'

'The bugger,' snarls Auntie Val.

'I imagine you sorted him out, didn't you Norman?' smiles Gerald.

'Well ... you know ... more wine Gerald?' says Dad.

'Don't mind if I do. That's a nice Chardonnay. So what do you do for a living Amy?'

I pick at my apple crumble. It just doesn't taste the same with the smell of kipper wafting around me.

'I'm a mortician,' I say with a little smile. 'I prepare the dead for their funeral.'

'Goodness, that's a bit gruesome,' he splutters.

'I don't murder them first,' I laugh.

'Do we have to discuss your job?' says Auntie Val with a shudder.

'For some reason I thought you did something more creative, like an artist or an event organiser?' says Gerald. 'Val told me how you organised your wedding.'

Yes, what a shame it never actually happened.

'Have you thought of doing that for a living?' he asks.

What a stroke of genius. Why didn't I think of that? I'd make a brilliant wedding planner. After all I had planned my own wedding meticulously, and I loved it. There wasn't a single loose end, apart from the groom not turning up and the garter disaster. Fortunately the feeling returned to my leg twenty-four hours later, but I would have had the perfect wedding. Sadly it didn't happen but why not plan perfect weddings for others? That way I would have all the pleasure and no disappointment. It is a win-win plan.

'Gerald, you're a genius,' I beam.

'I am?'

And at that moment I have a clarity and excitement that I'd not felt before. I will start my own business and begin a new life. I will put the past behind me, forget about Greg and move on. I will be the perfect wedding planner. In fact, I will call my business 'Perfect Weddings'.

Chapter Eight

Five weeks later

'Okay ladies, swing those hips and shake those buttocks.'

Monica gyrates and beckons us to do the same. I lean on the bar to rest my legs. The exercise bar, that is, not a drinking bar. I should be so lucky.

'Christ,' I groan, 'this is going to kill me. I'm too bloody overweight to be doing this.'

'And I'm too bloody old,' agrees Rosie. 'And you're not that overweight now.'

'And you're not old, you're twenty-eight, the same as me,' I say, my heart thumping in my ears.

'I won't live to be thirty if I keep this up,' she groans.

'No slacking girls,' calls Monica.

'She won't be happy until we're dead,' I grumble. 'I can't believe I'm paying her to kill me.'

'I don't think she'll have long to wait,' moans Rosie. 'They should have oxygen on tap if you ask me. At least I can rely on you to make me look good after the big event.'

'I'm not touching your dead body.'

'After all I've done for you, it's the least you can do. I fully expect you to turn me into Audrey Hepburn when I'm dead,' pants Rosie.

'I'm an embalmer not a miracle worker.'

'Just think what this is doing for your Fitbit,' says Monica gleefully.

'Sod the Fitbit,' says Rosie. 'I'm more worried about what it's doing to me.'

'I hate Fitbits,' I say scornfully. 'I bet they've killed more overweight 28-year-olds than anything else.'

'You're not overweight,' repeats Rosie.

'I am,' I insist.

'You're like an anorexic in reverse.'

She's quite right. I still try on size twenty clothes in the shops and get a shock when they hang on me like sack. I'm a size fourteen now and I really can't believe it.

Rosie blows her fringe from her eyes and wipes the sweat from her forehead.

'Reese Witherspoon never looks like this when she leaves the gym,' she says, before downing her water.

'The only thing we share with her is Evian,' I say, breathing heavily.

'Speak for yourself, I'm on Lidl flavoured.'

'Five minute break ladies,' barks Monica.

I flop onto the bench.

'I'm not altogether sure why I'm doing this,' Rosie says, draping a towel around her shoulders.

'To support me, remember?'

'I knew it wasn't from choice. I've never been so fit in my life.'

'I appreciate it, I really do.'

'So you should. Not many women would risk life and limb for a friend.'

A slight exaggeration, but I know what she means. We stagger from the gym looking like we've had hip replacements, but it's working. I've lost pounds. Lilian said I must burn off the fat and build up muscle. At the moment all I've got is bloody cellulite. I can't win. I get rid of one and gain another. I'm destined to have fat issues for ever and I'll never win Greg back. Not that I know where bloody Greg is. I'm seriously thinking of liposuction but I daren't tell Rosie. She'd have a fit. Rosie thinks I should accept myself for the person I am with or without cellulite.

'We've all got a bit of cellulite,' she'd say.

'I'm thinking of doing Pilates.'

'Are you insane? You already do three exercise sessions a week and the days in between you can't sodding walk. You run on a Saturday and basically die on a Sunday.'

'I thought you might like to come.'

'Like?' she exclaims. 'I've not liked anything we've done so far, so why would I *like* Pilates?'

'Because it's good for us, that's why.'

'So is a spa weekend but you never suggest that do you? You'll be getting me to skydive next.'

'Actually I'm thinking of liposuction.'

She looks about to faint.

'Have you lost your noodle? Swimming with sharks would be safer. Do you realise how dangerous liposuction is, not to mention that it costs the earth. You can barely afford your rent. Just buy yourself a Slendertone belt.'

'That's like electric shock treatment. Anyway, I'm thinking of branching out on my own. So money won't be a problem.'

'Do-it-yourself liposuction? Now I know you're crazy.'

'And box, one, two, three, four, come on people, rest time over,' shouts Monica.

'If you're expecting me to be your assistant with do-it-yourself liposuction you can think again. What are you going to use, Henry the hoover?' shouts Rosie over the music.

I punch the air, narrowly missing Monica's face. Well, if she will come so close.

'I'm not going to give myself liposuction you mad cow.'

'That's a bloody relief,' she sighs, punching the air for all she's worth.

'I'm thinking of becoming a wedding planner,' I announce.

Rosie stops punching and stares at me. I do my side punch and she blocks it expertly with her hand.

'A wedding planner?' she repeats with a look of horror on her face.

Anyone would think I'd said *call girl*.

'Yes,' I reply. 'I'll be the best. I'm going to call it Perfect Weddings.'

It's the most determined I've been since Greg jilted me.

'Perfect Weddings,' she repeats. 'You're going to give other women the perfect wedding?'

I nod.

'You don't think that's just a touch masochistic?'

'I love weddings,' I say. 'Just because I didn't have the perfect wedding, doesn't mean I can't plan them for someone else.'

In fact, I really can't think of a more perfect job.

'Well, at least your clients will be breathing for a change,' laughs Rosie.

'Exactly.'

Perfect Weddings here we come.

Chapter Nine

Three years later

'Ready to go Amy love?'

I look at my bouffant hair and sigh.

'The hair isn't quite ...' I begin.

'She's a bit sweaty. Joan, can we get that shine off? Someone get her some water. We can't have this coughing during the take,' barks Craig.

I'm sweaty and shiny because it's hotter than a sauna in the studio and I'm coughing like a fifty-a-day smoker because Craig's eighty-a-day smoke is seriously clogging up my lungs. I'll be lucky to get out of here alive. I try to pat down my backcombed hair before the cameras roll. My forehead is dabbed with cotton wool and Craig shouts 'action'. I clear my throat, smile and look straight into the camera, not that I can see it that well. There's more smoke here than at a Madonna concert.

'*I'm Amy Perfect from Perfect Weddings. Let's talk about the most important day of your life: your wedding day. You want your day to be magical, just like you always dreamt it would be and I, Amy Perfect, want to make your dreams come true. That special venue that you've always dreamt of? Perfect Weddings will book it. The wedding cake? We know the contacts. The perfect dress? The make-up? Flowers to enhance your eyes? Perfect Weddings will bring out your natural beauty to make you the most beautiful bride ever. And for that special magic to make your day unforgettable, Amy Perfect will wave her wedding wand ...*'

I wave the wand that Craig had pushed into my sweaty hand, in the most magical way I can muster. I suppose I should be grateful they didn't tart me up as a fairy godmother. Craig gives me the thumbs up and I continue.

'*Don't leave it to chance, leave it to Amy Perfect, and turn your wedding day into a Perfect Wedding day.*'

'And cut,' screams Craig. 'Great work Amy love.'

He blows smoke in my direction and I fight back the urge to cough. This was my sixteenth take and I'm convinced I now have emphysema.

'Let's see it,' he says and I wait with dread for him to say, 'one more.'

'It's perfect, just like you Amy Perfect,' he laughs. 'It will go out on the local show tomorrow.'

Great. I'm Amy Perfect, wedding planner fairy godmother and now television star. Shame about the Cilla Black sixties hair but you can't have everything. This should bring in lots more business. I love weddings. I just don't want one myself. There is no one I will ever want to marry. I made that decision three years ago and I'm never going to change my mind. So, why not have the next best thing: someone else's wedding. What can be better than giving a woman the wedding she deserves? Her special day will be my special day and that way I get married over and over again. I get to choose a beautiful wedding dress every week. All my brides are my best friends. I've even been maid of honour for some of them. I give them a wedding like no other. My real name is Amy Fisher of course, but that doesn't sound right for a wedding planner, whereas Amy Perfect smacks of success and perfection, and a change of name means a change of luck and in my case that is certainly true.

I am Amy Perfect, the success. I only wear designer clothes. My hair is coloured at Toni and Guys. I'm not mousy brown wavy-haired Amy Fisher any longer. I'm now blonde bombshell Amy Perfect. I have my shoulder length hair straightened every eight weeks and a facial once a month at the Sarah Chapman boutique. After all, a wedding planner has to look like a perfect bride every day. I am the envy of the girls at the gym. I have a healthy shake for breakfast and a healthy shake for lunch. I'm the ultimate health freak now. I always look immaculate when I leave my flat in the mornings. I run twice a week. I wear size ten clothes with ease. There is nothing I want that I cannot have, aside from chocolate of course. I fly to hot sultry places twice a year and have my own little honeymoon. I've just bought the perfect flat in Chelsea. I have a doorman greet me when I leave in the morning and when I arrive home in the evening. And now I am a television star. I am the woman with everything. That was until one Tuesday morning ...

Chapter Ten

'Perfect Weddings, Amy speaking, how can I help?'

'Is that Amy Perfect, *the* Amy Perfect?' says the excited voice at the other end of the line.

I can tell by the voice that she is about thirty, medium build, slightly disorganised and with a wedding date approaching. I know my girls before I even meet them. I'm not called Amy Perfect for nothing.

I smile.

'Yes it is. How can we make your wedding day perfect?' I say pleasantly.

There is a heavy sigh.

'I'm getting married in eight weeks. It's too last minute for an Amy Perfect wedding isn't it?' she says breathlessly. 'But I so wanted Amy Perfect to plan my special day.'

Anyone who knows anything about weddings wants Amy Perfect. If you want the best then there is no one else.

'We had to bring the wedding forward,' she adds.

I detect a hint of embarrassment in her voice. A shotgun wedding no doubt, last-minute weddings usually are. I gesture to Lucy to hand me the Big Red Book. She looks aghast when I say.

'Of course I can help you. Eight weeks is plenty of time.'

Lucy pulls a face and shakes her head, red curls bouncing around her cheeks. The Big Red Book is the Perfect Weddings' bible. Nothing is planned or changed without the Big Red Book being consulted first.

'We're fully booked,' says Lucy fluttering her heavily mascaraed eyelashes. 'We can't possibly.'

'There is no such word as *can't* at Perfect Weddings, Lucy.' I say chidingly, pulling the book out of her hands along with one of her false nails. I look at it in disgust while Lucy stares in horror at her finger.

'Twenty quid they cost,' she grumbles.

'At that price are you surprised they drop off at a mere touch?'

I go back to the phone.

'Now let me see. What date is the wedding?' I ask, throwing the bright red painted nail in the bin.

'I'd like the 25th of May, but I understand ...'

'A spring wedding, how perfect is that? Already you are on your way to the perfect wedding,' I say, flicking through the pages. 'I'm just going to put you on hold so I can check the date for you.'

The Big Red Book spills open with photos of brides in beautiful dresses, gold-lined invitation cards, honeymoon brochures, and wedding venue flyers. I've never been so busy. In fact, some nights I'm that knackered that I'm out for the count in seconds. I couldn't have a man in my life even if I wanted one, not that I do of course. Let's face it, all they are good for is leaving hair in the sink and piss on the toilet seat. I don't have time for a man in any case. Even the batteries in my vibrator have turned well and truly rusty.

I flick through to May 25th. Lucy opens her mouth to protest as the other line rings. She picks up the phone while giving me her best dirty look.

'Perfect Weddings, Lucy speaking, how can I help? Oh,' she says, glancing at me. 'Yes, of course you can change the date Marcia. So we're cancelling the 25th May. Yes that will be fine.'

I have the most wonderful luck. But then I believe we make our own luck. A red marker pen is scratched through Marcia's wedding date and I pick up the phone.

'How fortunate for you,' I say. 'We have one slot left for the 25th May. We are very happy to help you plan your wedding. Now, I just need a few details from you. Is there any reason for the hurry? Do we need to look at a special type of wedding dress?'

'I don't think so,' says the voice warily.

'Not a little bump we need to be aware of?'

Lucy winces.

'Hell's bells no. I see what you mean. No, the other date clashed with the football season, you see. I originally wanted it in August and then I thought maybe June but there are a lot of friendlies in June. July is fully booked at the church. So we've had to come forward to the end of May.'

I roll my eyes. What kind of man puts football before his wedding?

'Okay, let's book you in right now. What's your name, and the name of your fiancé?'

'I'm Georgina Winters and my fiancé is Greg Martin. It's Gregory Martin actually, that's what will go on the marriage certificate isn't it?'

My hand grips the phone until the knuckles turn white. My heart flutters unmercifully and my breath becomes shallow until I think I won't breathe at all. It can't be. It can't possibly be. Not Greg Martin, not my Greg Martin. Yes, it must be. Only my Greg Martin would put football before his wedding. My hands shake and my head spins. It's been three years since Greg jilted me at the altar, well, at the church gate to be precise. I've not seen hide nor hair of him since and now here is his new fiancée asking me to plan his perfect wedding. This has to be the ultimate kick in the teeth doesn't it?

'Right,' I stammer in a shaky voice, 'wonderful, and where is the lovely Greg from?'

Maybe it's not my Greg. There are probably hundreds of Greg's with the surname Martin.

'Are you having one of your panic attacks?' whispers Lucy, rattling a bottle of pills in front of me.

I do wish Lucy would stop asking me that. I don't have panic attacks. I just stammer when I'm anxious, that's all.

'My Greg is from Reading but he's been in Spain for the last two years. Does that matter?'

Spain? How did he cope in bloody Spain? He wouldn't move more than six feet off the couch if there was a match on the tele.

'Does the lovely Greg have a middle name?'

'Do you need mine too?' she asks.

'No, just his,' I snap.

'Middle name,' mouths Lucy. 'When did we start asking ...?'

I wave dismissively at her.

'Philip,' says Georgina.

Oh God, it is my Greg. How many Greg Philip Martins can there be? He's here, in London. I stare at the Big Red Book. I can't marry Greg Martin. I just can't. I don't mean I *can't* marry Greg Martin. I would give anything to marry Greg Martin. I just can't help marry Greg Martin to Georgina Winters. I can't, no I WON'T help make Georgina's wedding day perfect. I slam the book shut making Lucy jump.

'Take three of your *Quiet Life*,' she says, shaking the pills from the bottle. 'In fact, take four.'

'If I took half the bottle it wouldn't make any difference,' I hiss under my breath. 'Those things are sodding useless.'

'Can you plan my wedding?' asks Georgina hopefully.

'Of course,' I say sweetly. 'Let's book an appointment for Thursday. Just you though Georgina. Can I call you Georgie?'

'Oh yes, please do.'

'I find men so tedious in the early stages. It's much better if we girls work out the basics before we involve the men.'

'Oh, that's okay,' Georgina says pleasantly. 'Greg is in Spain tying up all the loose ends before he moves back to England, so it will only be me.'

'Shall we say eleven o'clock?'

'That's great. My diary is free that morning. I'll see you then. I'm so excited.'

I'm Amy Perfect. I create the perfect wedding day. I make wedding dreams come true. I can turn your day into the happiest of your life, or I can make it a total nightmare. I hold your special day in the palm of my hand and right now I hold Georgina Winter's special day in the palm of my hand. I pick up my marker pen and write *Greg and Georgie* in the Big Red Book and stare at it until the words blur.

Chapter Eleven

'You won't like this. I did consider hiding it but I know how much you love *Vanity* magazine. You're bound to find it eventually.'

'Is it featuring one of our weddings?' I ask, trying to prepare myself.

'Something like that,' says Lucy with a wince, hugging the magazine to her chest.

'Hand it over then.'

My stomach churns.

'Are there photos?' I ask.

A feature in *Vanity* is no small feat. It will bring in tons of business. Lucy hands over the magazine and I find myself staring at a photo of myself. It's a print from the TV advert. The piece is titled *Wedding Planners: Are You Being Ripped Off?*

'Oh God,' I moan. 'I'm too scared to read it.'

'It's by our heart-throb, Ben Garret,' Lucy says wistfully.

Ben Garret is known as the wunderkind of journalism. He is the most respected writer in Fleet Street. Just about every magazine in the country has headhunted him but *Vanity* won. He's been on numerous chat shows and is the best-looking journalist in the country. At least Lucy and I think so. We're often drooling over his picture in the magazine.

'Ben Garret,' I say in awe.

Lucy rattles the bottle of Quiet Life.

'You might need these. We're the last wedding planner in the article.'

'Oh God, is it that bad?' I groan.

'Just read it.'

I lay the magazine flat on the desk and scan the article until I see *Perfect Weddings* highlighted.

'Amy Perfect of Perfect Weddings is the most sought after wedding planner in London. Her fame has reached television proportions. She is also the most expensive wedding planner in

London. Amy Perfect's claim to fame is that she will make your dreams come true no matter how crazy they are. For the fee she charges I would expect that and much more. There are many wedding planners in London but Amy Perfect is the crème de la crème, at least her prices are. But in this day and age do intelligent and creative women really need a wedding planner? How hard is it to choose wedding invitations and a cake or am I simplifying things too much? Personally, I would never be ripped off by a wedding planner. If you'd like to book Amy Perfect for your perfect wedding the details are below. Note, prices aren't quoted on the website. The old adage of If you need to ask the price you obviously can't afford it, clearly applies here. But, if you want a perfect wedding, then it seems Amy Perfect is the one to hire.'

Ben Garret is the Editor in Chief of Vanity. The opinions stated in the article are Ben Garret's and not that of the magazine.

'Oh,' I say, struggling to breathe. Haven't I got enough on my plate right now?

'It's out today. I think we'll get some business from it,' says Lucy trying to appease me.

'What?' I explode. 'Didn't you read it?'

'Yes. He bangs on about our prices a bit, I know.'

'Bangs on?' I groan. 'He couldn't have given us a worse review if he tried. Get *Vanity* on the phone.'

'What, are you serious? I didn't think it was that bad.'

'I want a public apology. How dare he? I've not let one single bride down. How dare he say I charge too much?'

Lucy shrugs and chews her nails.

'Do you think we charge too much?' I ask.

'I ...'

She hesitates too long for my liking.

'Nobody has ever complained. Get him on the phone.'

I'm that angry that my body is trembling. I swallow three Quiet Life tablets and try to calm down.

'One moment, Mr Garret,' says Lucy, her face turning bright red.

'He's got a lovely voice,' she whispers, putting her hand over the mouthpiece.

I grab the phone.

'Mr Garret,' I say in a trembling voice.

'Miss Perfect,' he responds. Lucy is quite right. He has a warm sensual voice. Well, it won't pack any punches with me.

'I've just read your slanderous article on wedding planners and ...'

'Whoa, Miss Perfect, it's far from slanderous,' he drawls.

'You're clearly insinuating that I'm overcharging,' I snap. 'That is slanderous.'

'I believe for the service you offer, that you are overcharging.'

'I would like you to retract your comments and put an apology in the next issue,' I say bluntly.

He laughs and I grip the phone tighter.

'There is nothing to apologise for. It was an opinion. I also stated that you are the most popular wedding planner in London, and that if the reader wanted a perfect wedding then you were the person to hire. I'm not too sure why you are so upset?'

'Because you claim I rip people off and ...'

'It's an opinion,' he interrupts.

'I await your apology,' I say through gritted teeth.

'You'll wait a long time.'

'I could sue you for slander,' I say angrily.

Lucy winces.

'You could try,' he says with a smile in his voice. 'I'm sure you could afford to.'

'Piss off,' I retort before slamming the phone down.

'Oh no, did you hang up on him,' cries Lucy.

'He's a tosser.'

I grab the magazine and throw it into the bin.

'Oh dear,' says Lucy.

'That's the last time I drool over his picture.'

Although I can't deny he had a sexy voice but that's the only good thing you can say about him. The phone rings and I widen my eyes.

'It can't be,' says Lucy, picking up the phone. 'Perfect Weddings, Lucy speaking, how can I help?'

I hold my breath.

'Yes, that's right. We were featured in the magazine today. Yes, of course you can make an appointment.'

She winks at me. I pull the magazine from the bin and glance again at the piece. There's no such thing as bad publicity I suppose. Maybe it's worth keeping after all.

Chapter Twelve

Georgina stares at me wide-eyed. She's prettier than I envisaged but a little on the plump side. Those thighs have certainly seen one too many Cornish pasties. I can't deny that she is attractive though, with her baby blue eyes and cupid bow lips, but what I can't take my eyes off is her huge engagement ring. The obscene sapphire bling dazzles me. I think of my little solitaire that sits in a pad of cotton wool at the bottom of my jewellery box and fight back a sigh. Greg hadn't been so generous when we'd got engaged. Still, he wasn't flush then. Maybe he's gone up in the world.

'I can't believe I'm standing in the same room as Amy Perfect,' says Georgina in a breathy voice.

I can't believe it either. I'm amazed there is room for both of us, that bling and Lucy too.

'Well I can assure you that you are,' I smile. 'And I am going to give you everything you deserve.'

I gesture to Lucy for the Big Red Book. She gives me her usual sulky look.

'Everyone is amazed you could fit me in,' says Georgie, settling into the chair opposite me, her dress riding up to reveal her white chubby thighs. 'Greg doesn't know I'm here. He thinks wedding planners are a waste of money.'

Is that right? She fumbles in her battered leather handbag and pulls out a crumpled photograph.

'This is me and Greg, just after he proposed. We went to Yarmouth to celebrate.'

Oh, Greg proposed did he? Well, that makes a change.

'You can't get more romantic than Yarmouth can you Lucy?' I say. 'I hear it is nice there this time of year. They do nice fish and chips, so I'm told.'

Lucy raises her eyebrows and hands me the book, careful to make sure her hands don't connect with mine.

'Absolutely,' Lucy agrees. 'I've always thought Yarmouth was the place to go.'

To die maybe.

Georgina's waistline certainly smacks of too much candyfloss and chips if you want my opinion. I look at the photo she is holding out and have to hang onto the side of the chair to stop myself reeling. I fight back a gasp at the sight of Greg. He's older of course, but still as heartbreakingly handsome as when I last saw him three years ago. His arm is slung around an even chubbier Georgina. He is looking at the camera and for a second I feel he is looking right into my eyes. I swoon and feel my legs turn to jelly.

'Are you all right?' Georgina asks.

'You're not having one of your panic attacks are you?' asks Lucy.

'I don't have panic attacks Lucy. I just get a little anxious sometimes.'

'Same thing though isn't it?' says Georgie.

'I just feel a little faint,' I say waving a hand airily. 'Lucy, some fresh air please.'

Lucy rolls her eyes.

'I'll just pop out and get some shall I? I'd forgotten how the mention of Yarmouth sends you into a faint.'

'Are you on the 5.2 diet?' asks Georgina. 'My friend gets faint all the time on that. I've been okay so far.'

Lucy flings open a window and glares at me.

'How much fresh air would you like?'

I do wonder what I pay Lucy for.

'You're on a diet?' I say.

Georgina smiles shyly.

'Greg says he loves me just as I am but …'

I clench my fists.

'Well, so he should. You shouldn't ever try and change yourself for a man.'

Look who's talking.

'But every bride wants to look her best for her wedding doesn't she?' says Georgina, tugging the photo from my grasp and pushing it back into her bag. 'And I would like to be slimmer.'

'It's important to accept yourself for who you are.'

I really can't believe I'm saying all this and from Lucy's bewildered look, neither can she.

'Shall we get down to the nitty-gritty, Georgie?' I say, hurriedly changing the subject.

'I'll make coffee and as we're getting serious I'll bring in some choccy biscuits,' says Lucy, slamming the window shut.

Lucy obviously didn't hear the diet word. Georgina leans towards me and says in a conspirator's voice.

'I haven't chosen a dress yet. Do you think I should? It's just I thought I had longer. I was hoping to lose a bit more weight, you see.'

'Absolutely, but I think the dress should be the first thing we do. You need time for alterations. Let's talk about budget ...'

'Oh money isn't an issue,' she chirps before I can finish. 'My dad has pots of money and I'm a journalist for *Vanity* magazine.'

'*Vanity* magazine?' Lucy and I repeat in unison.

She nods proudly.

'The same *Vanity* magazine that Ben Garret works for?' squeals Lucy.

'He's the editor in chief,' smiles Georgina.

Lucy and I drop our jaws. We must look like we're catching flies.

'Lucky you,' swoons Lucy. 'I wouldn't mind working late with him. All shirtsleeves and no tie, and ooh those eyes.'

I slap her with a serviette.

'We've had experience of Ben Garret,' I say hotly.

'Yes he featured Perfect Weddings didn't he?' says Georgina. 'He can be a bit contentious. But it's good publicity.'

'Yes, well back to business,' I say in my efficient Amy Perfect voice.

'Is Ben Garret coming to your wedding?' asks Lucy eagerly.

I bloody hope not.

'I hope so,' says Georgie, 'he's the best man.'

'He's my best man too,' drools Lucy. 'He's a bit of a flirt though isn't he, so they say?'

'Coffee please, Lucy,' I say firmly.

'I have so many questions,' Georgina says excitedly, wriggling in her seat. 'I'm thinking black, pale green and white. What do you think?'

'For your wedding dress?' I say shocked. Is she going for the Halloween look? 'It's slightly unusual but why not?'

'Colour schemes,' she laughs.

'Of course, that sounds wonderful. A lovely colour scheme,' I say.

It's the most common theme ever. Lucy returns with the coffee and biscuits.

'Ooh I daren't,' says Georgina, her eyes feasting on the biscuits. 'Although, it is one of my five days, so I suppose I could.'

In that case let's pack in as much as we can, shall we? I have to admit to feeling an overwhelming desire myself. Just one won't hurt will it? No, that's a sign of weakness isn't it? One chocolate biscuit will lead to a praline chocolate and then before I know where I am I'll be on a box of Thorntons. My mouth waters and I have to pinch my hand very hard to stop myself reaching for a chocolate digestive.

'Are you sure you're not having a ...?' begins Lucy.

I shoot her a filthy look.

'I suppose the dress could be altered near the time,' says Georgina thoughtfully.

'Of course,' I say, taking a sip of coffee.

Georgina spends the next thirty minutes chatting about her wedding dreams, while munching her way through half a pack of chocolate digestives. She's getting married at St Andrew's in St John's Wood she tells us. There will be almost 100 guests. She would like a nice venue. Is it the wrong time of year for sweet peas?

'Only I love sweet peas,' she sighs. 'They're so delicate.'

'I'd like Greg in top and tails,' she says wistfully, helping herself to another digestive.

Oh yes, I remember Greg looked good in a top hat and tails. Just a shame the only time I saw him in one was at Fran's wedding a month before ours. I sway, and reach out for a chocolate biscuit, only to see they have all gone.

'We have Jaffa Cakes,' says Lucy, as the last digestive disappears into Georgina's mouth.

'We do?' I say.

'For emergencies,' explains Lucy.

This is as close to an emergency as I'll ever come. Just one won't hurt will it?

'Shall I get them?' Lucy asks questioningly, her lips quivering in anticipation.

You'd think we were talking about a secret stash of coke instead of innocent Jaffa Cakes wouldn't you? Although on reflection Jaffa Cakes are far from innocent.

'I love Jaffa Cakes,' Georgina enthuses.

'Wedding dress,' I say sternly

'Gosh, you're quite right,' says Georgina. 'I knew I was right to come to you.'

'It will be the best decision you ever made.'

Lucy pulls out an emery board and manically files her nails while shooting me daggers. Amy Perfect saves the day. You'd think she'd be grateful.

Chapter Thirteen

'You're kidding. I'd hoped he'd been abducted by aliens,' says Rosie between pants.

'Well he's back, at least he will be and what's more his fiancée wants me to plan their perfect wedding. I mean, honestly.'

'Holy shit, Amy, I really don't think you should do that.'

'Why not?' I ask innocently.

'Because it's not healthy is it?'

We skirt around an elderly couple walking their dog.

'I'm helping her plan her wedding. That's my job. What's unhealthy about that?'

'Bollocks. You don't plan your ex's wedding. That should come with a health warning.'

I stop running and rest my hands on my knees.

'Oh God, Rosie, just think, I could bump into him at any time.'

'For your sake, I hope you don't. You really can't plan his wedding. It's abnormal.'

'What would you have done, then?'

'You're asking the wrong person. I couldn't organise a bunk up in a brothel.'

She wipes her forehead, pushing back wisps of hair.

'But I guess I would have suggested another wedding planner.'

I continue walking at a brisk pace.

'I'm the best there is.'

'And modest with it,' she laughs.

'I can't watch someone marry Greg,' I say. 'I have to be sure he is making the right decision. Supposing he loses his nerve and dumps her at the altar too.'

'If he was a serial altar dumper I think he would have done it a few more times since you.'

'Maybe he has.'

'Do you know that he has?'

'Well no but we don't know he hasn't either do we?'

'So you're doing this to protect Georgina?' she says, checking her Fitbit.

'Well, not exactly ...' I begin.

'You don't think this is going to be rather torturous? I really think you should find yourself a nice boyfriend. Look, I know this great guy ...'

'I don't want a blind date. I'd rather know who I'm going out with thank you very much.'

'You don't go out with anyone, blind or otherwise.'

'I'm quite happy.'

'Happy planning everyone else's wedding but your own. It's not healthy,' she says, unscrewing a bottle of water.

'Anyway, who are you to talk? You go through men quicker than toilet roll.'

'I'm still looking for Mr Right, that's why. But at least that's not unhealthy.'

'Will you stop telling me that everything I do is unhealthy? You'll be telling me running is unhealthy next.'

'My knees are starting to think that. Look Amy, you can't win Greg back by sabotaging his wedding.'

'Why can't I?'

She sighs.

'Because it's ...'

'Unhealthy,' I finish.

'It is. And it's immoral and you're not that kind of person. Anyway, I don't know how you can still love the bastard, I really don't.'

'I don't think he knew what he was doing.'

'He was pretty brainless I agree.'

'Rosie,' I snap, checking my Fitbit. 'We really should do another mile.'

Rosie sighs.

'You can do another mile if you want. I stop at killing myself. That kind of defies the object of what exercise is all about doesn't it? Honestly Amy, you're gorgeous, you're not in the least overweight now. Your obsession with weight is ...'

'Don't tell me, unhealthy.'

'Well, it is. You look great, you really do.'

'Exactly,' I say triumphantly. 'If Greg could just see me, then surely he would realise that he lost a good thing. He wouldn't want to marry Georgie.'

'Maybe he loves her,' she says.

I gasp.

'How can you say that? She's overweight and could seriously do with a proper bra fitting. She wobbles like a half-set blancmange. There is no way Greg would marry a woman like that. He's obviously been tricked into this marriage.'

Rosie opens her mouth to speak as my BlackBerry trills. It's Lucy.

'Oh my God Amy, it's a disaster, an absolute disaster,' she cries down the phone.

'What is, what are you talking about?' I ask feeling my stomach churn.

'Did you forget?' she hiccups.

'Forget what?'

Oh shit.

'I've sent you six texts, haven't you seen any of them? I've had that sheikh on the phone. Not that I understood much of what he said mind you, but I certainly got every word of Laureta's when she rang.' She struggles to breathe. 'I think I'm having a panic attack. Can I take some of your Quiet Life?'

'Bugger,' I moan.

'You did forget,' she squeals. 'I don't believe it. They're at the airport waiting for the limo which *you* were supposed to be organising. It's a disaster. Laureta screamed at me. I tell you, I've only heard builders use words she came out with. She's not a happy bride-to-be. What are we going to do? I phoned the limo company but they don't have any record of our booking and all their cars are out.'

Shit, shit and triple shit.

'I'll collect them. Message me the flight number. Phone Laureta and tell her the limousine was involved in an accident and that I'm going to collect them in person.'

'Right,' says Lucy.

There is silence for a second and then she adds, 'But isn't your car at the garage for its service?'

Bollocks.

'Blimey, you've turned white. What's up?' asks Rosie as I click off my phone.

'Where's your car?' I say, turning quickly and colliding with the couple we passed earlier walking their dog. I somehow manage to get entangled in their cocker spaniel's lead and find myself going around in circles with the bloody yapping dog following me. Rosie struggles to release me while the elderly couple look around for help.

'What's the matter with you?' asks Rosie.

'I need you to take me to Heathrow Airport,' I say, disentangling myself from the lead.

'What? Why do you want to go to Heathrow? I thought we were going for a milkshake at Penny's. You never mentioned going away. This business with Greg has affected you more than I thought.'

'We're going for a shake all right. I'll explain later. You need to get me to Heathrow.'

'What now? It's a bit far to go for a shake isn't it?'

'Like yesterday,' I say, dragging her out of the park. 'I forgot to arrange the limousine to pick up the sheikh.'

'What kind of shakes are we talking about that need a limousine to collect them? I know you've got expensive tastes but ...'

'The prince kind of sheikh,' I snap.

'Who's the bloody sheikh when he's at home?'

'He's only bloody royalty, Prince Abdullah. He's also my client's best man. She's none too pleased apparently.'

'Holy shit,' Rosie groans. 'You can't meet a sheikh looking like that and certainly not smelling like you do.'

I look down at my jogging pants and sweat shirt. Things are just going from bad to worse.

'We'll have to stop at mine so I can grab some clothes.'

We run from the park as fast as our legs will carry us.

'I think my Fitbit might blow up,' pants Rosie as I fly past her.

'I'll be down in five,' I yell, diving through the entrance doors of my apartment block. 'Be outside with the car.'

'This kind of stress isn't good for you,' she pants. 'It's ...'

I don't hear the last word but I feel sure it is *unhealthy*.

Chapter Fourteen

I stare at Rosie's Fiat and wish I had a gun to shoot myself.

'I don't believe it,' I groan.

How could I forget how small her car was?

'It's the same car I've always had. I'd magically convert it into a four by four but I'm not the one who makes dreams come true,' she apologises.

We couldn't get a smaller car if we tried. I yank the door open and climb inside. I stare in horror.

'For God's sake Rosie,' I snap. 'Have you never heard of cleaning? The whole car needs valeting.'

'If you think we've got the time?'

'Not now. If we had time to valet the bloody car I wouldn't be changing in it would I?'

'I don't have to do this, you know,' she complains, climbing in beside me. 'I'm not the one who forgot to order the limo.'

'This is ridiculous,' I mutter, grabbing a carrier bag from the back seat and throwing chocolate bar wrappers and empty McDonald's cartons into it. 'What are you doing eating a McDonald's anyway?'

'It was only the once,' she says, guilt written all over her face.

'There are two cartons here,' I say accusingly.

'Okay it was twice. Arrest me.'

She starts the car and *Hava Nagila* begins playing on her car stereo. I cock my head.

'What's this?'

'Hava Nagila, it's the soundtrack from *Snatch* and unfortunately the CD player is buggered and it plays the same track over and over again.'

'Can't you turn it off?'

She pulls out onto the busy London road.

'No. It's stuck.'

I groan.

'We're collecting an Arab sheikh. You can't possibly be stuck on bloody Jewish *Hava Nagila*.'

'I'm sorry. But you did rather spring this on me. If you'd given me a few weeks' notice I could have got a belly dancing CD stuck instead.'

'I don't believe this.'

'You can always use someone else's car,' she snaps.

'You are kidding me? You can turn it down can't you?'

She shakes her head.

'The bloody thing is jammed. What do you think it's like for me? I'm singing sodding *Hava Nagila* in my sleep.'

I throw my head back and groan.

'I'm dead, I'm seriously dead.'

I pull open the glove compartment and rummage through her stash of sweets.

'Amy, what are you doing?'

'I need sugar.'

'Remember what Lilian says.'

'Sod what Lilian says.'

'One is the beginning of a downhill slide into hell.'

'I'll shake hands with the devil then,' I say, before swallowing half a Milky Way.

'Bloody black cabs,' she says, braking suddenly, before opening her window and yelling. 'Get over; you don't own the road you know.'

Traffic screeches around us and I grab the sides of my seat. The car stalls and motorists hoot us from all directions.

'Shit,' curses Rosie. 'I hate driving in London.'

'What are you doing lady?' shouts a driver. 'Masturbating at the wheel?'

I gasp.

'I wish I had time,' screams Rosie.

'So do I,' I say. 'You'd be much better tempered.'

She turns the key in the ignition several times and finally the thing starts again. We get going and I check the time on my BlackBerry. We're never going to do it. I rummage through the glove compartment for another Milky Way. I look up to see we are fast approaching an amber traffic light.

'Slow down,' I yell.

'I can do it,' she says.

'You can't,' I argue.

'I can.'

'Stop,' I shout pushing my foot onto an imaginary brake.

'I can do it,' she repeats, slamming her foot down on the accelerator.

'No you can't,' I cry.

'I can.'

'You can't,' I say, as the little Fiat roars. The light changes and we speed through the red like something out of a Bond movie. A bright flash blinds us for a second and Rosie curses again.

'Oh shit,' I groan.

'Those cameras never normally work,' says Rosie.

I sigh.

'Well that one did. Either that or we're being chased by paparazzi.'

My phone trills and I snap it open.

'Amy,' squeals Lucy, 'are you at the airport?'

At the speed Rosie is going, I reckon we'll be there in a few seconds.

'We're almost there,' I say.

'Are you insane?' says Rosie. 'We've barely started. How fast do you think I can drive?'

I check the speedometer.

'One hundred and ten miles an hour,' I say.

'What's that music?' asks Lucy.

'*Hava Nagila*,' I say, wincing.

'*Hava Nagila*,' repeats Lucy. 'Do you think that's a good idea under the circumstances?'

'No I don't. I think it's a terrible idea but the CD player is stuck,' I say lamely.

'Oh,' says Lucy, like CD players getting stuck on *Hava Nagila* is the norm. 'Never mind, I just phoned to tell you they will be waiting by WH Smith.'

'They?' I repeat.

'The sheikh, and his wives, and their maid, and I reckon they've got tons of luggage. Amy, are you there? Amy?'

'How many wives?' I ask, finding my voice.

I'm dead. I'm seriously dead. There's absolutely no way that I'm not.

'I don't know, but it's more than one.'

Why couldn't I get a monogamous sheikh?

I manage to change clothes as we burn down the A4. I rub a wet wipe under my armpits and then check my reflection in my handbag mirror. I look wild and my hair is still sticky with sweat. I comb it back and secure it in a hairband before slapping on some make-up.

'Am I in the right lane?' asks Rosie.

'What?' I say, turning sharply and smearing red lipstick across the bottom of my cheek.

'Bugger,' she curses, swerving to take the exit. 'Which terminal?'

I'm shaking so much that I can barely tap into my phone to check Lucy's message.

'Terminal 3,' I say.

She zooms into a parking space only to get a filthy look from a black cab driver.

'You can't park here,' he says.

'I'm picking up a sheikh,' she retorts.

He looks at her Fiat and bursts out laughing.

'Yeah, right, and I'm picking up Barack Obama.'

I check my reflection in the mirror. I've got lipstick across my cheek and down my chin. I resemble a clown. I drag a wet wipe across my face and climb from the car, relieved to finally be free of *Hava Nagila*.

'Are you available?' I ask the cab driver. 'I'm desperate.'

I'll need more than the Fiat for the sheikh, his wives and a maid.

'Desperate are you? Well, I'm free darling but the cab's all booked up I'm afraid.'

'She's not that desperate,' scoffs Rosie, grabbing my arm and pulling me into the terminal. The heel of my Prada shoe gets wedged in a crack. There's a snap and I groan as my ankle twists. I hobble forward, heelless.

'Oh no,' Rosie cries. 'Not your Pradas.'

I fight the urge to cry. Amy Perfect has never looked so imperfect. If someone dragged me through a bush backwards I couldn't look any worse. I limp towards WH Smith at arrivals.

'I've never met a sheikh before,' says Rosie. 'I've read about them in Mills and Boon, but never met a real one.'

So, here we are, or at least here I am at Heathrow Airport limping on a broken Prada to collect a sheikh. And there he is, queued up outside WH Smith with his harem. Oh my God, how many are there? We freeze at the sight of them.

'How can we squeeze all of them into my Fiat?' asks Rosie, panicking.

I shrug.

'Let's go,' I say, patting my hair and limping forward with my head held high.

'Work it,' says Rosie. 'Strut your one-legged stuff.'

I paste a wide smile onto my lips and head towards them.

'Should we curtsy or something?' asks Rosie.

'I don't know,' I whisper.

'There must be some kind of etiquette, didn't you check?'

'I didn't know I'd be collecting them,' I snap. 'But *Hava Nagila* in the car is definitely not the best etiquette going is it?'

'It's not my fault.'

'Smile,' I say.

'Perhaps we should bow or something,' she says.

It suddenly occurs to me that my dress may be a bit too short for the sheikh. I quickly pull it over my knees, managing to stick a nail through my tights in the process. A ladder snakes up them and I sigh. I'm starting to look like a trashy hooker.

'Shalom,' says Rosie, bowing to the sheikh.

'Have you gone mad?' I whisper. 'It's Salam isn't it, or something like that? It's people like you who start bloody wars.'

'I don't know do I? They don't have greetings in Mills and Boon.'

Meanwhile the sheikh and his many wives, who all look the same in their burkas, continue to watch us.

'Shalom is Jewish,' I hiss as we get closer to them. 'You don't think *Hava Nagila* is enough?'

'Bugger,' groans Rosie.

I hold out a hand to the sheikh who is looking at my feet. He looks up. His tanned face stares out at me from beneath his headscarf. He is dressed from head to toe in a long sleeved robe.

'I'm so sorry,' I say loudly.

'Why are you shouting?' asks Rosie, nudging me. 'He's foreign, not deaf.'

'I'm so sorry we're late,' I say, staring at my hand which he still hasn't taken. 'The limousine had a problem. Is this your lovely wife … wives?'

He lifts a hand and for a moment I think he is going to take mine but instead he gestures to a porter who rushes forward pulling a trailer of Luis Vuitton bags. God, there's hundreds of them. Bags that is, not porters.

Rosie shakes her head.

'Well, *they* won't go in the boot.'

The sheikh looks down at my feet. Being shoeless and a woman is probably the height of disrespect, not to mention the laddered tights, and an above the knee dress.

'I tripped and …' I begin.

He pulls me away from Rosie and the wives. Oh God, I'm going to be publicly flogged in the middle of Heathrow arrivals. Oh, well, I suppose all publicity is good publicity. I'm dragged unceremoniously towards a shoe shop in the airport where he replaces my Pradas with a new pair.

'Oh no, I couldn't possibly,' I say, conscious of his three wives watching us.

He plonks the shoes onto my feet and gestures for me to lead the way. I feel like Cinderella.

'We follow you,' he says in soft broken English.

Rosie sidles up to me.

'I might get my handbag lodged in the lift or something. I could do with a new one.'

'Just keep walking,' I snap.

The Fiat and Hava Nagila are waiting for us, and I feel my face turn red. So, here we are, or at least here I am, trying to

'Keep your hair on. At least you got a pair of shoes out of it. All I got was a parking ticket,' she moans.

I have a feeling I have a bit more to come yet.

Chapter Fifteen

'It was totally unacceptable,' shrieks Laureta, wagging her finger in my face.

'I'm so sorry,' I say, for what feels like the hundredth time.

Lucy pours more tea with trembling hands

'*Hava Nagila*?' Laureta spits. 'Had you lost your mind?'

'That was a mistake,' I say, fumbling for my Quiet Life.

'It certainly was, Amy,' she snaps.

'The limo had an accident. I did the next best thing and raced there myself and ...'

'You have a Mercedes convertible,' says Laureta.

'It was being serviced.'

'Jaffa Cake?' offers Lucy, popping a whole one into her own mouth.

'Well ...' Laureta hesitates, 'maybe just the one. You're lucky my mother is having her boobs done, because if she even got a whiff of this ...'

'It's okay, we don't often have Jaffa Cakes,' consoles Lucy.

'I meant the airport debacle, obviously,' Laureta retorts stiffly.

We'll have to make sure she doesn't get a whiff of anything won't we? After all, it is mummy who is paying my bill.

'Did the operation go well?' I ask pleasantly, trying to change the subject.

Although the chance of a private Harley Street boob job going wrong is pretty slim isn't it?

Laureta's eyes sparkle.

'If she didn't have these awesome breasts she wouldn't even have known she'd had an operation. I'd have mine done for the wedding if there was time. Have you ever thought of having yours done Amy?'

Lucy chokes on her Jaffa Cake. That will teach her. I look down at my breasts, which if I do say so myself, I've always considered to be little bobby dazzlers. Not huge, more medium sized and certainly well defined.

'Well, no, I haven't …'

'They do start sagging after thirty you know.'

I'm not sagging am I? I glance down again and see Lucy also having a good gander.

'I'm not thirty yet,' I say.

Laureta has the nerve to look surprised.

'Oh, I figured you were a bit past thirty actually. Ever thought of having Botox?'

I grit my teeth and force a little laugh.

'Oh God, yes, they deliver it with the milk where I live.'

She laughs and Lucy joins in, fluttering her eyelashes rapidly.

'Well …' I say, deliberately glancing at the clock on the wall.

'Yeah, I need to get off too. I'm meeting Jeremy for lunch.'

And I'm meeting Georgie to look at wedding dresses.

'We'll let this little incident pass,' she says, swinging her Burberry over her shoulder and stealing another Jaffa Cake. 'If you want the name of the boob guy just let me know.'

She waltzes out of the door and Lucy and I let out a collective sigh.

'That was close,' says Lucy.

'It was fine,' I say. 'She wouldn't have terminated. We make dreams come true Lucy. No one will give that up.'

'I still can't believe you forgot,' she says.

Neither can I. I'm Amy Perfect, the success. I don't make mistakes. My diary has an entry for everything. I just had a little glitch. It was a shock discovering Greg was around, and getting married. But I'm over that now and back in control. I swallow three more Quiet Life and straighten my shoulders.

'It was just a blip,' I say, popping another Quiet Life, just to be on the safe side.

'Should you take that many?' asks Lucy anxiously.

'They're only herbal,' I say dismissively, opening the fridge for a shake. I stare nonplussed at the empty shelf.

'What happened to my shakes?'

'You drank them all.'

'Are you sure?'

'Trust me,' she grimaces. 'I wouldn't drink them if you paid me.'

'Oh,' I mumble.

'I get blips all the time when I'm premenstrual,' she nods. 'It's not unusual.'

'I don't get premenstrual,' I snap. 'Women don't have that. It's all in the mind.'

Lucy opens her mouth to protest but I hold up a finger to stop her. I check the diary on my phone and grab my bag.

'I'm meeting Georgie. I'll be back at four.'

'Oh,' she says, glancing at the diary on the desk.

'What?' I ask. Surely I haven't forgotten something else.

'You have an appointment at the health centre.'

I scroll through my phone. There is no mention of an appointment.

'Are you sure?'

She nods.

'Is everything all right Amy?' she asks. 'You never used to forget things.'

No, everything isn't all right. Ever since Georgina Winters came into my life I've started to lose the plot.

'It's fine. I'll make a note now.'

I must get a grip. Nothing else is going to go wrong. I have my car back. There are no more sheikhs to collect from the airport. Today I just have Georgina Winters to deal with. What can go wrong?

Chapter Sixteen

Georgina is waiting outside Petunia's wedding salon and I am about to wave to her when I see she is with a man. Georgina points to a dress in the window and the man drapes an arm around her shoulders and looks to where she is pointing. They are laughing. I fumble for the Quiet Life and pop a couple more. My legs go weak and I feel sick with nerves. Greg looks taller than I remember. He's lost weight too. And what happened to his bald patch? Surely he hasn't had a hair transplant as well? What is the woman doing to him? How on earth can he love a woman who does nothing but change him? As I move closer, I see the man isn't Greg at all. I exhale with relief and a small wave of anger runs through me. Does Greg know that his fiancée is looking at wedding dresses with another man? How insensitive is that?

Georgina sees me and waves coyly, whispering to the man as she does so. He turns and smiles and I'm stopped in my stride. It's Ben Garret and he's totally gorgeous and I mean, totally. His hair is cut perfectly and his deep blue eyes are mesmerising. He seriously is better looking in real life than in his photos. He takes his arm from Georgina's shoulders and pushes a hand into the pocket of his jeans. His gaze is steady as he looks at me. His eyes hold mine for a few seconds and I feel hypnotised. His brown hair has been tumbled by the wind but he's still extremely attractive and beguiling. I get the feeling he knows more about women than I could ever know about men.

'This is Ben. He's our best man and one of my closest friends,' says Georgina, squeezing Ben's arm and turning sparkling eyes on me.

'Mr Garret,' I say stiffly.

'Miss Perfect, we meet at last,' he says in his warm sexy voice.

He stretches out a hand towards me. I take it and find myself holding it longer than is necessary. Wait till I tell Lucy. She'll be dead envious.

'Hello,' I say, 'I wasn't expecting Georgie to bring anyone with her. I usually deal just with the bride and groom.'

He seems to swim before my eyes and I grasp the door handle of Petunia's to steady myself.

'Ben is practically family, aren't you Ben?' says Georgina.

I raise my eyebrows. Well, if that hug I saw earlier was brotherly then I'm a monkey's uncle.

'Are you okay?' Ben asks. 'I know I have an effect on women, I just never realised it was that potent.'

He's smiling broadly and I can't help admitting he is very appealing but doesn't he know it? Is he arrogant or what?

'I'm fine,' I say. 'I assure you it has nothing to do with your potency.'

Although I can't deny he smells as gorgeous as he looks. He looks into my eyes while his hand still clutches mine. His is warm and soft and I fidget uncomfortably under his stare. It's like he is looking right through me.

'I've seen your advert,' he smiles and I find myself staring at the little dimples in his cheeks. 'You look good on TV.'

Is he trying to say I don't look good off it?

'Part of your research was it?'

'I see you haven't forgiven me,' he says with a twinkle in his eye.

'And I see you haven't printed your apology,' I shoot back.

'Ah, I hope you're not holding your breath,' he grins.

'I rather think I'd be dead if I were,' I retort.

'Shall we go in?' Georgina interrupts.

'I'm not quite the groom but I promised Gina that I'd check out the dress with her,' he smiles.

Gina? They are obviously close. I wonder how Greg feels about Ben checking out the dress.

'I hope you have plenty of time to spare. We girls can take some time choosing a dress at the best of times but a wedding dress ... now that is something else.'

'Ben has given me the afternoon off,' smiles Georgina, pulling me into the shop. 'So we can take as long as we like. Come on, I'm so excited.'

I trot behind her and feel Ben's eyes on us as he follows.

'I don't usually have much contact with men,' I say.

Hang on, that didn't sound right. I must not take any more Quiet Life.

'I mean, I don't have much contact with best men,' I correct, struggling to see the rose coloured couches.

'What kind of men do you have contact with then?' smiles Ben.

'Doesn't the groom normally choose the best man?' I ask, turning on him.

'How do you know he hasn't?' he asks, meeting my eyes again.

'I think I'd know if ...' I begin, and then stop. What am I saying? 'You work with Georgie don't you?'

'I do. In fact I'm her boss, any other questions?'

Georgina chats to Petunia, the owner, who waves on seeing me.

'I think it's lovely that you're supporting Georgie, but I'm her wedding planner and I would appreciate it if you would let me to do my job, even if you do think I'm overcharging for it.'

He pretends to take a step back.

'Whoa, you don't let go easily do you?'

'I'm just clarifying my position,' I say firmly, sounding like Jean Brodie. I couldn't be primmer if I tried.

He nods, a grin playing on his face.

'Got it. I'm just here to support and besides, it's good for my ego to be seen with two pretty women.'

Oh, he's smarmy too. He is certainly true to his reputation.

'Please don't try and flatter me. I'm a professional and that kind of thing just doesn't work on me.'

'Right,' he says, holding up his hands. 'I've been suitably told off. I will try not to compliment you again. I don't think it will be that difficult somehow.'

I clench my fists and am about to give him a sharp retort when Georgina squeals.

'Ooh I love this. What do you think Amy? You're the expert.'

I drop my bag onto the satin covered couch and follow Georgina to the mannequin. She's stroking the dress lovingly.

'This is just the kind of dress I had in mind.'

'It's perfect,' says Ben from behind us. I spin round and glare at him.

'I really don't think you know what is best for Georgie,' I say.

'Prosecco?' asks Petunia, while air kissing me.

'Lovely, Petunia,' I say. 'This is Georgina. We're choosing her wedding dress today. I hope you have plenty of Prosecco and cake.'

Petunia and I laugh while Ben looks on.

'Of course, Amy, just say what you need.'

'Lots of cake I think. You know how stressful buying a wedding dress can be.'

'I'm not sure cake is a good idea,' says Ben softly. 'You do realise Gina is on a diet?'

I glare at him.

'It's one of her five days.'

'I don't think the idea is to eat lots of cake though, even on a five day.'

I sigh loudly.

'What do you think?' calls Georgina, holding the dress against her chubby body.

'You should try it.' says Ben.

He's *trying* me and it's only been fifteen minutes.

'What do you think Amy?'

I feel Ben's eyes on me.

'Try it on, absolutely,' I smile.

She disappears into the changing room while I browse the other dresses and make a concerted effort to avoid Ben Garret. Fortunately his phone rings. I sip my Prosecco and listen to his irritating laugh.

'Hello Sophie? Do you want to come over tomorrow?'

I cock my ear to hear better but he wanders off, lowering his voice as he does so. Moments later he is busy texting. What a whirlwind of a love life he has.

Georgina steps from the fitting room and parades self-consciously in front of us. The dress looks hideous. I struggle not to grimace.

'Mmm,' mumbles Ben.

'It makes me look dumpy doesn't it?' sighs Georgina, studying herself in the mirror.

'Not at all,' I lie. 'It really becomes you.'

'Are you sure?' asks Georgina.

'Absolutely.'

Ben grunts.

'You look dumpy,' he says flatly.

I gasp.

'That's a bit blunt isn't it?' I say.

'It's better than telling her she looks great when she doesn't.'

'Do you really think it becomes me?' she asks.

'Yes, I do,' I say.

Georgina turns back to the mirror and grimaces. I throw back half the Prosecco.

'I guess you're the expert,' she says glancing at the price tag.

'But we have loads to try on,' I say, ignoring the fresh cream éclairs that Petunia has placed on the coffee table.

'What is madam's budget?' asks Petunia, while leading Georgina towards a rail of dresses.

Ben flops down onto a couch and my heart sinks. I was so hoping he would go.

'Oh, daddy's paying, so the sky is the limit,' laughs Georgina.

'If you're determined to stay,' I say turning to Ben, 'then please don't interfere.'

He scoffs a chocolate éclair.

'Trust me I wouldn't interfere with you if someone paid me. But I'm the best man. I need to make sure everything goes smoothly. I've promised Greg that while he is tied up in Spain I would oversee things on his behalf.'

'And I'm the wedding planner. I've been paid to make sure everything goes smoothly.'

'Yes, and you charge a hell of a lot don't you?' he grins.

Not that again.

'How dare you ...'

'Amy, I think I will try this one and how about that veil?' calls Georgina, holding up a Vera Wang dress.

'Lovely,' says Ben.

It's going to be a long session. I stare yearningly at the éclairs and then pinch my hand. I'm Amy Perfect, the success, I never give in.

Chapter Seventeen

Don't puke. Please don't puke. My ringing phone vibrates through my head and I fumble to find it my Chloe handbag. Don't throw up in the bag. In fact, don't throw up, period. Ben is slouched on the pink satin couch surrounded by garters. He's texting one of his numerous girlfriends. Georgina is now parading in her seventh dress and I can barely see my hand let alone anything else. The Quiet Life and the Prosecco are having a profound effect on me. Either that or I'm having a brain haemorrhage. I flip open the phone to Lucy's squealing. That's all she does these days. I really don't know what is wrong with her.

'Amy, where are you?' she yells.

'In Pertulips,' I stutter. 'I told you. Georgie is tying wedding gowns.'

God, am I slurring?

'That was five hours ago. You're supposed to be at the health clinic. They just phoned. Your appointment was at four.'

I groan.

'Is everything okay?' asks Georgie, parading in front of me in yet another gown. It feels like we've been here forever.

Oh no, don't puke. Don't puke on the wedding dress.

'I have an appointment at a health clinic,' I say, grabbing my bag.

'They've moved you back forty minutes. It's a good job it's not the NHS. You'd be moved back six months,' snaps Lucy, before hanging up.

'Are you all right?' Georgie asks again. 'You've turned a funny colour.'

'I'm fine. It's just a check for, you know ...' I point to my crotch. 'Private health clinic,' I mumble.

What am I saying, and even worse, why am I pointing at my crotch?

'A check?' repeats Georgina looking shocked.

'I thought you didn't have contact with men?' grins Ben.

How rude.

'Not that kind of check,' I say, feeling my face grow hot.

Oh God, don't puke, don't puke.

'Right,' says Georgina, looking uncomfortable.

This is terrible. They think I'm going to an STD clinic.

'It's not that kind of check,' I laugh. 'I mean, you can't catch anything from me.'

Oh God, do shut up Amy. It now sounds like you're planning on having sex with them.

'If there was anything to catch, which, of course, there isn't. I mean, it's not like we're going to do anything is it?'

Talk about opening your mouth and putting your foot in it. I'm just digging a bigger hole for myself aren't I?

'What a shame you have to leave,' Georgina says, while looking quite relieved that I am. 'Greg is on his way. You could have said hello.'

Oh shit. I can't see Greg looking like this. Come to think of it, I probably wouldn't be able to see him anyway. How can I drive in this state? How can I even walk in this state? I've only had one and half glasses of Prosecco. What is the matter with me?

'I'll phone you, Greganna,' I say, heading towards the door. At least I think I'm heading towards the door.

She looks at me oddly.

'I think I'm going to take the fourth dress, what do you think?' she asks. 'I'm torn between the Dior and the Oscar La Renta.'

I don't even remember seeing a fourth dress, or a Dior gown, come to that.

'Where's your car? I'll drive you to the health centre and then home. That Prosecco seems to have gone to your head,' Ben says, taking my arm.

Either that or I'm having a stroke, maybe I should ask him to take me to hospital instead. Oh God, I'm going to die before I hit thirty.

'I'm perfectly fine,' I say, falling over a mannequin and apologising to it.

'Yes, I can see that,' he smiles.

'Oh dear,' says Georgina, following us outside.

The cold air hits me and I struggle to stay upright. I'm led to my car just as Georgina screeches Greg's name. I slide down in the passenger seat and hold up my handbag to hide my face. Don't throw up. Not in the Merc.

'Nice car,' compliments Ben. 'The wedding business must be booming.'

The truth is I only bought the Mercedes because I thought Greg would be impressed if he ever saw it. I've never been into fancy cars myself, but Greg was always big on status symbols, not that we could afford any at the time, but he liked to dream.

'I hope you have insurance,' I mumble, hearing Georgina scream 'byeee' as we pass.

'Insurance?' he grins. 'You've got to be kidding. I've not even passed my test.'

I gape at him and then feel something rise up in my oesophagus. Oh no, don't puke, please don't puke. I let out an enormous burp and sigh with relief.

'Feel better for that?' he asks.

'You haven't passed your test?' I repeat. 'Are you insane? You're not fit to drive my Mercedes.'

'And you think you are? Of course I have insurance. I wouldn't even consider driving someone else's car without it. It was rather a dumb question wasn't it? Now, where is this clinic?'

'Harley Street,' I sigh, leaning back onto the head rest.

'I really don't think you should encourage Gina to drink so much. She's very conscious of her weight you know. She hasn't got the makings of a lush like you,' he says giving me a sidelong glance.

'I'm in the middle of a brain haemorrhage,' I say, 'so this really isn't the time to pick an argument.'

'The excuses women use,' he says, turning into Harley Street. 'What number is the clinic?'

'Number twenty-three.'

He stops the car outside the clinic, orders me to wait and comes around to the passenger side to help me out. I stumble on the kerb and he supports me in his strong muscular arms. He leads me up the steps and to reception.

'Amy Perfect,' I slur. 'I have an appointment.'

The receptionist checks her notes and looks up at me.

'There's no need to be nervous,' she smiles. 'It's just a smear, but I'll tell the nurse you're a bit edgy.'

'I'm not …' I begin as Ben leads me to the seating area and lowers me into a chair.

'Magazine?' he asks.

'Can't you just go?' I sigh.

'You're not safe on your own,' he says, flicking through a copy of the *Reader's Digest*.

Seconds later I am called in and a prim looking nurse gives me a disapproving stare.

'We recommend not drinking before a smear, Miss Perfect.'

'Quite right,' I say. 'We wouldn't want to be scraping a drunken vagina now would we?'

I climb onto the couch, tearing the white paper that covers it as I do so. The nurse turns, waving the biggest speculum I have ever seen. Or does it just look bigger to my blurry eyes?

'That's huge,' I say.

'Relax Miss Perfect. There's nothing to it.'

I open my legs and think of Georgina's wedding and that, of course, leads me to think of Greg, lovely, blond Greg, with his electric blue eyes and little nose. I feel my heart thump in my chest.

'It may feel a little cold,' says the nurse.

How could he? How could he marry someone else? More importantly, if I was too overweight for him how can he marry Georgina? I feel myself tense with anger. After all the weight I lost too. I can't just give up can I? I can't let him marry her.

'Try to relax Miss Perfect,' says the nurse, probing with her speculum. 'Now, where's that vagina of yours?'

Hopefully where it has always been, if not I'm in trouble.

'Ah, there you are,' she says gleefully. 'We lost you for a moment.'

Good God, she's talking to my vagina. I only hope it doesn't talk back.

'We're looking nice and pink and very healthy,' she says.

Now I know she's not talking to me.

'All done,' she announces a few seconds later.

I wobble to the door and the waiting area where Ben is chatting to another patient. I ignore him and head to the entrance.

'Whoa there, don't you need to rest or something?' he says, jumping up and taking me by the arm.

'It was a smear test,' I say, 'not major surgery.'

I ask him to take me to the office and we drive there in silence.

'Thank you so much,' I say when we arrive. I pull my purse from my Chloe handbag and hand him a twenty pound note.

'That should pay for a cab,' I say and head towards the revolving doors, only to swing myself around in a circle and back into the street and straight into Ben Garret's arms.

'You have such charm, Miss Perfect,' he says, leading me to the doors.

'I'm glad you think so,' I say, allowing him to glide me through them.

'Which floor?' he asks.

'Second, but really, I'm fine,' I say, tripping into the lift.

'Yes, I can see that.'

The door closes and I have an overwhelming urge to jump him. Seriously, it's all I can do to control myself. I'm sex starved, that's the problem and the fresh musky smell coming from him is playing havoc with my sexual urges. Much to my relief the doors open and I exhale.

'Thanks so much,' I say, holding out my hand.

'I'll see you to the door,' he says, coming over all Victorian.

'It's only there,' I say, pointing.

'It won't exert me then will it?' he smiles.

I allow him to take my arm and escort me into the office, where an anxious Lucy jumps from her seat and begins her usual squealing.

'Where have you been? Did you get to the clinic? I can't believe you forgot again and ...' she stops when her eyes clap on Ben Garret.

'Oh,' she breathes. 'Hello.'

Her breasts heave in excitement.

'Hello there,' Ben returns. 'I've brought Amy back. She's a bit unsteady after her procedure.'

Lucy gapes.

'What procedure, what's happened?'

'You know,' I say nodding.

'Oh my God,' she cries, rushing forward. 'Are you okay?'

'Of course I am,' I say irritably.

I turn to Ben Garret.

'Thank you so much, but I assure you I am fine. Would you like Lucy to call you a cab,' I say removing my coat.

'That's fine. See you ladies.'

He walks from the office, leaving behind a gentle fragrance.

'Oh my God,' mouths Lucy. 'That was Ben Garret.'

'You don't say.'

'He's just gorgeous.'

'And arrogant with it,' I say, banging at the water machine. 'This thing never works.'

'The bottle needs changing,' says Lucy, rushing to the window. 'Look at that sexy walk.'

'Do you have any painkillers?' I ask.

Lucy turns and looks at me anxiously.

'I'll get you some. Are you in pain?' she asks, looking concerned.

'I'm fine. It's just a headache. I think it was the Quiet Life.'

She takes some painkillers from her bag.

'You don't look good. What kind of procedure was it?'

'What are you talking about Lucy?'

'Ben Garret,' she says and sighs. 'He said you'd had a procedure.'

'Well, prevention is better than cure.'

She gasps.

'I don't think that is the best way to prevent it Amy,' she says primly.

I cock my head to one side. Just what are we talking about?

'I have them every three years,' I say.

'Every three years?' she repeats, her eyes widening.

'That's the norm.'

'The norm?' she repeats.

'It was a smear test Lucy, what do you think we're talking about?'

'Oh God,' she stutters. 'I don't know. I just thought …'

'You thought I got pregnant every three years?'

'Well …'

And you think I'd tell Ben Garret? I hardly know the man.'

'Yes, I did think that was a bit odd. Ooh, just wait till I go to the pub tonight and tell everyone I met Ben Garret.'

'I'm glad you're excited,' I say, putting my feet on the desk.

That's the last time I take Quiet Life.

Chapter Eighteen

'I'm surprised Greg puts up with it,' I say.

'Are you breathing Amy?' asks Miriam, putting a hand on my diaphragm.

'Yes,' I say, 'it's something of a habit.'

'And stretch,' orders Miriam.

I pull my leg up and hold it.

'Shit,' cries Rosie, 'I've got bloody cramp.'

'Breathe,' suggests Miriam.

'I'd rather swallow a quinine tablet.'

'Honestly, he's like the maid of honour. She takes him everywhere with her,' I say irritably.

'Even the loo?' asks Rosie rubbing her leg.

'You know what I mean.'

'I really don't think you should be planning this wedding. It's unhealthy.'

'Flex those feet ladies.'

'She's having a bridal shower.'

'Are you going?'

'I'm planning it, and you're coming,'

'What?' exclaims Rosie, dropping her leg. 'Now hang on a minute Amy.'

'Lift that leg Rosie,' orders Miriam.

'I need moral support, especially if Ben is there. She's talking about having it next Thursday.'

'I go to Zumba on a Thursday,' she says with finality.

'You hate Zumba. You hate anything that makes you fit.'

'I really don't think you should be doing this. Besides, Ben won't be there will her? Men don't go to bridal showers.'

'I wouldn't put anything past him,' I say scathingly.

'If you ask me this is all very ...'

'Unhealthy,' I finish.

'Well it is,' she argues. 'And you've lapsed with the shakes, so it is getting unhealthy isn't it. Oh, and talking of shakes. How is the Prince?'

'I haven't lapsed ...'

My leg is jerked back and I see Miriam standing over me.

'This is a Pilates class, not a women's meeting. You can join a slimmer's club for that,' she snaps.

'Ooh bitchy,' mutters Rosie, lifting her leg and groaning.

I look suitably chastised and roll onto my tummy for a back stretch.

'And you're forgetting things,' whispers Rosie. 'You need to tell her to find a new wedding planner. There must be others who do what you do.'

'Not as good as me,' I say between breaths. 'Besides, I'm having cocktails with Georgie and her maid of honour later. I'm in too deep.'

'I think I'm getting too old for this. I can hear my joints creaking,' Rosie moans.

'Will you come to the shower?' I ask.

She sighs.

'Is there going to be booze?'

'Yes, Georgina wants sparkling wine. I tried to tell her it was tacky but ...'

'What's tacky about it?'

'Whose side are you on?'

'I like sparkling wine, what's wrong with that?'

'Okay ladies let's wind down, on your backs,' instructs Miriam.

'My favourite position,' laughs Rosie.

'So you're coming?' I ask pleadingly.

'It will all end in tears,' Rosie sighs.

I check the time on my BlackBerry. I've just enough time to order Louise's bouquet before my next bride arrives, and then I have venue viewing, cocktails and food tasting with Georgie. It has been three days since the dress fittings and there has been no sign of Ben. Georgie had phoned, saying she had settled on the first dress which I had assured her looked delightful. Fortunately it was one of the few dresses she tried that I can actually remember seeing. Of course, it would have looked far more delightful had she been just a touch slimmer. Greg might be expecting a trim bride but I'm going to do all I can to make sure he doesn't get one. After all, a man should love his bride for who she is. Isn't that what Bridget Jones preached? Far better for Georgie to discover what her future husband is really like before he actually becomes her husband, and if that means being jilted at the altar then that is far better isn't it? After all, nobody wants to get divorced do they? I shuffle the assortment of invitation cards and place the red and white design on the top.

Lucy strolls in from the outside office. She is a vision in black. That is aside from her bright red lipstick. She grimaces and says,

'Chardonnay Storm is here for her one o'clock appointment.'

'Great, send her ...'

Before I can finish the door swings open and I'm met by a cloud of Poison perfume. Lucy coughs and heads for the water dispenser.

'Hello, honey,' Chardonnay gushes, before grabbing me in a tight embrace and almost knocking me off my chair. 'I'm thrilled to meet you.'

For one awful moment my hair gets dangerously tangled in her chunky necklace.

'Oh my gawd,' she exclaims.

She's so close that I can see the swell of her breasts straining inside her push up bra. She releases my hair and stands back. Chardonnay Storm is not my normal run-of-the-mill bride, but everyone is entitled to a perfect wedding aren't they? Provided they can afford to pay for it of course. Chardonnay looks at me with wide eyes, framed in long false eyelashes. Come to think of it, there isn't much about Chardonnay that isn't false, from the fake snakeskin handbag to her thick highlighted hair extensions.

'Can I sit down babe? It's been a hell of a journey from Saffend,' she says, flopping into a chair opposite me.

'Saffend?' I question.

'Southend,' explains Lucy with a roll of her eyes.

'Ah,' I say.

Seems my name is getting into the most unsavoury places too. Not that I've got anything against Essex you understand. But you only have to watch one episode of TOWIE to know what I mean.

Chardonnay fingers her chunky necklace with great concentration.

'Luckily it's okay. I've only 'ad it a week you see,' she says. 'Gary bought it from Ratners so he'd be gutted if it got broke. It's gorgeous ain't it?'

'Lovely,' I say.

'Tea or coffee, Chardonnay?' asks Lucy.

'Ooh, do you 'ave a sweet white wine?'

'We don't have alcohol on the premises,' I say.

She looks surprised.

'I ain't never 'eard that before.'

'We'll be planning the most important day of your life. It is the one time you want to keep a clear head.'

'And Amy knows all about that, don't you Amy?' quips Lucy before gliding out of the room.

'I love your office,' says Chardonnay, pulling off her jacket and revealing her leopard print top in all its glory. 'I knew it would be posh like this.'

'I hope you received all the information,' I say, trying not to inhale her perfume fumes, 'our prices and everything.'

'Oh yeah, that's okay. Gary's bruvver Dave is helping to pay. Gary was a bit dan in the maff that he couldn't come today but he 'ad a lot on at the garage. He wants to get 'is own garage one day, so it's good to keep in wiv the punters ain't it?'

'Oh yes,' I agree. 'And who's Dan?'

'Dan, I don't know nuffink about a Dan.'

'You said Dan in the maff.'

She laughs, her gold hooped earrings swinging along with her merriment.

'Nah, down in the mouth,' she says, widening her mouth to articulate the words. 'You know, *gutted*.'

'Ah,' I say.

'I wanna do me own make-up. I wanna tell ya that right away. That's what I do, you see, I'm a make-up technician. I don't want no one else doing it.'

Lucy flies back into the room her cheeks red. She gestures with her thumb.

'There's someone to see you.'

I sigh.

'Well, they'll have to wait Lucy.'

'I don't think so,' she says, hopping from one foot to the other.

'Everyfink all right?' asks Chardonnay.

'I'll be one minute, Chardonnay. Have a Jaffa Cake.'

I shove the plate under her nose and follow Lucy into the outer office.

'What's the matter with you? It's not professional to ...'

I stop on seeing Ben Garret.

'He insisted on seeing you immediately and I thought as it's Ben Garret. I did try ...'

'I'd like a word,' he snaps.

'Only one?' I say making an attempt at humour.

You don't have to be a brain surgeon to work out he isn't happy. There's a deep line etched in his forehead where he is frowning and his lips are drawn tightly together.

'I'm with a client,' I say. 'Can we discuss this later perhaps? Lucy has the diary and ...'

'I don't care if you're with the Queen Mother. What are you doing telling Gina to buy that grotesque wedding dress?'

Oh, for goodness' sake.

'Who's Gina?' asks Lucy, looking confused. 'I don't think we have a Gina on our books. I think there's been a ...'

'The dress is perfect for her,' I argue. 'That's what I create, the perfect wedding.'

'The perfect catastrophe more like, because that's what it will be if she wears that dress. You know damn well she looks ...'

'Fat,' I finish for him. 'I think Georgina will look fat in any dress she wears, because she *is* fat.'

Lucy gasps and looks behind me where Chardonnay is watching from the open door.

'Perhaps we could do this at another time?' says Lucy, nodding her head towards Chardonnay.

'Every fink all right?' asks Chardonnay.

'Everything is fine, isn't it, Mr Garret?' I say.

'Look, I know I'm a man and I don't know much about wedding dresses, but I know when someone looks terrible and that dress just isn't right.'

I fight back a sigh.

'I'll have a chat with Georgie this afternoon if that makes you happy, but I'm starting to think that maybe I'm not the right person to plan this wedding. I cannot possibly arrange her perfect wedding if you are harassing me all the time.'

'Don't flatter yourself. I've got better things to do than harass you,' he snaps, before striding to the door. He stops and holds out a twenty pound note.

'I believe this is yours,' he says curtly. He slams the note down onto the desk, opens the door and stops again. I hold my breath.

'That perfume of yours would kill at ten paces. Don't get Gina to wear that either.'

'It's not my ...' I begin but the door has closed behind him.

'Faaackinell, he was a bit miffed weren't he,' says Chardonnay, shoving a Jaffa Cake into her mouth. 'But I agree wiv ya. You can't be a fat bride. Mind you, he was a dish. Is it his bride that's fat?'

'I can't really talk about other clients,' I say, leading her back into the office.

'That was Ben Garret,' Lucy says finally.

'Tell me something I don't know,' I snap.

I swallow three Quiet Life tablets with my coffee and force Chardonnay's attention back to her own wedding while I struggle to push away the image of Ben Garret's cross but handsome face. What a bloody cheek, barging in here telling me my job. I'll have to speak to Georgina about him. This has got to stop. At that moment my BlackBerry trills and Georgina's name lights up the screen.

'You're dead popular ain't you?' says Chardonnay.

'I won't be a sec,' I say, hurrying out of the room.

'I'm so sorry to bother you,' says an apologetic Georgie, 'but Greg is in the UK for a few days and I told him all about you and ...'

Oh no, she's not cancelling is she? This is my only chance to win Greg back.

'He wants to meet you.'

'Oh,' I say, 'the thing is, I'm pretty tied up so ...'

'So is Greg,' she laughs.

At least we're not tied up together which is something of a shame. I feel myself grow hot at the thought and grab an envelope from Lucy's desk to fan myself.

'Are you okay?' asks Lucy wearily.

I nod.

'Are you free for dinner on Saturday?' asks Georgina.

'I have a wedding,' I say.

'That's a shame. Greg is going back to Spain next week. Oh well, we'll have to arrange it for when he gets back. At least he is fine about us having a wedding planner. Isn't that great?'

'Great,' I say trying to calm my pounding heart.

'Can we meet for cocktails at four? I'm really sorry to change the time but my meeting has been put back and I'm not going to get away before that.'

'Four is fine,' I say, without looking at the diary.

Lucy's head jerks up and she begins gesturing at me.

'See you then,' says Georgina.

I click off my phone.

'Who are you meeting at four?' demands Lucy. 'You haven't put anything in the diary.'

'Georgina, she's put it back by an hour. We have food tasting and cocktails.'

Lucy exhales.

'Did someone drop you on your head at Pilates?'

'Don't tell me I've got a flu jab or something?'

'Four o'clock is Michelle's wedding rehearsal. If you'd checked the diary you would have seen it clashed.'

Bugger, how could I forget that?

'But I have to meet Georgie,' I say.

'Every fink okay?' calls Chardonnay. 'The fing is I have to be back in Saffend by five. Gary and I are going for a slap up meal with our mates.'

'You'll have to change Georgie to another day. After all her wedding is seven weeks away,' says Lucy.

'I can't.'

If there's one bit of advice that I've learnt it's to *keep your friends close and your enemies closer*. Well, that's what the Godfather said in the film wasn't it, and he ought to know, and although Georgina is not strictly my enemy, she is marrying my Greg. If I can get close to Georgina it will get me closer to Greg.

'I don't understand why you're so obsessed with this one wedding.'

'I'm not obsessed,' I say, looking for my Quiet Life.

'Don't start with those. Remember what happened last time,' reprimands Lucy.

'You'll have to stand in for me,' I say.

'You always go to the wedding rehearsals, they expect it. They want Amy Perfect, not me.'

'Shit, shit,' I mumble.

'Almuch longer you gonna be?' calls Chardonnay.

'Phone Georgie, see if she can do four thirty,' I say, fighting the urge to pop the entire contents of the Quiet Life bottle. Why do people have to keep chopping and changing?

'The wedding rehearsal will last longer than thirty minutes,' sighs Lucy.

'I'll work something out,' I say, hurriedly making my way back to Chardonnay.

I'm Amy Perfect. I create perfect weddings. I make dreams come true but right now I'm in danger of giving myself a perfect breakdown.

Chapter Nineteen

How can the bride be so bloody late? I check the time on my BlackBerry and curse.

'She's here,' cries Michelle's mum.

'You're late,' I say accusingly as Michelle walks through the church doors.

'I thought I was supposed to be,' says Michelle, looking at her mum for support.

'On the day,' I say gently. 'Not for rehearsal. It doesn't really matter for rehearsal does it?'

At times like these, I seriously consider chucking in Perfect Weddings and taking a job in Waitrose, scanning loyalty cards and asking people, 'how's your day been so far?' Why is this happening to me? I can't be late meeting Georgie.

'If we can move on with things,' I say to the vicar. 'Get the show on the road so to speak.'

The organist begins to play The Wedding March and I draw an imaginary line under my throat and he stops abruptly.

'I think we know that bit don't we. Shall we jump ahead to the ceremony?' I say.

'I'd like to go through everything if you don't mind,' says Michelle's mum huffily. 'After all, a girl only gets married once.'

I hate to tell her that only fifty-four per cent of them do, but probably best not to mention that. After all, mummy and daddy are paying my bill so I simply nod in agreement.

'Of course, it's just that Michelle is so on the ball with everything that I thought we could cut to the chase and ...'

'Cut to the chase?' she snarls.

I wish the brides wouldn't bring their mothers to rehearsals. I give the thumbs up to Dennis, the organist, and he starts again. I follow behind Michelle and her bridesmaid, while tapping out a quick text to Georgie.

Running a bit late, will be there soon

I circle my hand at Dennis gesturing him to speed things up a bit. Michelle walks faster and her little bridesmaids do a skip to keep up. We finally reach her fiancé Michael, and I breathe a sigh of relief before checking my phone. There's a text from Georgie.

No worries see you later.

'Don't you think that was a bit fast,' says Michelle's mum.

Mothers are such a headache for wedding planners. If I had my way I'd have them blindfolded and gagged in a cellar somewhere, at least until the big day arrives.

'I thought it was fine,' I say, nodding at the vicar.

'I thought it was a bit fast,' says Michael.

We all stare at him. I've never known Michael voice an opinion. Clearly neither has anyone else as we are all struck dumb. Finally, Michelle says,

'If Amy says it is okay, then it is okay.'

Michael nods nervously in agreement. I don't think Michael will be jilting Michelle at the altar. He'd be too afraid. My mind wanders back to my own wedding and I forcefully push the memory away.

'Shall we continue?' asks the vicar.

I nod in irritation.

'Was the walk okay?' Michelle asks worriedly. 'Did the girls cope behind me?'

'Fabulous, it looked fabulous.'

'She won't be able to walk that quickly in her dress,' says Mum. 'She has a long train.'

'Dennis will slow it down on the day, won't you Dennis?'

'I wouldn't have gone so ...' he begins.

'Great,' I say interrupting him. 'Shall we press on?'

We perform a shortened version of the ceremony and I check my BlackBerry again.

'Perfect,' I say. 'We're all ready for Saturday week.'

'I wanted to check with you about the flowers and ...'

'Can you email me?' I say shuffling backwards.

'Email you?' repeats Mum.

'Yes, email any last-minute concerns.'

'Don't you think we should discuss the concerns here?' says Michelle's dad, blocking my way.

Is it any wonder I'm stressed? And why don't churches have mini bars in the pews? I can't think of a better place to have them.

'I always advise my brides not to get bogged down with the details a week before the ceremony. Too much attention to detail is how mistakes happen.'

What on earth am I saying?

'But you said ...' begins Michelle.

'I think we should all go for coffee and discuss Michelle's concerns,' says the mother of the bride.

'That's a good idea. What do you think Michael?' asks Michelle.

I roll my eyes and discreetly check my BlackBerry.

'Well ...' begins Michael.

My phone trills and I flip it open gratefully.

'It's me,' says Lucy.

Why does my heart sink whenever Lucy phones?

'Lucy,' I say, 'is it urgent?'

'No, I'm just phoning to tell you that the sheikh has sent you an enormous bouquet of flowers. I've never seen one this huge in my life. We could barely get them through the door. That's nice of him don't you think, especially after what happened?'

'Oh no, that's just terrible,' I say, letting out a gasp. If I play this right I may be able to get them to believe this is an emergency and make my escape.

'It is? I thought it was rather nice of him. The card says, *To Amy with grateful thanks.* I think he fancies you.'

'Oh no,' I say, placing a hand on my heart. 'Should I come immediately?'

'Well, no, not unless you think you should. I just wondered if you could bring some vases back with you. We've got nowhere near enough for this lot, but there's no rush for them.'

'I'm speechless,' I say.

'Yeah, I was when I saw them.'

Michelle looks at me wide-eyed.

'I feel quite faint hearing this. I'll go straight to the hospital.'

'God, Amy, are you okay? It's only a bouquet of flowers. Are you having a panic attack?'

'It's just the shock. It's just when I last saw him he looked perfectly normal.'

'He is normal isn't he? It's not unusual for a man to send a woman flowers is it? Oh God, is there more to this than meets the eye?' asks Lucy in a trembling voice.

'We'll have to discuss the ceremony. It may have to be cancelled.'

'Blimey, is it that serious? Does it mean something else when a sheikh sends flowers? Is it a coded threat or something? Oh my God, they're safe aren't they? Should I leave the office?' asks Lucy in a panic-stricken voice.

'I'm on my way,' I say and hang up.

'An emergency,' I say to Michelle. 'I really have to run. Email me, or phone Lucy if it's urgent. I'll see you early Saturday.'

I fly out of the doors before she can even blink. I've got exactly two minutes to get to The Ivory Hotel.

Chapter Twenty

I fly through the revolving doors of The Ivory Hotel and find myself spinning around like a top. Are all my meetings with Georgina destined to be like this? I stop to catch my breath and feel my head thump. I really don't do revolving doors.

'Good afternoon, madam,' says the doorman, pleasantly. 'Are you coming in or going out?'

Buggered if I know. I seem to be all over the place these days.

'Actually, I was trying to turn myself into Superwoman,' I respond. 'But, as you can see, it didn't work.'

'I'm sorry to hear that madam, how can I help otherwise?'

'I'm meeting Georgina Winters and ...'

'Ah yes, they're waiting for you in the bar. May I take your jacket?'

I hand him the jacket, straighten my dress and head to the loo where I phone Lucy.

'Thank God you phoned. I don't know what to do. Mike said I should phone the bomb squad but I don't know their number, do you have it?' she squeals.

Who the hell is Mike?

'Oh yes, of course. I'm always phoning the bomb squad. What are you talking about Lucy?'

'The flowers, what do you think I'm talking about? Are you calling from the hospital?' she says, her voice rising.

'Why would I be at the hospital?'

'I don't know. You said you were going there and ...'

I exhale and pull a hairbrush from my bag.

'Lucy, the flowers are fine. I had to escape from Michelle's wedding rehearsal. Your phone call was a godsend.'

'But I thought there was a big problem,' she sighs.

'You did say we didn't have enough vases.'

'I don't know you any more, Amy,' she says dramatically.

'I'm sorry, but I'm getting really stressed. Are there any other messages I should know about?'

'Just the sheikh phoning and oh yes, Laureta called twice. She asked if you could phone her.'

I really don't understand these brides. They cannot do anything themselves. I managed perfectly well without a wedding planner for my big day, not that it ever happened of course, but that's not the point.

'And who's Mike?'

'The plumber, he's fixing that leaky tap in the loo.'

'Oh,' I say, 'I didn't know we had a leaky tap.'

'You haven't noticed much at all since you took on that client, Georgina. I don't know why you're so obsessed with her wedding. Are they paying extra or something?'

'I'll tell you later. I'd better go, Georgie will wonder where I am,' I say hanging up.

I check the time and tap in Laureta's number as I walk out of the loo.

'Ah, good. Amy, you got my message. Prince Abdullah wants to take you out for dinner this evening and ...'

'I can't. I've ...'

'You can't say no to the Prince,' she snaps.

'But isn't he married?' I say nervously.

'He's been married three times, what's that got to do with it?' she says dismissively.

I would have thought quite a lot.

'Hasn't he got enough women? I'm sure he doesn't want another.'

She sighs.

'What am I paying you for Amy?'

Not to sleep with Arab princes that's for sure, and I hate to remind her but she isn't paying me at all, her mother is and she's paying me to plan a wedding, not entertain Arab princes.

'To plan your wedding,' I say gently.

'Jean Maurice's at eight. Don't be late. He likes punctuality.'

Oh God, there must be something I'm doing at eight this evening.

'Amy, there you are,' calls Georgina.

I spin round to see her waving from the bar.

'I've got to go,' I tell Laureta and hang up.

'Oh Amy, I was getting worried,' Georgina cries. 'I just said to Patsy, it's not like Amy to be late.'

Georgie looks fantastic. There's a glow to her face that I would die for. Her thick wavy hair has been pulled back into a perfect bun and her full figure is hugging a fluffy white cardigan over a black silk top. I look behind her to a big boned, bespectacled, brown haired woman wearing a plaid skirt and black fluffy cardigan.

'This is Patsy, my maid of honour,' says Georgie.

'Oh,' I say.

Admittedly, I wasn't expecting Beyoncé but by the same token I wasn't expecting Olive Oil from Popeye either.

'She's deaf in one ear so you may have to shout a bit,' whispers Georgie.

Patsy smiles, revealing crooked teeth. Doesn't Georgie mean matron of honour? Patsy must be forty if she's a day.

The breath is knocked out of me as I'm engulfed in a bear hug. Jesus, the woman may look like Olive Oil but she has the strength of a sumo wrestler. She releases me and I stumble to stay upright. She shakes my hand manically.

'Hello, Amy doll, I've heard so much about you. I'm overwhelmed, really overwhelmed,' she says loudly.

She isn't the only one. I'm as overwhelmed as anyone can be. I would speak but bits of her fluffy mohair cardigan are stuck in my mouth.

'You're slim,' she says, 'very slim in fact.'

'Thank you,' I reply, discreetly removing the mohair before it chokes me.

'It must be nice to be slim,' she comments, looking pointedly at my hips.

This feels too much like a *Fatal Attraction* moment to me.

'You like animals, Amy doll?' she asks.

I told you it was a *Fatal Attraction* moment. I'm beginning to wonder if she thinks my surname is Doll.

'I don't like rabbits,' I say.

Best to establish that at the beginning isn't it? Although, I don't believe I'm having this conversation.

'Who does like rabbits?' she asks, meeting my eyes.

'Well, Dan had one in the film *Fatal Attraction*, didn't he?'

What am I saying?

'Ooh yes, and that horrible Alex boiled it,' says Georgina shivering.

'He was totally in the wrong having that affair,' says Patsy, still looking into my eyes, while all I can see is my reflection in her glasses. 'Women who steal other women's men deserve all they get.'

Why do I feel she's warning me?

'Well,' I say, shrugging nervously. 'People make mistakes.'

'I love animals,' says Patsy. 'I've got three cats and a dog.'

'Lovely.'

'Patsy works for a vet,' says Georgie. 'She's their receptionist.'

'Oh, that's nice. It must be rewarding helping sick animals.'

'We put a lot of them down,' she says bluntly.

Right, I can't very well say 'lovely' to that, can I?

'Oh well,' I shrug. 'You can't win them all.'

She just looks at me.

'Patsy's got two weeks off to help with the wedding,' says Georgie.

'Lovely,' I say.

I must sound like some of the parrots she sees.

'Cocktails?' suggests Georgina.

I can't think of anything better.

'Great idea,' I say, throwing my bag over my shoulder. I stroll into the bar and they follow me. What is Greg doing with these people?

Patsy pulls her mohair cardigan down over her plaid skirt and nudges me so hard I almost fall over.

'See that hunk over there,' she says pointing with a nod of her head.

I discreetly look to the end of the bar where two attractive men are sitting.

'I think he fancies me,' she says, hitching up her bra. 'He's been eyeing me up ever since we arrived,' she blushes.

'He has?' I say, trying to hide my surprise.

But come to think of it, Patsy could be very appealing if she plumped up that lifeless hair of hers, and she does have lovely oval shaped eyes. It's just a shame you can't see them through her specs. And the plaid skirt and plain cardigan just don't do her justice.

Georgina wanders over to the bar to look at the cocktail menu.

'The names of some of these cocktails are very rude,' she says, blushing.

'Ooh they are a bit,' says Patsy.

God what planet are these girls on?

'I know what I'm having,' says Patsy, tossing her hair back and sending an earring flying across the room.

'Sex on the Beach,' she whispers. 'I had it in Ibiza once. It was lovely.'

'The drink or ...?' I ask with a laugh.

She gives me a deadpan look.

'Well, the drink of course.'

This is going to be a bundle of laughs, that's for sure.

We climb onto bar stools and study the drinks menu.

'What are you having?' asks Georgina.

'I expect you've had loads of cocktails haven't you Amy, doll?' says Patsy loudly.

'It's Amy Perfect, actually,' I say, ordering a daiquiri.

'Shall we get pissed Amy doll?' asks Patsy.

Evidently I'm not talking into her good ear.

The barman places our drinks in front of us, gives Patsy an odd look and then walks away. Patsy takes a gulp of her drink and smacks her lips.

'What's yours like Georgie?'

'Very nice,' says Georgina shyly.

Patsy nudges me and I slide ungainly from my stool. She's not only got the strength of a sumo wrestler, but the muscles too.

'How's yours?'

'Aside from it being all over my dress, it's lovely.'

'I so love planning the wedding,' says Georgie excitedly.

I pull the wedding invitations from my bag and lay them out on the bar.

'I thought these red and white ones would be perfect. We ought to get them ordered so we have time to check them and get them sent out on time,' I say pushing them towards her.

She claps a hand over her mouth and lets out a tiny 'oh'.

'Do you not like them?' I ask.

'They're gorgeous,' she replies in a breathy voice.

'I'd love invitations like that when I get married,' says Patsy wistfully.

'Do you have your guest list?' I ask Georgie guiltily.

Georgie rummages in her bag and pulls out a notepad.

'Oh, this is so exciting,' she squeals.

I try to ignore the burden of guilt that weighs heavily on my shoulders. But, let's face it, if she doesn't know the Arsenal team colours, then she really isn't the woman for Greg, is she? Football is everything to him. Georgie ought to know that. I can't imagine what Greg is thinking of, marrying her.

'He's coming over,' Patsy whispers, hitching up her bra before patting at her lifeless brown hair. 'What do I do?'

I look to see the blond guy walking towards us. I would do anything to slink down in my seat and disappear, but you try doing that on a stool.

'Hi ladies, sorry to bother you,' he says pleasantly.

Georgie smiles while Patsy removes her glasses and attempts to flutter her eyelashes, except she rolls her eyes instead and looks like she's about to have an epileptic fit. I wouldn't mind but she's fluttering her eyelashes at me. She's clearly blind without her specs on.

'You're not bothering us,' she responds nervously. 'What can we get you to drink?' she adds, stroking her neck seductively.

I cringe and throw back the remainder of my daiquiri.

'I've already got a drink but thanks for the offer,' he smiles and then holds out an earring. 'I think this is yours.'

Georgie and I look at the earring while Patsy continues to smile feverishly, her eyes glittering. It must be rather terrifying for him.

'Thanks so much,' says Georgie, taking the earring.

By the time Patsy has put on her glasses he is well gone.

'I do believe it's time to view the banqueting hall,' I say, climbing from my stool.

Patsy and Georgie follow me and my heart races as we get near the entrance. I open the doors with their ornate handles and try not to gasp at the beautiful sight in front of us. Glass chandeliers hang from the ceiling and the walls are decorated with burning sconces. I close my eyes and visualise Greg and I entering the packed ballroom and feel myself sway with ecstasy. We were going to have our reception here. I'd arranged to have candles all around the room. I had pictured the crystal shimmering under their lights. Every table was to have a single rose in a tall crystal vase. It was to be the most blissful reception ever and then Greg had ...

'Oh,' breathes Georgie, 'this is amazing.'

I open my eyes.

'It's perfect isn't it? Every bride wants this venue but it is so expensive, but of course, money isn't an issue for you.'

'Awesome,' whispers Patsy.

I'm not so sure Greg will agree of course. The last thing he'll want is a reception in the same hall as we had booked for our wedding.

'Greg will adore this,' says Georgie, trembling with excitement.

'It is available for your date,' I tell her.

'Wow, how abfab would that be?' booms Patsy.

'Can Greg see it? He's home for a few days so that would be great.'

'Just let me know when and I'll arrange it with the hotel.'

Georgie pulls me into a hug and her Paul and Jo fragrance has such a calming effect on me that I barely feel the twinge of guilt that taps me on the shoulder yet again.

'Georgie, about Ben ...'

'Isn't he just brilliant?'

'It's just ...'

'Food tasting,' says Patsy before I can finish.

'Thank you so much Amy,' gushes Georgie. 'I just knew you would give me the best wedding ever.'

I lead them to the doors.

'Time for some food tasting I think,' I smile.

I must avoid the puddings at all cost. I'm slowly heading down the slippery road to hell. Greg won't want me if I get fat again. I need to get my act together. Just one drink to calm my nerves and then I will drink less alcohol and eat less food from this day forth. Yes, great plan.

Chapter Twenty-One

'I couldn't eat another thing,' groans Patsy, belching loudly.

We've eaten and drunk so much that a gastric band, coupled with liposuction is looking like the only option for my extended stomach. This is a disaster. I never drink at my clients' tasting sessions. Mind you, Patsy is enough to drive a nun to drink.

'How are we doing ladies?' asks Charles, the chef.

'Lovely,' replies Patsy. 'I never knew wedding food tasting could be so much fun.'

Georgina tucks her arm into mine.

'I love you Amy,' she slurs. 'You're giving me the purrfect wedding.'

I feel a stab of guilt. The thing about being pissed is that you always feel you can tell the truth, the whole truth, and nothing but the truth, and everything will be all right. At that moment, while feeling Georgie was my best friend, I open my mouth to tell her everything.

'Georgie,' I begin, 'I really should ...'

'The bridal shower,' she squeals, almost deafening me. 'We have to plan it.'

'Let's make it *dirty*,' suggests Patsy, lurching out of her seat to grab the last bottle of wine.

Crikey, a few glasses of wine and Patsy becomes a right little raver.

'Oh, I don't know if Greg ...' begins Georgie.

'He won't even know,' says Patsy, her glasses lopsided.

'I was thinking a trip to Brighton might be more fun instead,' giggles Georgie.

I try to stand up but the room spins.

'You're pissed,' laughs Patsy.

'So are you,' I retort.

'Its great fun though isn't it? I love getting married,' Georgie laughs.

'Where are we going onto from here?' Patsy asks, struggling to get the last drop of wine from her glass.

'We could go onto a club, what do you think Amy?' asks Georgie.

'What's the time?' I ask, growing hot.

Georgie fumbles with her phone.

'Seven thirty,' she says. 'Why?'

'Shit,' I mutter. 'Shit, shit.' I'd completely forgotten my dinner date with Prince Abdullah.

God, I'm exhausted. I don' think I could squeeze any more into this day if I tried.

'What's up chick?' asks Patsy, lurching from her seat.

'I'm supposed to be meeting the Prince for dinner. God, I'm going to have to hurry.' I say anxiously, standing up again. I so wish the room would stay still.

They both gape at me.

'Prince Harry,' says an amazed Patsy. 'You lucky cow, how did you swing that?'

'He's an Arab sheikh,' I say, grabbing the back of a chair for support.

'No, he's not,' argues Patsy.

'I'm not meeting Prince Harry, I'm meeting Prince Abdullah. My job depends on it.'

Holy shit, how can I meet the sheikh in this state? I look down at my creased dress and want to sob.

'Have you ladies decided?' asks Charles.

'Oh yes,' sighs Georgie, 'I know exactly what I want.'

She flops back down in her chair only to have Patsy yank her out of it.

'She's got to meet the Prince.'

'He's a sheikh actually,' says Georgie dreamily, 'isn't that romantic? It's just like a Mills and Boon romance.'

'I can assure you it is nothing like a Mills and Boon romance,' I say.

'Phone me your choice later, that will be fine,' says Charles.

'Everyone Amy knows is so lovely,' Georgie purrs, pecking him on the cheek.

'We'd better get you to the ladies,' says Patsy, grabbing my arm. There's no way I can resist her. She's as strong as an ox. God knows how many Weetabix she has for breakfast.

I stare at my reflection in the loo mirror and groan. My face is flushed and my hair a mess.

'I look like crap,' I moan.

'I can't disagree,' nods Patsy.

There are also small red stains on my dress where I had spilt some raspberry juice.

'Get that off,' demands Georgie. 'We'll tidy that up while you sort yourself out.'

'I can't go,' I whine.

But I have to go don't I? If I don't, Laureta will pull out of her contract. For the first time in my life I really don't want to be Amy Perfect. I just want to be Amy Fisher, sitting in a nice quiet mortuary. Not dead, obviously. Even I don't think things are *that* bad. But what I wouldn't do to be back in my old job with a lovely boyfriend waiting at home for me. Is that too much to ask?

'You're ready,' says Patsy, squinting at me through her glasses.

The truth is I am far from ready.

Chapter Twenty-Two

So, here we are, or at least here I am, standing outside Jean Maurice's with my heart pounding. I'm twenty minutes late. Seriously, who keeps a prince waiting? Patsy and Georgie wave from the cab, encouraging me to go in. Jean Maurice's is known for its celebrity clientele. Anyone who is anyone frequents it, so God knows what I'm doing here. My head is still spinning from all the wine we had drunk. I have no idea why I am doing this. I'm Amy Perfect, the success. What's the worst that can happen if I don't have dinner with the sheikh? Laureta will cancel her contract, that's what. And then her mother will tell everyone what a cock up Amy Perfect made of Laureta's not so perfect wedding and I'll have clients dropping off my list like flies. No, that won't do at all. Reputation is everything in the wedding business. I know a lot of women would give anything to be wined and dined by a billionaire prince, but I'm not one of them. I hesitate at the door and am about to turn away when it opens.

'Good evening,' greets a waiter.

Soft jazz music plays in the background.

'Hello,' I say, giving a little cough.

'How can we help?'

'Believe me; it's too long to go into.'

I scan the tables but can see no sign of the sheikh. Let's face it; he's pretty hard to miss in that get up of his. I feel a momentary sense of relief. Maybe he has changed his mind. I never thought I'd be grateful at being stood up.

'Do you have a reservation?' asks the waiter.

'I was meeting someone,' I say, 'but I don't think they're here. It's not a problem.'

I turn to the door.

'Let me check for you madam. Who are you meeting?'

'Prince Abdullah,' I mumble.

The waiter doesn't flinch. They obviously have princes here every day.

'One moment madam and I will check.'

He disappears and I cast my eyes around the busy restaurant and then I see him, not the sheikh, but Ben Garret. He's at a table with a group of people. I turn away before his eyes have time to meet mine. Oh no, what is he doing here? I must talk to Georgie about him.

'This way madam,' says the waiter.

'Really?' I say, trying not to look disappointed.

I reluctantly follow him to a table by the window, skirting past Ben Garret's table as inconspicuously as I can. A man in a pristine white shirt and pale blue jeans rises from his chair. I look for the sheikh but can't see him anywhere.

'I think ...' I begin.

'Good evening, Miss Perfect,' says the man, leaning forward to kiss my hand.

'Prince Abdullah?' I say, surprised.

'Of course,' he smiles.

'Oh, I thought you would be wearing ... erm ...'

I can't say garb can I, and I'm far to pissed to think of a more appropriate word.

'When in Rome,' he grins.

He's rather good looking out of his garb. He's also married I remind myself, and not married just once. I wonder what his wives are doing while he's out wining and dining another woman. Or are they here too, watching me with their beady eyes from another table?

'May I take your jacket madam?' asks the waiter.

I slip it from my shoulders and hand it to him.

'And what can I get you to drink madam?'

'Just water please,' I reply, fumbling in my bag for some paracetamol.

'You look very lovely,' Prince Abdullah says in his soft accent. 'You have the English rose look.'

I have the English pissed look, more like.

'You may have wine. I don't drink but I'm happy to get it for you.'

I can't say I've had plenty already.

'I'm fine with water,' I smile.

After all, I need to keep a clear head, or at least a somewhat clearer one. The waiter pours my water and I give Abdullah a sideways glance as he studies the menu. He's younger than I thought and rather good looking too. The white shirt he's wearing stands out against his dark complexion. He lifts his sultry eyes and meets mine.

'I hope you liked my flowers.'

I'd clean forgotten about those.

'They're beautiful.'

So Lucy says anyway.

'Although I'm sure you get men sending you flowers all the time.'

'I wouldn't say that.'

'There must be a boyfriend. I hope he isn't too cross about our dinner this evening?'

'There isn't a boyfriend,' I say quickly, feeling the urge to cry. Honestly, it's all I seem to do these days. One thought of Greg and I'm like a running tap. It's ridiculous.

The sheikh looks at me intently and I'm relieved when the waiter returns. I glance down at the menu.

'May I order for you Amy?' asks the Prince.

On his tongue my name sounds like a caress.

'Yes, of course.'

I'm totally stuffed and seriously couldn't manage another thing. I hope the portions are small. They normally are in posh restaurants aren't they?

'The quail salad for starter,' he orders.

'And for madam?' asks the waiter.

'The same and we'll have the sea bass for main course.'

His voice is soft and sensual and totally hypnotising. The waiter leaves us and Abdullah looks at me over his glass.

'What are your wives doing this evening?' I ask, just in case he's forgotten about them.

'They are resting. It was a long journey.'

'I'm so sorry about *Hava Nagila*,' I stammer. 'And the awful drive to the hotel.'

He raises his eyebrows.

'We had ordered a limo but there was a bit of a cock ...' I bite my lip and blush profusely. 'A mess up,' I correct.

'It was ... different,' he smiles, 'but your company made it worthwhile.'

Oh my God, is that his foot travelling up my leg. I fight back a gasp and tuck my legs under the chair. I bet you don't get this in Mills and Boon. He'll be selling me off to a white slave trader next. I need to drink plenty of water.

'So, are you available Miss Perfect?'

'Available?' I repeat hoarsely.

Do they normally ask if you're available for white slave trade? His eyes ravish me and he licks his lips sensually.

'For some romance, Miss Perfect, you have heard of romance?'

Oh yes, I've heard of it. It's just never come my way.

'Please call me Amy.'

Please call me a cab more like. We've not had dinner yet and he's coming on to me. You'd think he'd be exhausted with those three wives wouldn't you?

I gulp down some water and struggle to think of a reply. I don't want to upset Laureta any more than I already have. I've got enough on my plate with Georgie's wedding as it is.

'I'm far too busy for romance,' I say, unless of course it is with Greg. How I so wish I was having this dinner with him.

'No woman should be too busy for romance,' he says, his eyes appraising me. 'Am I right in thinking that a man has let you down?'

I think that being jilted fits that description. The waiter places the quail in front of us with his legs sticking up like a can-can dancer. The quails legs that is, not the waiters.

'Looks wonderful, do you agree?' asks Prince Abdullah.

'Lovely,' I say, feeling nausea rise up in my stomach.

'I'm not here for long. I'm sure you can find some time for me,' he says, slicing through the quail with a knife.

His eyes defy me to say no.

'I've got a lot on,' I say nervously, picking at my food.

'I think you can give me some time,' he smiles; his voice soft, but firm. 'Come to my hotel tomorrow.'

Oh my God. This is getting more and more sordid by the minute. Surely he isn't thinking of a foursome. I feel the quail rising up.

'If you'll excuse me, I'm just going to pop to the ladies,' I say breathlessly.

He stands up immediately and waits for me to leave. I dive into the loos and flop down onto the toilet seat my head between my hands. My head is thumping unmercifully. The restaurant is boiling hot. I'm barely able to concentrate on anything. The only thought that is going round and round in my head is how can I say no to the sheikh and keep the contract with Laureta? I can't possibly go to his hotel. I'll end up in the Sunday tabloids. I'm in turmoil. One minute my life was as perfect as Perfect Weddings. Everything was going swimmingly and then Georgina burst into my life and nothing has been the same since. I can't possibly have a romance with a thrice married man, can I? I shouldn't even be having dinner with him. I create perfect weddings and that's it. It's not a call girl agency. It's not obligatory for me to have dinner with the best man is it? I stand up and stride from the loo. I am resolute. I cannot spend any more time with Prince Abdullah. I open the door and walk straight into Ben Garret. I feel his hands on my arms and shudder as the most delicious tingle runs through me.

'Whoa, sorry,' he smiles, steadying me. His eyes meet mine and his smile turns into a frown.

'Ah, Miss Perfect, good evening,' he says, quickly releasing me.

'Mr Garret,' I say, acknowledging him.

I go to walk past but he sidesteps, blocking my way.

'Have you had a chance to speak to Gina about that dress?' he asks bluntly. From the corner of my eye I can see Prince Abdullah watching us.

'If you'll excuse me I should get back to my companion,' I say briskly.

'You haven't answered my question,' he says, placing a hand on my arm, sending yet another tingle all the way down my right arm. Of course it may have nothing to do with Ben

Garret and may simply be the first stirrings of a coronary. After all, let's face it, my stress levels are fit to burst.

'I really haven't had the time.'

'Don't you think you should find the time?' he says, his voice hardening. His hand is still on my arm and the tingling has spread to my loins. It seems Ben Garret awakes the animal in me.

'I assure you I will speak to her.'

His warm brown eyes lock onto mine.

'I don't want to step on your toes ...'

'Then maybe you shouldn't,' I say sharply.

'But I really can't allow Gina to wear that dress.'

'Can't allow?' I repeat. 'I think Georgie has a mind of her own.'

'Yes, but unfortunately she trusts your judgement where weddings are concerned. I can't say I share her confidence but ...'

'You really are the rudest man I have ever met. Now if you'll excuse me.'

'Have a good evening Miss Perfect,' he says, before removing his hand but not before sensually stroking my wrist.

'You too Mr Garret,' I say, struggling to breathe. I feel his eyes on me as I return to the table. Abdullah stands as I approach.

'Who was that?' he asks possessively.

'He is the best man for another wedding I'm planning,' I say as I watch Ben leave.

Abdullah leans across the table and grabs my wrist.

'I hope you don't go out with all the best men?' he says, his gentle tone turning menacing. His grip is tight and I try to pull my hand away.

'I don't go out with any of the best men Prince Abdullah and I really shouldn't be here. Please remove your hand, I need to leave.'

'But we haven't had dinner,' he protests, his eyes boring into mine.

I tug my hand from his grasp and stand up, scraping my chair back noisily.

'I have to go,' I say firmly, picking up my bag.

I hurry from the restaurant before he has time to follow.

'Is everything all right madam?' asks the waiter as he rushes after me.

'Could I please have my jacket?'

'Certainly madam, is there anything else we can help you with?'

'I just need some air,' I say, trying not to panic as I see Prince Abdullah striding towards me.

I throw the jacket over my shoulders and dash out of the restaurant.

Chapter Twenty-Three

I rush into the street and am about to hail a cab when a hand grasps my shoulder.

'I can't allow you to leave like this.'

My heart thumps in my chest.

'Let me go please. You're a married man and I really shouldn't be having dinner with you.'

'Then why did you come?' he demands.

'Because I didn't want to upset Laureta,' I say, holding back my tears.

I try to hail a cab but he pulls my hand down.

'I don't want you to leave yet,' he says harshly.

This is not in the least Mills and Boon, is it? I feel tears running down my cheeks.

'Is everything okay?' asks a voice behind us. Relief floods through me when I turn to see it is Ben Garret.

'Oh Ben,' I say.

He raises his eyebrows. I never call him Ben. I also never thought I'd be so pleased to see him.

'Everything is fine, thank you,' says Abdullah.

'I was talking to Amy,' says Ben firmly.

He turns to me and frowns.

'Are you okay?' he asks, ignoring Abdullah.

I give him a pleading look. I really don't want to antagonise Abdullah any more than necessary.

'I was just escorting Amy to my car,' Abdullah says, brusquely taking my arm. I try to pull away but he has a vice like grip.

'I'm not sure Amy wants to go,' says Ben, stepping between us.

'Please let me go Abdullah,' I say quietly.

'You heard the lady,' says Ben, removing Abdullah's hand from my arm. 'She doesn't want to go with you.'

Prince Abdullah gives Ben a scathing look before gesturing to two burly men standing by his limousine.

'Oh no,' I groan.

'Great,' mumbles Ben. 'I don't need a starring role in *The Essex Boys*.'

I watch them approach and feel my breath catch in my throat.

'I really don't think this is your business,' snarls Abdullah. 'You move on, perhaps?'

'Laureta won't be happy if you cause trouble,' I say, trying to hide the tremble in my voice.

'Then go in the car Amy,' he says firmly.

'You can beat me up,' grins Ben, 'but expect to make the headlines tomorrow. I've a lot of contacts in the media.'

'Ben is the editor in chief for *Vanity* magazine,' I say. 'He's very well respected.'

'Thank you,' smiles Ben.

How can he be so bloody calm? Abdullah looks at us suspiciously. The two monsters stop in front of us and my stomach clenches. Ben can't take on these bullies and win.

'We'll discuss this matter another time Amy,' Abdullah says finally.

He walks to the car with the burly men following. I exhale with relief.

'Nice company you keep,' says Ben as the limousine drives off.

My legs turn to jelly and I grab his arm for support.

'It wasn't my choice,' I say.

'You don't look good. My flat is around the corner. Come for a cup of sweet tea and when you feel better I'll get you a cab.'

I nod weakly. The events of the last few hours have finally taken their toll.

'Thank you,' I say gratefully.

He hooks my arm into his.

'I'm sorry about Abdullah's men,' I say.

'I could have taken them on. I probably wouldn't have won mind you,' he laughs. 'But hopefully you would have visited me in the hospital. What were you doing with him anyway?'

'He's my client's best man. She wanted me to have dinner with him. I felt obliged because I messed up collecting him and his wives from the airport.'

'Wives?' he questions.

'He has three.'

'That's a bit greedy don't you think?'

I laugh.

'He's a sheikh,' I say, as if that explains everything.

'I see.'

'Thank you for rescuing me.'

'I rescue damsels in distress all the time. Think nothing of it.'

We turn the corner and stop outside a newly built apartment block.

'This is me,' he says. 'Are you happy to come up?'

He might be a bit flirtatious but I don't somehow think Ben Garret will be selling me to white slave traders. Not tonight anyway.

'Yes,' I say, following him through the doors. It is warm inside and the smell of leather upholstery hits me. A doorman greets us and pushes the lift button.

'Good evening Mr Garret.'

'Hi Bob, how are you this evening?' smiles Ben.

'I'm great, Mr Garret.'

I follow Ben into the mirrored lift and we travel up to the fifth floor. I follow him along the carpeted hallway.

'Here we are,' he smiles.

I step into his flat and gasp. It's enormous. I'm faced with a wall of windows and the view is amazing.

'You can see most of London from here,' he says wandering into the open-plan kitchen.

I step over a rolled-up rug and marvel at the lights of the city.

'It's better during the day. But I'm not suggesting you stay the night,' he calls.

I glance at a pile of CDs on the floor and wander over to take a closer look.

'Sweet tea,' he says.

I turn to see him standing behind me with a tray.

'Sorry about the rug,' he apologises. 'It came a few days ago but I've just not had time.'

I take a few sips of the tea.

'Have you just moved in?' I ask enviously.

Boxes are scattered around the room and in one corner a pile of books cover the floor. Paintings lean against one wall and against another is a piano. In the centre of the room is a rolled-up carpet.

'I moved in two months ago. I just haven't had time to get things organised. There's been a load of fashion shows and … well you know how busy work gets.'

I look for evidence of a woman living with him but I can't see any. I sip my tea while he fiddles with the rug. He's really rather nice when he's being pleasant.

'If you take that end we can roll this out,' he says.

His cool blue eyes meet mine and I have to fight that overwhelming urge to jump him. I take an end of the rug and help him roll it across the floor.

'At least it's the one I ordered,' he says with a twinkle in his eye.

'You haven't looked at it until now?' I say.

He grins. We stand back and admire the Moroccan style rug.

'It looks nice,' I say, helping him straighten it.

'Can I ask you about Georgina?' he says turning to face me.

Oh dear, just when things were going so well.

'I really don't want to talk about weddings.'

'You can't seriously think she looks good in that dress. You don't seem stupid but …'

Well it didn't take long for him to be insufferable again did it? I let out a sigh.

'It's as though you want her to look terrible on her big day,' he adds.

I feel myself blush.

'Don't be ridiculous,' I say.

'I hope you're going to talk to her about that.'

'I will. I'm also going to talk to her about you.'

'Me?' he says, feigning shock. 'What have I done apart from rescue you this evening?'

'You're interfering with me,' I say and blush when I realise what I just said.

'I beg to differ on that one,' he says with a twinkle in his eye.

'Interfering with me doing my job,' I explain.

'I'm just doing my duty as best man,' he says simply. 'And that means making sure the wedding goes smoothly. Georgina looking plump and not her best is not a good start for a perfect wedding. But hey, what do I know? Perhaps you think differently?'

'It's my job to make sure weddings are perfect,' I say defensively.

'You're pretty bad at your job then, that's all I can say.'

'You just don't give up do you? Isn't it enough you insulted me in your stupid magazine?'

'Here we go again,' he says, rolling his eyes.

I fight back my anger and pick up my jacket.

'You really are quite insufferable,' I say angrily. 'Now if you could call me a cab I will be on my way.'

'I didn't mean to insult you ...'

'Well you did,' I say sharply, turning to the door.

I've really had enough of men this evening. I hurry out of his flat and straight into the lift. The doors close and I lean against the wall as the lift descends to the ground floor.

The doors open to the foyer and the doorman greets me.

'Good evening mam, would you like me to hail a cab for you?'

'That will be wonderful, thank you.'

A taxi arrives within seconds and I reach for my bag only to find it isn't there. Damn, I'd only gone and left it in Ben Garret's flat.

'Where to?' calls the taxi driver.

'Just a sec,' I say, struggling to think what to do. What's happening to me? I'm Amy Perfect, the success. I never forget my handbag.

'Everything okay mam?' asks the kindly doorman.

I shuffle my feet.

'Do you want the cab or not?' asks the driver.

'Yes, it's just …'

The driver sighs.

'I left my bag behind,' I whisper to the doorman.

'Hold it,' yells a voice. I turn to see Ben striding from the lift waving my handbag.

'You forgot this,' he says.

I turn to the cab but it has gone.

'Oh no,' I groan.

'Shall I hail another?' asks the doorman.

'It's fine Bob,' says Ben. 'I can do that.'

'Certainly Mr Garret, good evening mam,' he says with a nod.

I snatch my handbag from Ben and walk along the street.

'You're very stubborn,' he says, following me.

'And you're insufferable.'

'So you keep saying.'

'Because, it happens to be true,' I say, quickening my step.

'I only want Gina to look her best on the day, that's all.'

'So do I,' I say reeling around to face him.

'You could have fooled me.'

I glare at him.

'Okay, I'm sorry. I didn't mean to insult you earlier. I'm sure you're a brilliant wedding planner. Admittedly I'm no expert on weddings and maybe I don't know a nice wedding gown when I see one but can I just introduce Gina to our wedding fashion editor. I'd rather do it with your approval.'

Now, I can't very well say no, can I?

'Fine,' I agree.

'Great,' he sighs. 'How about we drink to it, there's a place around the corner that does great milkshakes. Let's go there and make up,' he suggests.

His gentle fragrance washes over me. He raises his eyebrows and waits.

'I really don't see the need to make up with you Mr Garret. I just want to go home. It's been a very tiring evening.'

'So, end it on a milkshake. They're really good.'

'I do know the place,' I say, thinking of the lush chocolate brownie milkshake that was always my downfall. This really isn't something I should be considering, especially now. I could turn a corner and bump into Greg at any moment.

'Then you'll know how good they are,' Ben smiles.

He's really quite hard to resist with his gorgeous eyes and warm lips, and the truth is I would like to spend a little longer in his company, although I couldn't tell you why. It feels so natural with him, even when he is being insufferable.

'Just one,' I say, giving in. After all, one won't hurt will it?

'Trust me, one is enough.'

I slow my pace as we walk to Pepi's Parlour. It's warm inside and busy, but we find a table. The background music is drowned out with the chatter and laughter of the other customers.

'What would you like?' asks Ben.

'The Chocolate Brownie shake,' I say without hesitation.

'Ah, you have been here before,' he grins.

His phone begins to ring and he gives me an apologetic smile before answering it. I sigh, one of his many girlfriends no doubt.

'How are you doing?' he says into the phone.

It seems forever since I was last in Pepi's. I had missed the ambiance, and the smell of cinnamon and chocolate mixed with the aroma of freshly roasted coffee. I close my eyes and drink in the atmosphere. After all, I won't be here again for a long time.

'Sure,' he is saying, 'how about ice skating?'

He sure has a busy social life doesn't he?

He hangs up a few seconds later and wanders over to get the shakes. I close my eyes and reminisce. Greg and I used to love coming here. Oh, Greg, I miss you so much. I open my eyes to see Ben coming back from the bar with the milkshakes and my mouth waters. I scoop some off the top with a spoon and nearly die from the flavour. It's heaven. I've so missed it.

'They're good aren't they?' he says, pulling off his jumper.

'The best,' I agree.

He really is a dish. I'm not the only one to think so either judging by the number of girls glancing at him. I can see his well-toned body through his white shirt.

'What will you do about the sheikh?' he asks, handing me a serviette.

'Drinking it seems a good idea.'

He laughs.

'I was thinking more along the lines of the real sheikh.'

'Oh, I'm not sure,' I answer. 'I expect the bride will get a new wedding planner.'

'One that doesn't mind sleeping with sheikhs you mean?'

I shrug.

'I suppose so.'

He leans across the table and touches my cheek, making my body tingle.

'You've got cream on your face,' he says, wiping it gently.

Our eyes meet and my hand trembles.

'Thanks,' I say, pulling away.

Thankfully, at that moment my mobile trills and I pull it nervously from my bag. Please don't let it be Laureta. I really don't feel strong enough to deal with her yet. I look at the screen and see it is Georgina.

'Amy,' she says in a hoarse voice. 'I'm sorry to bother you. I know you're with the sheikh and everything ...'

'No I'm not actually ...'

'You're not? Is everything okay?'

'Well …'

'Oh Amy,' she blurts, bursting into tears. 'Everything is going wrong. Greg called me a stupid woman. I didn't realise the invitation colours were Arsenal football colours, he hates Arsenal.'

Oh shit.

'We had a terrible argument and he stormed out saying I didn't understand him. You don't think it's all over do you? Oh Amy, what shall I do?'

Chapter Twenty-Four

I grip the phone tightly. Ben looks at me with interest. I daren't tell him what is happening.

'If you're not with the sheikh, can I come round and see you. I don't know what to do Amy.'

'Of course you can. I'll be home in fifteen minutes.'

Ben raises his eyebrows.

'Thank you Amy.'

Oh God. I didn't think things would come to a head this soon. I'm racked with guilt. But let's face it, she really should have known about the Arsenal colours shouldn't she?

'You have to go?' Ben asks as I stand up.

I grab the milkshake. After all, who knows when I'll get another one?

'One of my brides is a bit upset. I need to see her.'

'It's a twenty-four hour job isn't it?'

'Thanks so much for the shake,' I say, pulling on my jacket.

'I'll see you into a cab.'

Two minutes later we are on the street. I'm about to climb into the cab when he steps closer and kisses me on the cheek, his lips soft and warm on my skin.

'Thanks for a pleasant evening, burly men aside,' he chuckles.

'Thank you for the milkshake and of course the tea.'

'Anytime, just say the word,' he grins, handing me a card.

He closes the car door and I give a little wave. The cab pulls away and I lean back in the seat and look at the number on the card.

Of all the men in the world, why do I have to be attracted to Georgie's best man, and why now of all times? The memory of Georgie jerks me back to reality. Surely Greg hasn't broken off the engagement? Not this soon. My heart flutters at the thought of Greg being available. I really shouldn't be having this milkshake. My phone trills again and I glance at it warily. It's Laureta. I grimace and decline the call.

Georgie is sitting outside my apartment block when I arrive. She looks terrible. Her cheeks are mascara-streaked and her eyes puffy and red. Her hair has come loose from its bun and tendrils hang around her neck. She's cradling half a bottle of wine between her legs.

'Amy,' she cries. 'You've got to talk to Greg.'

'Oh Georgie,' I say, hugging her as guilt engulfs me. She trembles as I hold her.

'I don't believe this is happening,' she says.

I pay the cab and hurry her into the building. She sobs as we make our way up the stairs.

'I'll make some tea,' I say, throwing a roll of loo paper her way.

'I've brought brandy,' she says, pulling a bottle from her bag.

I could certainly do with a glass of that.

'Did you know about the Arsenal colours?' she sniffs.

'Erm … I …'

She slaps her hand.

'That was terrible of me, of course you didn't. You're giving me the perfect wedding, or at least you were. Please forgive me Amy. I don't know what's wrong with me. Bloody football, I hate it,' she sobs, pouring brandy into a glass.

'Is that wise?' I ask, looking at the glass. 'You've already drunk a lot today.'

She blows her nose into a wad of loo roll.

'If I kill myself drinking it will serve Greg right.'

'But you'll be dead, so what's the point?'

'Then he'll be free of me.'

Oh dear.

'Perhaps he doesn't want to be free of you.'

What am I saying? I want him to be free of her don't I?

She grabs my arm and hurls herself onto the couch next to me.

'He's my whole life Amy. I can't live without him,' she says, bursting into hiccupping sobs.

I pour brandy into a glass for myself and knock it back.

'That's a bit extreme isn't it?' I say.

'Have you ever been in love, Amy?' she asks, blowing her nose.

I picture Greg in my mind and feel tears prick my eyelids.

'Yes, I was madly in love,' I admit before pouring more brandy into my glass. I don't think I've ever had so much alcohol pumping through my veins as I have tonight. Georgie pulls her legs under her and looks at me expectantly.

'What happened?'

'He dumped me on our wedding day,' I say and then burst into tears myself.

'Oh Amy,' she exclaims, throwing her arms around me. 'What a bastard. I'd just die if Greg did that to me.'

Yes, well, I hate to tell her that he may do just that.

'Oh Amy, no one deserves that. Do you know why he did it?'

'I never saw him again,' I say miserably.

What am I doing? I must not drink any more. I'll be telling her everything next.

'I can't imagine your pain Amy. Or maybe I can,' she says, fighting back tears. 'If I lose Greg I'll want to kill myself. I'll take poison like Juliet.'

God, that's rather dramatic. Even I wouldn't take poison for Greg.

'Will you phone him Amy? Explain that you gave me the invitation cards. You can tell him that you didn't know they were Arsenal colours.'

Me, phone Greg? Is she insane? I take a gulp of brandy.

'I don't think that is a good idea,' I mutter.

'But I know if *you* explain it will make all the difference,' she pleads. 'Everything was going so well. I showed him the brochures of The Ivory Hotel and he was pleased, more than happy to come and see it with me and ...'

'He was?' I say. Surely he remembered our wedding was to be held there?

'Yes,' she sniffs, 'and then I showed him the invitation and he went crazy.'

'Has he called the wedding off?' I ask breathlessly.

'I don't know. He said he didn't think I was the right woman for him. I can't help it if I'm not interested in football can I?'

My phone trills and I sigh. Ever since I started planning Georgina's perfect wedding my own perfect life has gone to pot. I look at the screen and wince. It's Laureta again.

'Perhaps he needs a woman who's into football like him,' I say cautiously.

'Do you think?' she asks, before draining her glass.

Her cupid lips tremble.

'I could try and like it.'

'Maybe it's all for the best,' I add, refilling my glass. 'If he's going to get this angry over a few colours, is he the man for you?'

She nods in agreement and rummages in her battered handbag.

'Do you want one?' she asks, producing a bag of jam doughnuts.

Oh no, this is a disaster.

'I don't think we should.'

'But why not, after all, I was only dieting for the wedding,' she scoffs, pushing one into my hand. The temptation is too hard to resist, even if her fingers have been all over it. There are times when needs must.

Three doughnuts and four brandies later and Georgina is brandishing her phone like a dangerous weapon.

'You have to phone Greg,' she slurs, pointing it at me.

I back away as if it was a loaded pistol.

'I think that's a bad idea,' I caution.

'But if you tell him that you told me that those colours were perfect for our perfect wedding, then he'll know it's not my fault,' she slurs.

'But you should have known the Arsenal colours,' I protest.

'I don't even know the Tottenham colours,' she weeps, shaking the brandy bottle. 'Why would I want to know them?'

'It shows an interest in him,' I say.

'I'll phone him then,' she says passionately. 'I'll phone him and tell him that you're sorry,' she hiccups.

'Hang on Georgie ...'

'I've nothing to lose,' she sobs.

'But it has gone midnight.'

'Well if he can sleep after what has happened, then he is not the man I thought he was,' she says crossly.

Before I can stop her she has punched in Greg's number. My heart races and my hands turn clammy.

'Greg, oh Greg,' she cries before bursting into tears and pushing the phone at me.

'Talk to him Amy. Explain.'

I lift the phone to my ear and hear Greg say, 'Georgie, are you there?'

My heart beats so fast that I can barely breathe. His voice sends shivers through me. I down some brandy to wet my dry mouth. I haven't heard his voice in three years and it sounds heavenly.

'Please,' Georgie pleads.

'Hello,' I say, attempting to disguise my voice.

'Who's that?' he snaps.

'It's Amy Perfect ...' I say, sounding like a Liverpudlian with a Scottish accent.

'Who? Is Georgie there?'

'I'm the wedding planner,' I stutter.

And the woman that loves you and would always know the Arsenal colours.

'Oh, are you?' he says in a scathing tone. 'Did you suggest those colours for the invitations?'

Greg, oh Greg, it's me, I want to shout down the phone.

'Well ...' I begin, stupidly.

'Amy suggested the colours,' Georgie screams before I can stop her.

'Georgie didn't say they were Arsenal colours,' I say defending myself.

'She should have known,' he barks.

Well I can't disagree.

'What did you say your name was?' Greg asks, curiosity in his voice.

Bollocks, he's recognised me.

'Amy Perfect. I'll hand you back to Georgie,' I say, throwing the phone at her.

She belches into it before saying, 'Greg, I love you. I don't want the Arsenal colours either.'

She stares at the phone for a few seconds and then bursts into loud sobs.

'He hung up. It's all over,' and with that she grabs my Yves Delorme cushions and sniffles into them.

'I could just die,' she declares.

So could I. Those cushion covers were from Harrods and they cost me 160 quid. I so wish she would put them down.

'Crying isn't going to help,' I say tugging gently at the cushions. 'You need a good night's sleep. Everything will look better in the morning.'

That is, except my cushions, of course.

'I expect you're right,' she says, clambering up and revealing her chubby thighs.

'I'll ring for a cab,' I say.

Getting her into a cab was easier said than done. Two refused to take her and the third only agreed when I offered to pay double.

'She'd better not throw up,' he grumbled.

I flop onto the couch and look in dismay at my cushion cover. I dab at a small blob of raspberry jam only to spread it over more of the cushion. I leave the empty glasses and brandy bottle on the coffee table and crawl into bed fully clothed, my mind full of Greg. My head spins and my stomach churns but the thought of Greg makes everything okay. I push away all thoughts of the sheikh and Laureta. I'll deal with that tomorrow. A pang of guilt hits me when I remember all the food and drink I've had this evening. Still, one night won't hurt will it? Just think, soon I'll be back with Greg. Georgie really isn't the right person for him, and it will be for the best if they break off the engagement. I am sure Georgie will thank me for it in time. It's what's best for Greg.

With Greg's name on my lips I doze off to sleep and, strangely, dream of Ben Garret.

Chapter Twenty-Five

Lucy frowns as I walk into the office.

'Good afternoon,' she grunts. 'Nice that you found time to come in.'

'It's not *that* late,' I argue. 'And please don't start on me, I have a terrible hangover.'

'It's almost midday. I've sent you five texts. I tried phoning you. I've Whatsapped you. I almost tried contacting you through a medium.'

'Do you think, just one day, you could greet me with a smile Lucy?' I ask wearily.

'I'd love to but you give me nothing to smile about. I feel like a hamster in a cage. The phone hasn't stopped ringing. I've not had a break. My head is splitting and these flowers are making me sneeze.'

She should have my head. It feels like someone's demolishing a tower block in there.

'I really don't need a lecture Lucy,' I groan, reaching for the water dispenser.

I have to agree about the flowers though. The office looks like a funeral parlour. Oh well, I won't be getting any more flowers from the sheikh will I?

'And,' she continues, 'the sheikh has been on the phone, so has Laureta, several times, and Georgie too. Don't you check your phone any more?'

'The battery's dead. I forgot to charge it last night.'

'That's not like you.'

I haven't been like me for several weeks.

'I've got a hangover,' I groan.

'You don't say. Don't worry I'll always hold the fort,' she says sarcastically.

'I've had a terrible night,' I moan, swallowing an aspirin. 'Greg broke off his engagement to Georgie. She didn't leave my flat until 2am. The sheikh made a pass at me and tried to sell me off to a white slave trader. Ben Garret rescued me and almost got beaten up by two thugs for his trouble.'

Lucy gapes at me.

'That all happened last night?' she asks.

I nod.

'How did you escape?'

'Escape what?'

'The white slave trade?'

I close my eyes and sigh.

'Well, obviously it didn't get that far. It could have though if it hadn't have been for Ben Garret.'

'How did he get to be there?' she quizzes.

'He was in the same restaurant.'

'Is he okay?'

'Yes of course.'

'But you said he got beaten up.'

'*Almost* beaten up, luckily the sheikh called them off,' I explain.

'You're sure you didn't dream all this?' she sniggers.

'No, of course not.'

'Your life is one big adventure isn't it?' she quips.

'If Laureta phones, tell her I'm out of the office all day. I won't be back until very late,' I say, grabbing the Big Red Book and walking into my office.

I open the book to Georgie and Greg's wedding day. I bite my lip and consider what to do. I really should give Greg some time to come to terms with breaking off his engagement. I plug in my phone and wait anxiously. A second later it bleeps as the messages arrive. There are Lucy's messages, three from Laureta asking me to call and two voicemails. It then rings and I take a deep breath before answering.

'Amy Perfect speaking,' I say hesitantly.

'Oh hi, you sound different.'

I drop the phone in shock at hearing Greg's voice. I fumble around the floor and retrieve it.

'Hello,' I say, disguising my voice again. I'm sure this time I sound like Stephen Hawking.

'Hi Amy, its Greg Martin, we spoke last night.'

My legs give way under me and I fall onto my chair knocking the Big Red Book off the table.

'Everything okay?' he asks.

'Oh yes, everything is fine.'

Absolutely fine, couldn't be better in fact.

'I wanted to apologise for yesterday. I was a bit sharp on the phone …'

'Oh no, not at all, it was a bit stressful.'

How did he get my number?

'I overreacted,' he says.

He did?

'Not at all,' I say.

Oh God, I'm in danger of sounding like a parrot.

'We should really meet.'

We should?

'Oh erm …' I begin.

'Georgie gave me your number, she said I should apologise. She is right as always.'

She is? The blood roars in my head.

'You spoke to Georgie?'

'Hang on a second Amy.'

My body turns to jelly at the sound of my name on his lips.

'I have to go, sorry Amy. Georgie will call you and arrange the time.'

Arrange a time for what? With that he hangs up and I'm left dangling. Before I have time to breathe it rings again. I answer it immediately, expecting to hear Greg's voice again, but it's Laureta.

'Amy, what's wrong with your phone?' she demands.

Right, that's it. I've had a terrible night and I'm not taking any more shit from Laureta and that bloody sheikh. I don't care if he looks like Omar Sharif. I'm not sleeping with him.

'Laureta, I'm really sorry but …'

'What are you sorry for? The Prince loved you. He said you've got balls. He didn't use those exact words obviously. Anyway, we need to meet. I want the Prince to take a bigger role in the wedding and I need to update you.'

I must be dreaming. I obviously haven't woken up yet from my terrible night. Laureta should be firing me and the sheikh should be livid and Greg, oh Greg, shouldn't be phoning me.

'Can you meet for lunch at Bar Meze? Do you know it? It's close to the Embankment?'

'Yes, of course, what time?'

'See you in an hour?'

'Great.'

Amy Perfect the success is back. I tap in Georgie's number. She answers on the first ring.

'Amy, I was going to call you. Thank you so much for last night. I hope you're not too hung over. I'm so happy. Greg was so apologetic. He sent me a huge bouquet of flowers this morning and admitted to being a fool. It's only football colours, he said. Can you believe it?'

No I can't.

'Can you make lunch? He really wants to meet you before he goes back.'

'I can't, I've already got a lunch date,' I say miserably.

'Oh what a shame, Bar Meze do great lunches too,' she says enthusiastically.

'Bar Meze?' I echo.

Oh no, this surely isn't happening.

Chapter Twenty-Six

I've worked through every possible scenario and there is no way out aside from entering Bar Meze with a brown paper bag over my head, I'm well and truly fucked. I've got just forty-five minutes to think of something and right now I can think of absolutely nothing. I walk into the outer office and look vacantly at Lucy.

'Now what's wrong? You look like you lost ten quid and found ten pence.'

'Okay, I'm coming clean ...'

She holds up her perfectly manicured hands.

'Don't tell me you've been at the Jaffa Cakes? We only had a few left,' she scolds.

I feel a small surge of comfort.

'We've got Jaffa Cakes?' I say hopefully.

'Is that a question or a statement?'

'A question, because if we've got Jaffa Cakes then I need them,' I say desperately.

'Oh dear, I don't like the sound of this. I'll get them.'

She hurries from the room and returns with a flowery tin. She opens it and I grab two Jaffa Cakes.

'Has it got something to do with the sheikh?' she asks nervously.

I take a deep breath.

'Georgina, our bride ...'

'Not her again,' she groans. 'You've not been the same since she booked her wedding.'

I take another deep breath and say,

'Her fiancé Greg was once my fiancé.'

She stops with her hand poised over the tin.

'Not the one that jilted you?'

'How many fiancé's do you think I've had?'

I stuff the Jaffa Cakes into my mouth.

'Does he know you're planning the wedding?' she asks.

'No, he doesn't, but now he wants to meet me, or at least meet Amy Perfect.'

'Oh God, this is terrible,' she says, taking another Jaffa Cake.

'But I said I couldn't meet them ...'

She sighs with relief.

'However, Laureta wants to meet me for lunch to discuss the Prince, who apparently thinks I'm ballsy,' I continue.

'Who, the Prince or Laureta?' she asks, perplexed.

'Does it matter Lucy?' I snap.

'I don't know, does it?'

'The Prince thinks I'm ballsy, but he also wants to, you know...'

'Fuck you?'

'I wasn't going to be that blunt. Anyway, I'm meeting Laureta in half an hour in Bar Meze, but that's also where Georgina and Greg are lunching. I'm bound to bump into them, but if I don't go we'll lose Laureta's contract, and her wedding is only four weeks away.'

I grab another Jaffa Cake while Lucy stares at me.

'I need to get my head around this,' she says pressing her fingertips to her temples.

'It's not a bloody conundrum Lucy.'

'But how can you plan the wedding of your ex-fiancé?'

'It hasn't been easy.'

'No wonder you've had a meltdown,' she says sympathetically.

'Lucy, what do I do about Bar Meze?'

She bites her lip.

'So, let me get my head around this. You don't want Greg to see you because you don't want Georgie to know that you were once engaged to Greg?'

'And obviously I don't want Greg to know I'm planning his wedding.'

'Right,' she says, wagging a finger. 'But you have to meet the Prince even though he wants to fuck you because we can't afford to lose Laureta's contract.'

'Right, well, we could lose it but I don't think we could cope with the bad publicity and knowing Laureta's mother she'll make a stink.'

'This is terrible,' she agrees.

'Tell me about it.'

She stands up excitedly and claps her hands.

'I've got it. I'll come with you,' she announces.

I know I was hoping she would come up with something but I rather hoped it would be a little more imaginative than that. I rub my eyes and sigh. It's no good. I'm well and truly up Shit Street and it's a one way Shit Street at that. I know I wanted Greg to see my new slim body, but not like this.

'Hang on a minute,' says Lucy, giving me a suspicious look. 'Why didn't you just tell Georgie you couldn't plan her wedding because Greg was your ex-fiancé?'

I grimace.

'Oh no Amy, please don't say you were trying to break them up.'

'Well … the thing is I'm in too deep now,' I stutter.

'But why did you do it in the first place?'

I pull a face.

'Oh Amy, you're not still in love with him?' she groans.

'I've never loved anyone other than him,' I sniff.

'I'll have to come with you?'

'And do what? Guide me into the restaurant because I'll have a brown paper bag over my head?'

'I can keep a check on Greg and Georgina so you can relax. I'll make sure you stay out of their sight and as soon as the meeting is over we'll leave. No hanging around. We need to work out some codes.'

'Some codes?' I question. This is turning into a *Mission Impossible*.

'Whenever I see Georgina or Greg I'll cough like this.'

She puts her hand to her mouth and clears her throat.

'If you need to leave the table for any reason then you have to let me know in a subtle way. So …'

'I don't think this is going to work,' I say anxiously.

'It will. You need to yawn if you want to leave the table. Then I can check. I'll blow my nose if it's all clear and if it isn't I'll cough.'

'But what if you cough naturally?'

'I hardly ever cough.'

'You do around flowers,' I argue.

'They don't have flowers in restaurants.'

I check the time on my BlackBerry and gasp. Shit, we have fifteen minutes to get there. We both dash to the tiny loo and fight for the mirror. I want to look my best just in case Greg sees me. The thought of seeing him again has me in a dither. I empty my make-up bag over the sink and begin re-doing my face.

'What are you doing? We haven't got time,' exclaims Lucy. 'Put some lippy and blusher on, that will do.'

'Damn,' I mutter, pulling a brush through my hair only to find it's full of static.

'My hair's like cotton wool,' I moan.

'Chuck some of this on,' says Lucy, shoving a bottle into my hand. 'Not too much though.'

By the time she'd warned me I'd rubbed three squirts in and now my hair looks limp and flat.

'It looks ten times worse now,' I cry.

'You don't need that much.'

'Shit and bugger everything,' I say, fighting back tears.

'Pull it back,' Lucy suggests.

I tug it into a hair band and clip it into a bun.

'Let's go,' she says, yanking me by the arm. 'Operation G, here we come.'

'Your codes had better work,' I say.

If they don't then I'm well and truly fucked.

Chapter Twenty-Seven

'Put these on,' says Lucy, pulling a pair of black rimmed glasses from her bag. 'They're my reading glasses, and wrap this scarf around your head.'

I gawp at her.

'You are joking?'

'No I'm not,' she snaps. 'It's only for when we first go in. Supposing Greg and Georgina have a table by the door. They'll recognise you immediately.'

I suppose she's right. I wrap the scarf around my head and pop on her glasses.

'Jesus, these are strong. I never realised you were so blind. I can't see a thing.'

'Don't exaggerate,' sighs Lucy.

'Seriously, I can't see anything. I'm not exaggerating. Everything is blurry.'

'You won't see Greg then will you? At least you won't panic.'

'I could bump straight into him and I wouldn't know it.'

She hooks her arm into mine.

'Ready?' she asks.

'No,' I tremble.

'Mind the step,' warns Lucy as I trip into the restaurant.

This is terrible. I'm as blind as a bat. All I can see is a collage of colours and a sea of blurry faces.

'Hi,' says Lucy to a figure in front of us. 'We're meeting Miss Dobson.'

I lower the glasses and look around. The restaurant is all wicker chairs and candles. It's not flashy but it isn't McDonald's either. My eyes travel around the room until they feast on Greg. He and Georgie are sitting at a corner table. My knees give way at the sight of him and I grasp Lucy's arm for support. He looks adorable. He hasn't changed at all, apart from his receding hairline. He laughs at something Georgie says and my heart goes into overdrive. That beautiful smile always made my heart flutter. He's wearing a salmon shirt and I stare in disbelief at his bulging stomach. Okay, not bulging but it's certainly evident. When did that happen? Probably caused by too many second helpings of paella, no doubt and to think he had the cheek to dump me because I was overweight? Seeing him again in the flesh brings back the memories of our time together. It's no good. I have to ask him. I have to know why the love of my life left me at the altar. I take a step towards him but am dragged back by Lucy.

'What are you doing?' she whispers.

'It's Greg,' I say, barely able to find my voice. 'I have to ask him what happened between us.'

'Don't be crazy. You've got to keep your head.'

Georgie looks over and waves and I almost pass out.

'They've recognised us,' I say, panicking.

'Ben Garret just walked in,' she whispers, pushing the glasses back up my nose. 'Don't look round. They're waving at him.'

This is getting worse. I let Lucy pull me along. I haven't got much choice have I? I can't see a damn thing.

'Take your glasses off.'

'What?'

'We're almost at Laureta's table,' she says, whipping off my scarf.

I pull the glasses from my face and find I'm standing in front of the sheikh.

'Miss Perfect,' he drawls, taking my hand and kissing it. What a nerve. I pull it back and diplomatically wipe it on my coat.

'We thought you weren't coming,' says Laureta.

If only she knew how close to the truth that is.

'This is Lucy, my assistant,' I babble. 'Lucy may I introduce Prince Abdullah.'

Lucy stands with her hand extended. The Prince takes it and plants a kiss on it.

'Delighted to meet you Lucy,' he says seductively.

She stares into his eyes. This is all I need isn't it? I nudge her in the ribs. I don't want her going all dewy-eyed.

'Think *white slave trade*,' I hiss. 'And don't go forgetting Operation G.'

'Chardonnay?' says Laureta.

'Where?' I say, looking around.

'The drink, not the client,' whispers Lucy. 'Do try and relax Amy. Have a glass of wine.'

Laureta swishes her hair back and says,

'Abdullah feels he has offended you.'

The Prince studies me and it is all I can do not to kick him in the balls.

'No, not at all,' I lie.

Lucy coughs and I freeze in my seat. Oh God, this is it. This is the end of Amy Perfect the success. I'm terrified to turn around. I put on the glasses and study the now indecipherable menu.

'I didn't know you wore glasses,' says Laureta.

'I have them for reading.'

'Are they near?' I whisper to Lucy.

'No, they're eating.'

'Why did you cough?'

'The wine went down the wrong hole.'

'Can you make sure everything goes down the right hole from now on? For God's sake Lucy, my career and your job depend on this.'

'It was all a misunderstanding,' says the sheikh.

A misunderstanding my arse. I pull off the glasses to look at him.

'We understand each other now, don't we?' I say, giving him a steely look.

'I like a woman with spirit,' he smiles.

'We've ordered a selection of hot meze's,' says Laureta, 'unless of course you would like something different?'

'I can't see anything else I fancy,' I laugh.

Lucy coughs again and I raise my eyebrows at her. She gives a little nod and I feel my heart lurch. From the corner of my eye I can see Greg approaching. I can't breathe. He's getting closer and closer. Oh my God, he's coming straight towards us. Lucy looks at me wide-eyed and before I know what I'm doing I dive under the table.

'Amy, what on earth are you doing?' exclaims Laureta, peeking under the tablecloth.

'I've dropped a contact lens.'

'But I thought you were wearing glasses?' she says, banging her head on the table.

I scramble around the floor pretending to search for the non-existent contact lens.

'I have glasses for my long-sightedness and contact lenses for my short-sightedness,' I say, trying not to panic.

'It's okay Amy,' says Lucy cheerfully. 'I've got your spares so you don't have to search.'

I lift my head and look. There is no sign of Greg. Prince Abdullah peers down at me.

'They're little bastards these contact lenses. There one minute and gone the next,' I say, clambering from under the table.

'I don't remember you having glasses yesterday,' he says suspiciously.

'You were wearing your special contacts yesterday, weren't you?' Lucy interrupts.

I throw back some Chardonnay and fight the impulse to look at Georgina's table.

'He's gone to the loo,' whispers Lucy. 'He's got to come back this way though.'

My shoulders are stiff from the tension. I knock back my glass of wine in an attempt to relax. The waiter arrives with the food and there is silence as we eat. Lucy obviously gets completely side-tracked by the meze's because she doesn't cough at all. So when a familiar voice calls my name I jump out of my skin.

'I don't believe it,' says Georgie. 'You're having lunch in the same restaurant as us. What a coincidence.'

I feel certain my heart stops at the sound of her voice. I give Lucy an evil look.

'Oh fiddlesticks,' she mutters through a mouthful of meze's.

Fiddlefuckingsticks more like.

Chapter Twenty-Eight

Amy Perfect the success is no more. I watch Georgina's mouth move but can't hear what she is saying above the roaring in my ears. Lucy kicks me under the table.

'What a coincidence,' Laureta says.

The sheikh stares at me. I can feel perspiration run between my breasts. Laureta is chatting to Georgie and Lucy is looking intently at her phone. Any minute now Greg will return and Georgie will introduce him and then I'll be toast.

'I hope you don't mind me interrupting,' says Georgie. 'Amy is planning my wedding.'

'And mine,' says Laureta.

'That is a coincidence,' says Prince Abdullah. 'So where is your groom?'

Why is he looking at me?

'Greg has gone to the loo.'

'This is Prince Abdullah, he's our best man,' says Laureta, lifting her head proudly.

Georgie's eyes light up with surprise.

'Oh, hello, pleased to meet you,' she says, giving me a quick sidelong glance.

'Good luck with your wedding,' she smiles at Laureta. 'Isn't Amy just the best? We're so lucky to have her.'

Amy Perfect the best is thinking she will be planning her own funeral at the rate things are going.

'Oh dear, oh dear oh dear,' utters Lucy, 'Judy Brannigan has been taken to hospital.'

'Oh no,' I cry, trying to remember if we actually do have a Judy Brannigan on our books.

'You'd better phone her fiancé immediately,' Lucy orders. 'Judy Brannigan is one of our brides,' she explains to the others. 'She was getting married next week. You must phone her Amy.'

I stare dumbly at her.

'I think you should phone her, like now,' urges Lucy.

'Yes, you're right,' I say, pulling myself up.

'That's awful, poor Judy,' says Georgina. 'She must be so upset.'

'Excuse me,' I say shakily. 'Sorry to leave like this Georgie.'

'It's fine, your brides must come first,' she says giving me a quick hug.

'Absolutely,' agrees Lucy.

I stumble across the restaurant and make it to the ladies just as Greg emerges from the Gents. I dive into a cubicle and lean against the door. Perspiration runs down my face and I dab at it with some toilet roll. This has to be the worst day of my life. No, that's not true. My wedding day was the worst day of my life. But this is surely a close second. What am I going to do now? Georgina has seen me. She isn't going to give up. I pull out my BlackBerry and phone Rosie. Pick up, I pray. My prayers are answered and her chirpy voice has me in floods of tears.

'What's the matter?' she asks.

'I'm in Bar Meze with Laureta and the Prince, which would be great if only Georgie and Greg weren't here too. I'm stuck in the bloody ladies. Georgie only wants me to meet Greg. Everything is going tits up. Oh God Rosie, what do I do?'

'How did you end up in a restaurant with Georgie and the Prince?'

'It's a long story,' I sob.

'I told you all this stuff with Greg was unhealthy.'

'What do I do? Georgie has seen me now. I'm finished Rosie.'

'Bloody hell Amy, how do you manage to get into these situations?'

'It takes a lot of practice,' I say, trying to muster up some humour.

'You can't stay in the loo all day. You have to go out and face the music. Get it over and done with.'

'Are you sure?' I ask incredulously.

'What else can you do? Unless you can create some kind of an illusion, I don't think you have much choice. The worst that can happen is you lose the contract.'

She's quite right of course. I either go back into the restaurant and face the music or climb out of the loo window and make my escape. I take a deep breath and open the cubicle door. I shall face the music because the truth is I could never squeeze through that tiny window. I splash my face with cold water and check my reflection. A few blotches and slightly swollen eyes but it's not too bad. I pause at the door, trying to muster up the courage to go back out into the restaurant. The door swings opens and a woman sails through. She stops and holds the door open for me. Little does she know that she's sending me to my execution? Okay, a slight exaggeration, but it certainly feels like that. I step through the door like a woman condemned. The place is still buzzing. I nervously look over to our table and see that Georgina is no longer there. My eyes scan the restaurant but there seems to be no sign of her, or Greg. I gingerly walk towards the table when the door to the Gents opens. I freeze. Relief washes over me when I see it is Prince Abdullah. I'm a walking wreck.

'Allow me to escort you,' he says, taking my arm.

It is then I see Greg. He's walking from the cloakroom and he looks so gorgeous that I want to throw myself at him and beg for answers. Behind him is Ben, who stops to chat with one of the waitresses. The man has no control when it comes to women it seems. I see Greg coming closer and panic.

'Is everything okay?' asks Prince Abdullah, his eyes following mine to Greg.

'I just feel a little faint,' I say, leaning against the Prince and hiding my face in his robe as Greg passes. From the corner of my eye I see him open the door and escort Georgina out of the restaurant. Prince Abdullah supports me with his arms, his spicy aftershave overpowering me.

'You're shaking,' he observes.

My nerves are in shreds. I need a bottle of Quiet Life. I straighten my shoulders and pull myself free from Prince Abdullah's embrace to find Ben Garret standing in front of us. I wince and meet his accusing eyes.

'Hello,' I say, burning with shame.

Ben glares at Prince Abdullah before turning his eyes back onto me.

'This is a strange situation after last night,' he says his voice hard.

'It's not ...' I begin, as tears well up in my eyes. 'I think you've misunderstood. It's not at all ...'

'No, you're right,' he bristles 'It's not my business. Enjoy your lunch Amy.'

Before I can answer he walks away and out of the door. I have to fight the impulse to chase him. How dare Ben Garret judge me? What right does he have? And why do I care what he thinks of me? He's nothing but a womaniser. But now he thinks I am with the sheikh, and worse than that, the sheikh thinks I am with the sheikh. Damn it. I dab my eyes and look at Lucy. What the hell happened to her bloody codes?

'After you,' smiles the Prince as he leads me to the table.

'These are the changes to the speeches,' says Laureta, pushing a sheet of paper across the table.

I pick it up with shaking hands.

'Are you okay Amy?' asks Laureta. 'I saw you bump into that arsehole, Ben Garret. Lucy told me about that piece he did in *Vanity* about you.'

'Oh that,' I laugh dismissively.

'We're going back to The Savoy as the Prince's guests', says Laureta as she stands up. 'Are you coming with us?'

'Of course she is,' says the Prince.

Not again.

'I can't,' I say forcefully. 'I have some wedding work to do.'

Laureta looks at the Prince and I wait nervously. I feel Lucy's eyes on me. Here it comes, the end of my contract.

'Oh well, never mind,' says Laureta, gesturing to a waiter for her coat.

Lucy and I sit in silence as the Prince pays the bill.

'I'll be in touch,' he says, and then they are gone.

'And what happened to your codes?' I say to Lucy.

'That all went very well I thought.'

Oh yes, great. Ben Garret thinks I'm with the Prince. Greg has forgiven Georgina and I'm still alone. Oh yes, it went very well.

Chapter Twenty-Nine

'That's a lovely one,' I say, fighting back a sigh.

I'm so depressed. I'm drowning in photos of Greg. Greg in nappies, Greg with pimples as a teenager, Greg making sandcastles, Greg at uni and Greg around the time I first met him. I'm surprised Georgie hasn't got photos of Greg having a piss. She's got pictures of Greg that I didn't know existed. We are putting together the slideshow for the wedding and it's killing me. I'm almost expecting her to pull out a photo of me and Greg at any moment.

'I love this one,' she says gleefully, handing me a photo strip of her and Greg.

'We did this in Yarmouth,' she reminisces.

They're hugging each other, their cheeks touching. It seems all good things happen for Georgie at Yarmouth. Maybe I should make a trip there myself. Throw myself off a cliff or something. It would be quite fitting to do it there wouldn't it? Greg would always remember me then.

I hand the photo back and wait with dread for the next one.

'This is me as a baby, we'll use this one,' she says placing it with her other choices.

Jesus, she was chubby as a baby too.

This is agony. The coffee table is covered in photos of Greg looking just as I remembered him.

'Ooh this is fab,' cries Patsy, diving into the shoebox and pulling out a black and white picture.

'Oh, I don't want that one,' says Georgie crossly. 'It shouldn't even be in here. That's Greg's ex, Amy Fisher. I keep meaning to cut her out. I like Greg in the Star Wars outfit though.'

My stomach lurches. I remember the day that photo was taken. We had gone on a studio tour and had a souvenir photo taken. Greg was dressed as Luke Skywalker and I was a

Stormtrooper. I snatch the picture from Patsy but fortunately my face is hidden in the helmet.

Patsy clucks.

'I wouldn't worry about her. She's really fat. You're in a whole other league. Don't you agree Amy?'

What a bloody cheek.

'Oh yes,' I say, agreeing that Georgie is in a whole other league to me.

Georgie helps herself to more cheesy balls. That's really going to help the diet isn't it? At this rate the dress will never fit. Did I tell you that Georgie has chosen a Chanel wedding gown? Ben Garret organised it. It costs the earth and unfortunately she looks quite spectacular in it but at least Ben will stop banging on about the dumpy dress that I had suggested. In all fairness it was mean of me to suggest that dress. Mind you, if she keeps popping cheesy balls like this she'll end up looking like a cheesy ball herself.

'I've got tons more photos on my laptop,' she says, pulling it out from under the coffee table.

Oh no. I love Greg but there is a limit.

'More wine?' asks Patsy.

A bottle and a half later we're listening to music while putting the photographs in order.

'This one next,' Georgie says.

We've got photos of Greg and Georgie everywhere.

'Not with Greg in that jumper,' I say. 'He hates it.'

Georgie's head snaps up.

What?' asks Patsy.

I bite my lip.

'I mean, he'll hate it won't he? That jumper is so outdated.'

'That's the idea,' says Georgie. 'So people can see that time has passed. Let's listen to *Both Sides Now* by Joni Mitchell,' she says, jumping up to change the CD. 'I want that for the slideshow.'

I stare at her.

'You don't think it is a bit melancholy?'

I curl up on Georgie's couch and prepare myself. I feel like I'm a guest at *An Evening with Greg Martin*. I'm inundated with photos of him and drowning in his favourite music. I have to listen to the account of how they met and the chronicles of the Greg and Georgie romance. I'm feeling quite suicidal by the end of it.

'Aw, these are lovely stories aren't they Amy?' says Patsy.

'Lovely,' I say feeling an urge to retch.

'Are you okay, Amy doll?' she asks. 'You're so pale you'll blend into the walls.'

'I feel a bit sick,' I say, resting my head.

'Too much wine,' scolds Georgie.

Too much Greg more like.

'I should get going,' I mutter grumpily.

'What about the photos?' asks Georgie in her politest voice. 'Will you get them scanned?'

'Of course she will,' pipes up Patsy. 'That's her job.'

I grab a couple of chocolates from the box on the table. I see it as doing Georgie a service. After all, she can't get any bigger can she? Not if she wants to marry *my* Greg. I wish I could tell her he is *my* Greg and not hers. But I don't really want to admit to being that *fat, out of Georgina's league, woman*, do I? I take the photos with a smugness I didn't think I was capable of. At last, I have some new photos of Greg, and no one will think it strange that I'm scanning them. As Patsy said, it's my job after all. It's five weeks to the wedding and I'm no closer to stopping it than I was at the beginning. I just can't let Georgie marry my Greg, but I have no idea how to stop her.

Chapter Thirty

I sit on the duvet and hug my knees. For the first time since becoming Amy Perfect, I feel the stirrings of loneliness. How can everything go so wrong? I shiver and pull the duvet over me. How can Greg even think of marrying Georgina? How can he come to London and not contact me? How can I love a man who clearly loves someone else?

I can't think about Greg and expect to get some sleep. I force my weary body from the bed and totter to the kitchen. What a night. It could have ended in disaster if there had been a photo of me amongst that lot. I open the fridge door and grimace. It's full of healthy shakes, which remind me of Prince Abdullah. I grab a bottle of chilled wine and pour myself a generous glass. I don't even want to think how many calories I have consumed tonight. Anyway, what does it matter? It seems Greg doesn't care if his women are fat. An awful thought occurs to me … Oh God, if Greg didn't dump me because I was fat then why did he? I huddle under the duvet with my glass of wine and feel tears prick my eyelids. That must have been the reason. Maybe he'll do the same to Georgina if she doesn't lose some weight. I must stop thinking about Greg. I need to get my mind on something else. So with that thought in mind I pick up the *Vanity* magazine from the floor. The magazine falls open at Ben Garret's article and his gorgeous face stares back at me. The lunch was a nightmare and now Ben thinks I'm with Prince Abdullah. I must look so two faced. What must he think of me? What is happening to me? I'm Amy Perfect, the success. Amy Perfect, the perfect spinster more like. After all, let's face it, who does spinsterhood as well as I do? I sit for what seems like forever. The words of the *Vanity* article blurring in front of me. Why does Ben Garret hate me so much? I've done nothing to upset him. The memory of his lips on my cheek sends my pulse fluttering. He is insufferable, but there is something about him. I push Ben Garret from my mind and reach into the bedside cabinet for the photo of Greg. His image has me refilling my wine glass and crying into the pillow. After another glass of wine I start thinking that topping myself isn't a bad idea. The only problem is I don't have anything to kill myself with. The flat is new so it isn't equipped with gas. I rummage through my handbag for pills but all I find is a pack of Windeze and three Imodium. I don't think they'll do much good will they? I'll just be wind free and constipated for a month. See what I mean? I can't even kill myself without cocking it up. It's impossible to jump from the window as they're fitted with these special contraptions so the window only opens a few inches, and I'm not that bloody slim. I suppose I could electrocute myself in the bath, but seeing as there are no power points in the bathroom, I'd have to drive to Homebase first to buy an extension lead and I can't do that as I've been drinking. That's a point. I could drink myself to death. I surely have more than one bottle of wine in the fridge. I stumble into the kitchen where I find a bottle of Merlot. I try to remember if I've ever heard of anyone topping themselves with two bottles of wine. Then I remember the cooking wine and take that into the bedroom too, along with some dried prunes. I don't think the prunes will contribute much to the deathly cocktail but they'll satisfy my sweet craving. I turn the heating up and slide back under the duvet. Three glasses of wine and ten prunes later and I'm not only still alive but I've worked myself up into frenzy over the article in *Vanity*. Ben Garret has no intention of printing an apology or he would have done it by now. How dare he insinuate I charge inflated prices? Doesn't he realise that some of these damn brides give me a breakdown over their bloody nuptials? I tip the contents of my handbag onto the bed and rummage through them until my prune sticky hands land on the white card with his phone number.

'Right, I'll tell the little git what I think of him,' I mumble drunkenly.

His sexy posh voice answers on the second ring. Yes, that's what he is, a posh upstart. Well, I'm not taking this shit from him.

'Are you going to publish an apology or do I have to get legal?' I slur, while trying to focus on Greg's photo.

'Who is this?' he asks his tone hard and suspicious.

'Amy Perfect, why, how many other people do you owe an apology to?'

I hear him sigh and feel my anger boil.

'Miss Perfect, it's one in the morning. Have you been drinking?'

'Are you calling me a lush?' I say, checking the time on the bedside clock. Shit, what am I doing phoning Ben Garret at one in the morning?

'Most certainly not, but you don't sound yourself. Isn't there a sheikh or some other royal that can assist you?'

I gasp.

'You are so rude,' I cry.

'And you're not?'

'At least I haven't slaughtered you,' I say.

'I'm so hoping you mean slandered, Miss Perfect?'

Wasn't that what I said?

'And I haven't slandered you. Where are you?'

'I'm not telling you,' I retort.

'Are you at home? Because if you are I suggest you turn on the television and watch the rest of *Four Weddings and a Funeral*. It's right up your street. That way I can see the end too. It's on the film channel.'

I slurp my wine and switch on the TV. I fiddle with the remote until Hugh Grant pops up on the screen. It's the funeral and I find myself getting weepy all over again.

'I love this film,' I mumble.

'Me too,' he says and I can hear the smile in his voice.

'I never understood why he decided to marry Duckface,' I say.

He laughs.

'Me neither. I was always very in love with Kristin Scott Thomas myself.'

We both take a sharp intake of breath as Hen lashes out at Charles when he says he loves someone else.

'Ooh painful,' says Ben.

'He deserved it. There's nothing worse than being let down at the altar,' I say and after all, who knows better than me?

'I hope that never happens at one of your weddings,' quips Ben.

The love scene at the end is so moving and of course makes me think of me and Greg. I swallow down my tears with more wine. The film reaches its climax and I reach for the Kleenex. I'd forgotten how good the film was.

'Great ending,' he says as the credits roll.

'A classic,' I say.

'So, why are you up so late?' he asks, letting out a yawn.

'I couldn't sleep. What about you?'

'I couldn't sleep either.'

'Nice to chat to another insomniac,' I say, before popping a prune into my mouth. My head is spinning and I slide down under the bedcovers.

'You were totally wrong about the sheikh,' I say sleepily.

'Was I?'

'I'm no more interested in him than the man in the moon.'

'It didn't look that way,' he says softly. His voice is almost hypnotising me.

'I'm not interested in the opposite sex,' I say forcefully. 'They are nothing but trouble.'

'I feel the same about the female sex,' he chuckles. 'We finally agree on something.'

'You do? But you're such a flirt.'

I bite my lip. I've drunk far too much that's for sure.

'Goodnight Amy, it was nice watching *Four Weddings* with you.'

'Night,' I say, clicking off the phone.

I switch the bedside lamp off and sigh.

Chapter Thirty-One

The vintage bus pulls up with Patsy hanging from the platform like some forties *Vogue* model. She's wearing a polka-dot swing dress and on her head are a pair of willy boppers, not something I imagine was very popular in the forties era. The dress code was swing dress and Rosie and I had gone all out. Rosie has donned a red polka dot with matching socks while I had gone for a black and white polka dot with matching white socks. The bus door opens to a backdrop of screams and giggles.

'Hey chick,' screeches Patsy on seeing me.

Well, there's no doubt she's had a few drinks is there?

I open my mouth to speak but I'm struck dumb. Close up I can now see that Patsy has her hair tied into a neat ponytail. Her glasses are steamed up and she has to look over them to see us, but her soft dusty brown eyeshadow really brings out the colour of her beautiful almond shaped eyes. The dress highlights her figure perfectly. It's just a shame she has pulled the ponytail back so tightly.

'Where have you been Amy doll?' she cries, pulling me onto the bus. Rosie follows reluctantly.

'My God, is that her? How old is she?' whispers Rosie as we shuffle to the back of the bus where big band music deafens us. 'She looks like she was born in the forties. Greg is marrying *her*? No wonder you're trying to stop this wedding.'

'That's Patsy, the maid of honour and I don't think she is as old as she looks. She just tends to wear old-fashioned clothes. By the way she's deaf in one ear.'

'I can tell,' groans Rosie.

'Amy,' Georgina squeals as she bounces from her seat. Her full figure is encased in the most beautiful red and white flowered dress. She's fresh faced, her cheeks glowing pink with her happiness and her cherry red painted lips widen at the sight of me. Her hair is styled in a perfect victory roll and as she hugs me I feel my hair get tangled in her vintage slide.

'I'm so happy you're coming,' she says. 'I booked this fabulous bus, what do you think? It's got a loo and everything.'

'We'll need it,' laughs Patsy. 'We've got tons of booze on board.'

I tug my hair from her slide and pull myself gently from her embrace.

'This is Rosie,' I say, as she hands her our gift.

'Oh, you shouldn't have. Having Amy Perfect plan my wedding is the best gift I could ever have,' Georgie says, hugging me again. 'We're going to have such a great time in Brighton.'

Rosie gives me a sidelong glance which I suitably ignore.

'Is everybody here?' calls the driver.

'Yes, let's get this show on the road,' yells Patsy.

We settle into our seats and Patsy hands us both a little party bag.

'There's chocolate willies, glitter and balloons,' she squeals. 'You can forget the diet this weekend.'

I rather think the diet has been forgotten every week since I met Georgie but best not to dwell on that.

'Looks like fun,' I say uncertainly.

The bus's CD player is turned up.

'Let the party begin,' bellows Patsy. 'Who wants a Hanky Panky cocktail?'

'Sounds different,' laughs Rosie.

'Want to help with the food?' asks Patsy. 'The menu is on the ration card, look,' she waves a replica war ration card in my face.

Rosie and I nod and follow her to the back of the bus

'This Hanky Panky is good,' says Rosie, helping herself to more.

'You seen that prince again?' asks Patsy excitedly.

I sigh.

'He was all for selling me into white slave trade,' I say.

'No way,' Patsy screams, perforating my eardrum. 'Did you hear that Georgie?'

I think everyone heard that.

'He looks intimidating,' says Georgie. 'I'm glad you're not involved with him.'

'I won't be seeing him again,' I say, placing sausage rolls onto paper plates.

Patsy pulls bottles of Prosecco from a cool bag. 'Now we can really get this party going.'

There is laughter and popping of wine corks for the next fifteen minutes. Food is handed around and the music is turned up. I push the Strictly Come Slimming Club from my mind and stuff myself full of sausage rolls and mini chicken fajitas. Just one day off the diet won't hurt will it? Georgie taps on her glass for everyone to shut up.

'A toast to Amy Perfect, my perfect wedding planner and true friend,' she cries, pulling me from my seat and hugging me tightly. Guilt washes over me and I feel myself turn red. I hug her back and feel genuine warmth for her. If only she weren't marrying my Greg.

The music is starting to give me a headache. I watch Patsy pace up and down the bus and start to feel dizzy. I take a chocolate willy, after all that's sure to help. Let's face it, this is the closest I've come to a penis in two years, and knowing my luck it will be another two years before I see another one.

'They're a scream,' says Rosie, gesturing to the bus party. 'Georgie seems nice too.'

'What are you saying?' I snap.

'I'm not saying anything. I just said Georgie seems nice.'

The truth, is I think Georgie is nice too, but not nice enough to marry *my* Greg. I must not weaken. I am Amy Perfect, the success. I'm here on Georgie's hen weekend for one reason only. I must stay focused on my mission and get my man back.

Chapter Thirty-Two

We roll into the town at midday like the girls from Sex and the City, albeit not as glamourous. We're windswept and tipsy, and the hotel proprietor is already looking anxious.

'Afternoon,' says Patsy as she approaches the reception desk. 'Are you the owner?'

I yank a bit of dress that is tucked into her knickers and smile politely at the man behind the desk.

'We're the hen party,' I say by way of explanation.

'Is that right?' he says miserably. 'Looks more like a fifties convention to me.'

'Forties,' corrects Patsy. 'And we are THE hen party, we booked you on Tripadviser.'

'They're nothing but trouble in my experience.'

'Tripadviser or hen parties?' I ask, hiccupping.

'Both,' he says dryly.

'I booked the rooms,' says Georgie, stepping forward with a bottle of Prosecco clutched in her hand. Rosie straightens her tiara.

The proprietor widens his eyes.

'Will there be a lot of this?' he asks.

'A lot of what?' asks Patsy innocently, pushing the willy boppers back from her forehead.

'I think he means *penises* and *drunkenness*,' says Rosie softly.

'I bloody hope so,' shrills Patsy. 'It's a bloody hen night. You weren't expecting a bus of bloody nuns were you? It's bloody Brighton after all.'

I'm thinking it might be a good idea to keep Patsy's booze intake to a *bloody* minimum.

'There's no need for bad language,' he says firmly.

Good job he wasn't on the bus.

'We don't have noise after ten,' he says bluntly. 'Drunken behaviour is not tolerated. And ...' he hesitates, 'no men are to be brought back to the rooms.'

'We won't be bringing back men,' says Georgie. 'I'm getting married.'

'Everyone got that?' yells Patsy. 'No bloody noise, no bloody drunkenness and no bloody men. In other words no bloody good time for anyone.'

'She's playing havoc with my eardrums,' grumbles Rosie.

'Them's the rules,' says the man resolutely. 'Take it or leave it.'

We take our keys, rush to our rooms for a shower and assemble back in the foyer thirty minutes later for a night on the town. The only change is the colour of our swing dresses. Georgie is now wearing a bride-to-be sash and I have succumbed to a pink feather boa.

'Let's party,' screams Patsy.

We march past the terrified proprietor and head to the town.

I don't know about you, but I'm not a great lover of hen nights, even though I plan lots of them. So when Patsy leads us to the Funky Lounge nightclub, I feel apprehensive. A burly ginger-haired doorman counts us in while another searches our handbags. I feel my stomach lurch when he fishes a small tin from my bag. He opens it and stares at the white powder. Georgie gasps in surprise while Patsy, with several others, leans over to take a look.

'Oh my God,' shrieks Patsy. 'You do drugs, awesome.'

'I never knew you did drugs,' says Georgie, looking shocked.

'I don't,' I say defensively.

A girl named Kate pushes forward and juts out her chin angrily.

'I don't approve of drugs, Georgie,' she says firmly.

'It's not drugs,' I sigh.

'So, what's that then?' she asks, her eyes lighting up.

'Is that coke?' asks Georgie.

For God's sake, do I look like someone who does coke?

'No, of course it isn't,' I say, but I don't seem able to say it without stammering, which you have to agree doesn't do much for my credibility.

'What is it then?' asks Rosie.

'It's sweetener,' I say, blushing.

The doorman looks at me suspiciously and dips a finger into the powder. Everyone holds their breath as he pops it into his mouth. He pulls a face and swallows.

'It's sweetener alright,' he grunts and everyone lets out a sigh of relief.

He continues to search my bag, obviously keen to catch me out with something.

'What are these?' he asks, pulling out my bottle of Quiet Life tablets.

'They're herbal tranquilisers,' I say.

'You carry a lot of meds don't you,' says Patsy.

'I'll have to take them off you,' he says. 'Don't want you selling them.'

I'm sure I'll make a mint selling Quiet Life in a nightclub.

'Fine,' I say.

'I don't want no trouble,' he says, pointing to me when he finally lets us go in.

'My friend the drug pedlar,' Rosie sniggers.

The music here is a hundred times louder than on the bus. If Patsy hasn't already deafened me then this surely will.

'This is brilliant,' someone yells. 'Let's get a drink.'

I look around with a sinking heart. We're not the only hen party in the nightclub. Rosie and I look at each other.

'A drink,' nods Rosie.

I couldn't agree more. In fact, I think there will be plenty of drinks. That's one of the hotel rules that we'll be breaking for sure.

'Make mine a large one,' I say as someone treads on my boa and almost throttles me.

This is going to be a long night.

Chapter Thirty-Three

So, here we are, or at least here I am, doing the limbo in the Funky Lounge nightclub. I've never done the limbo in my life and after this I don't think I'll be in a fit state to do it again.

Don't you just hate hen weekends? Maybe you don't. Perhaps you're one of those people who always have a hoot. I'm not one of those people. I'm surrounded by neon pink sashes and tiaras. *Disco inferno* thumps in my ears and stale sweat assaults my nostrils. I'm overdosing on L plates and rosettes. What's more, there seems to be an overabundance of soon-to-be-brides in Brighton. I blow the boa feathers out of my eyes, spit out yet another one and bend my back even more. I feel sure I hear a crack. I emerge from under the bar to Rosie's screams of 'she did it'.

'You couldn't have done that two years ago,' she reminds me. I feel quite elated. Georgie slips an arm through mine and drags me to the bar. She hitches up her bride-to-be garter and drunkenly orders a round of shots for our group. The tempo changes and *All the Single Ladies* begin to play.

'Yes, yes,' shouts Patsy, as if she's in the throes of an earth-shattering orgasm.

I groan.

'Let's go,' says Georgie, dragging me onto the dance floor. I definitely need more shots if I'm to get through this. I've not long ago endured a male stripper who thankfully was happy to dangle his rope and tackle in front of Georgie. I'm now feeling quite fragile. I feel sure had he brought it anywhere near me I'd have thrown up.

'Come on ladies, let's be having you,' shouts the DJ.

'What's the time?' I ask Rosie.

'Time for another drink,' she replies.

Another stripper jumps onto the stage and another bride undergoes the torture. His hip thrusts make me feel quite nauseous. I'm obviously still nowhere near pissed enough to cope with this debauchery.

'*If you like it, you should have put a ring on it,*' everyone screams.

'And preferably keep it there,' I mumble drunkenly.

Another bride-to-be slips on some spilt wine and falls ungainly onto the floor, giggling loudly. Her bright red lips gape open as she lets out a loud burp. I grimace. Georgie clutches my arm and drags me to a group of girls who are doing a very drunk rendition of *Single Ladies*. I force a smile and head towards them when I'm yanked back by my boa. I feel myself choke as it tightens around my neck. Oh no, please don't let me die at the hands of a pink feather boa. That would be the ultimate humiliation. I gurgle as the boa tightens and struggle to pull it from my neck. A feather tickles my throat and I pray when I fall unconscious that my stocking tops don't show. This is not how I planned to end my days. Death by feather boa is as far from my agenda as anything could be. The boa loosens and I fall forward into the arms of a John Travolta lookalike.

'Sorry. I stood on your feathers,' he says.

'That's an original line,' I gasp.

Does he realise he almost strangled me? He dirty dances with me for a second and then shimmies on past. I sway and look for Georgie and her gang. I must be very drunk. I'd never dance with a John Travolta lookalike if I were sober.

'More shots,' yells someone pointing to a tray.

'Count me in,' shouts Patsy, shimmering towards us.

'Come on.' She herds me and Georgie through the dancing throng towards the tray of shots.

'I'm nowhere near drunk enough,' giggles Patsy knocking back a shot.

I throw back mine and shudder. Georgie wraps her sweaty body around mine and kisses me.

'I'm so glad you're here,' she says, leaning heavily on me.

'I'm enjoying it,' I lie, lifting my aching foot from the floor and slipping it out of my heels. I sigh with relief.

'I'm so glad,' she says. 'More drinks. I'm still not off my face.'

Not much.

'I'll get them,' I say, removing my other shoe and carrying them to the bar with me. It's so hot in the nightclub. I'd styled my hair in a loose bun and can feel escaped hairs on my neck. I imagine my make-up is smudged too.

'Four sea breezes,' I yell to the barman.

What I wouldn't do for a nice sea breeze.

'Enjoying your night?' shouts the DJ, turning up the volume.

'I wish I'd worn a fancier costume,' says Karen, sidling up beside me.

I don't know Karen, or Maggie or the dozen other women that Georgie invited. But I'm Amy Perfect, the wedding planner, and it needs to be remembered that these women are future clients.

'You look great,' I say.

'Come on,' calls Georgie. 'We're off to Miss Wong's.'

Just when I thought it was time to go home too.

Miss Wong is down a dark alley just off the main street. Patsy flings open the door and Asian music greets us which, I have to admit, is much calmer than the 'Night Fever' which we'd just left. We are led to a table by a girl clad in Chinese dress and given a cocktail menu. I feel suddenly huge. I swear the heat in the nightclub has made me double in size. Either that or my dress has shrunk.

'This is more like it,' I whisper to Rosie. 'I've less chance of getting throttled here.'

'Someone tried to throttle you?' gasps Rosie.

'Not deliberately.'

'Someone tried to accidentally throttle you?'

'It really isn't important,' I sigh.

'Let's all try the Indochine Martini,' suggests Patsy. 'A few of those should get us well and truly wasted,' she laughs.

I feel well and truly wasted already, in more ways than one. It's hard work being twenty-eight. Everyone expects you to have a good time. In fact everyone thinks you want a good time and that includes lots of sex. Frankly, I'm not getting much of either. I look around the dimly lit club and sigh with relief to see there are no other hen parties here. The tables are either taken by couples or groups of men. One rowdy group wave at us and I'm about to turn away when one of them stands up and calls,

'Hey, Amy Fisher, is that you?'

Oh no, it's Jack. It's been three years since I've seen him and of all the times for him to turn up it has to be now.

'Did he say Amy Fisher?' asks Georgie, looking around. 'Where is she?'

'No I don't think so,' I say.

The waitress returns with our cocktails. She sets them down and eyes Georgie's huge bling.

'Beautiful,' she says.

I see Jack heading towards our table and quickly jump up.

'I desperately need a pee,' I say.

'Is that Jack?' whispers Rosie. 'He's looking good.'

'Don't look his way,' I hiss, before staggering to meet him.

I grab his arm.

'Amy, it is you? You look so different, I barely recognised you. Where are we going?'

'To the loo,' I say, glancing behind me. Fortunately, Georgie is side-tracked by the cocktail waitress.

'Don't you think we're moving a bit fast here? I've not seen you in three years. Shouldn't we have a drink first before having sex in the loo?'

I pull him into the corridor that leads to the toilets.

'Don't flatter yourself Jack. I didn't fancy you three years ago, so I certainly don't fancy you now.'

'Thanks for that blow to my confidence.'

'I'm not Amy Fisher any more. I can't have anyone overhearing you call me that.'

Jack looks sceptical.

'So who are you now then, Jane Bond under cover?' he laughs. 'I have to say you are looking great. I wasn't sure it was you. You've lost tons of weight and look so different. I like the blonde hair, it really suits you. But why do you have to be incognito?'

I see Georgie approaching and my heart jumps into my mouth.

'Just don't call me Amy Fisher,' I say quickly.

'Hello,' says Georgie.

Oh God.

'This is Georgie,' I say, feeling my legs buckle. 'It's her nuptials in a few weeks.'

'Congratulations,' Jack smiles.

'Are you with Amy Fisher?' she asks bluntly.

'Well ...' Jack looks at me confused.

'I thought I heard you call her name.'

'No,' I laugh, 'he called Amy Pisher, isn't that right Jack?'

I can almost see Jack's brain whirring.

'Yeah, that's right. When I hung out with Amy she was always pissed you see and ...'

I gape at him.

'Not always pissed,' I say, forcing a smile.

'She used to say, *I'm so pished* and then throw up on someone's carpet. After a while we just started calling her Amy Pisher.'

What the fuck?

'Really,' says Georgie doubtfully. 'I just can't imagine you being permanently pissed.'

'Well, I wasn't ...' I begin.

'Oh yes,' chimes in Jack. 'I can't remember a time she was ever sober.'

What the buggery is he playing at?

'Georgie,' screams Patsy, 'what are you doing?'

'Well, it was nice meeting you,' she says, giving us both a suspicious look before walking back to our table

'Jack, what the hell was that about?'

'You tell me, you did rather put me on the spot.'

'That's Greg's fiancée, I'm planning their wedding. He doesn't know that and she doesn't know I was his previous fiancée.'

'What a tangled web we weave. Look, here's my number. Let's have a drink when we're back in London.'

Frankly, if Jack couldn't make contact with me after the wedding debacle, I don't see why I should bother meeting him now, but I take his number anyway.

'Is that Rosie with you?' he asks.

'Yes, but please don't speak to her, it will just complicate everything.'

'It would be nice to say hello.'

'Please,' I plead. 'Don't stir things.'

'How is Greg doing these days?'

'I wouldn't know and can you please keep your voice down. I'm not supposed to know Greg. Now, I really must have a pee. After all, we wouldn't want me doing that on the carpet too would we?'

He smiles and kisses me on the cheek.

'It all sounds a bit complicated to me but I'll leave you to it. We're off to somewhere a bit livelier but give me a call sometime and give Rosie my love,' he says, giving her a wave. 'She looks good but then she always did.'

When I return to our table two cocktails are waiting for me.

'You're not keeping up,' reprimands Patsy.

'She ought to. Apparently she's known as Amy Pisher, because she got pissed so much,' announces Georgie.

Not quite a reputation to be proud of.

'Amy Pisher,' repeats Rosie and then mumbles 'unhealthy' under her breath.

'I could have sworn that guy said Amy Fisher,' says Georgie.

I'm starting to wish that the John Travolta lookalike had throttled me with my feather boa.

'I feel like I'm in Thailand,' giggles Georgie. 'It's all very decadent in here isn't it?'

'Who needs decadent,' slurs Patsy, throwing back her cocktail.

'Who's for another?' she asks, 'before we have our Vichy massage treatment.'

Vichy massage, what Vichy massage?

Before Rosie and I know what's happening, we're being led through a beaded curtain with our cocktails still in our hands to a massage room. Now, in my opinion, anything that involves water jets being blasted at you from every quarter comes under the heading of torture, and not therapy, and should be avoided at all costs. Not even the calming Asian relaxation music make it any more bearable. I swear I would have revealed all had Georgie asked me.

We return to the bar, where I now most certainly need a drink. My skin tingles from the force of the water and my head aches from the Indian massage that my overenthusiastic therapist gave me.

'I feel totally invigorated, don't you?' asks Georgie.

I feel totally dead.

'I feel like I should be reporting them for war crimes,' mutters Rosie.

The small stage is illuminated with a spotlight. The music changes to something exotic and we all stare mesmerised at the stage as a drag artist floats on dressed in a fur shawl and silk kimono.

'More cocktails over here,' yells Patsy.

'Shush,' Rosie and I snap in unison.

The music changes to the *St Louis Blues* and the drag artist begins to strip erotically. Oh well, I suppose it's better than a man exposing his meat and two veg. We all stare wide-eyed.

'Holy shit, it's only a man,' exclaims Patsy.

'It's a drag artist,' squeals Karen.

His fur coat is thrown and lands in Georgie's lap who giggles with pleasure. The waitress brings more cocktails along with a bowl of nuts.

'Have the nuts on me darlings,' calls the stripper. 'I don't often have ladies in.'

The nuts and cocktails are shortly joined by a garter.

'I just love gay men,' bellows Patsy as she jumps up and joins the stripper on stage.

Let me tell you, there is nothing worse than a drunken bespectacled woman strutting her stuff next to a half-naked drag queen. I can barely look as Patsy thrusts her hips so forcefully that she almost falls off the stage.

'Christ,' says a stunned Rosie.

'We really shouldn't let her drink,' I say.

'It's a bit late telling us that now,' Rosie winces.

Georgie screams with delight while my head screams in agony. Watching Patsy is torture and the only thing that helps is another cocktail. One final hip thrust and Patsy stumbles from the stage and back to our table.

'We're going to get tattoos after this,' she pants.

Will this night ever end?

Chapter Thirty-Four

'Tattoos?' I echo.

Greg hates tattoos. He thinks they are unfeminine. My eyes feel gritty and I resist the urge to rub them. Georgie lurches towards us.

'I can't believe I'm getting married in four weeks,' she sighs.

Neither can I.

It's well gone midnight and we're all wasted.

'Who's getting one?' asks Patsy, heading for the tattoo parlour.

'Not me,' I say, hanging onto Rosie. 'They bloody hurt.'

'I'm getting a heart with Georgie and Greg on it,' slurs Georgie.

'Me too,' says Patsy.

'With Georgie and Greg on it?' asks Rosie.

'Don't be a silly mare,' laughs Patsy. 'I'm having Brighton rules on mine. I've always wanted a tattoo but I've never had the nerve to do it before. You guys are great. You give me such confidence.'

'We should talk them out of it,' I whisper to Rosie.

'It's their bodies,' she argues. 'They can decorate them however they want, can't they?'

'But Greg hates tattoos.'

'I thought you wanted Greg to call off the wedding? Anyway, you can't tell her Greg hates tattoos. How would you know that?'

That's a point.

'Besides, isn't that what you want?' asks Rosie.

The truth is I don't know what I want any more. The tattoo parlour looms ahead, its neon lights enticing us forward.

'I don't think you should do this Georgie. We've all had too much to drink and ...' I say.

'It'll be romantic. It will show Greg how much I love him.'

It will show Greg how irresponsible you are. I can't believe I am thinking so rationally after so much booze.

'I really fancy some chips,' says Patsy sniffing the air.

The smell of fish and chips reaches my nostrils and my stomach cramps. None of us had eaten since getting off the coach.

'I'm starving,' agrees Rosie.

Our stomachs override the desire to get a tattoo and we glide past the parlour without as much as a second glance. We burst into the chippy and buy chips and curry sauce and then eat them sitting on benches outside, all of us shivering as a cold wind blows along the sea front.

'This has been the best night ever,' says Georgie, dipping her chips into the curry sauce.

'It's not over yet,' screeches Patsy. 'We've still got to pull, and get our tattoos.'

She spears a chip and dunks it in the sauce, managing to drip it down the front of her dress. Now, we'll have curry smell everywhere we go.

'We should get back to the hotel,' I say, checking the time on my phone. It's almost two in the morning.

'I've got to get my tattoo,' slurs Georgie, swigging from a bottle of vodka.

'Where did you get that?' I ask primly.

'Karen gave it to me, or someone,' she says, looking confused. 'Anyway it's mine.'

I sigh.

'Let's get you back to the hotel,' I say, taking her arm.

She snatches it away and stumbles to her feet.

'I've got to get my tattoo,' she asserts.

Patsy takes her arm and they stagger to the tattoo parlour.

'It's closed,' I call, hurrying after them.

'They're open till four,' says Rosie.

That's just great. My name will be mud if Georgie gets a tattoo and Ben Garret will no doubt murder me, and of course the wedding will most certainly be off. If there is one thing that Greg detests it is tattoos.

I stop in mid stride and take a deep breath. But that's exactly what I want isn't it, for the wedding to be off? Rosie and I watch as Georgie enters the parlour.

'This is bad,' says Rosie with a wince. 'This is not going to go down well with Greg is it? It looks like your plan to stop the wedding is about to happen.'

I galvanise my drunken legs into action. I've got to stop her.

Chapter Thirty-Five

'I don't think you should do this, Georgie. You really ought to be sober when you make these sorts of decisions,' I plead.

The greasy haired tattooist gives me a scathing look.

'I'd never do it if I was sober,' she giggles.

'Greg might not like it,' I say urgently.

Might not, that's an understatement. Greg will go ape shit.

'He will. I know he will,' asserts Georgie.

He won't. I know he won't.

'Please, Georgie, won't you change your mind? You can't do a thing about it once it's done.'

'I want it,' she says petulantly.

I rummage in my bag to find Ben Garrett's phone number. I hurriedly punch it into my phone and wait.

'Who's next?' asks the tattooist.

'Hello,' says a sleepy voice.

'Hi Ben, it's me, Amy,' I say hesitantly.

'Amy Perfect?' he questions.

How many Amy's does he know?

'Yes, that one ...'

'Don't you ever sleep?' he asks.

'I'm in Brighton,' I say.

'I want this one,' Georgie says. 'Can you put GG in the middle?'

Oh my God, it's just getting worse.

'Is that a different time zone?' Ben chuckles.

'I'm with Georgie on her hen weekend ...'

'Oh yeah, how's that going? I didn't know you went too.'

'I need your help,' I say anxiously.

The tattooist gets his kit together and I'm starting to feel very nauseous.

'Have you been drinking? You only seem to phone me when you're drunk.'

Is that disappointment I hear in his voice?

'Georgie is about to get a tattoo, and I can't seem to stop her. I've tried everything. Will you speak to her?'

'A tattoo,' he echoes, he sounds wide awake now. 'I thought you promised the perfect wedding? I think a tattoo is going to put the damper on that.'

'I didn't tell her to have it. In fact, I've spent the best part of fifteen minutes trying to talk her out of it,' I say angrily.

'Doesn't sound like you did a good job does it?'

The tattooist looms closer to Georgie's arm.

'Can you wait a minute,' I scream, pushing towards him. He recoils, knocking over his tray of tools.

'What the fuck is wrong with you? You're bloody demented,' he explodes.

'Hell's bells Amy, what are you doing?' says Georgie.

'Speak to Ben,' I say handing her my phone. 'He wants to talk to you.'

'What's going on Amy?' whispers Rosie. 'I thought you wanted Greg to call off the engagement.'

I sigh.

'I can't let her do this. She's far too nice.'

'I can't disagree with that.'

Georgie climbs from the couch and steps outside with my phone to her ear.

'You can do mine then,' chirps Patsy. 'I want something that flies.'

'I'll buy you a kite,' I say, pulling her out of the chair.

'You lot are nuts,' says the tattooist. 'I don't want to do any of you.'

That's a relief.

Georgie is weeping softly by a rubbish bin when we join her. She hands me the phone.

'Thank you Amy. Ben wants to speak to you.'

'Hello,' I say cautiously and prepare myself for an ear-bashing.

'I've talked her out of it,' he says flatly.

'Thank you.'

'She never mentioned you were going to this Brighton malarkey.'

'Well I'm here,' I say, still reeling from the whole tattoo debacle.

'That's a shame. I was going to ask you if you'd like to come to the flea pit up the road. They're showing Notting Hill tomorrow afternoon. I thought you'd enjoy it.'

'Oh,' I say.

'It would be nice to go with a friend, but if you're in Brighton ...'

'That would have been nice. I'm not back until tomorrow night though,' I say hopefully.

'I'll check the days it's on and call you back. Is this your phone?'

'Yes,' I say, my heart fluttering.

'What's going on with Ben Garret?' smiles Rosie after I hang up.

'Nothing,' I say. 'I'm not interested in men.'

Not interested in men indeed. If that's the case, why is it that night, with my head spinning from cocktails, do I toss and turn with thoughts of Ben Garret?

Chapter Thirty-Six

My relief at arriving back in London is short lived.

'Okay, don't panic,' says Rosie.

Don't panic, she says. Don't bloody panic. It's easy for her to say isn't it? It's not her life that is about to fall apart. Does she have any idea what this means? It's the end of me, that's what it means and the end of *Perfect Weddings*. I can just see Ben Garret writing a great piece about this.

'I'm sure everything will be fine,' she adds, but this time there is a tremble in her voice. 'Just don't panic.'

Okay, she's said it too many times now. What she really means is I *should* panic. We'd just got off the coach from Brighton. The vintage bus was a bit too expensive for both trips. I look around for somewhere to hide but aside from jumping back onto the coach there is nowhere. Not even a sodding rubbish bin to dive behind. There is a hiss of air as the coach door closes. That's it then. I'm well and truly buggered.

'Rosie,' I say urgently. 'What do I do?'

'I don't know,' she says shakily.

Then, everything seems to happen in slow motion. From the second Greg's eyes land on me to the moment the coach driver's brakes squeal. I feel my legs move and Rosie's hand pulling me back. I hear Georgie calling Greg. The other girls are ahead of us and for a second I can't see him. Then the girls part and there he is. Greg in all his glory, wearing a white shirt tucked into cream canvas trousers. His eyes meet mine and they lock. He looks puzzled for a second and then he smiles uncertainly. He begins to skirt around the girls. He steps into the road and my breath catches in my throat. A cyclist swerves around him only to see the coach too late.

'Greg!'

For a moment I think it is me that has cried out, but it is Georgie who is now screaming hysterically. Greg is on the ground with the cyclist on top of him. His dazzling white shirt now covered in dust from the road. There is stillness for a few seconds and then everything goes crazy.

'Greg, Greg,' screams Georgie.

If only Greg hadn't seen me. I feel sure none of this would have happened.

'He's unconscious,' someone shouts. 'Call an ambulance.'

'I don't understand,' cries Patsy. 'What was he thinking?'

I stare at Greg's prostrate body. Please God, I pray, Let him live. I promise to be good for the rest of my life. I'll never covet another woman's fiancé ever again.

'Greg,' wails Georgie. 'Wake up, come on babe wake up.'

A bump on his head swells in front of our eyes.

'He's breathing,' someone says and I sigh with relief.

'Greg, it's me, can you hear me?' Georgie says, dripping tears onto his cheek.

'It's the knock on the head what did it,' says a man. 'He'll come round soon.'

Oh God, I so hope so.

There is mayhem. Thankfully the ambulance soon races around the corner, with a police car at its heel. People rush forward to give eyewitness accounts and all I can do is kneel at the side of Greg and look at him.

There's a small graze on his cheek but apart from the bump on his head he looks fine.

'He seems quite unscathed,' I whisper to Rosie.

'Unscathed?' gasps Rosie. 'Who knows what a knock on the head like that can do?'

'It's terrible,' sobs Georgie. 'He'll be all right won't he?'

'Of course,' I say as Georgie follows Greg's prostrate body into the ambulance.

'We'll be right behind you,' I promise, grabbing Rosie's arm and jumping into a stationary cab.

'Follow that ambulance,' I say dramatically.

'He's got a siren darling and I don't, but I'll do my best.'

'Oh God,' I groan. 'Do you think he'll have brain damage?'

'Nah, you've got to have a brain to do damage to it,' scoffs Rosie.

How she can be so scathing, I do not know.

'Rosie,' I admonish. 'That's a terrible thing to say.'

'Terrible but true.'

'It's my fault,' I whine. 'It was the shock of seeing me.'

'For goodness' sake, you didn't push him in the road did you?'

'My thoughts may have done.'

She rolls her eyes.

'You're not Superwoman.'

The cab pulls up at the hospital and we dive out. Please let Greg be alive and with all his brain intact.

It's been one hour, thirty minutes and ten seconds since we arrived at the hospital and still there is no sign of Georgie.

'At least we know he hasn't died,' says Rosie. 'She wouldn't be sitting there all this time with a corpse.'

Rosie has such a comforting way with words.

'Maybe she can't pull herself away,' I say miserably.

'I'll get us another coffee,' offers Patsy.

At that moment Georgie appears at the end of the corridor and bursts into tears at the sight of us.

'He still hasn't come round,' she chokes.

Patsy and I stare at her in disbelief.

'Even now?' says Patsy. 'But it's been ages.'

'It's only been just over an hour,' says Rosie.

'How about if we take it in shifts to talk to him,' suggests Patsy. 'That's what they do when someone's in a coma isn't it?'

'But he's not in a coma,' I say, 'is he Georgie?'

'I don't think so,' she answers thoughtfully.

'He could be like it for years,' says Patsy.

'He's been like it for years already,' mutters Rosie.

I elbow her roughly in the ribs.

'I'm not turning off the machine,' cries Georgie suddenly.

'What machine?' I ask.

Rosie rolls her eyes.

'He's not on life support is he?' she says. 'He's only been unconscious for a short time. You lot will be planning his funeral next.'

'Oh, please don't say things like that,' sobs Georgie.

'I've got a great idea,' pipes up Patsy. 'We should play him Spanish music and dance the flamenco.'

She's full of great ideas isn't she?

'Dance the flamenco?' I repeat.

'Well, he's in Spain a lot isn't he?'

'Better still, why don't we stage a bull fight,' scoffs Rosie. 'That's bound to bring him round.'

'You don't have to take the piss,' snaps Patsy, 'I'm only trying to help.'

'Please don't argue,' cries Georgie. 'I just couldn't stand it.'

'Why don't we let him rest? You can visit again tonight Georgie. Things may have improved by then,' I say hopefully.

She hugs me.

'You always speak perfect sense,' she says.

'Bring in his football videos,' suggests Patsy.

'What a great idea,' says Georgie, forcing a smile. 'I must stay positive. After all, it could have been much worse.'

Personally, I can't think how much worse it could be, but I don't say anything.

Chapter Thirty-Seven

It's been eighteen hours, fifteen minutes and twelve seconds since Greg hit his head, and he's still unconscious. The hospital room looks like a harem. The four of us sit around the bed and stare at him. Georgie's eyes are dewy with tears, mine anxious and guarded while Rosie and Patsy look confused. Greg lies silently in the starched white sheets. He looks like an innocent cherub. Patsy had tried the Spanish music but that didn't elicit any response. Georgie babbles on about the wedding and what needs to be done while Rosie and I just look at each other.

'Shall I try the music again?' asks Patsy.

'I really don't think I can take any more flamenco,' groans Rosie. 'I'm starting to forget what country I'm in.'

'I'll try something else then,' says Patsy and waves a Tottenham programme in Greg's face and sings an off key rendition of *You'll Never Walk Alone*.

'You'll miss the matches if you carry on like this,' she shouts.

Anyone would think a bang on the head affects the ears the way she's yelling at him. For a second his eyelashes flutter.

'Did you see that?' cries Georgie.

'I think it was the breeze from the programme,' says Rosie. 'And anyway, isn't that Liverpool's song?'

'I'll get us some coffee,' I say.

I really can't look at Greg's lifeless body any longer. Even the hospital café is better than this. I wander down the corridor, my heels clicking on the floor.

'Hello,' says a voice. I stop at the entrance to the café to see Ben Garrett walking towards me.

'How's Greg?' he asks.

The sound of his voice sends a tingle through me.

'He hasn't come round yet. We've been trying everything from flamenco music to football programmes. If Patsy had her way we'd be dancing around his bed.'

'In that case do you blame him for not coming round?' he smiles.

I raise my eyebrows.

'Georgie is very worried,' I say.

'I know, but I'm sure he'll be fine,' he says confidently.

'I was just about to get coffee, would you like one?' I offer.

'I'll get them,' he says, strolling ahead of me. 'By the way, Notting Hill is showing tonight if you wanted to come?'

'Oh,' I say, trying to hide my pleasure. I thought he had forgotten.

'I was going to phone you,' he adds. 'Unless of course you wanted to stay with Georgie. I fully understand if you do.'

'Oh no,' I say, much too quickly. Never seem too keen, that's the key isn't it? And let's face it, the last thing I need is to be in the room when Greg comes round. 'It will be nice to get away from the hospital.'

Now it sounds like I don't care about Greg.

'Great. Shall we get a bite to eat first? We could meet at Joey's burger bar.'

I'm about to answer when Patsy flies into the café and grabs us both by the arm.

'He's come round,' she cries, pulling us towards the door.

Oh no.

'Is he okay?' I ask nervously.

'Not really, he seems confused.'

'He's probably disorientated' says Ben, following us.

I can't decide if this is a blessing or a curse. I enter Greg's room nervously and avoid looking at him. A doctor is checking his vitals and I glance at Rosie.

'Perhaps we should leave,' I say. 'We don't want to crowd him.'

Or be around when he recognises me.

'Good idea,' says Rosie, nodding in agreement. 'It's *unhealthy* all of us being here.'

'I've got to get ready for my wedding,' Greg says anxiously, trying to get out of bed.

'Just relax, Mr Martin,' says the doctor, gesturing to a nurse.

'But I've got to get to The Ivory Hotel. There are things to check.'

Rosie and I tiptoe to the door.

'Don't worry about The Ivory,' says Georgie patting his hand. 'It's still four weeks before our wedding. I'm so glad you're okay.'

He gawps at her.

'Who the hell are you?' he growls, turning on her. Rosie and I stop in our tracks. Georgie lets out a tiny gasp.

'It's me, Georgie, your fiancée.'

He cocks his head to one side.

'I've never seen you before in my life,' he replies sharply.

What happened to the angelic Greg that was lying under the white sheets?

'Oh dear,' mutters Rosie.

'Who are you people?' says Greg, his voice rising. 'Why are you in my room?'

He looks around and his eyes land on me. I try not to meet his eyes but it's impossible.

'Don't try to force things, Mr Martin,' the doctor says. 'You had a nasty bump on the head and are a little confused. You must rest and I'm afraid your visitors need to leave now. They can come again tomorrow.'

'What kind of bump on the head? What the hell happened to me?'

The nurse steps forward with a hypodermic. Greg sees it and struggles to get out of the bed.

'You don't understand, I'm getting married, I can't be here,' he shouts.

'Our wedding is four weeks away, Greg ...' begins Georgie.

He glares at her.

'I'm not marrying you,' he snarls. 'I'm marrying Amy.'

All eyes turn onto me. I shrug helplessly while Rosie lets out a tiny groan.

'But ...' falters Georgie.

'Where is she, where is Amy Fisher, my fiancée?' he demands.

Chapter Thirty-Eight

So, here we are, or at least here I am, finally with my dreams coming true. Not only does Greg Martin remember me but he also remembers that he is marrying me, or at least, marrying Amy Fisher. The truth is he doesn't recognise me at all. I'm not the curvy, out of condition, Amy Fisher that he remembers. I'm Amy Perfect, slim blonde and successful. Slim and blonde anyway, the successful has gone out of the window these days. I turn on my phone to find Lucy has left three hysterical messages. What have I forgotten now? It rings and I reluctantly answer.

'Where are you?' Lucy demands. 'I've been trying to reach you. When did you get back from Brighton?'

'I'm at the hospital,' I reply indignantly.

'Yeah right, I've heard that before, remember?'

'Greg was rushed here in a coma,' I say, trying to make her feel guilty.

'Oh my God, what happened? Is he okay?'

'Kind of, he's lost his memory, well bits of it.'

'Which bits?'

'The important bits, like who his fiancée is.'

'Jesus. Well, I hate to tell you this but he's not the only one. You were supposed to meet Rebecca Marshall at one for the flowers, and then at three you were taking Chardonnay and Gary to look at venues. You didn't lose your memory too did you?'

'Bollocks, I totally forgot.'

'Don't worry, it's what I've come to expect. I told them you had your pet dog put down this morning, straight after returning from a hen do, so you were a bit frazzled. I assured Chardonnay you would rearrange.'

'I don't have a dog.'

'Not any more you don't. What else was I supposed to say, that you keep forgetting things since you discovered your ex-

173

fiancé was marrying your client? Fortunately for you Rebecca cancelled.'

This is a disaster. Rosie was right when she said taking on Greg's wedding was unhealthy. It's killing me.

But what luck, right? The man I love, the man I want to marry, the man I would have done anything for, well almost anything, cannot remember the woman he is marrying in four weeks' time. But he remembers me, Amy Fisher. That must mean something, mustn't it? So why aren't I elated? Why am I more excited about going to see *Notting Hill* with Ben Garret?

'Talking of your ex-fiancé, does this mean the wedding is off? I don't suppose he can marry someone he doesn't remember,' says Lucy.

'That's the thing. He does remember that he's getting married and that the reception is at The Ivory Hotel. The problem is he thinks he's marrying Amy Fisher.'

There is silence, All I can hear is Lucy breathing.

'He's remembered you?' she says finally.

'He's remembered Amy Fisher,' I sigh.

'But you are Amy Fisher.'

'Yes, but he doesn't recognise *me*.'

'You just said he did,' she says tetchily.

'He remembers the Amy I used to be.'

'What will you do?' she asks.

'Aside from dye my hair blue? I haven't got a clue.'

Ben, Georgie, and Patsy emerge from Greg's room. Georgie looks devastated.

'I have to go,' I say quickly, hanging up.

'Oh Amy, what am I going to do?' Georgie sobs, throwing herself into my arms. 'He doesn't know me. All he can talk about is Amy Fisher.'

'Whoever that bitch is,' quips Rosie.

Charming, and she calls herself a friend.

'It's probably that fat cow in the Star Wars photo,' says Patsy with a sneer. 'Don't worry, he'll soon forget her.'

That fat cow in the Star Wars photo? Honestly, it's all I can do to bite my tongue.

'I didn't think she looked *that* fat actually,' I say, 'maybe just a little overweight.'

'Give him time,' says Ben, throwing a comforting arm around Georgie.

'I don't understand it,' says Georgie frowning. 'I thought she broke the engagement off. Why would he think he's marrying her?'

I wince. The little bugger told her I broke off the engagement? What a shit.

'Do you think I should find this Amy Fisher? Get her to explain to Greg that she isn't his fiancée any more?' says Georgie sadly.

'It does sound like he is in a time warp,' agrees Patsy. 'What do you think Amy?'

'Erm, well ...' I stutter.

'Could you find Amy Fisher for us?' Georgie asks eagerly.

'I'm sure she'd have no trouble finding her,' says Rosie.

I glare at her.

'Perhaps we should give it a while. It's not fair to pull her into this. She's probably moved on, and may be married to someone else, who knows?' I say, feeling the perspiration run down my back.

'We'll chill with a takeaway and a movie,' says Patsy, 'then pop back later. See if he remembers anything else.'

'When can you visit, Amy?' asks Georgie. 'The more of us that do, then the more likely we'll jolt his memory.'

'I'll pop in tomorrow to give you moral support,' I hear myself say.

Am I insane?

'Thanks so much Amy. I don't know what I'd do without you.'

'I'll get the car,' says Ben.

'I'm so glad you and Ben are friends now,' Georgie whispers. 'He has been a bit lonely since his break up from Davina.'

'Davina?' I question.

She looks guilty.

'Maybe I shouldn't have said anything. It's just I think you two would make such great friends, and he lacks female company.'

My impression was that he always got plenty of that.

'But ...' I begin.

'Oh, he flirts,' she smiles. 'But there is never anything in it. You're both so similar. Neither of you are interested in settling down. You'll be great friends for each other.'

'I'll see you later, say, around seven?' says Ben as he returns. He takes Georgie by the arm and leads her from the building.

'I'll see what else I can dig up to jog Greg's memory,' says Patsy.

As long as she doesn't bring along half the Tottenham football team.

'You'll pop in tomorrow to give her moral support?' hisses Rosie. 'Have you lost your marbles? He already remembers you. The shit is well and truly going to hit the fan isn't it? I hope you're happy.'

'What else do you suggest I do? I can't wipe myself off the face of the earth can I?'

'More's the pity.'

'Rosie,' I say. 'What's wrong with you?'

'Seriously, don't you think that girl has had a big enough shock without discovering the Amy Fisher her fiancé thinks he is marrying is actually you? You may be a bit slimmer ...'

'A *bit*,' I say, insulted.

'And somewhat fitter than when he last saw you, but you haven't had a face transplant,' she continues. 'The only difference is that you look two years older, your hair is blonde and longer, and your clothes are a few sizes smaller. It's just a matter of time before he recognises you, and frankly, I don't know what you see in him.'

I have to agree he isn't the same Greg Martin that I remember, or is it Amy Fisher that has changed?

Chapter Thirty-Nine

I've played every song that ever mattered to Greg and me. I've surrounded myself with his photographs. I've willed those old familiar feelings to come back but they just don't. It's as though someone has clicked a switch and turned them off. I gaze at the infamous Star Wars photo. Obviously, I overlook the supersize me and focus on Greg. I turn the volume up on one of our favourite songs but still I feel nothing. Even my little solitaire engagement ring has no effect. This is not at all what I imagined. I thought seeing Greg close up would drive me insane. Instead, I'm going insane trying to drive myself insane. I expected to feel all kinds of emotions when up close and personal with him but the truth is nothing happened, nothing at all, absolute zilch down there in the loins. Now that can't be right can it? After all, Greg is the love of my life. But the Greg lying in the hospital bed isn't my Greg from three years ago. I'm starting to think that the Greg I carried around in my head for the past three years doesn't actually exist at all.

I scan the photos and email the folder to Georgie. I don't even bother making a copy for myself.

I sigh when my phone rings. It's either going to be a hysterical Lucy, a sobbing Georgie, an angry Rosie, or a randy sheikh. I'm about to answer it when the door buzzer goes. I push the button on the entry phone.

'Miss Perfect?' asks a voice.

'Yes.'

'I've got a delivery for you.'

I buzz him in and answer the phone.

'Amy,' says Lucy, and my heart sinks.

'What have I forgotten now?' I ask.

'Nothing, I just thought I'd phone to see how Greg is doing.'

The delivery man steps out of the lift carrying a Harrods box.

'He's the same,' I say. 'I've not had any updates.'

I sign for the package and close the door, trying to remember if I had ordered anything.

'I also thought I'd go through the diary with you. You know, just to be on the safe side.'

What she means is, to check if I have forgotten anything.

I slice a knife along the parcel tape.

'We've rescheduled Chardonnay and Gary for tomorrow at nine.'

'Yes, okay got that,' I say, checking it against my own diary.

'Laureta's rehearsal is at two thirty, so that gives you plenty of time.'

'Next Saturday is her wedding, one p.m., St George's. I'm giving you plenty of notice for this one.'

'Check,' I say, pulling at the package.

'Oh, and of course there is the sheikh's dinner on the Thursday.'

I pull the long black evening gown that is wrapped in tissue paper from the box. A string of pearls drops to the floor and I take a sharp breath.

'What dinner?' I say breathlessly.

I remove the small card that is attached to the tissue paper.

'He phoned today to remind you. A special pre-wedding dinner, I presumed you knew all about it. It's at The Savoy.'

The card reads, *'To Amy, please wear this for our dinner next Thursday. I'm sure you wouldn't want to let Laureta down at such short notice.'*

I fight back a gasp. I don't believe this. The bloody Savoy is where he's staying. Now what is he playing at?

'I presume the whole wedding party is going,' says Lucy.

'Laureta hasn't said anything,' I say, placing the dress and pearls back in the box. 'Can you phone The Savoy and check how many people are booked for the dinner?'

'Oh dear,' she mutters. 'I don't like this sheikh business. I keep thinking you'll disappear to Saudi Arabia.'

My fear exactly but I don't tell her that. I search for the dress on the web and discover that the dress and pearls cost five thousand quid. What is he going to expect for that? My mobile trills and I grab it.

'It's me,' says Lucy.

'How many are booked for the dinner?' I ask, tensing my shoulders.

'Two,' she groans.

'Shit.'

'What are you going to do?' she asks.

Complete panic stations. Everything is crowding in on me. What has happened to my life? I hang up after telling Lucy not to worry. After all, there's nothing to worry about is there? I punch in the number for The Savoy and with a racing heart ask to speak to the sheikh.

'Ah, Miss Perfect, I hope you liked the dress,' he says, in his broken English drawl.

'Prince Abdullah, I thought I had made myself very clear. I can't have dinner with you. You're a married man.'

'Is that right Miss Fisher?'

For a second I think I must have misheard him. I swallow. I can't speak. It's as though someone is squeezing my voice box.

'It is Miss Fisher isn't it?' he asks, clearly proud of himself.

'I'm really sorry but I can't make the dinner,' I say, trying to keep my voice steady.

'That's a shame. I was very much looking forward to it. You see, Miss Perfect, I always know when someone is keeping a secret and I really couldn't believe a beautiful woman as yourself would not have a boyfriend. You always seemed so on edge, especially during our lunch meeting,' he says menacingly.

A cold shiver runs through me.

'But I can understand how difficult it must be planning a wedding for the man you clearly love.'

I gasp.

'How did you …?'

'Miss Perfect, when one has contacts like I do, nothing is difficult. I am, of course, presuming that his fiancée knows nothing of your relationship with her soon-to-be husband, or is your plan for him *not* to be her soon-to-be husband?'

'How dare you,' I say breathlessly. 'I don't have to explain myself to you and I'm afraid I can't meet you next Thursday.'

'Are you quite sure? You see I have no qualms in telling Miss Georgina Winters that you were once engaged to her fiancée and that you still love him.'

What I wouldn't do to cut off his balls. I can't let him tell Georgie the truth. If anyone tells Georgie the truth, it will be me.

'You see, when I want something, I get it. Everyone has a secret Miss Perfect, I just didn't realise yours would be so easy to discover. I think I will see you on Thursday.'

The phone clicks and all that goes through my head is the most painful way I can castrate the bugger. I'm having beautiful fantasies of doing just that when my BlackBerry trills again. I sigh and answer it.

'Amy, it's me Georgie. I thought you might like an update on Greg.'

Not really, in fact Greg updates are giving me palpitations and I seriously don't think I can take much more.

'How is he?' I ask. 'Has he remembered anything else?'

She gives a little sob.

'I don't understand it Amy. He seems to be remembering loads of things but he must be delirious or something because they make sense but they don't make sense. He remembers The Ivory and the reception but he thinks our best man's name is Jack.'

Oh shit.

'He's still saying he doesn't know me, and keeps asking for Amy Fisher.'

'The fat cow,' Patsy shouts down the phone.

'He can't remember anything about the time we spent in Yarmouth,' she says tearfully. 'I'm pretending to be a friend otherwise he gets so agitated. He doesn't understand why this Amy Fisher isn't with him at the hospital.'

'What does the doctor say?' I ask.

There's a little gulp from Georgie before she says,

'He thinks its post-traumatic amnesia and it could last up to a month. It's like he's stuck in a time warp and the doctor reckons Greg must have done something traumatic or something made him really happy around that time which is why he can't get past it.'

'Bloody trauma I reckon, especially if that fat cow Amy Fisher had anything to do with it,' says Patsy scathingly.

I wish Georgie wouldn't put her phone on speaker.

'Oh Amy, what am I to do? The wedding is so close. We've only got four weeks. Do you think I should cancel it?'

A few weeks ago and I would have said 'yes' in a heartbeat. My dream is coming true, except now I'm not so sure I want it to.

'There's still time,' I say positively. 'Don't do anything rash.'

'There's only one thing for it,' Patsy yells down the phone. 'We have to find Amy Fisher.'

My stomach churns.

'That seems a bit extreme,' I say shakily.

'We don't have a choice,' says Georgie. 'Amy Fisher is the only person who can get Greg out of this state and get his memory back in time for the wedding. We need you to help us find her. You will won't you?' she implores.

She sounds so desperate that before I know what I'm doing, I'm agreeing to look for myself.

Chapter Forty

Ben is standing outside the burger bar. He grins when he sees me and my heart flutters.

'Am I late?' I ask, while knowing full well that I'm not.

I'd had to wear my strapless bra as it was the only one not in the wash. I really haven't been functioning at all since Georgie came into my life. I'd thrown on an old River Island top and covered it with a multi-coloured kimono. I'm beyond caring how I look. I have more important things on my mind, like, how the buggery do I get out of sleeping with Prince Abdullah?

Ben kisses me on the cheek sending a tingle up my spine. I'm in a zomboid state. I hope he doesn't notice. Mind you, I've been in this state from the day he met me so he must think this is the norm for me. I've turned my BlackBerry off. Let's face it, the damn thing only rings to give bad news. God, what if Greg still loves me? I'd never thought of that. I'd just kind of presumed I would need to get him to love me again now that I'm slim, fit and trendy. Mind you, the way I've been eating recently I won't be slim, fit and trendy for much longer, and he'll be falling out of love with me quicker than you can say 'calorific'. But you have to admit, it is strange how he only remembers the time when we were together. Maybe he was happy. But if that is true then why did he abandon me at the church?

'Joey's is quite busy,' says Ben, taking my arm. 'Are you happy to wait or shall we get fish and chips?'

Oh, how I love fish and chips.

'Sounds great,' I say.

Do you know how many calories there are in fish and chips? Nine hundred, that's how many. But it has been a challenging few weeks hasn't it? I need food for sustenance. My arm is tucked in Ben's and I feel myself relax.

'Greg is stuck in a bit of a time warp isn't he?' says Ben.

It seems I can't escape my nightmare no matter where I go. I can smell the fish and chips and God, it smells so good.

'Yes, but I'm sure he will remember the wedding soon.'

'He remembers a wedding,' he smiles, 'just not the right one.'

We enter the shop and join the queue. Ben orders a large portion of chips, curry sauce and two pieces of cod. We sit at a table outside and eat them from the paper. We reach for a chip at the same time and our fingers connect and it feels like someone just shot hundreds of volts through me. Ben's eyes meet mine and I smile weakly.

'So are you going to help Georgie?' he asks.

I raise my eyebrows.

'She said she was going to ask you to help her find Amy Fisher. Georgie thinks you have contacts in the marriage business and could track her down from Greg's previous wedding.'

'I'm a wedding planner not a private detective.'

He spears a chip and dips it in the curry sauce.

'There you go getting all defensive again.'

'I'm not getting defensive,' I argue, cutting into the cod.

I can't begin to tell you how fabulous the chips are. Forget the diet. I've well and truly fallen off the wagon. There's nothing like chips in curry sauce is there? They're heaven. Add a pickled onion and you're in paradise. Except of course, it's no fun kissing someone once you've indulged in a pickled onion. Not that I'm expecting Ben to kiss me. He's made it very clear that he only wants a friend, not like the sheikh I am sorry to say.

'How is the sheikh these days?' he asks, as though reading my mind.

I can't tell the truth can I? Not without spilling the beans and telling him that I am, *the* Amy Fisher, the Amy Fisher that everyone wants to find. How did I get into this mess? One minute I was happy and successful and the next a complete wreck. That's karma for you. I really shouldn't have talked Georgie into booking her reception at The Ivory Hotel. The only person it hurt was me. Greg was obviously more than happy to have his second wedding reception at the same place. That could mean one of two things; either he had good memories of it because of me, or he didn't have any memory of it as our reception venue and so it didn't matter to him. The invitations backfired too and Ben stepped in when he realised the dress was hideous. So far I haven't managed to do anything to stop the wedding, apart from putting Greg in hospital with a case of post-traumatic amnesia. I've behaved like a total bitch. Now I'm really up Shit Street. If I come clean then Georgie will find another wedding planner, Ben will never forgive me and if there is one person I want to stay friends with it is Ben. If only Greg would get his memory back. I could then discreetly change the venue, disappear into the background and let them have their perfect wedding.

'Penny for your thoughts?' says Ben.

I pull myself from my reverie and help myself to a few more chips.

'I was just thinking about weddings,' I smile.

Well it's true isn't it?

'They're a bit overrated don't you think?' he grins.

'I love them,' I say passionately.

'Well, you do make quite a lot of money from them.'

Oh no, not that again. I feel my lips tighten.

'So you keep pointing out.'

'It's not a criticism, it's a compliment.' he says, pushing the chips towards me.

'Here, treat yourself.'

'Is this usually how you wine and dine your women?' I say.

He reclines in his chair.

'I wasn't aware I was wining and dining you.'

I blush. How stupid of me. He doesn't see this as a date at all, just two friends sharing chips and seeing a film.

'Shall we go?' he asks.

We stroll to the cinema only to find the screening has been cancelled due to lack of interest.

'Oh dear, not everyone has got great taste like us it seems, Still, *Four Weddings* was good wasn't it?'

I try not to let my disappointment show. I was so looking forward to losing myself in another world for a few hours and forgetting my problems.

'The fish and chips were nice,' I say.

'I know how to wine and dine a woman,' he laughs. 'Talking of which, fancy the pub? I usually go to The Hive.'

'I've not been there, it sounds great.'

We enter the busy pub to shouts of, *Hey Ben, thought you weren't coming tonight, what you having Ben, and evening Ben.*

'This really is your regular,' I say.

'What would you like?' he asks, leading me to the bar.

The barman gives us a wide grin.

'Hi Ben, your usual?'

'Hi Mike. I'm not sure; maybe we'll have a bottle of wine. We went to see Notting Hill but they've cancelled the screening.'

Mike laughs.

'That's because most people prefer new films.'

'Not us,' says Ben, throwing an arm around me. 'We like the old ones, don't we Amy?'

My body tingles at his touch and I struggle not to let it show but my ovaries are having a party. Ben Garret is perfect baby making material and don't my ovaries know it. He takes off his coat to reveal an open necked white shirt over his pale blue jeans.

'Fancy sharing a bottle of plonk?' he suggests

I nod, while thinking I must not drink more than two glasses. I don't want to be spilling the beans.

'So, what's your take on this wedding business with Greg and Amy Fisher,' he asks once we've sat down.

I almost knock over my wine glass.

'My take?' I ask. 'What do you mean?' I try not to look guilty.

'Do you think it is a good idea for Georgie to go searching for Amy Fisher? I think it will cause more problems. It could open a can of worms.'

'Well ... I ...'

'Don't want to talk about weddings on your night off, right?' he smiles.

I take a gulp of wine and nod. His phone rings and he looks at me apologetically.

'Sorry, do you mind if I get this?'

I shake my head.

'Hello princess,' he says with a smile on his face.

I shift in my seat. That's just great isn't it? If there is one thing guaranteed to make you feel small it's your date talking to another woman. He really is proving himself to be an insufferable, rude man. He stands up and walks to the bar.

'It's not really the best time,' he says into the phone before turning to smile at me.

Honestly, what a nerve.

'Okay. I'll be home in fifteen minutes. See you then.'

I don't believe this. I force a smile as he returns. He's going to dump me for another woman, and another woman that goes by the name of Princess. God, my life revolves getting dumped. I'm a serial dumpee. I must be giving off something and it isn't pheromones. He sits opposite me and takes a sip of wine before saying,

'I'm really sorry about this. Can we take a rain check? Something's come up and I can't get out of it I'm afraid.'

'Oh,' I say, trying to hide my feelings. What a fool I am.

'It's a good job we weren't in the cinema,' I say, with a smile but the words come out bitter.

'Can we do it another time?' he asks shyly.

What a bloody nerve he's got.

'I don't think so. I have a lot on the next few weeks,' I say shortly.

He looks into my eyes and I melt.

'I'll call you,' he says, standing up. 'I've paid for the wine so need to rush off.'

He walks out of the pub and I'm left feeling like a spare part at a wedding.

Chapter Forty-One

So, here we are, or at least here I am, drowning my sorrows in someone else's local. What a nightmare day. Everything that could go wrong has gone wrong. The one time I find a nice man and he turns out to be the biggest dick on the planet. I should have known. Let's face it, a good-looking successful guy like Ben Garret must have women throwing themselves at him left right and centre. The blonde, long-legged and glossed lipped model types, no doubt. What's wrong with me that all the men I meet dump me? Okay, two of them, but let's face it, two is two too many, and what do I do? I just sit and take it that's what. I finish the last of the wine and head for the door.

'You off?' shouts Mike the barman.

'Yes, thanks so much,' I smile.

I head out into the cold and stand uncertainly for a few seconds. I've every right to confront Ben Garret and his squeeze haven't I? After all, he did abandon me in a strange pub for a blonde bimbo with long legs, glossed lips and who answers to the name of *Princess*, no less. What a cheek.

I walk along the wet streets until I come to the entrance of Ben Garret's block. The same friendly doorman greets me.

'Good evening mam,' he says pleasantly.

'Hello, can you remind what number Ben Garret's flat is?'

'Number 93. Would you like me to get the lift for you?'

Before I can change my mind, the lift doors swish open and I'm stepping inside. I tidy my hair and touch up my lipstick. My hands are shaking and my heart racing. I step from the lift and walk nervously to Ben's door. The sound of *One Direction* reaches my ears and I frown. Then I hear a giggle and feel my anger rise. God, she sounds like a teenager. There's nothing more insulting than being dumped for a younger model is there? Before I know what I'm doing, I'm rapping on the door. I pull back my shoulders and push out my chin just as the door is swung open. Ben stands in his jeans and open neck shirt. He's holding a bunch of playing cards.

'Amy,' he says. 'What a surprise.'

I bet it is.

'I just wanted to tell you that you're a dick of the highest order. You're so up your own arse that if you're not careful you will ...'

'Hang on a minute Amy,' he interrupts, stepping into the hallway and pulling the door closed. One Direction disappears into the background.

'Just because you have a dick it doesn't mean you have to behave like one,' I say angrily. 'Honestly, you men are all the same. Well, you can shag Princess's brains out but don't you dare ...'

The door opens and a little flushed face peers around it.

'Uncle Ben, it's your turn.'

'Amy, may I introduce *Princess*.' His tone is hard and angry. Bollocks.

'Hello, I'm Sophie,' she says, her face beaming. 'Do you want to play Top Trumps with us?'

'Come in,' says Ben, frowning.

I step into the flat.

'I'm so sorry,' I say, 'I didn't know.'

'No, you just presumed that I was some kind of dick who walks out on a date so he can shag someone else?' he says quietly.

God, it sounds awful when you put it like that. We step into the living room. On the coffee table is popcorn and lemonade.

'Let's start a new game,' says Sophie, bouncing onto the couch.

'You deal the cards while I get Amy something to drink,' he says, taking my arm and leading me into the kitchen.

'Would you like some wine, or would you say you've had enough?'

'I'm really sorry. It's the last thing I imagined.'

'I don't even want to ask what you imagined.'

'I'm so sorry but what else was I to think?'

'Sophie's my niece. My sister is having some problems in her marriage. There's a lot of stuff going on and when things get a bit too much she'll phone me and ... I should have been more honest about it.'

He clinks his glass against mine.

'Here's to misunderstandings.'

'It's okay. I know that sometime it's hard to share things.'

He looks at me curiously.

'I've done something terrible,' I say, 'and I've no idea how to put it right.'

Oh dear, I really shouldn't drink so much. One, it is far too calorific and two, I always spill the beans.

'You've done something terrible since I left the pub?'

I laugh, although I'm not sure why.

'No, I did it well before then.'

'Uncle Ben, are you playing?' calls Sophie irritably.

'You're welcome to stay if you don't mind playing Top Trumps. Sophie will be going to bed soon.'

'Not until I've had ice cream,' she says, peering round the doorway. 'We've got chocolate and vanilla. Do you like ice cream?' she asks.

Do you know how many calories there are in ice cream? Two hundred and forty-eight in a tub, that's how many.

'I love ice cream,' I say, following her into the living room which looks very different to the last time I was here. The paintings are hanging on the wall and the once tidy room is now strewn with Sophie's things.

'This is my favourite game at the moment,' she says, showing me her set of cards.

'One game, and then we'll have ice cream, and then bed young lady. Your mum is coming to collect you early tomorrow.'

Sophie pulls a face.

'I wish I could stay more days,' she pouts.

'Well you can't because I have to work,' he grins. 'Come on, deal those cards.'

I could listen to his soft sexy voice forever. While Ben gets the ice cream, Sophie rummages through my make-up bag.

'Can I put on your lipstick?' she asks. 'Mum always lets me.'

I've only just wormed my way out of one sticky situation with Ben so I really don't want to fall in to another, but before I can stop her she swipes the stick along her lip.

'Let me show you how to do it properly,' I say, taking it from her.

By the time Ben returns she is wearing blusher, lipstick and eye shadow. I hold my breath and wait for his explosion.

'Look at you,' he smiles. 'You look like a film star.'

'Amy showed me how to do it. She's a wedding planner. She's going to plan my wedding when I'm older.'

'Have you told her your prices?' he quips, handing me a bowl of ice cream.

'Can Amy come on the picnic with us on Saturday?' asks Sophie.

'I imagine Amy has a wedding to go to.'

The mention of weddings brings back the memory of my conversation with Prince Abdullah. If only I could ask Ben his advice but I'd then need to tell him who I am. Once he finds out I've misled Georgie, and that I tried to stop her wedding, he'll want nothing more to do with me.

'Yes I do, actually. I have weddings most Saturdays; otherwise it would have been lovely. Where are you going?'

'Regent's Park,' says Sophie excitedly.

Ben refills my glass and offers Sophie more ice cream.

'This is the last bowl and then bed,' he says firmly.

I feel all cosy and warm inside knowing that Ben doesn't have a blonde floozy in tow and that he would have spent the evening with me if it hadn't been for Sophie needing a sitter. I've actually met a man that I like more than Greg, and I never thought that could happen, but it couldn't have happened at a worse time.

Sophie makes the ice cream last for as long as possible. Finally with a wink at me Ben says,

'Bed, Sophie. I want you up bright and breezy when Mum comes. If she finds out that I let you stay up late she won't let you come any more.'

'Okay, I'm going,' she smiles.

'Won't be a sec,' he says, following her.

I refill my glass and go to the kitchen to wash up.

'There's no need for you to do that,' Ben says, following me in. 'I just throw it all in the dishwasher.'

It feels uncomfortable to be around him now Sophie has gone.

'Tell me about this terrible thing that you've done.' he asks, beckoning me back to the living room. 'And what music do you fancy?'

'I don't mind.'

No amount of music is going to make my dirty deed sound any better is it? He puts on an Ed Sheeran album and sits opposite me.

'Sorry about this evening,' he says, looking into my eyes. 'I don't normally walk out on dates. My sister, Julia, is really trying to work things out and it just isn't always possible with Sophie there.'

'It's fine.'

He called it a date. Does that mean he sees us as being more than friends?

'You didn't think so earlier,' he says, his eyes twinkling mischievously. 'I'm getting the impression you have a pretty low opinion of men.'

'I have a low opinion of one man,' I say truthfully.

'Ah, I knew it,' he says triumphantly.

'How about you?' I ask curiously.

'I have a low opinion of one woman,' he smiles. 'Did you marry yours?'

I wince.

'Not quite. He didn't actually make it to the wedding. Unfortunately I did,' I say softly.

He reaches his hand out to mine.

'I'm so sorry Amy, that's a bummer.'

I nod. It was a bummer all right. On a scale of one to ten it's a number ten bummer, and as far as breaking my heart, nothing has come anywhere near since.

'That's why I started Perfect Weddings. I knew I would never plan another one for me so I thought, why not plan the perfect wedding for others.'

I take a gulp of wine. He nods thoughtfully and says,

'I got married, her name was Davina. She left me the next day. She realised it wasn't what she wanted after all.'

I gasp. God, that's worse than being dumped at the church gates.

'That's terrible, I'm so sorry.'

He gets up and takes a bottle of whisky from a cabinet.

'Something stronger needed I think,' he says quietly, pouring a good measure into a glass. 'Do you want some?'

I nod and hold out my glass.

'Here's to never getting married,' he smiles.

'To never getting married,' I agree.

'And now *Notting Hill*. I've got the DVD. Not as good as watching it at the flea pit but the next best thing. What do you think?'

I think this is the nicest evening I have had in a long time. What a shame Prince Abdullah's shadow has to ruin it. We clear away Sophie's things and Ben sets up the DVD.

'I was going to suggest it in the pub but then Julia phoned and it all got a bit complicated. Thanks for doing the make-up with Sophie. That's the kind of thing I can't do with her when she's here. I imagine she gets sick of Top Trumps,' he says, opening a pack of crackers. 'I've got some cheese in the fridge.'

Oh no, do you know how many calories there are in cheese? Thousands, absolutely thousands.

'I'll open another bottle,' he adds, strolling into the kitchen.

Not to mention the thousands of calories in the wine.

I tuck my legs under me and relax on the couch. I won't think about Prince Abdullah, not tonight. I'll worry about that tomorrow. Everything will sort itself out I'm sure. I just don't quite know how.

Everything was going really well. The film was brilliant. Well, what film with Hugh Grant in it, isn't? And then it got to that part where Ronan Keating sings, *When You Say Nothing at All,*

in that heartbreaking way that he has. Anna and William walk around the garden and then she reads the inscription on the bench. I don't know about you but when she says 'some people do spend their whole lives together' I'm done for. Tears run from my eyes and I remember the wonderful feelings I had had on my wedding day and how Greg had tossed them aside when he hadn't turned up for the wedding.

I feel Ben's arm slide around my shoulders and I lean into his body.

'A bit too much?' he whispers.

I sigh and dab at my eyes.

'Time for the interval,' he says pausing the DVD. 'Do you want to talk about it?'

I'd love to talk about it but how can I possibly talk about Greg to Ben. His muscular body is far too close and all I can think of are his kissable lips. I close my eyes and move ever so slightly on the couch.

'He's back,' I say.

'Your ex, the one who didn't turn up for the wedding?'

I'm grateful he doesn't say jilted.

'It's really complicated. But the terrible thing I've done is to do with him.'

He removes his arm from my shoulder and I feel suddenly bereft.

'I'm sure it's not that terrible. You haven't murdered him have you?'

'Not exactly,' I smile, 'but I'd like to.'

Well, I almost did.

'I don't know what this terrible thing is, but for what it's worth, I can't imagine anyone wanting to leave you standing at the altar. I happen to find you very appealing, apart from that sharp tongue of yours, and your insistence on being right all the time.'

'I'm not sure how to take that.'

He strokes my cheek.

'I like you, Amy Perfect, even if your tongue spits venom every so often,' he says, his voice strangled.

I have an overwhelming urge to jump him again, except this time I don't resist it. The need for him rushes to my groin.

His lips meet mine and his arms enfold me. Oh, the pleasure of feeling his tongue against mine. His firm body pushes me back onto the couch. His lips are urgent and I match his urgency with my own. The feel of his skin against mine sends tingles of pleasure through my body. The taste of him overpowers me and then suddenly he pulls away from me and for one awful moment I feel guilty as though I'd done something terribly wrong.

'What's the matter?' I ask, unable to keep the tremble from my voice. My whole body is on fire with desire for him.

'I'm sorry Amy, you've been drinking, and I really shouldn't have taken advantage. I know you only want a friend.'

God, I so wish I could take that back.

'No, it's ...' I begin.

'Please forgive me.'

'Uncle Ben, can I have a glass of water?'

He jumps up from the couch and I have to fight to stay on it. Sophie stands in the doorway and looks at us curiously.

'Can you read me a story Uncle Ben, I can't sleep.'

He looks at me shyly.

'I should be going,' I say.

'There's no need ...' He begins.

'It's getting late.'

'Bye,' says Sophie before I've even reached the front door. I stand in the street and the magnitude of what I've done hits me. Finally, after three years I find a man I could love, but when he finds out what I've done he won't want to know me. In my desperation to win Greg back I've lost everything. Don't you just hate it when karma comes back and bites you in the bum?

Chapter Forty-Two

'Thanks so much babe, it's been a blast, ain't it Gary?'

'A blast,' yawns Gary.

Chardonnay plonks a wet kiss on my cheek.

'We love the posh hotel you showed us, don't we Gary?'

'Yeah,' Gary yawns.

'It's not too expensive?' I ask. 'There are more reasonable ones than The Majestic that we can look at.'

'Nah, I want that one. What do you think Gary? That was the best one weren't it?'

'Yeah,' says Gary.

I'm seriously wondering if yeah is the only word he knows.

'I'm gonna treat meself to some retail therapy,' says Chardonnay draping her leopard print jacket around her shoulders. 'All this wedding thinking is bloody stressful ain't it? Gary 'ates the shops don't ya babe?'

'Yeah, 'ate 'em,' agrees Gary.

'Where are you off to now, Amy?' she asks.

'I was going to walk to Costa Coffee,' I say without thinking.

'Ooh great, I'll come wiv ya. Give us a bell when you get back to Saffend Gary.'

Before I can protest she has dragged me down the street to Costa.

'What do ya think of my Gary?' she asks.

'He's very nice. Not very talkative though.'

She laughs loudly and everyone in the coffee shop turns to look at us.

''E don't get a look in wiv me does 'e?'

Georgie spots us and waves.

'You didn't let on you were meeting someone.'

I didn't get much of a chance did I? Rosie sits beside Georgie with a face as long as a kite.

'Hi,' says Georgie excitedly.

'This is Chardonnay, one of my brides,' I explain.

'Ello,' says Chardonnay, plonking herself into a chair.

'I'm a bride too,' says Georgie and promptly bursts into tears.

This is all I need.

'Oh my gawd, what's wrong?' asks Chardonnay.

'I'll get some coffees,' says Rosie with a sigh.

'My fiancée had an accident and doesn't know me any more,' hiccups Georgie.

'Oh my gawd, that's terrible,' comforts Chardonnay, putting an arm around Georgie. 'What kind of accident?'

I leave the table and join Rosie at the counter.

'I can't believe you're serious about this,' she snaps. 'I told you this was unhealthy. It's like a virus, it just keeps spreading.'

'I can't tell her the truth, not this close to the wedding. I told her that I'm going to help her find Amy Fisher and that's what I'm going to do.'

'What are you talking about? You are Amy Fisher,' she hisses.

'I know that, of course I know that.'

'You could have fooled me. I sometimes don't think you know who you are. I'm having a coffee and then I have to get back to work.'

I gawp at her.

'But I thought you were coming to help find Amy Fisher?'

'Will you stop saying that? How can I find you if you're already here?' she demands.

'Keep your voice down,' I whisper. 'I'm just trying to bide some time until I can work out what to do.'

'I just know I'll give the game away if I come. I'll end up putting you in it.'

We take the coffees to the table where Chardonnay looks up with tears in her eyes.

'Isn't it awful about Greg? We 'ave to find this Amy Fisher so we can get his memory back. I don't know what I'd do if Gary forgot me.'

I somehow think Gary has already forgotten her, but I don't say anything.

'Good luck,' says Rosie. 'I can't come with you. I have to get back to work. I hope you find her though,' she adds, giving me a mean look.

'How is Greg?' I ask. 'Has he remembered anything else?'

'The doctor said he can leave the hospital in a few days. Luckily he finished everything up in Spain so he doesn't need to go back. He just keeps asking where Amy is and what's happening about the wedding. Why is he stuck at that stupid wedding to her? I thought it was all over with Amy Fisher.'

I check my BlackBerry to see if Ben has left a message but there is nothing. He's probably getting one of his spooks to check me out.

'Drink up,' says Chardonnay eagerly. 'The sooner we look for Amy Fisher, the sooner we find her.'

'Here's her address,' says Georgie. 'I found it on the electoral roll.'

'You did?' I say, feeling my heart start to thump.

Chardonnay's eyes light up when she sees my Mercedes convertible.

'Wow, that's what I call a car.'

'I've got a map,' says Georgie, pulling a crumpled sheet of paper from her handbag. 'It's not in the best part of London.'

What a cheek. It happened to be a good neighbourhood when I lived there. We clamber into the Merc and with a leaden heart I move off into the busy London road. We drive for a full twenty minutes until Georgie says,

'You take the next left.'

'Are you sure?' I ask.

If I remember it was the next right, but what do I know, I only lived there. I take the left turn as directed, and Georgie instructs me to stop.

'It should be here,' she says doubtfully.

'Well, according to Google maps we should 'ave taken the turning on the right instead of the left,' says Chardonnay, studying her phone.

'Oh,' says Georgie. 'Maybe that's right. I'm a bit nervous.'

I turn the car around, take the turning and suddenly we're in gangland New York, or at least it feels like it.

'Oh my gawd, this is worse than Essex,' says Chardonnay.

My old block is now daubed with graffiti. A burnt out car sits outside and is surrounded by yobs standing in a blue haze of smoke. I wouldn't like to say what it is they're smoking.

'Amy Fisher lives here?' gasps Georgie as a football hits the car window.

'Oy, you little sod, 'ave some respect,' shouts Chardonnay.

I somehow feel this is not a good start to the proceedings.

'Perhaps she doesn't any more,' I say, doing my best to protect my reputation. God, the place has gone to the dogs since I lived here.

The yobs look at the Mercedes and nudge each other.

'I'm thinking they're thinking your car is worth a bit,' says Chardonnay nervously. 'I wish Gary were wiv us. He always carries a knife.'

'He does?' I say shakily. My clientele *is* going downhill.

'I think we should go,' I say, putting the car into reverse.

'No,' screams Georgie, 'we have to find Amy Fisher.'

'I'm really not happy about leaving the car,' I say, trying not to sound too materialistic.

'Maybe one of us should stay with it,' suggests Georgie.

'I ain't volunteering. They're stoned,' mutters Chardonnay, looking at the yobs.

'Perhaps if we pay them?' says Georgie.

There's a tap on the windscreen and we all jump out of our skin.

'Oh God,' I squeal as a greasy haired man pushes his face against the window.

'Oh my gawd,' cries Chardonnay.

'Don't open it,' screams Georgie.

He bangs on the window again. This is all so unfamiliar. How can a street change so much in three years? I feel like I've gone *Back to the Future* in a DeLorean.'

'Can we help you?' I say politely.

'Just tell 'im to fuck off,' says Chardonnay, cringing in her seat. 'We should never 'ave come 'ere in a posh car.'

'You want me to watch it?' asks the man. His alcohol enriched breath seeps through a gap in the window. I wind the window down halfway.

'We need to go into those flats,' I tell him, jerking my head as I do so.

'One of us does anyway,' nods Georgie.

'We should stick together,' says Chardonnay.

'I'll make sure the buggers don't go near it,' he says, producing a gun from his pocket.

'Oh my gawd,' repeats Chardonnay. 'It's worse than back 'ome.'

I so wish she would stop comparing my old street to Essex.

'Cost you.'

''ow much?' asks Chardonnay.

''undred quid.'

'A hundred quid?' I gasp.

'Cost more than that to fix if it got beat up, but it's up to you,' he says and turns to walk away.

'Wait,' calls Georgie. 'Surely between us we've got a hundred pounds haven't we?'

This is wonderful. We're paying a hundred quid to a complete stranger so we can go and look for me. It would be funny if it wasn't so tragic. I suppose I should be flattered. We all rummage in our bags.

'I've got forty,' says Georgie.

The man's eyes light up at the sight of the money.

'I've only got thirty,' I say.

'I've got twenty quid. I didn't bring any more as I was gonna do all my shopping on Gary's Barclaycard,' says Chardonnay.

Chardonnay is smarter than I gave her credit for.

'We're ten pound short,' says Georgie.

''ang on,' says Chardonnay, digging deep into her bag. 'I've got a tenner 'ere somewhere. I remember shoving it in me bag.'

She produces a ten pound note like a magician and we hand the money over to the greasy haired man.

'Don't ya worry about ya motor,' he says confidently. 'Anyone tries to get near it and I'll put a bullet through their skull.'

'That's very kind of you, thank you,' I say.

Best to be polite in these situations, I find.

'Do you think we can trust him?' asks Georgie.

I grab a hat from the back seat and pull my sunglasses from my bag.

'Do we have much choice?'

'Let's go,' says Georgie. Chardonnay and I climb reluctantly from the car and follow her to the entrance of the flats.

Chapter Forty-Three

The yobs give us a threatening look.

'My fella knows people,' says Chardonnay as we pass. 'People who knew the Krays, you get me? And don't for one minute think we ain't tooled up.'

I give her an impressive nod. Although anyone who knew the Krays would have to be getting on a bit, but still, it sounds good.

'Looking for someone special are ya?' asks one, spitting just a few inches from my new Prada shoes.

'Amy Fisher,' says Georgie, 'do you know her?'

They look at each other.

'Nah, never 'eard of 'er, what does she look like?'

'She's fat,' says Georgie.

I wince.

'Lot of fat people around these days,' they laugh.

I pull Georgie into the flat foyer and Chardonnay follows. The place stinks of urine and I wrinkle my nose. Georgie studies the name plates.

'According to the electoral roll, Amy lives at number 106.'

Amy is certainly glad she doesn't live here any more.

'Let's go,' says Chardonnay, heading to the stairs.

'You ain't leaving that motor outside are ya?'

We turn to see four of the yobs standing in the doorway.

'Good little runner is it?' asks another.

'I wouldn't go near that if I was you. Not unless you wanna bullet frough your skull' says Chardonnay menacingly.

I wouldn't want to get on the wrong side of Chardonnay.

'Do you think we should pay them?' asks Georgie.

'We haven't got any more money,' I remind her.

It seems finding me is becoming an expensive pastime.

'Are you sure you want to find this Amy Fisher chick?' asks Chardonnay. 'She might be a nasty piece of work.'

Georgie ignores her and starts climbing the stairs.

'Bleedin' 'ell,' groans Chardonnay as we reach the third floor. 'I can 'ardly breathe.'

Georgie pants beside her.

'Just another two flights to go, I think.'

We climb the last two stairwells and stand panting at the top.

'Hell's bells,' gasps Georgie. 'How does Amy Fisher manage these stairs?'

'Yeah, she's fat too ain't she?' agrees Chardonnay.

'There must be more to Amy Fisher than her being fat,' I say defensively.

The yobs bound up the stairs behind us.

'What's this Amy Fisher done then?' asks one of them.

'You really don't want to know,' I say, and follow Georgie with Chardonnay close behind.

'They're following us,' whispers Chardonnay.

I really shouldn't be putting my brides in such danger. Can you imagine what Ben Garret would say about this? I can almost see the headline, *'Amy Perfect, the not so perfect wedding planner, gets brides lynched in 'worse than Essex' tower block.'* Talking of Ben, I pull my BlackBerry from my bag and see there is a text from him.

If you're free later do you fancy a repeat of last night but minus Sophie? Fish and chips or a restaurant of your choice? Let me know.

It's all I can do not to jump up and down with happiness. I look up to see Georgie standing at the front door of my old flat.

'What do I say to her?' she says, her voice shaking. 'I never really thought about that.'

Before I can reply, Chardonnay bangs on the knocker and we wait with our breath held, although I'm not sure why I'm holding mine.

'Shall I try again?' suggests Chardonnay, after a minute of waiting.

'Ain't no one going to answer that door,' says one of the yobs from behind us.

We look nervously at each other.

'Why not?' asks Chardonnay.

'Oh God, she's dead isn't she?' utters Georgie. 'I knew it.'

She claps a hand to her mouth.

'Oh Jesus, you don't think Greg murdered her do you and that's why he's stuck in a time warp. That must have been the trauma.'

For a future wife she has a very low opinion of her soon-to-be husband.

'Bloody 'ell,' says Chardonnay, 'that's a bit extreme isn't it? Men don't kill their girlfriends because they're a bit chubby.'

I sigh.

'They're in the nick ain't they?' says the yob. 'Ave been for months.'

Georgie sways.

'Amy Fisher is in prison?' She gasps. 'Why, what did she do?'

The flat door behind us is flung open and we come face to face with Mrs Slater. I quickly pull down my hat.

'What's all the racket about? I'm trying to watch Jeremy Kyle.'

'We're trying to find Amy Fisher,' says Georgie.

'Do ya know what prison she's in?' asks Chardonnay.

Oh no. It will be all round the street that I'm in prison now.

'Good God, what did she do? Poor cow, she was out of her mind, of course, after what happened,' says Mrs Slater with a sigh. 'No girl deserved that.'

Quite right, I couldn't agree more.

'Well, thanks very much,' I say, trying to pull Georgie away.

'What 'appened to 'er,' asks Chardonnay. 'Is she … you know?'

'It's probably not our business,' I say. 'The thing is, she doesn't live here any more. That's all we need to know isn't it?'

I'm not too happy at how closely Mrs Slater is looking at me.

'Killed him did she? Well, I'm not surprised. The bastard had it coming,' she scoffs.

'Killed who?' asks Georgie breathlessly.

'Yeah, who did she kill?' asks the yob curiously.

'You'd better come in,' says Mrs Slater, opening the door wider.

The smell of cat piss hits us and Chardonnay puts a hand over her nose.

'Faaackinell, it smells like somefink died in 'ere too,' she groans.

'What's that?' snaps Mrs Slater.

'Nothing,' I say, trying to disguise my voice.

'Who did Amy Fisher kill?' Georgie asks insistently.

'We don't know she killed anyone,' I say.

'Why are ya talking funny?' asks Chardonnay.

'I'm not talking funny,' I mumble.

'You girls want a cuppa?'

'No thank you,' I say quickly.

'Who did Amy Fisher kill?' demands Georgie.

'Greg Martin, I presume. Why else would she be in prison? I'd have killed the bugger too if he had jilted me at the altar.'

Georgie sways and I reach out to steady her.

'She didn't kill my Greg,' Georgie says hoarsely.

'Oh my gawd,' says Chardonnay. 'The bugger jilted 'er. What a sod. That's the worst thing ever.'

I couldn't agree more.

'My Greg wouldn't do that,' argues Georgie.

'But why is Amy Fisher in prison,' asks Chardonnay, 'if she didn't kill your Greg?'

'I didn't say she was, you did,' huffs Mrs Slater, opening the kitchen door to let in her cats.

'We should go,' I say, turning to the door.

'You sound familiar,' says Mrs Slater suspiciously. 'What are you girls here for?'

'Oh my gawd,' cries Chardonnay, looking out of the window. 'They're only taking the wheels off the Merc.'

'Whose Merc?' asks Mrs Slater.

'Mercedes,' I correct, diving out of the door. 'And it's mine.'

Chapter Forty-Four

This whole thing is becoming a terrible nightmare. The blood pounds in my head as we fly down the stairs. We get to the entrance door to see Mr Grease Hair waving his gun around like a mad fiend. Two of the yobs have their hands in the air and thankfully all my wheels are intact. Okay, I must keep my head and I mean literally keep my head. The way Mr Grease Hair is waving that gun around anyone of us may lose ours.

'Don't move a fucking inch,' Mr Grease Hair shouts at the yobs, 'or I'll blow your brains from here to kingdom come.'

He swings around and the three of us duck.

'Holy shit,' cries Chardonnay.

'Everyone just keep calm,' I say, while shaking like a leaf.

'I never realised 'ow bad London was. Essex is a walk in the park compared to this,' whispers Chardonnay.

'I ain't let 'em near your motor,' Mr Grease Hair smiles, while still aiming the gun at us.

'That's brilliant,' I say shakily. 'But we're ready to leave now, so we'll need to get into the car.'

'You speak for yourself,' says Chardonnay.

I walk unsteadily towards the Merc with Georgie clinging to my arm.

'You fucking stay back, do you 'ear me.'

'We're not going to get out of here alive,' cries Georgie hysterically.

'I told you that chick Amy Fisher was bad news,' trembles Chardonnay.

'We need to leave now,' I say quietly.

'Okay, come on,' he says, beckoning us forward.

We take a few steps when he screams and waves the gun angrily.

'I told ya to stay back.'

'I wish he'd make up his bleedin' mind,' groans Chardonnay. 'Somethink ain't right 'ere.'

'Oh God, he's schizophrenic,' cries Georgie. 'No wonder Greg jilted Amy Fisher.'

'What's she got to do with it?' asks Chardonnay, cowering behind a rubbish bin.

'If she lives somewhere like this she can't be all the ticket can she?' Georgie weeps, her tears soaking my jumper.

'I ain't moving,' one of the yobs shouts from behind us. 'Don't shoot.'

'Thanks so much for looking after the car,' I shout. 'We're coming out now, so can you lower the gun?'

'Come on,' I say to Georgie, stepping forward nervously.

Mr Grease Hair keeps the gun pointed at the yobs behind us. We carefully skirt around him and clamber into the car.

'Hit it,' shouts Chardonnay as I start the engine.

I screech off in third gear and take the corner on two wheels with my heart hammering in my chest. In the rear-view mirror I can see Mr Grease Hair waving his arms angrily.

'Oh God,' moans Georgie, dropping her head into her hands.

I cannot believe what we've just been through. How can a place change in three years? Rosie won't believe it either. We sit in silence and all that can be heard is Georgie's rapid breathing.

'My head is throbbing,' she says finally.

'Here,' says Chardonnay, handing her two aspirin.

I take the next turn at break neck speed and it's then we hear the police sirens.

'They're chasing us,' exclaims Chardonnay. 'Stop the car.'

I see the flashing lights in the rear-view mirror and groan. How can this be happening? I slow down and pull the Merc into a bus lane.

'We can't tell them what happened,' I say.

'Why not?' asks a tearful Georgie.

Because Ben Garret will hear about it and that's all I need.

'It'll be bad publicity for 'er wedding business,' explains Chardonnay.

'But you *were* driving too fast,' Georgie accuses.

'I was trying to get us away from a madman with a gun.'

I watch through the rear-view mirror as two officers climb from the patrol car and stride towards us with an arrogant swagger. I wind down the window and smile sweetly.

'Sorry officer, was I speeding?'

'I'll need you to step out of the car,' he says bluntly.

''ello,' calls Chardonnay from the back seat. 'Was we going too fast? Poor Georgie is so upset that ...'

'Would you step out of the car too, miss,' he says sharply.

'Sure,' smiles Chardonnay. 'Although I ain't gonna be a miss for much longer. This is Amy Perfect, she's my wedding planner, and she's the best there is in London. I've come all the way from Saffend to see 'er and ...'

'And you,' he says looking in at Georgie.

Georgie steps from the car and bursts into tears.

'We didn't mean it,' she says, between hiccups. 'I just wanted to find out about her. I didn't imagine she would be in prison and we didn't know he had a gun. I'd never have gone if I'd known.'

Chardonnay and I stare at her. Oh God, what is she saying?

'It's okay Georgie,' I say, 'you've been dreaming.'

'Have you taken something, miss?' the officer asks, looking at her closely.

'Only two pills,' she says innocently. 'Greg is in this time warp you see and ...'

'Pills is it? I see. I need you to step into the police car, miss.'

''ang on a minute,' interrupts Chardonnay. 'You can't just take her like that. She ain't done nothink wrong. It's not illegal to take pills.'

'Step into the car too, miss,' he says, taking her arm.

'I ain't going nowhere wiv you pigs,' she cries, pulling away. 'We ain't done nothink apart from drive a bit too fast.'

'Fifty miles an hour in a thirty mile an hour limit is more than a bit too fast,' he says firmly.

'I didn't think I was going that fast,' I argue. 'I thought it ...'

'Is that right?' he butts in. 'Can I see your driving licence Miss Perfect,' he says with a smirk. 'I shouldn't have to tell you that driving under the influence of Ecstasy is a criminal offence.'

I gulp, did he say Ecstasy? He must be joking. I've not felt anything close to ecstasy since Greg accepted my proposal years ago in the Little Chef.

'Ecstasy?' I repeat. 'I wouldn't even know what it looks like.'

'I'm arresting you ladies on suspicion of being in possession of and under the influence of illegal drugs.'

Oh great.

Chapter Forty-Five

So, here we are, or at least here I am, sitting in a cold police cell, with my two brides, Chardonnay and Georgie. This can't be happening.

'I can phone Ben,' suggests Georgie. 'He'll know what to do.'

'I don't think you should bother him,' I say.

'I can call Gary but it'll take him an 'ell of a time to get 'ere,' says Chardonnay.

We're being charged with being under the influence of illegal drugs, although they can't find anything on us apart from a packet of aspirin. We've had blood tests so it's just a matter of time before we'll be released. Meanwhile, Chardonnay and I have also been charged with assaulting a police officer. Things got just a touch out of control. Chardonnay decided not to get in the police car without a fight and I was all for being a bystander until the police officer said,

'If your fella's got any sense he'll jilt you at the altar. No man needs to put up with this.'

Well, you can imagine can't you? It was like a red rag to a bull, and I did charge at him like a woman demented. I think I called him a sexist pig or something worse. It must have been something worse because he got quite mad at that point. I vaguely remember him yelping when I stamped on his foot. Chardonnay came to my aid and whacked him around the head, which didn't go down at all well.

'We need someone to bail us out,' I say.

'Gary always says you should never go peacefully with the pigs. So I didn't,' Chardonnay says proudly.

'It's my fault,' Georgie groans as she fiddles with a ladder in her tights. 'I wanted to find Amy Fisher.'

'At least you know Greg didn't murder her,' says Chardonnay.

'But how can she help Greg if she's in prison?' says Georgie, wiping away her tears. 'And we don't even know what prison she's in, or why she's there. Poor Greg, what am I going to do? I'll have to cancel the wedding.'

'There must be somethink we can do,' says Chardonnay.

Right now, all I want to do is get out of this police cell. I'm falling apart. My life is a mess. The love of my life turns out not to be the love of my life after all. His fiancée thinks I'm in prison. The sheikh is blackmailing me. The man I do like is never going to forgive me once he finds out the truth. Sooner or later Georgie will find out who I am and hate me too. I'll never have the perfect wedding. I'm doomed to be a spinster for the rest of my life. I might as well go back and let Mr Grease Hair blow my brains out, what brains I have, that is. Let's face it, if I'd had more than two brain cells in my head I would never have thought of sabotaging Georgie's wedding. The only person I've hurt is me and Greg will still love Georgie when he comes round.

The cell door swings opens and we all jump up.

'Alright ladies?' the officer asks, giving us an evil grin.

'Can we go?' asks Georgie, as hopeful as ever.

'You're lucky this time. Your blood tests came back normal. Unfortunately it will be a few hours before we're done with the paperwork. You did assault a police officer.'

'You assaulted us,' Chardonnay reminds him but he's already slammed the door shut.

'I'll phone Rosie,' I say.

'I'd better phone Gary, or he'll think someone has run off wiv me,' laughs Chardonnay.

There is no answer from Rosie's phone. It's no good. I have no choice but to phone my mother.

'Hello darling, how are you? We're at Val's yet again,' she says proudly. 'She's started this gin rummy club. It's great fun. Your dad is proving to be a bit of a champion. Gerald's here too. He's very good. In fact,' she adds, dropping her voice, 'he's really rather nice. Maybe you should rethink things about him and ...'

'Mum, can you come and get me?'

'You want to play gin rummy? How lovely,' she says.

'No, I'm more of a Monopoly girl. I need a get out of jail free card.'

'I don't understand dear.'

'I've been arrested, along with two of my brides.'

She gasps.

'Arrested, what on earth for?'

'Who's been arrested,' I hear Auntie Val ask.

'For being under the influence of drugs and assaulting a police officer,' I say bluntly.

'With your brides, what were you thinking of? I don't believe it. What drugs have you taken? Oh my goodness, you've not been shooting off, have you?'

'I think you mean shooting up, and no, I haven't. It was two aspirin and Georgie took them.'

'The police don't arrest you for taking aspirin?' she says doubtfully.

'And I stamped on his foot. Mum, can you come and get us out?'

'Oh dear, I never thought I'd see the day. What police station?'

She hangs up after promising to come right away. Georgie then phones Patsy. We hear her scream down the phone.

'Holy shit. That is so awesome Georgie. I'm on my way.'

My mother turns up incognito. For a few seconds I think Joan Collins has come to rescue me. Her hair is wrapped in a scarf and her eyes are hidden behind huge sunglasses. She's wrapped in a fur coat which I've never seen before. Auntie Val strolls in behind her.

'What the ...' I begin.

'Val said there might be paparazzi outside. So ...'

'Paparazzi, why would there be paparazzi?'

'Well, you were on the tele.'

'In an advert, I'm not exactly Cate Blanchett am I?'

'I can't believe you're on drugs,' says Auntie Val gleefully. 'That's very decadent of you.'

I sigh.

'I'm not on drugs.'

Patsy rushes in behind them and screams at the sight of us.

'Hey guys, how did you get busted?'

'They took drugs,' says Auntie Val proudly.

'I took two aspirin,' says Georgie.

'And we assaulted the pigs, ain't that right Amy?' adds Chardonnay.

At that moment Lucy bursts through the door.

'You're in a cell,' she says.

Lucy has a knack for stating the bloody obvious.

'What happened this time?' she asks. 'Your mum phoned me. She thought I might be worried.'

'This time?' questions Mum. 'Have there been other times?'

'Not where I've been in prison,' I explain, glaring at Lucy.

'Hey babes,' says Chardonnay, 'can one of you bail us out? Only I've got to get back to Saffend.'

'Saffend?' repeats Auntie Val.

'Southend,' translates Lucy.

'It's been a real larf though,' giggles Chardonnay, 'apart from the gun. That was fucking scary.'

'Gun?' repeats Mum. 'What gun?'

'Can we just get out of here,' cries Georgie, 'I can't take much more. What if Greg's memory has come back? I won't be there for him.'

'Greg?' echoes Mum, 'Greg who?'

Oh no. I need to get us out of here before things get out of hand.

'My fiancé Greg,' says Georgie. 'Greg Martin.'

'Greg Martin?' exclaims Auntie Val. 'Not the little git who ...'

'Auntie Val,' I say sharply.

'No, I don't think so,' says Lucy in a shaky voice, while looking worriedly at me.

'Who you calling a little git?' says Georgie angrily.

'I'm getting very confused,' says Mum.

'We're all het up,' I say. 'We need to get out of this cell. Mum can you sort out the bail please.'

Mum and Auntie Val wander out to the reception desk.

'How does your auntie know Greg?' asks Georgie suspiciously.

'They don't. They've been playing gin rummy,' I say, as if that somehow explains everything. The police officer opens the cell door and gives us a surly look.

'Seems you're free to go but just watch yourselves.'

'And you watch yourself,' says Chardonnay.

I grab her arm and pull her out of the room.

'You've got Laureta's wedding next Saturday,' hisses Lucy. 'I hope you haven't forgotten because you didn't turn up for the rehearsal this afternoon. Do you think you could possibly stay out of prison before the ceremony?'

Damn, I totally forgot about the rehearsal.

'I told her your piles were playing up.'

'My piles?' I gasp.

'She caught me unawares. If you must know I was in the middle of a very intimate phone call with Frank.'

'Frank?'

Who's Frank?

'My new boyfriend and I didn't have time to think of a better excuse, so piles it was.'

It's no good. This Greg and Georgina thing is taking over my life. I need to get this sorted once and for all and get my life back to normal. Great plan.

Chapter Forty-Six

I arrive at The Hive to find Ben pacing up and down outside. My ovaries start partying the minute I set eyes on him. He looks so appealing that I just want to take him home and shag the life out of him. I can't remember ever feeling this randy about anyone. I certainly didn't feel this horny when with Greg, but it's not just that. Ben makes me feel so feminine. I get butterflies when Georgie mentions his name or when I hear his voice at the other end of the phone. He has an effect on me that no other man ever had. I'd fastened my hair onto the top of my head and chosen a simple black evening dress. I'd covered it with a pashmina but am now wishing I'd brought my coat.

I rush to his side.

'I'm sorry I'm late,' I say, 'I got held up.'

I can't very well say I got arrested can I?

'Have you been waiting long?'

'No, not at all,' he smiles.

I'm feeling quite desperate if truth be known. Hiding this whole Greg scenario from everyone is taking its toll. I can't keep it up for ever. I'm a bag of nerves. I'm swallowing Quiet Life left right and centre. I can't think clearly, although that probably is the Quiet Life. I must not drink. Alcohol and Quiet Life really don't make a good partnership. I've got to keep my head. I've got Laureta's wedding coming up. I need to be on top of things. Although the only thing I really want to be on top of is Ben Garret. I sigh and smile at him.

'Won't you be cold?' he asks.

'I must admit it's chillier than I thought.'

He removes his jacket and drapes it around my shoulders.

'Now, I've got a confession to make,' he says shyly. 'I tried to book a table but I couldn't get anything until nine. I booked a table at Lorenzo's. I hope you like Italian?' he says, his eyes sparkling.

'I love Italian food.'

'Great. In the meantime do you fancy a drink? A friend of mine has his wine bar opening tonight. He's not really expecting anyone to turn up except a few of his friends so I'd feel bad letting him down,' he laughs. 'He's been getting this wine bar ready for months. What do you think?'

'I'd love to,' I smile.

'I'm sorry about last night,' he says taking my arm.

'It can't be helped. Sophie is very sweet.'

'I meant about the kiss. I shouldn't have. I'm well aware that you don't want anything too deep.'

'I wouldn't say ...'

'Happy to be friends?' he asks.

I don't believe this is happening to me.

'Yes, of course.'

Not really.

'Great,' he says with a grin. 'Let's go and try this wine.'

I feel more like jumping off London Bridge. What is it with me and bloody men? Greg dumps me at the altar, Ben only wants to be friends and sodding Gerald is more interested in sticking his sausage in the oven. It says a lot about me doesn't it? Here I am, slim, fit and trendy at last, and no one is bloody interested, apart from the sheikh. Oh, why did I have to think of Prince Abdullah now? I think I'll enter a convent after Georgie's wedding, that's if the wedding happens of course. Yes, that's what I'll do. I'll become celibate and pure. I'll devote my life to God. Let's face it, I couldn't be any more celibate if I tried, so I might as well put it to good use.

The wine bar is buzzing when we arrive and a young frazzled guy with a ponytail greets us, his face lighting up at the sight of Ben.

'Hey man, you made it. This is good for my reputation. Float around a bit won't you,' he smiles before grabbing two glasses of bubbly from a tray.

'A toast to *Pearls,* the newest and best wine bar in London.'

We clink glasses.

'This is Amy Perfect,' says Ben, 'and this is Seb, he and his girlfriend Pearl own the wine bar.'

'Not *the* Amy Perfect, the wedding planner?' asks Seb.

I blush.

'The one and only,' grins Ben.

'We might well need you sometime soon,' says Seb, raising his eyebrows. 'I'd better circulate as they say. Have a great time. Drink plenty of champagne, there's buckets of it.'

And so we do. We find a quiet corner and talk about everything under the sun while soft blues music plays in the background. I haven't felt this relaxed in months. We discover that we share a love of tenpin bowling and agree to go the next day. Seb was right when he said there were buckets of champagne. Our glasses never seem to empty, so much for my great plan not to mix alcohol with Quiet Life tablets. We share a plate of nachos, compliments of Seb and Pearl, and chat to people who recognise Ben. A small area of the restaurant is cleared for dancing and as Adele's *When We Were Young* begins to play, Ben takes my hand firmly in his and drags me onto the dance floor.

'I'm not a great dancer,' I say quickly. Greg used to tell me I had two left feet.

'Just copy me, how hard can it be?' he smiles.

I breathe in the manly smell of him and allow him to glide me around the dance floor. He is so different to Greg. Ben is so self-assured, capable and so manly. Oh yes, that is the word alright. Ben Garret is manly. His muscular body glides me expertly around the dance area.

'You look beautiful tonight,' he says looking into my eyes.

I feel my cheeks grow hot under his stare.

'Thank you,' I reply softly. 'You don't look so bad yourself.'

I have to look away from his warm appealing eyes before I drown in them.

'You still haven't told me what the terrible thing is that you've done. Should I be afraid?'

His eyes sparkle with humour.

'No,' I say, and then to change the subject quickly add, 'You're a good dancer.'

It feels strange being so close to him, to feel the solid muscle of his chest and to breathe in the scent that is uniquely his. He gives a lazy smile.

'I'm not doing very much.'

He's got no idea what's he doing but I can assure you it is a hell of a lot. I feel my cheeks grow hot under his stare. His warm hand strokes my back as we dance and I shiver with pleasure. He pulls me closer. Close enough for me to feel his arousal and I fight back a gasp. My desire throbs low in my groin. The sexual tension between us is so tangible it almost takes my breath away. My heart thuds and I pull him closer.

'Are you enjoying yourself?' he asks huskily.

'Yes,' I whisper as his lips move closer to mine.

'Ben ...'

'You talk too much,' he says before bringing his lips down onto mine and then we're kissing with a passion I didn't know I possessed. I tremble under his touch. His tongue teases mine and I feel sure I will faint with my desire for him.

'Enjoying yourselves guys?' Seb asks. We pull apart so suddenly that I sway on my feet. I hear Ben sigh before he smiles at Seb.

'It's a great night mate, but we've got to push off. We've got a table booked at the Italian around the corner but it's been great,' he says.

I kiss Pearl on the cheek and hope my face isn't as red as it feels.

'I expect you to come back,' she says, hugging Ben. 'We need your influential presence.'

Ben laughs and we step out into the cool night. He tucks my arm into his.

'I hope you're hungry,' he says and it's as if the kiss never happened.

We're given a table in a corner and Ben orders a bottle of wine before I can protest. Oh well, one glass won't make any difference now will it? Not after all that champagne.

'It's been a great evening,' he says lifting his glass in a toast. 'Maybe later we can carry on where we left off. Seb can be a bit tactless sometimes.'

The butterflies flutter in my stomach again.

'I'd love to,' I say, feeling myself blush. Honestly, I'm acting like a seventeen-year-old.

'So, have you had a busy day?' he asks, helping himself to a bread stick.

'You could say that,' I smile.

'Greg is being discharged tomorrow. He still hasn't remembered the wedding. Poor Gina, it's not looking good for her big day is it? Any luck with finding Amy Fisher?' he asks.

'Amy Fisher?' I say.

'Gina said you were going to her flat today,' he says, looking at me closely. 'Didn't you go with her?'

'Oh yes, that Amy Fisher.'

As if I could forget.

'She doesn't live there any more.'

Amy doesn't live here any more. I'd make a good film title wouldn't I? My great plan not to drink too much has gone out of the window as Ben is already topping up my glass. Quiet Life and wine seem to produce something akin to a truth serum where I'm concerned, and by the time our main course arrives I'm ready to spill everything. I open my mouth to tell him about Greg but instead say,

'Did Greg ever tell you about Amy Fisher?'

'Not much. I haven't known him that long. Gina introduced us. He only said that Amy ended the relationship just before their wedding and that he was glad.'

The lying little sod.

'Have you had many girlfriends?'

He raises his eyebrows.

'Enough, how about you?'

'I've never had a girlfriend,' I giggle.

Oh dear, I must slow up on the wine.

'Parmesan madam?' asks the waiter.

'Have you had many boyfriends?' Ben asks with a wink.

'Not really,' I reply, picking at my carbonara. 'I've not had a boyfriend since Gr ... my fiancé let me down.'

'You mustn't blame yourself. He really should have told you well before the day.'

I feel tears prick my eyelids and take another sip of wine.

'It was supposed to be the happiest day of my life.'

'If it's any consolation it's much worse when they dump you the day after.'

'I'm so sorry,' I say reaching for his hand.

'It wasn't your fault,' he smiles. He seems to hesitate and then says, 'Amy, how do you feel about taking this a step further. I don't mean run before we can walk but move past the friendship stage. What do you think? I know I'd like to.'

I think this is music to my ears.

'I ...'

'I understand if you'd rather not.'

'Oh God,' I groan as I see Prince Abdullah walk through the door.

'The thought of it, is that bad is it?' he asks with a smile. 'Too soon for you?'

It's too much for me more like. Fortunately Ben has his back to the door so doesn't see Abdullah enter but Abdullah sees me and that's all I need.

'No, I would really like that,' I say, turning my eyes away from Abdullah. 'I'd like that more than anything.'

'I'm glad,' he says, reaching his hand across to mine.

What is Abdullah doing here? If I didn't know better I'd think he was stalking me. I discreetly try to see who he's with. I hope it isn't Laureta. The waiter moves away from their table and I see he is with his three wives. He surely won't approach me if they're with him.

'Are you okay Amy? You look a bit pale.'

'I'm fine. I've got Greg and Georgie on my mind.'

Haven't I just. It feels like my life revolves around Greg's wedding. I feel more involved in his second wedding than I was in his first, and I was the bloody bride then. I discreetly rummage in my bag and find my Quiet Life tablets. I swallow three and try to relax. The sheikh is busy ordering his meal and seems to have forgotten about me. I must keep calm. There are only so many bad things that can happen in one day aren't there? I just need to get some perspective on everything. I'm sure things aren't as bad as they seem. Hopefully, one day I'll be able to look back on all this and laugh. I glance slyly over to Prince Abdullah's table. Another man has joined them and everyone is laughing and enjoying their meal. Good, I just need to get through our meal and we can leave.

'Anything on the dessert menu takes your fancy?' Ben asks.

I really just want to get out of here as soon as possible. I'm almost shaking with fear. Perhaps I should warn Ben, but what do I say?

'I'm going for the ice cream,' says Ben smiling. 'Sophie has shamelessly got me into ice cream.'

And there was me hoping we could skip pudding. I'm about to reply when I see Abdullah stand up and my body freezes.

'Ben, I need to talk to you about Greg and Georgie,' I begin.

I'm struggling to breathe and feel that any minute I might collapse and fall to the floor.

'The wedding is quite close isn't it?' he agrees.

'Can I get you dessert?' asks the waiter.

I'm getting my just desserts all right.

'What do you fancy Amy?' asks Ben.

'Erm ...' I say, lowering my head as I see Abdullah approaching.

Oh God, please make him walk straight past. I'm sorry for what I've done. I know it was wrong. I'd do anything now to give Greg and Georgie the perfect wedding.

'I'd recommend the ice cream,' Ben says, although I barely hear him. The blood is thumping in my ears and I feel dizzy. I look up to see Abdullah standing over me.

Chapter Forty-Seven

In that moment I knew it was over between me and Ben. I was getting everything I deserved. Karma had not only bitten me on the bum, it had well and truly kicked me hard in it too, and there was nothing I could do. I never thought there would be a man in my life again and then along he came. Insufferable at first but I felt more for him than I ever felt for Greg, and I wasn't going to be given the chance to get to know him. It is all I can do to fight back the tears.

'Hello Amy, fancy seeing you here,' says Abdullah with a triumphant smile.

Ben looks at me intently.

'It's not so surprising is it?' I say bitterly. 'You seem to end up in most places I go to.'

'The food is good here, you agree?'

'I *was* enjoying it,' I say between gritted teeth.

He leans towards me and I see Ben tense.

'I'm looking forward to seeing you in the dress I bought you,' Abdullah says seductively. I have to fight the urge to slap his face.

Ben cocks his head and looks me in the eye.

'Amy?' he questions.

'I'm sorry,' says Abdullah, acknowledging Ben for the first time. 'I'm interrupting your dinner. I'll see you for our dinner on Thursday, Amy. I'll send a car for you.'

He strolls away towards the loos and I lower my eyes so as not to meet Ben's.

'It's not what you …' I begin lamely.

'No, I remember you said that last time,' says Ben, folding his napkin and throwing it on the table.

'Please let me explain Ben …'

'Are you having dinner with him?' he asks flatly.

'Well … I …'

'Are you, or aren't you having dinner with him?'

'I am and I'm not.'

Yes, well, that makes a lot of sense doesn't it?

'You just said you wanted to take our relationship past the friendship stage ...'

'I do,' I interrupt. 'I really do.'

'But you're seeing someone else and you never even mentioned it. It's a very strange situation Amy. I thought you disliked that guy.'

'You've only just asked me if I'd like to be more than friends. I was entitled to see other people before.' I say angrily and then bite my tongue. What a stupid thing to say. I've not even been seeing the sheikh.

'But of all the men?' he says, surprised.

'But the thing is, I do dislike him. I need to tell you about ...'

'He bought you a dress?' he says angrily. 'And you presumably accepted it.'

What's the point of trying to explain myself if he won't let me bloody speak? I throw back the remainder of my wine and stand up.

'What's the point?' I say angrily. 'If you think that badly of me why should I even bother to explain?'

'I don't understand any of this, Amy, and I don't know that I want to,' he says standing up with me.

'Ben ...'

'There's no rush to leave. I'll pay the bill.'

Before I can speak he has turned from me and I watch as he strides to the door. I struggle to fight back my tears but they come unbidden and I run to the loo before Abdullah can see me. I have to fight the urge to dive into the Gents and cut off his balls. I lock the cubicle door, pull my phone from my bag and call Rosie.

'What's happened now?' she asks patiently.

'The shit's hit the fan,' I say hiccupping. 'It's all over with Ben.'

'I didn't know it had started.'

'I'm really close to cutting off Abdullah's prick,' I say viciously. 'He's right next door in the Gents. It will take about two seconds to chop that little prick's cock off.'

'Holy shit, that's a bit extreme don't you think?'

'I can't go on like this,' I cry in frustration. 'It's all getting too much. I'm so stressed. Today we tried to find me, and I ended up getting arrested for possessing Ecstasy ...'

'What?' she gasps. 'What are you doing taking Ecstasy? My God, what's happening to you? Was it that Chardonnay? That's what you get for taking on Essex girls.'

'Georgie took two aspirin and the police thought they were Ecstasy tablets.'

'That's a bit odd,' she says disbelievingly.

'Anyway, we didn't find me.'

'Are you surprised?'

I grab some toilet tissue and dab my eyes.

'Then,' I continue, 'Ben asked me out for dinner and it was going so well and he even asked me if I'd like to take our relationship further ...'

'But that's great news Amy. You could do with a man in your life.'

'But he doesn't know I'm Amy Fisher. He knows I was jilted but not by Greg.'

Even I'm having trouble keeping up with this. I pull myself up off the loo and leave the cubicle. I splash my face with cold water and look at my sorrowful reflection in the mirror.

'Abdullah was here tonight. I think he's stalking me.'

'Amy, do you want me to come and get you?'

'No, I've made a decision. I can't be blackmailed. You see, Abdullah has discovered my Amy Fisher secret and has threatened to tell Georgie unless I meet him at his hotel on Thursday.'

'I don't need to read Mills and Boon with you around.'

'What do I do?'

'I'm erring on the side of cutting his balls off,' she says. 'But I'm sure if you explain to Ben ...'

'No,' I say. I pull a brush from my handbag and tidy my hair.

'There's only one thing for it. I need to tell everyone the truth.'

Chapter Forty-Eight

I make a quick phone call to Georgie to check Greg hasn't been discharged.

'They want to do a few more tests first but at least he's in a private room now. Patsy and I have just been. I'm feeling a bit stressed so Patsy suggested a drink. She wants to hear all about our little adventure today,' she laughs. 'Do you want to come along too?'

I try to laugh with her, but it's too difficult.

'I thought I would visit Greg,' I say. 'See if I can help trigger something.'

'I do hope you can,' she says hopefully. 'Sometimes I think his memory is never going to come back.'

I scroll through my contact list until I see Jack's number. He answers on the first ring.

'Jack, it's Amy Fisher,' I say bluntly.

'Hi Amy, how are you? I don't hear from you in three years and now twice in one week.'

'Greg's had an accident,' I say without preamble. There is a moment of silence.

'I thought he was getting married, what happened?'

'He was in a road accident and bumped his head. It happened the day we got back from the hen do. He's now got a form of amnesia and doesn't remember his bride, but he does remember that he's getting married. The problem is he thinks it's me he's marrying.'

'My God, sounds like a bit of a mess. You do know he tried to find you after the ... well, you know?'

I'm glad he doesn't say the jilting. If I had my way I'd have the word banned. I take a sharp intake of breath.

'I didn't know that.'

'It was a year after the bridge incident, he tried to contact you but it was like you had disappeared off the face of the earth. You weren't at your old address and ...'

'What do you mean *the bridge incident*?'

'Oh God, you don't know about that?'

Would I be asking if I did?

'I think Greg should be the one to tell you about that,' he says hesitantly.

'Was that why was he trying to get hold of me?'

Please don't say he wanted to put things right. That he'd changed his mind and wanted to marry me after all. The truth is the last thing I need right now is for Greg to still be in love with me. Who'd have thought that I, Amy Perfect, would be hoping that Greg doesn't love me any more?

'There was something he had to tell you. He was really upset about not going through with the wedding.'

So he should be.

'The thing is, he has to marry Georgie,' I say urgently. 'I have to get his memory back. I think perhaps you can help with that. Can you visit him? I can meet you at the hospital.'

He is silent for so long that I feel sure he is going to say no.

'I don't see how I can help,' he says finally.

'It's worth a try, surely?'

He agrees reluctantly and I give him the name of the hospital and arrange to meet him there. Ambulance sirens greet me and I feel nauseous with nerves. I walk hesitantly into the main entrance and make my way to reception. The receptionist directs me to Greg's private room. I dive into the nearest toilet to check my appearance. I redo my make-up and let my hair down and don my sunglasses. Finally, when there is nothing else I can find to do I walk out and stride purposefully to Greg's room only to find he isn't there. David Beckham's autobiography sits by the bed. He can't be far away I conclude but do I have the nerve to wait? What am I doing here anyway? Once Greg discovers the truth I will lose everything.

'Hello.'

I turn at his voice to see him standing at the entrance. He's wearing a dark blue dressing gown and carrying a towel. Nerves get the better of me and I fall into a chair.

'Can I help you?' he asks.

I try not to stare at him. It feels odd to be so close to the man I was once going to marry. There was a time when Greg Martin was the only man that existed for me. Now, looking at him, I find myself wondering what I saw in him. He rubs his eyes and climbs onto the bed.

'I've come to visit you,' I say with a smile.

'Well, thanks for coming, especially this late, but I don't know you, just like I don't know anyone who visits.'

'I'm your wedding planner.'

'Amy's planning our wedding,' he says sharply. 'She wouldn't let anyone else do it.'

'I'm helping,' I say, attempting to appease him. 'How are you feeling?'

He looks at me closely.

'The doctor's say I have lost my memory but I don't think I have. I feel fine,' he smiles. 'I just wish someone would tell me where Amy is. I have to say you do look familiar which is more than most people do. Do you work with Amy? You sound like her.'

He studies me and opens his mouth to speak again when Jack strolls in.

'Well, who'd have thought I'd be in the same room as you two,' Jack laughs.

'Jack,' exclaims Greg. 'Thank God, where the buggery have you been? I've wanted to call you but I don't seem to have your number in my contacts? How can that be?'

'I guess you haven't needed it. What happened, why are you here?'

'Apparently I had a knock on the head. They keep telling me my memory has gone but it hasn't. The only thing I don't remember is banging my head. When's the wedding and where the hell is Amy? And what do you mean I wouldn't need your number? You're my bloody best man aren't you? Why haven't you called me?'

Jack looks at me and I shrug.

'Blimey, one question at a time mate,' laughs Jack. 'You have lost your memory Greg. I've come to try and help you get it back. But the wedding to Amy isn't going to happen.'

'What are you talking about mate? Don't play silly buggers. You pulling my leg or what? Where the hell is Amy?'

My throat is dry and my heart is hammering in my chest. I have no idea if this is going to make things better or worse.

'A few days ago you went to meet your fiancée Georgina, and that was when the cyclist hit you and you knocked your head,' I say gently.

'I don't have a fiancée called Georgina. I'm engaged to Amy.'

'You've got to move on mate,' says Jack. 'We're here to help.'

Greg looks startled.

'What did you just say?'

'I said you've got to move on mate.'

'Oh,' says Greg, swaying on the bed. 'I don't feel so good.'

'Shall I get a doctor?' Jack says.

'No, I just had a kind of flashback,' says Greg in a shaky voice.

I hand him some water.

'What do you remember?' asks Jack.

'London Bridge, what happened at London Bridge?' Greg asks. 'You said it then didn't you? You said 'you've got to move on mate'?'

Jack nods.

'That's right I did. You phoned me from White Hart Lane. You were marrying Amy at three o'clock. You'd been drinking. You were wasted.'

'Didn't I turn up? Oh Christ. Have we postponed the wedding? Is that why she's not visiting me? Is she still angry with me?'

He phoned Jack from football? What the hell was he doing at football on our wedding day? He really takes the piss doesn't he?

Greg lies back on the bed and covers his eyes.

'Greg it's more complicated than that,' says Jack.

'I think you should go,' Greg says. 'I don't understand what's going on.'

'Greg?' I begin.

'Nurse,' he calls, making us both jump.

'I think we should leave,' suggests Jack.

I reluctantly follow Jack out of the room.

'Greg was so near to remembering,' I say, attempting to hide my disappointment but failing miserably.

'He's feeling a bit traumatised,' says Jack, taking my arm. 'I think you need to give him time.'

He's feeling traumatised. He should have been me three years ago. I'll give him sodding traumatised.

'He doesn't have time,' I say, 'His wedding is just two weeks away.'

Chapter Forty-Nine

GREG

Greg closes his eyes and takes a deep breath. He swallows the tablet the nurse gives him and feels his heart slow down.

'This should help,' she smiles. 'But don't fight it. If your memory is coming back that's a good thing.'

He doesn't disagree with her this time. Maybe he has lost his memory after all. That was most certainly Jack, and even he is saying that his marriage to Amy Fisher never happened. So what the hell did happen and where is Amy?

'You've got to move on mate,' he says quietly to himself. Why is that phrase so familiar and why does he remember London Bridge.

The relaxing effect of the pill begins to take effect and he feels his body unwind.

'You've got to move on mate,' he hears Jack saying, the words echoing in his head. And then with a jolt he is looking down at the Thames. He's standing on London Bridge but he's on the wrong side and he can't recall how he got there. He's so drunk that keeping his balance is becoming quite a challenge. It's so cold up here that he can't feel his hands any more. There are blue flashing lights below and a crowd of people looking up at him. He sways slightly and grabs the bars of the bridge tightly. He sees a fireman climbing up to rescue him.

'We're coming up mate, just hold on.'

He remembers the fear as his hand slipped.

Greg shakes away the memory and focuses his eyes on the glass of water by his bed. They're right, he has lost his memory and he's not so sure he wants it to come back. What in the world could have been that bad that he had wanted to end his life? Is it something he even wants to remember?

'You look amazing,' says Jack.

'Thanks,' I say before taking a sip of coffee.

'Greg's looking good too isn't he?'

I smile.

'You don't know what to say to me, do you?'

He lets out a relieved laugh.

'Honestly? No I don't. You were a wreck the last time I saw you.'

I was a wreck for about a year but I don't tell him that.

'Greg had a meltdown, poor sod.'

'I'm trying to find it in me to sympathise,' I say bitterly.

'There was more to it than meets the eye, although even I don't know half of it.'

'So, what do you know Jack,' I ask curiously, 'aside from the fact that Greg jilted me because I was fat?'

'Fat?' he repeats.

Don't tell me Jack never noticed that I looked like two ton Tessie.

'I think there was a hell of a lot more to it than you being fat,' he says.

I wish someone had told me this, three years ago.

Chapter Fifty

'You're that woman on TV aren't you?' says the girl pumping away on the cross trainer next to me. 'You sounded so clear and positive. I'm getting married next year.'

'How lovely,' I say, turning up the speed on the running machine. I need to get rid of my murderous feelings for Prince Abdullah.

'That's why I'm working out,' she pants.

'Good for you.'

'Yes, I'm really excited.'

Although, frankly I can't imagine why as I'm beginning to think that weddings are the worst thing that can happen to a woman. Or maybe they're just the worst thing that can happen to me.

'You sounded so passionate, you really inspired me and you're such a visionary,' she gushes.

Blimey, this is starting to sound like an Oscar acceptance speech.

'I know it's not the place to ask, but is it possible to book myself in with you?' she pants as Georgie bursts through the doors.

'I've cancelled the honeymoon,' she says calmly.

'You've what?' I explode, accidentally hitting the stop button and crashing into the console.

'The whole wedding is a shambles. Everything that could go wrong is going wrong. Nothing has gone to plan,' she says, fighting back tears.

The girl on the next treadmill diplomatically removes herself as I very undiplomatically untangle myself from mine.

'Once his memory comes back Georgie ...'

'He'll realise that he still loves Amy Fisher, that's what will happen. I could kill her, I really could. No, it's over. I'm telling him today. Not that he will care of course because he doesn't even know that he's marrying me.'

Oh my God, what was once my dream is now coming true, except now it is a nightmare and I can't let it happen. I just can't. Ben will hate me. Greg has to marry Georgie, he simply has to. Tell her, tell her now, my mind screams. But I can't. I just can't bear to see the pain on her face when she discovers her beloved Amy Perfect is that fat bitch Amy Fisher. Well, that bitch, Amy Fisher anyway.

'Let's visit him and see if he remembers anything else,' I say limping to the changing room.

'All he talks about is London Bridge,' she says angrily. 'Anyway, I've had my lunch break. I just wanted to let you know that I'm calling it off.'

'But you can't Georgie, you just can't. He loves you,' I say desperately.

'If he loves me, why does he only talk about Amy bloody Fisher? Oh, that woman, that bloody bitch,' she says fiercely. 'I wouldn't mind but she's nothing but a common criminal.'

Now, hold on a minute. She's quite right though. Not about me being a criminal, I don't mean, but I am a total bitch and let's face it, I'm getting everything that was coming to me.

'How about if I visit again today ...?'

'I really don't see how you can help. It's Amy bloody Fisher we need and God knows where she is. I've contacted every prison and no one has even heard of her.'

'I could try, you never know. I know a lot about weddings and he seems to want to talk about his. I may be able to bring something back.'

She sighs heavily.

'It's just not happening though is it? I'm sorry. I know it's not your fault Amy. You're a fabulous wedding planner. If only Greg hadn't stepped in front of that cyclist. I still don't know what made him do that.'

He saw me that was why. But now, if I'm truthful, I don't think he was overcome with desire or anything. In fact I'm not even sure he recognised me. I may have looked familiar but I feel sure that was all, else why hasn't he recognised me since? And if I'm being totally truthful, I'm not sure that I actually loved Greg at all. I loved the idea of being in love with Greg and of course having a magical white wedding, like a wedding in a magazine, but love, well that's something altogether different isn't it? And it certainly wasn't sexual compatibility that brought us together. Greg never was one for experimentation in the bedroom. His motto was, 'never attempt anything in bed that you can't pronounce'. The only time we got into bondage was when Greg's pyjama cord got caught around the bed post. No, when it comes to love, I feel quite certain that that was not what I felt for Greg. I was in love with the idea of getting engaged and I loved weddings so much that I got caught up in the romance of it all. I was more in love with the idea of our marriage then I was with the man I was marrying.

'You can visit him if you like. I need to get back to work,' says Georgie abruptly.

I wrap a towel around my shoulders and am about to walk to the changing room when she says,

'Ben says you're seeing that sheikh.'

I spin round.

'It's a misunderstanding Georgie.'

'Be careful Amy, I really think he is trouble.'

Tell me something I don't know Georgie.

'Don't cancel the honeymoon Georgie. I'll see Greg this evening, you never know. He may remember something.'

'Okay,' she agrees reluctantly. 'I'll give it one more day.'

'One day,' I exclaim. 'Give it a few more than that.'

'Okay, four days, but if he doesn't remember me or the wedding by then I really don't see the point in continuing,' she says tearfully.

I run my hands through my sweaty hair and wonder how I can time travel Greg's mind back to the present in the next four days.

Chapter Fifty-One

It's been two days since my dinner with Ben and I still haven't heard from him. I dive for my phone every time it rings in the hope it will be him, but of course it never is. I've tried to call him several times but always lose my nerve at the last minute. After all, what am I supposed to say? There is absolutely nothing I can say that will redeem me.

The afternoon is a blur of activity. Laureta is dragging me around her wedding venue but the only thing on my mind is my conversation with Georgie.

'The lighting is too dim,' she complains. 'I thought you were getting that sorted.'

I flip through the Big Red Book but can see nothing about lighting. I turn to Lucy.

'It's the first I've heard about lighting,' she says nervously.

'Well, you're hearing it now, so sort it,' barks Laureta.

She pulls out a large black leather-bound book and my heart sinks.

'The Prince has to have special music to announce his arrival. You need to get that sorted.'

And I know just the song.

'Make a note Lucy,' I say.

'I'll send someone over with a CD and for Christ's sake don't lose it,' snaps Laureta.

The only thing I'm likely to lose right now is my cool.

'You're getting stressed darling,' says Henrietta, Laureta's mother. 'Lucy, run to that juice bar and get her a ginseng shake.'

Lucy's eyes widen.

'Cool,' says Laureta. 'Also I need a sugar lift, so get some chocolate.'

Lucy opens her mouth and fearful of what may come out of it, I say,

'That's really great of you Lucy, thanks.'

She strides angrily to the door, which is opened for her by the sheikh, and my heart sinks. He's wearing jeans and a black sweater. I think I prefer him in his garb. What the hell is he doing here? He stares at me with his hypnotic eyes and smiles.

'Your Majesty, we're so glad you could make it,' says Henrietta, curtsying. I swear I hear her boobs hit his knees.

'Oh good, I was just telling Amy about the music to announce your arrival at the reception. You do know the music don't you Amy? Only you did miss the rehearsal,' Laureta reminds me.

I wondered when she'd throw that at me.

'I know a wonderful surgeon,' says Laureta's mum, pushing her new breasts into my face. 'If he can make these I'm sure he can do something about your piles.'

'Yes well, I'd like them removed,' I say, 'not made bigger.'

What am I saying? I don't even have bloody piles.

'There are many remedies,' says Abdullah, eyeing me slyly. 'Maybe I can suggest something.'

He's a bloody pervert, that's what he is, a majestic one maybe, but a pervert nevertheless.

'Can we get on?' snaps Laureta. 'We're here to discuss my wedding not your piles. Now the doors are all wrong and ...'

The doors are all wrong? A door's a door isn't it? How can it be wrong?

'I don't ...'

'For goodness' sake Amy, do I have to explain everything in minute detail? The doors should open inwards not outwards.'

'I'm not sure that ...'

'Just get it sorted Amy. What are we paying you for?'

To perform miracles it seems. I mean, seriously how can I get the doors changed?

'Also, after the gifts are given to the parents, Jeremy will be giving me one.'

You'd think he'd wait till the wedding night wouldn't you? Oh well, at least I still have a sense of humour. I try to hide the little smile from my face.

'Right, does he want us to arrange ...?' I begin.

'He doesn't know yet. You don't think he thought of that himself do you? It will be a large bouquet of red roses. So you'll need to arrange that and some very romantic music and make sure they are red roses, no other colour will do.'

She takes a breath and studies her book.

'I can't think of anything else,' she says finally.

Thank God for that.

'How about you Mum?'

Lucy strolls in and Henrietta snatches the chocolate from her.

'She can't have that. Are you insane? Her wedding is on Saturday. She doesn't want to waddle down the aisle looking like a meringue does she?'

I personally can't think of anything more pleasurable.

'One square won't hurt Mother,' sulks Laureta.

She's got no idea has she?

'Your Majesty, can you think of anything else?' asks Henrietta.

'Amy and I are having dinner on Thursday. I'm sure we can iron out any misunderstandings then,' he smiles.

Lucy looks anxiously at me. Clearly her fears of me being abducted to Saudi Arabia are playing on her mind.

'How lovely,' beams Henrietta. 'I said Amy Perfect was the ideal wedding planner didn't I Laureta?'

'I'm not sure I can ...' I begin.

'I hope very much that you can,' he says, with a hint of menace in his voice. 'There would be serious consequences if you were to cancel.'

'Yes, it's all in your hands now,' says Laureta ominously. 'Don't bugger it up.'

The sheikh leans towards me, presumably with the intention of kissing me on the cheek, but I side step quickly and he bumps into Henrietta's breasts instead. He stutters an apology and Lucy and I have to fight back our giggles.

They file out of the hall and Lucy lets out a heavy sigh.

'Who's for chocolate?' she asks.

'Why not,' I say.

After all, it's the only comfort I've got these days.

Chapter Fifty-Two

I leave Lucy to return to the office while I make my way to the hospital. I check my phone for the hundredth time. Ben hasn't phoned. I don't really expect him to, so I don't know why I keep checking. I punch his number in, but again can't find the courage to press the call button. Half of me wants so much to explain everything while the other half can't bear the thought of his response. I check my phone one last time and then throw it back into my handbag. I reluctantly make my way to Greg's room. He's sitting reading his David Beckham book with a small rucksack by his feet.

'Hi, you just caught me. I'm hoping to go home in an hour. Mind you, they've been saying that all day,' he laughs.

'You seem better, more cheerful.'

'My memory is coming back. In small chunks mind you, but the doctor says that's normal.'

'That's great,' I say.

'Is Georgina with you?' he asks, putting the book down.

'No, I guess she's busy wedding planning.'

Best not to mention that she's calling the whole thing off, although I don't suppose it will matter to Greg as he can't remember what she's calling off anyway.

'I wish I could remember this damn wedding. More importantly, I wish I could remember the bride,' he says angrily, throwing the David Beckham book into his rucksack. 'I can't very well marry a woman I don't know can I?'

'But you remember Amy Fisher?' I say.

He looks at me curiously.

'I remember going to a football match. The strange thing is, I was wearing my wedding suit. Why would I go to a match in my wedding gear?'

He shakes his head in frustration and it is all I can do not to yell angrily at him, *what the hell were you doing at bloody football on our wedding day?*

'The first half was good, I remember that. The score was 3-0 to Spurs at half time,' he smiles.

That's good then. I guess that made everything worthwhile. His expression changes and he frowns.

'Of course they bloody blew it in the second half.'

Is football all he can think of? He shakes his head and sighs.

'What is Georgina going to do about the wedding? You're our wedding planner. You must know what's going through her head.'

'Well ...' I begin.

'Why do you always wear sunglasses?' he asks suddenly.

'I, well ... I have mi ... migraines,' I stammer.

He looks at me curiously.

'Have you always had a stutter?' he asks. 'You sound a bit like her.'

'Like her?' I repeat.

'Amy, she has a bit of a stutter when she gets anxious.'

Oh bugger, this really may well be when the shit hits the fan and flies all around Greg's hospital room.

'Only when I get a little anxious,' I say, biting my lip.

He looks closely at me and I shift uncomfortably under his stare. Thankfully the door opens at that moment and a doctor walks in.

'So, you're all packed I see,' the doctor says with sharp efficiency. 'Any more flashbacks?' he adds, while checking Greg's pulse.

'I remember being at football in my wedding gear. It was a good score too,' he says, his eyes becoming vacant. 'At half time I phoned Jack to tell him and I remember he was livid. It was my wedding day. I'd gone to football on my wedding day. That's all I can remember. Then I seemed to be on London Bridge ...'

That's so bloody typical of Greg isn't it? He buggers off to a Tottenham match on our wedding day and then doesn't make it back in time for the wedding. How selfish is that?

'And why would you have done that?' asks the doctor gently, pumping away at the blood pressure machine.

'I couldn't go through with it. I didn't know how to tell Amy. I thought after a few drinks I'd get the courage to say sorry and explain but I couldn't and ….'

'And what Greg?' encourages the doctor.

'I decided to jump off London Bridge instead.'

I realise I had been holding my breath and I let it out in shock.

'But why?' I shout. 'Nothing could have been that bad that you couldn't have told me …' I stop abruptly but fortunately neither Greg nor the doctor realise what I've just said. 'That you couldn't have told Amy,' I finish.

'I don't know,' he says miserably, 'if only I could remember.'

'It will come back,' says the doctor.

It better had. I'd like to know why Greg felt a football match was more important than our wedding. That says a hell of a lot about me doesn't it?

Chapter Fifty-Three

'You shouldn't be eating that,' says Rosie, 'but if you are then I'm going to.'

She cuts off a small slice of my apple strudel and groans with ecstasy.

'Don't you just love being sinful,' she sighs.

The truth is I have become well and truly sinful. There was a time when I would be up at five a.m. for an early morning run. I'm really sorry to tell you this, but the fact is I have seriously let myself go. I've gained at least five pounds and what's worse they've all gone to my stomach. I haven't waxed in weeks. I've reached the point of no return and have called a crisis meeting. They say a problem shared is a problem halved so I have decided to halve my problems by dumping it onto Mum, Auntie Val and Rosie. We're meeting at a little café just around the corner from Auntie Val's in Stanford Hill. I'm figuring no one is going to recognise us there. I've got just three days to make sure that Georgie marries Greg and I haven't got a clue how to do it. I'm facing the worst dilemma of my life. If I tell Georgie the truth she is bound to tell Ben and he is going to feel duty bound to write something about Perfect Weddings. After all he can't very well say I'm the best wedding planner in London now, can he? No matter how backhanded that original compliment was. I can't see the brides flocking to me after that and I will have lost Ben for good, that's if I haven't already. It's no good. I just can't crack this on my own. Although Auntie Val, Mum and Rosie aren't the best team in the world they are all I've got. I need help. Georgie seems intent on calling off the wedding and I have to make sure she doesn't.

'Well, this is lovely darling,' says Mum hugging me. She smells of stale Givenchy and I wrinkle my nose. 'Val gave it to me,' she whispers. 'It would have been rude not to wear it.'

'There were nicer places we could have had coffee,' says Auntie Val starchily, eyeing up the apple strudel dubiously.

'Everything has come to a head,' I say dramatically. 'I thought it was time to share and I didn't want to be overheard by anyone we knew.'

'Oh my God,' says Mum dropping into a chair. 'You're pregnant.'

'You've got to have sex first,' says Rosie. 'And trust me; there has been no action in Amy's life since Greg jilted her.'

'Rosie,' I say stunned.

'Call a spade a spade Amy. They're the facts, the bastard jilted you.'

'You've met someone at last?' questions Mum. 'Is that it?'

'I thought you'd want the whole world to know that and you couldn't do worse than Gerald. In fact he's ...' begins Auntie Val.

'Greg's back,' I say, stunning her into silence.

Mum gasps and Val falls into her chair in shock.

'He's alive?' says Auntie Val.

I didn't think there was ever any doubt about that.

'But what about Gerald?' Auntie Val asks.

'I'll get the coffees,' says Rosie. 'Anyone for apple strudel?'

Mum and Auntie Val shake their heads.

'There's worse to come,' says Rosie. 'Are you sure you don't want strudel, they do it with ice cream?'

'I will,' I say.

'Did something terrible happen to him, is that why he didn't turn up for the wedding?' asks Mum.

'He doesn't know why he didn't turn up because he's lost his memory. He was involved in a road accident a few days ago and banged his head.'

'That's bloody convenient isn't it?' scoffs Auntie Val.

'Oh dear,' mumbles Mum. 'You really don't need him popping up now dear, not with Gerald so interested and ...'

Rosie plonks the coffees and strudel onto the table.

'Can you please stop talking about Gerald? I assure you he's the last person I'm interested in.'

'You haven't told them have you?' says Rosie accusingly.

'Told us what?' asks Auntie Val, tucking into the strudel.

'Amy was, or still is in fact, the wedding planner for Greg's new wedding to his second fiancée Georgie.'

Auntie Val splutters on her strudel and Mum sits like a mannequin with her teacup halfway to her lips.

'How ... how ...?' Auntie Val begins, before turning blue. A waitress rushes over with a glass of water. Auntie Val knocks it back between chokes and finally asks in a hoarse voice,

'Have you lost your marbles girl? Have you forgotten so quickly the way that man dumped you? You should be planning his funeral not his bleeding wedding.'

I fight the craving for another apple strudel.

'Amy took on the wedding with the deliberate plan to win Greg back. Basically, she was going to steal him from Georgie. These past few weeks she has been sabotaging his wedding,' says Rosie in a matter of fact tone.

'Thanks for that Rosie. I couldn't have put it better myself,' I say sarcastically.

'Only speaking the truth, and talking of speaking the truth, you're gaining weight again. I told you this business was unhealthy didn't I?'

'I don't believe any of this,' says Mum. 'Do they sell wine here? This coffee isn't doing anything for me.'

'It's a coffee shop not a wine bar,' I say, and before I know what is happening, I'm blubbering into my cappuccino as the memory of Ben and I dancing in Pearls wine bar comes flooding into my mind.

'You need to read the book *Women Who Love too Much*,' says Auntie Val. 'You're a classic case you are. Fiona McKay swears by it. When she was jilted ...'

I glare at her.

'Well, anyway, it's only a pound, second-hand on Amazon,' she quickly adds.

'I don't think a book from Amazon is going to sort this mess out,' says Rosie.

'I don't know how you can still love him,' says Mum.

'Especially when you've only got to say the word and Gerald ...'

'Will you stop talking about Gerald and bloody Fiona McKay?' I snap. 'The truth is I'm not in love with Greg, in fact I don't think I ever was. I was in love with the idea of getting married.'

'Then why were you trying to sabotage his wedding?' asks Auntie Val.

'Because I thought I still loved him. But now I realise I don't. But the man I really want is Greg's best man.'

'Jack?' exclaims Mum. 'All this time you've been in love with Jack?'

Rosie sighs.

'No, she hasn't. It's me who's been in love with Jack all this time.'

'What?' I say, taken aback. 'You never said anything.'

'What was the point, he never noticed me.'

'Oh, but Rosie, he did. He always fancied you but you gave the impression you weren't interested.'

'This is the story of my life,' she groans. 'You might have said something.'

'I did have a wedding on my mind at the time and I didn't think you fancied him.'

Mum sighs.

'If it isn't Jack, then which best man are we talking about?' she asks.

'The best man at Greg's wedding to Georgie, and once he knows what I've done he'll hate me.'

'You didn't say you had a man,' says Auntie Val, clearly affronted. 'I'd never have put myself through all that torture of vegan cooking if I'd known.'

'Not to mention the sheikh who is blackmailing her,' adds Rosie, cutting into another strudel. 'He's an Arab prince, no less. Seriously, you couldn't make this up. She has a starring role in her own Mills and Boon novel.'

Mum grabs the table for support.

'I feel quite light headed,' she groans.

It's the Givenchy perfume that's doing it. It's playing havoc with my eyes too.

'How on earth do you know an Arab prince?'

'He's one of my bride's best men.'

'But why is an Arab prince blackmailing you?' asks Auntie Val.

'More's to the point, why couldn't you have fallen in love with that best man? We'd be able to live like Elton John for the rest of our lives if you had,' says Mum, ever the unrealistic one.

'He already has three wives,' I say irritably. 'Anyway ...'

'That doesn't stop them. They can have as many as they like can't they?' says Mum.

'Fiona McKay ...' begins Auntie Val.

'Don't tell me she had a sheikh blackmailing her too?' says Rosie.

I'm starting to think this Fiona McKay doesn't exist.

'She lived in one of those Arab countries. She said they can have as many wives as they like.'

'I thought it was four,' says Rosie thoughtfully.

'I don't care if it is forty. I don't want to marry the bloody Prince.'

'There's no pleasing her is there,' says Auntie Val.

I drop my head into my hands. It's all useless. No one can help me. I've ruined Georgie's life. Wasn't it enough that I went through all that pain when Greg jilted me? I can't put her through that. I just can't. Greg loves her. I know he does. You only have to look at their photos to see how much he adores her. He never loved me in that way. Georgie's eyes light up whenever she mentions his name but this week she has become a shadow of her former self. Georgie means everything to him and he needs to remember her and I seem to be the reason he can't. I can't be responsible for ruining Georgie's happiness. She deserves to be the most beautiful bride ever. I'm her perfect wedding planner and I'm not going to give up on her dream of a perfect wedding.

'Greg loves Georgie. Theirs is a true love story. I did a terrible thing. I've got to put it right. We have to get Greg's memory back,' I say resolutely. 'Georgie deserves the perfect wedding I promised her and you all have to help me give her that. The sheikh is threatening to tell her the truth and if I don't meet him at his hotel tomorrow he'll expose me. Who knows what he'll tell her. I've got to get Greg's memory back. He needs to tell Georgie how much he loves her. I need you to tell me I'm doing the right thing by telling them the truth. It may well mean I'll lose everything, my business, the man I really like and of course Georgie and Greg's friendship.'

Rosie leans over and hugs me.

'You can do it and we'll be backing you.'

'You've got to live with yourself,' says Aunty Val, philosophically.

'I agree with Val,' says Mum, 'and if it all goes wrong there's still Gerald.'

Thank God for family and friends.

Chapter Fifty-Four

Everywhere I go I think I see Ben. The guy ahead of me in the Starbucks queue, the guy who cut me up at the traffic lights and even the guy who phoned from Vodafone sounded like him. So much so that for the first time in my life I was polite to someone from Vodafone and that seriously is a first.

I can't stop thinking about his kiss. I can't think of a time when Greg had ever kissed me like that. In fact I can't think of a time when anyone had kissed me and left me feeling so shaken and so alive all at the same time. It was like we were on the verge of something so special and now it is gone. I've never felt so battered. If I close my eyes I can picture the passion that had flared in his eyes. I can't help wondering if he thinks of me too. How could he seriously believe that I was interested in Prince Abdullah? How could Georgie believe it? The thought of Georgie makes my stomach churn and I push my meeting with her from my mind as I approach the doors of The Majestic, where Chardonnay and Gary are waiting. A doorman opens them and welcomes me. I see Chardonnay and Gary waiting in the foyer and wave to them before pulling my ringing phone from my handbag.

'I hope this isn't a bad time,' says Prince Abdullah.

'I'm about to meet with a bride,' I say briskly.

'It isn't our friend Georgie is it? I won't keep you. I'm looking forward to our dinner. I'm sending over a little something for you. I do hope you'll wear it, under the dress of course.'

I don't reply but feel myself shiver.

'How's that friend of yours? Ben Garret isn't it?'

'I have to go, I'm with a client.'

'Of course, I'll see you later.'

I hang up and shakily throw my phone back into my bag.

'You awright babe?' Chardonnay asks.

'Yes, I'm fine. I think I'm coming down with a cold that's all.'

'Well, we're cheer ya up won't we Gary?'

'Yeah,' says Gary, with a yawn.

She pulls me up the red carpeted stairway into the ballroom, where several other guys are standing around.

'We've tested the acoustics,' says one, 'and they're well good.'

'It's a brilliant hall for a disco,' I say. 'You don't need to worry.'

'This is Dave, Gary's bruvver,' she says, introducing him. He shakes my hand vigorously.

'It's an 'onour to meet ya,' he says shyly. 'I ain't met anyone famous before.'

'Oh I'm not famous ...'

'You been on tele and everyfink,' says Chardonnay.

'And this is Del, our best man, and of course Gary's doing it, I mean obviously,' she laughs.

'Doing what?' I ask, confused.

'And Mick who can't be 'ere is gonna do it too.'

I sincerely hope I'm not doing it, whatever it is.

'Right, everyone get ready,' orders Chardonnay.

I watch in amazement as they don white criminal suits and trilby hats. I widen my eyes at Chardonnay.

'You're gonna love this,' she says.

The sound of spooky music echoes over the sound system and the guys stiffen. I wince when I realise what is about to happen. Michael Jackson's voice floats around the hall and Gary and his mates begin their dance rendition of *Smooth Criminal* while Chardonnay rocks from side to side in sheer delight. I watch in amazement as at one point they moon walk. Who would have imagined this from Gary? He may not speak much but boy can he dance.

'What do you fink?' Chardonnay asks.

I'm too speechless to reply and she smiles in pleasure.

'The timing is ...' I begin.

'Yeah, they need to practise that. It's good though ain't it?'

It's better than good, it's brilliant. It's the first thing in days to cheer me up and I hug Chardonnay.

'Blimey, what's that for?'

'You don't know how much it has cheered me up,' I smile.

'I knew you'd be impressed.'

'Chard thought you might know a good dancer that could learn us,' says Gary, using more words than I imagined he even knew. "ow to do that bit where he leans right forward, you know?'

'Chard says you're the best wedding planner in London,' says Dave.

Flattery will get you everywhere.

'And you know famous people.'

'I'm sure I could find someone. You'll need special shoes I think but it won't be …'

'Dosh ain't a problem,' says Dave throwing his jacket on with a swagger. 'Gary wants to do this for Chard.'

Oh, how romantic is that? I feel the tears well up and quickly turn away. Not fast enough obviously as Gary says,

'Blimey, was we that bloody bad that it made ya cry?'

'No, you were brilliant. Leave it with me,' I say, fumbling in my bag for a tissue. Chardonnay takes me by the arm and leads me out of the hall.

'I'll give ya a bell, laters Gal,' she says leading me to the loos.

'Blimey these are bleedin' posh ain't they? Wait till me mum takes a piss in 'ere. We'll never 'ear the last of it.'

I try to laugh but end up crying.

'Right,' she says, giving me a hug and tangling me up in her collection of chunky necklaces.

'What the fuck's going on? If this is 'ow I cheer you up remind me never to bleedin' upset ya.'

I pull my hair from her necklace and sigh.

'I've buggered up everything that matters to me. You know Greg …?

'Yeah the guy in 'ospital who's lost his memory. You ain't crying over 'im are ya? That won't 'elp the bugger.'

'Three years ago I was engaged to Greg. He jilted me at the altar …'

'Holy fuck,' she says, falling into a chair.

'Good job this is a posh loo, else I'd 'ave fallen on the floor. What ya doing planning his wedding? Does Georgie know about him dumping ya?'

I shake my head.

'No, she doesn't. I've been a real bitch Chardonnay ...'

'Call me Chard for Christ's sake, we're mates ain't we? And you're far from a bitch girl, let me tell ya.'

I smile. Who'd have thought Chardonnay would have been the one I'd be sharing this with?

'I hadn't seen Greg since the wedding that didn't happen and then this bride phones and asks me to plan her wedding. She desperately wanted Amy Perfect and ...'

She gasps.

'You're Amy Fisher,' she exclaims.

I nod.

'You ain't in the clink then? Did you really live in that shit 'ole?'

'It wasn't a shit hole when I lived there.'

'I can't believe you were under our nose the whole bloody time.'

'I took on her wedding because the truth is I thought I could spoil it and win Greg back. You see, he dumped me because I was fat and I thought now I'm slim he'd want me back, but it's all gone wrong. I don't love him at all. I don't think I ever did. Georgie is going to call off the wedding in two days' time and it's all my fault and then the man I really do like, Georgie's best man, Ben, thinks I'm seeing the sheikh so he doesn't trust me now ...'

'Right, this is too bleedin' much for my little brain without a drink. I need a sweet white wine. Come on, you can tell me everything over a bottle.'

That sounds like a good idea to me.

Chapter Fifty-Five

The Savoy doorman looks curiously at us. I guess he's not seen three Michael Jackson impersonators at The Savoy before.

'Can I help you gentlemen?' he asks cautiously.

'They're with me,' I say, stepping forward.

He takes one long look at my lacy fringed shawl that covers my pencil line Vivienne Westwood dress that the sheikh had sent me and apologies profusely.

'I'm sorry madam, I didn't see you.'

'No problem,' I say, giving him a bright smile. 'We're here to see Prince Abdullah. Is he in residence?'

'If you'll excuse me for one moment madam,' he says politely. 'Please take a seat.'

We watch as he walks to the concierge. They study Chardonnay and I, at first and then their eyes travel to Gary, Dave and Del. Even I have to admit they look a bit shady in their white jackets and trilby hats. I almost expect Michael Jackson to glide in and lead them into the Smooth Criminal dance. You've got to agree that would be a cool sight in The Savoy foyer wouldn't it?

The concierge makes his way towards us.

'I understand you wish to see Prince Abdullah?' he asks with a fake smile.

'I'm a close friend,' I say, giving a twirl. 'He bought me this dress and I so want to show him how it looks. Is he in or shall we come back?'

'If I could take your name madam, I'll see if the Prince is free to see you.'

'Tell him it is Amy Perfect.'

I wait with a pounding heart while Chardonnay and the boys make themselves comfortable on the luxury foyer couches.

'This is bleedin' awesome ain't it Gary. Shame we couldn't 'ave our reception 'ere ain't it?' says an awed Chardonnay.

'Miss Perfect, would you care to follow me?' beams the concierge, leading me to the lift. I look nervously at Chardonnay who simply nods. My shaky legs barely get me into the lift and when we arrive at the tenth floor I'm feeling quite sick.

'Suite 1025, Miss Perfect,' says the concierge. I step out of the lift and hear it hiss as the doors close behind me. I fight the desire to hit the lift button and take myself back down but instead pull my phone from my bag and text Chardonnay before walking slowly to suite 1025. The door is opened on my tap and the sheikh stands there in a white towelling robe.

'What an unexpected but lovely surprise, Miss Perfect,' he says, opening the door wider. 'You're early.'

I peek inside.

'I'm alone. My wives have their own apartments,' he explains, reading my mind.

'The dress looks even better than I imagined,' he says, with desire smouldering in his eyes. He takes my hand. The suite is exactly as I imagined it would be. It is the ultimate in luxury. He points to the sofa and I sit down. I must keep calm. Nothing can go wrong can it? Famous last thoughts, after all, let's face it just about everything has gone wrong since Georgina came into my life.

'Would you like some tea?' he asks, his eyes appraising me. 'The dress brings out the best in you,' he adds huskily.

I force my eyes from his towelling robe which clearly reveals his feelings about the dress.

'No tea for me, thank you,' I answer shakily.

He sits beside me on the sofa and I primly fold my hands onto my knees.

'Relax Amy. How about a brandy?' he says, draping his arm around my shoulders. 'Why are you so nervous? You must be keen, to visit me so early? Shall I order champagne?'

He strokes my hair and moves his hands down my neck, gently removing the wrap from my shoulders.

'You like the pearls, yes?'

I can barely swallow let alone speak. What on earth was I thinking of agreeing to this?

'Amy, you drive me crazy, you know that don't you?'

I keep my body rigid. He gives an evil laugh and pulls me roughly towards him, his strong spicy aftershave making me nauseous.

'I won't be what you want me to be Abdullah, I'm sorry.'

'I think you will Amy,' he says, his hardness pressing against me.

His hand slides down the back of my dress and panic kicks me in the stomach when I feel him undo my bra.

'Don't,' I protest, my voice trembling. I struggle to get up but his hold on me is too strong.

Oh God, where are they? I did give the right suite number didn't I? I can't very well ask him to hold on while I check, can I?

'Why not? You know you want it. That's why you came isn't it? You couldn't wait.'

He's breathing unsteadily and I turn my eyes away from the bulge in his towelling robe. A tap at the door makes me jump and he frees me.

'Who is it?' he demands angrily.

'Room service your 'ighness,' says Gary, attempting his best posh voice.

'I didn't order room service,' Abdullah shouts, jumping up and flinging open the door.

In the doorway stand the Smooth Criminal team, in their suits and hats with Chardonnay behind them in a short slinky black dress.

'What the ...?' Abdullah sniggers. 'You're not room service. What have you arranged for me my little Miss Perfect?'

'Can we come in?' Chardonnay asks, gazing at the bulge through his towelling robe with amusement.

I struggle to clip my bra up and Chardonnay leans across to help.

'You awright babe?' she asks.

'Nice gaff you got 'ere,' says Gary, looking over the place.

'What's this about Amy?' Abdullah asks, putting his arm around my shoulder again. I shrug it off angrily.

'These are my friends,' I say, backing away from him. 'You should be grateful to them. I was all for coming here and cutting off your balls.'

'And 'anging them out to dry,' smiles Chardonnay. 'That'd be a sight to see at the old Savoy, wouldn't it? Your balls 'anging out on the tenf floor of The Savoy.'

'Not sure why we talked 'er out of it,' says Dave, helping himself to a brandy from a silver decanter. 'Sounds like ya deserved it. Putting 'em to bad use if you want my opinion.'

'I didn't ask for your opinion,' snaps Abdullah.

'You give men a bad name you do,' says Del.

Abdullah looks at me and then makes a move towards the phone, which Gary quickly rips from the wall.

'We're from Essex mate. You'll never be as quick as us.'

'Essex?' repeats Abdullah, beads of perspiration beginning to form on his forehead. 'What's Essex?'

'It's a little county 'ere in England. Ain't 'eard of it? Let's just say we make your little bully boys look like pussies.'

Abdullah pulls his shoulders back. I note his erection has quickly dissipated.

'Do you have any idea who I am? I'm royalty. I'm well respected in this country.'

Chardonnay scoffs.

'I can't think why. Men who blackmail women into having sex with them ain't respected anywhere mate, so don't go thinking they are.'

'I don't know what you're talking about,' he laughs. 'Amy came here willingly to have sex with me. Amy will you please tell them and put an end to this nonsense?'

'That's the point Abdullah, I did tell them. I told them everything.'

Gary pushes Abdullah roughly onto the couch.

'Don't touch me. You've no idea how you'll pay for this. When your Prime Minister hears about this ...'

'You won't tell the Prime Minister anything mate and you know it,' says Del.

'Amy will give ya the dress back, and the bling, won't ya girl?' says Chardonnay. 'She never wanted 'em in the first place. And she'll tell Georgina Winters what she needs to know. It's for 'er to do, not you.'

Abdullah goes to stand up and to my horror Gary pulls a sawn off shotgun from his rucksack. I have to fight back a scream. Abdullah freezes. Christ, I know Chardonnay said Gary carries a knife but I didn't think he'd have a bloody shotgun as well.

'A little warning,' says Dave, with a hint of menace in his voice.

'Just in case you think you can mess wiv us,' Gary says, aiming the gun at Abdullah's groin. 'Don't even think of getting your heavies onto us, because believe me, I'll slice off your dick with a chain saw before you can say *inshallah*.'

Oh God, I'm in an updated movie of *The Krays*.

'Get the frock off girl,' Chardonnay says, tapping me on the arm. She hands me a carrier bag and I rush into the bathroom. The sooner we get out of here the better. Dear God, please don't let them blow his cock off while I change. That will certainly be the end of Perfect Weddings then wouldn't it? That would make the dailies let alone *Vogue*. '*Top Wedding Planner has best man's royal cock blown off.*' That would certainly finish my parents off too. Auntie Val would blame it on my being jilted and Rosie would be quoted as saying 'It always was unhealthy'.

GREG

Greg walked into the kitchen, filled the kettle and emptied the box of photographs that Georgie had left with him.

'They might bring something back,' she'd said.

The truth is they were all giving up on him. He couldn't blame them. What he didn't understand was why not one of these damn people could find Amy. He made a coffee and browsed through the photos, flipping them with disinterest to one side. He finished his coffee, sighed and was about to throw the photos back into the box when a black and white one caught his eye. He pulled it out and gasped as memories flooded like a haemorrhage through his brain. He remembered that photo. They'd had a laugh that day and then suddenly he was back at White Hart Lane dressed in his top and tails and knocking back his fifth beer while telling himself he couldn't go through with it. He just couldn't. It wasn't fair on either of them, he told himself. Amy would get over it and it would be for the best. Things would be worse if he went through with it. No, he had to call it off. Halfway through his sixth beer he'd phoned Jack.

'I can't do it mate, I just can't. Tell Amy I'm sorry. I'm a real shit. I should have been more honest with her. Tell her she can keep the ring.'

'Hey mate, hold on,' Jack had yelled down the phone. 'Where are you, let me come and chat with you, there's still time. We can get you there.'

'There's no point. Bloody Spurs lost as well, I ask you, I'm going to London Bridge, get some fresh air.'

He can't remember what the hell he was thinking of when he stepped over the side of the bridge. It just seemed easier than telling the truth. What a fool he'd been, a real bloody fool. It seemed too much booze and too much guilt had been his downfall. Now it's all come back to haunt him. God, to think he nearly went over the bridge. He shivers at the memory. Jack had been there for him, promising not to tell anyone.

'You've got to move on mate,' he'd said. 'No point going back all the time.'

He was right of course. It's now time for him to move on.

Chapter Fifty-Six

Lucy has become a force I no longer recognise. Her nostrils flare and her eyes bulge every time I walk into the office. She's like a rabid dog. I almost expect her to growl at me.

'You do realise I'm running Perfect Weddings single handed these days?' she says accusingly.

'I'm sorry, I'm going through a crisis,' I say, slumping in a chair.

'We've got more weddings than we can handle and you decide to have a crisis. There's nothing you can do about Greg so just let it go and as for that sheikh, call his bluff. I don't think he'll say anything. Laureta will have her wedding and he'll go back to Saudi Arabia.'

I gape at her.

'You mean Laureta hasn't phoned and sacked us.'

She sighs.

'She can't sack you for not having dinner with her best man.'

I pull a face.

'Oh no, there's more you're not telling me isn't there? What have you done now?' she says, exasperated and filling the kettle.

I don't believe this. I'd been expecting a call all evening from Laureta telling me I was fired. I figured for sure she would have phoned the office first thing this morning.

'Have you checked our emails?' I ask.

Her eyes bulge and for a second I think they might pop out of her head like an alien movie.

'I do everything around here,' she says, handing me a coffee. 'That includes answering the phone, checking the emails, sorting out things you've forgotten, reminding you of your own diary events and, calming you down when you have a crisis, and that was never in my job description.'

'I'm sorry Lucy. I do appreciate everything you do. In fact ...' I pull an envelope from my bag. 'I've booked you a holiday. You must be due one and ...'

'You've done what?' she says. 'Do you need your Quiet Life?'

'I've messed up Lucy. I'm trying to put things right. I'm telling Georgie the truth over lunch and I realise I haven't appreciated you nearly enough. I know you've worked hard on Laureta's wedding so I'm sorry that we won't be doing it.'

'But we are doing it. She won't fire us because you refuse to go to dinner with him.'

'No, but she might, when she finds out that last night Gary threatened to slice off the Prince's dick with a chainsaw.'

'Oh Jesus, please tell me you're joking?'

I shake my head.

'And what was his response in that deep sexy foreign voice of his?'

'At one point he threatened to tell the Prime Minister,' I smile.

'I guess its good publicity,' she says poker-faced and then she laughs so hard that tears run down her face.

'Thanks for the holiday,' she says finally.

'It's only a week in Majorca,' I mutter

She gives me a hug which I didn't feel I deserved.

'I'll love it. I may even take Frank. You do remember Frank?'

'Your boyfriend,' I say, amazed at my own memory.

'Right,' I say, walking to the office. 'I'm going to do some work. I've got an hour before I meet Georgie and my world crashes around me, so I'd better do some while I can.'

'I should think so too,' she smiles.

I check the time on my BlackBerry and feel my heart lurch. Two and a half hours to go. It's going to be the longest two and half hours of my life.

I'd agreed to meet Georgie at a sushi bar around the corner from her office during her lunch break. The closer I get the more nauseous I feel. The grey overcast sky isn't helping my feelings of doom either. I take a deep breath, turn the corner into the street where the café is and collide with Ben Garret, knocking a sandwich and yellow Minion from his hands.

'Goddam it,' he curses looking at the broken remains of the Minion on the pavement.

'I'm so sorry,' I say looking down at the yellow mess, a single Minion eye stares back at me.

'That was Sophie's birthday cake.'

He barely looks at me, while my whole body tingles with the pleasure of seeing him.

'I'm so sorry. I didn't see you,' I say apologetically.

'Trust me if I had seen you it wouldn't have happened. I'd have crossed the road,' he says angrily.

He must have seen the pain cross my face as his features soften.

'I'm sorry, that was unnecessary,' he says softly.

'I'll pay for the cake,' I mumble, fumbling in my bag.

'Don't be stupid,' he says crossly. 'I'll get another. It's just irritating and a bit sad for the poor Minion,' he smiles.

He looks gorgeous. His hair is freshly washed and he smells clean and manly. I inhale the wonderful unique smell of him and wonder how I look to him. But I don't imagine he has even noticed. I wish I had worn my boots, they look much better with leggings than these stupid pumps I'm wearing.

Soft drops of rain begin to fall and he moves into a shop doorway, gently pulling me in with him.

'How have you been?' he asks.

He sounds nervous and uncomfortable and all I can think of are our kisses.

'Fine,' I reply. 'How about you?'

'Busy, you know, work and all that.'

I nod.

The rain is heavier now and we watch as the remains of his sandwich and cake get washed away.

'I saw Greg. It's good he's home,' he says.

'Yes ...'

'Do you want a coffee, get out of this rain?' he asks quickly.

Oh why now, why does he ask now?

'I'm meeting ...'

'Yes of course,' he interrupts. 'How is the sheikh?'

'I'm meeting Georgie,' I say, 'to discuss the wedding and other things.'

'Good luck with that. She's all for calling it off but I suppose you know that?'

I want so much to hug him, to tell him that he has it all wrong about the sheikh. To ask if we can give things a second go but of course I can't. Once he knows the truth I'll be the last person he'll want to spend time with.

'Right, I'd better get another Minion.'

'Wish Sophie a happy birthday for me.'

'I will.'

I watch as he runs out into the rain and then stare at the sodden cake. How could I have been so stupid? I sigh and step out into the rain to face my meeting with Georgie.

Chapter Fifty-Seven

Rosie waves at me and any plans of turning back are thwarted.

'What bloody weather,' she says, hugging me.

'Do I look okay?' I ask foolishly.

'It's not a date.'

I'm feeling distinctively nervous and my hands shake as I fumble in my handbag for a tissue to dry the rain from my face.

'Here's Chardonnay,' she says.

I sigh with relief.

'Awright girlies, shall we get this over with babe?'

I nod, and push all thoughts of Ben Garret from my mind and focus on the matter in hand. Georgie waves from her table.

'I didn't know it was a girlie lunch,' she says

She looks stunning. In fact she has always looked stunning. I've just been in denial about it until today. I can see why Greg is in love with her. She's gentle, kind and homely and dazzling with it.

'Why not?' says Chardonnay, gesturing to a waiter. 'The more the merrier, that's what I say.'

The waiter places menus in front of us and I push mine aside.

'Just a white wine for me please,' I say.

'Me too,' says Chardonnay.

'I'll have a white wine too,' requests Rosie.

'Let's get a couple of bottles,' suggests Chardonnay.

Blimey, don't tell me they're racked with nerves too. I'm depending on them to get me through this.

'I think I'd better stick to something soft,' says Georgie, looking embarrassed. 'I've got to get to back to work.'

I don't think Georgie will be going back to work after this somehow.

'Oh you'll be awright,' says Chardonnay dismissively and orders two bottles of white wine.

'Is Patsy coming?' Georgina asks.

I think not. I don't think Patsy is going to take too kindly to me after this and as I don't have a pet rabbit to boil it's a bit worrying what she might go for instead, I imagine it will most likely be my head. We make chit chat until the sushi arrives and then Chardonnay asks nonchalantly,

'Has Greg remembered anything else?'

Georgie bites a trembling lip.

'I haven't been to see him. I find it all too much. Every time I go all he talks about is Amy Fisher. I feel sure if I find her now it will be all I can do not to kill her.'

'Shit,' says Chardonnay, throwing back her wine which she hasn't noticed yet is a dry white and not her normal sweet.

Rosie nods at me. I shake my head. I can't do it. I simply can't add to Georgie's pain. I'm Amy Perfect, the wonderful wedding planner she looks up to, and the woman who was giving her the wedding of her dreams and now I'm about to smash all those dreams by telling her that Miss Perfect, the perfect wedding planner, was trying to give her the most imperfect wedding ever, and in the process steal her fiancé. I should boil my own head, it's what I deserve. I pour myself some wine and try to ignore the looks Chardonnay and Rosie are giving me. I just need a few more glasses and then maybe I can do it.

'We've got great news,' announces Rosie.

We have? Rosie looks at Chardonnay who then looks at me. I lower my eyes.

'Is that why we're meeting?' asks Georgie, taking a small sip of wine.

Chardonnay digs me in the ribs so roughly that I nearly fall off my chair.

'It is, ain't it Amy,' she says, throwing back more wine. I don't like to point out that she's now drinking from my glass.

'We found Amy Fisher,' says Rosie, her eyes pleading with me.

'You have? Where? Have you spoken to her?'

I toss back the nearest glass of wine and say,

'I'm Amy Fisher, Georgie.'

You could hear a pin drop. It's as though for a few seconds we are transformed into mannequins and then Georgie stands up, snatches her drink and throws it in my face. Chardonnay grabs her arm before I get the remains of her sushi over my head too. The restaurant turns quiet as the diners turn to see what the raucous is about. A waiter makes his way over to us but Chardonnay holds up her hand and mouths,

'It's okay.'

She puts an arm around Georgie.

'Awright babe, let's calm down shall we? We're in a sushi bar after all. Have some wine that will help.'

'How could you?' Georgie hisses. 'All this time, why didn't you tell me? You've made a fool out of me.'

Rosie hands me a tissue and I wipe the water from my face along with my tears.

'How could you agree to plan my perfect wedding to your own ex? Especially when you knew he still loved you.'

'He doesn't love me Georgie. I can assure you he doesn't. He jilted me at the altar. Well actually we never got that far. It was at the church gates to be precise.'

'And you expect me to believe you over Greg. You dumped him.'

'He jilted her,' breaks in Rosie. 'I was there. I was the chief bridesmaid.'

'I'm sorry, I'm so sorry. Greg did jilt me. I still don't know why. I thought it was because I was fat ...'

'Greg would never dump a woman because she was fat. He's not like that.'

'He was the love of my life, or at the time I thought he was. I didn't see him for three years and then you phoned and asked me to plan your perfect wedding. I just saw it as a way to get back the man I loved so I could have my own perfect wedding.'

'You were trying to steal him from me?' she says appalled.

I give an ashamed nod.

'But I don't love him. I don't want him and he certainly doesn't want me. It's you he loves. He never looked at me like he looks at you. I've seen those photos ...'

'But I don't understand. Why doesn't he recognise you?'

'He will, eventually,' says Rosie. 'But she's changed. She was really fat …'

'Slightly overweight,' I correct.

'Her hair was shorter and darker. She was much chubbier in the face than she is now …'

'I think you've made your point,' I interrupt. 'The thing is Georgie, I made a terrible mistake and the worst part for me is that I've lost your friendship.'

I dab discreetly at my tears.

'Well it sounds like Greg ain't the total innocent 'ere,' says Chardonnay, biting into her sushi. 'Should 'ave told ya why he couldn't go through wiv it earlier.'

Georgie stands up abruptly.

'I'm going to have it out with him.'

'Oh right,' says Rosie, looking down at a California roll. 'Right now?'

Chardonnay grabs an unopened bottle of wine.

'And you're going to tell him you're Amy Fisher, right?' Georgie demands.

Looks like I have no choice in the matter.

'Right, let's pay for this uneaten nosh and go then,' says Chardonnay.

Chapter Fifty-Eight

Greg's flat is in the best part of Chelsea. He has gone up in the world.

'He's only renting,' says Georgie. 'We're buying a house in … well we were …' she breaks off and strides ahead of us to the red brick converted house.

I'm praying he isn't home, but of course he is, and the door is opened by Jack.

'Whoa, is the word on the street that we've got pizza?' he laughs. 'Hello Rosie, haven't seen you in a while.'

Rosie blushes and seems unable to speak. Our sombre expression soon wipes the smile off Jack's face.

'Is something wrong?' he asks.

'We're 'ere to see Greg,' says Chardonnay, sounding like a policewoman.

He opens the door and we file in. I've never felt more depressed in my life. I finally found a career I was good at, excellent at it in fact, and now it is all ruined. Frankly, I couldn't care if I never see another wedding again. I would prefer to go back and talk to dead bodies. God knows, they never caused me this much grief, if you'll excuse the pun.

Jack leads us into the lounge and Greg jumps up from the couch on seeing us.

'Georgie,' he says, his eyes softening. 'I've been trying to call you.'

'You have? I had my phone on silent,' she says startled.

'I'm so sorry darling. I can't imagine what you've been going through.'

Shit, it is all coming back to him.

'You remember me?' she says, falling onto the couch. Chardonnay takes a swig from the wine bottle and then hands it to me.

'There's somethink wrong with this wine. It ain't right some'ow,' she whispers, 'but it does the trick.'

'It's a dry white wine, that's why.'

'Fuck, that explains it. It's bloody awful.'

Why we're discussing wine at a moment like this I do not know, but it does kind of put off the inevitable for a while. Greg reaches out to take Georgie in his arms but she pulls away angrily.

'You have a lot of explaining to do, don't you think? Like her, for example,' she says, pointing at me. 'You do remember her don't you? The ex-fiancée you dumped. You failed to mention that bit didn't you?' she cries and burst into tears.

'I didn't forget her, I forgot you, and for that I am so sorry. You mean everything to me Georgie, you must let me explain,' he says tearing up.

'Blimey,' whispers Rosie. 'I've only ever seen him shed tears when Tottenham lost.'

Greg takes a step towards me but before he can speak Chardonnay yells,

'The bleedin' pizza is burning by the smell of it.'

Jack rushes into the kitchen to rescue the charred pizzas with Rosie behind him.

'You told Georgie I dumped you when the truth is you jilted me because I was fat,' I say crossly.

'That isn't true is it Greg? Please say it isn't,' Georgie gasps.

'It had nothing to do with your weight Amy,' he says softly.

'It had nothing to do with my weight?' I repeat.

All that dieting, all that sacrificing and all that killing myself, not to mention almost killing Rosie too, and it was all for nothing. Greg didn't have a problem with my weight at all. I really don't believe this. I try not to think of all the doughnuts I could have eaten. All the milk shakes I had denied myself. The amount of chocolate I had hungered for. That's it. I'm going to buy bags of everything when I leave here and overindulge until I feel sick.

He shakes his head.

'I don't understand,' I say. If it wasn't my weight that was the problem, what was?'

He hesitates, takes Georgie hand, and says,

'I was married to someone else Amy.'

Chapter Fifty-Nine

For an awful moment I think Georgie is going to faint. She lets out an anguished cry and sways on the couch. Chardonnay rushes to her and puts the wine bottle to her lips. I would have thought smelling salts would have been better, but if needs must. Georgie chokes and in a croaky voice asks,

'You're married?'

Rosie and Jack rush in, plates of charred pizza in their hands.

'What the hell happened?' asks Jack.

'I just told them.'

'You knew?' I said, turning on Jack.

'I was sworn to secrecy, what could I do?'

'You're married?' repeats Georgie, taking a swig from the bottle.

'Not now, I would never have proposed to you if that were the case. It was a stupid thing. I barely knew the girl. She was from Russia and wanted to stay in the country, get a job and make a life here. I'd been drinking and said I'd marry her. It happened two years before I met Amy.'

Greg rubs his eyes and looks shyly at me.

'Frankly, your proposal came out of the blue that day. I didn't know what to do, so I said yes.'

'You could have said no,' I say angrily.

'That's quite hard to do and you looked so happy that day.'

I was even happier on my wedding day but best not to mention that. After all, I wouldn't want to traumatise Greg and risk another bout of post-traumatic amnesia would I? I can't believe he expects sympathy after jilting me.

'I tried to find Lidiya so we could get divorced but I couldn't trace her. I didn't know how to tell you. When the day arrived I just knew I couldn't go through with it. I didn't love you enough Amy. I somehow ended up going to White Hart Lane instead ...'

'How unique,' Rosie scoffs.

'I drank too much. I was trying to get up the courage to tell you and then before I knew it I'd ended up on London Bridge. I don't quite know what I was doing but I think the intention was to throw myself off.'

'Shame you didn't,' says Rosie.

'You don't know what it was like,' he snaps.

'I knew what it was like for Amy. She's been convinced all this time that you jilted her because she was fat. No man should make a woman feel that way.'

'It didn't occur to you that you throwing yourself off London Bridge may have made things worse for me?' I say angrily.

'I felt so bloody useless Amy. But the truth is we were never really suited. I always found you too overpowering. Call me weak if you like ...'

'You're weak,' obliges Rosie.

'I'd never have proposed to you if I'm honest,' he says ignoring her. 'I tried to find you a year later to explain but it was like you'd disappeared. I'm so sorry, but let's face it, I didn't get any say in our wedding. You took over totally. We had nothing in common, not really, and if you're totally honest, you'll agree it would have been the biggest mistake of our lives. You just wanted someone to marry. I don't think you loved me. We had fun but that's not love is it?'

So I, Amy Fisher, was Greg's trauma.

'I think we should eat these pizzas before they're totally ruined,' says Jack with a smile.

'You can't seriously think our wedding is still going ahead?' Georgie says tearfully.

'I'd still like to plan your perfect wedding,' I offer.

'To a man who's lied to me?' she whispers.

'Georgie listen to me. I love you, I love you more than life itself,' says Greg pleadingly.

'Faaackinell,' murmurs Chardonnay. 'The day Gary says that to me will be the day 'ell bleedin' freezes over.'

'I was too scared of losing you, and that's what stopped me telling you the truth. I didn't want to jilt Amy, but I couldn't marry a woman I didn't love.'

Hello, I am still here.

'And the previous marriage meant nothing. It was a ceremony and I never saw her again. She contacted me a couple of years ago through a solicitor and divorced me on the grounds of desertion. Don't leave me Georgie. I don't know what I'd do if you weren't in my life.'

'Would you give up football for her?' pipes up Rosie.

I widen my eyes in anticipation of his response.

'I'd give up everything for her,' he replies.

'I'm the last person you should listen to,' I say. 'But I think you should marry him. I've never seen a more suited couple in my life.'

Her eyes fill with tears and then she throws her arms around his neck, and we all sigh with relief.

'Let's have this sodding pizza now,' says Chardonnay, wiping away her own tears.

'You'll still plan my perfect wedding then?' Georgie asks shyly.

'It would be my honour.'

This is too good to be true. Maybe karma does work after all.

'Thanks,' Greg smiles. 'It means a lot to her to have Amy Perfect plan the wedding.'

'You look so different these days,' he says suddenly.

'Amazing what three years can do,' grins Jack. 'Rosie looks pretty terrific too.'

Amazing what three years of a killer diet and extreme workouts can achieve more like. I didn't magically get like this with the passing of time, and neither did Rosie.

'You've lost a lot of weight,' Greg comments.

'I'm a size 10,' I say proudly.

'I never have understood women's sizes,' he smiles.

And there was me thinking he would be dead impressed.

'And now you're planning our perfect wedding,' he smiles. 'How ironic is that? I'm glad we've cleared the air Amy,' says Greg, leaning towards me.

His kiss is gentle on my cheek, a sweet innocent kiss that doesn't stir me in the least. At last, Amy Fisher is over Greg Martin. Who'd have thought it? If only this were the end. Just like the Mills and Boon novels. But it isn't a Mills and Boon novel is it? I've still got to face Ben, and when he hears about this he'll never want to speak to me again.

Chapter Sixty

Lucy fidgets next to me, checking her watch for the umpteenth time.

'I wish you would stop doing that,' I say. 'You're making me nervous.'

'I don't want it to look like I'm panicking,' she says, 'but I've never known a bride to be this late.'

I turn my head to see Abdullah standing at the door. He's biting his lip nervously. My heart jumps into my mouth as Henrietta creeps towards me from her pew at the front of the church, her huge breasts preceding her.

'Where is she?' she hisses.

I step back to avoid a black eye by the offending right breast, which I feel sure is slightly wonky compared to the left one, but who am I to criticise the best cosmetic surgeon in London.

'I've no idea,' I say.

'God, what if they've had an accident?' she asks worriedly.

'I'm sure ...'

'This is your fault,' she accuses. 'You're the wedding planner.'

Exactly, I'm the wedding planner, not bloody God. I can't stop accidents and I can't make brides or bridegrooms turn up if they don't want to.

Jeremy turns and attempts a smile but he fails miserably. For an awful moment I think he is going to burst into tears. God, no, I've never had a bridegroom tear up.

'Shall we call the police to see if there have been any accidents?' asks Henrietta, now close to hysteria. At that moment the sheikh waves from the entrance and give us a relieved smile.

'I'll murder her,' Henrietta mutters before allowing Abdullah to lead her back to her seat. I avoid his eyes and look at the church floor.

'I'm going to carry a hip flask in future,' I mutter to Lucy but she is too focused on the bride to hear me.

Laureta looks stunning in her Balenciaga wedding gown. Her make-up is immaculate. She's blooming in exactly the way a bride should bloom. Her train is held perfectly by her pretty bridesmaids and she glides down the aisle as a perfect bride should.

'My work is done,' I whisper to Lucy, who dabs a tear from her eye.

'It makes it all worthwhile doesn't it?' she says dewy-eyed.

The reception is being held at a stately home owned by friends of Henrietta and her husband Angus. A string quartet plays in the rose garden and the guests in dinner jackets and evening dresses wander through the grounds helping themselves to Bucks Fizz and canapés from smartly dressed waiters.

'Hello Amy.'

I take a deep breath and turn to face the sheikh.

'Hello,' I say, looking for someone, anyone in fact that I know or come to that, don't know.

'I see your friends from Essex are not here.'

'They're not acquainted with the bride and groom,' I say, waving to a strange man who gives me an appraising stare.

'That doesn't surprise me,' he smiles.

The strange man makes his way towards us. He must be eighty if he's a day.

'Hello there,' he says, leaning forward to kiss me on the cheek.

'Oh hello,' I say. 'Abdullah, this is ...' I tap my forehead and sigh.

'My memory,' I laugh.

'John,' grins the man.

'Of course, John, yes how could I forget? This is Prince Abdullah.'

The man's eyes widen.

271

'A prince, ooh I say. I didn't realise we had royalty amongst us. Is there a princess with you?'

Abdullah smiles and points to his three wives huddled together in a corner.

'Those are my wives.'

'You've got three at once?'

I try not to smile.

'Bravo. I've had two but never at the same time. Well, excellent, congratulations on your stamina.'

The Prince fights back a sigh, excuses himself and wanders to his wives.

'We've never met have we my dear?' asks John.

'No, sorry about that, but you were quite right about his stamina.'

He looks wistfully at the sheikh.

A gong sounds and we all head into the state room for the reception.

'May I?' asks John, holding out his arm.

'I'd be honoured,' I smile.

After all, this might be the best I can do now.

'Ladies and gentlemen, please be upstanding for Mr and Mrs Roland-Smyth.'

Rainbow by Robert Plant begins to play as Laureta and Jeremy enter the state room and a terrible thought occurs to me. I struggle to catch Lucy's eye.

'Lucy,' I hiss, but she is too busy clapping the happy couple. Shit and double shit. This could be catastrophic. I slide out of my seat and hurry around the table to Lucy.

'You did change the CD didn't you, the one to introduce the sheikh?' I ask anxiously.

'Fuck!' she exclaims. 'I totally forgot.'

'You forgot?' I repeat. Please say I'm not hearing this?

Holy shit, this is a total disaster. I spur my legs into action and run in my Jimmy Choos across the state room's polished floor, my heels tapping loudly as I do so. I reach the entrance doors and slide through them as my heels slip. I fall straight into Abdullah's arms where he stands, in his royal garb, waiting for his entrance music.

'Oh God, I mean, oh Allah, I'm so sorry, I've done something terrible. I switched your entrance music CD with the CD from Rosie's car. You are going to enter to *Hava Nagila*. It was my way of getting back at you. I'm so sorry.'

His face darkens and then a smile slowly crosses his face.

'Touché Miss Perfect, and I suggest as there is nothing you or I can do about it, that you enter with me. I accept your apology if you'll accept mine.'

Before I can answer the Prince is introduced and *Hava Nagila* booms through the speakers. He takes my arm and leads me into the state room twisting me around as he does so. Laureta's face has a look to kill and her mother's isn't any better. If I survive the end of this wedding then I certainly won't get paid. Lucy looks horrified and the only people smiling are me and Abdullah.

'The lovely Amy Perfect,' he says, bowing to me when we reach the top table. 'The wedding couple's brilliant wedding planner who taught me what it is to have a sense of humour.'

There are a few moments of silence and then the room explodes into loud applause. Laureta's face relaxes and Lucy looks about to collapse to the floor.

The sheikh leads me to my table.

'Have an enjoyable evening, Miss Perfect.'

Lucy looks at me and shakes her head.

'Nice touch,' says the man sitting to my right and Laureta looks over and gives me the thumbs up. I smile. Somehow I had managed to give another bride a perfect wedding. Next I have Georgie's and Greg's and I'm determined to make it the most perfect wedding ever.

Chapter Sixty-One

Tonight is Georgie and Greg's pre-wedding bowling night. I've bitten my nails down to my fingers fretting about it. There's no way out, everyone is going, even Chardonnay and Gary. I contemplate phoning Rosie and feigning a migraine but considering I've never had one since she's known me I really can't see that working. Anyway, I've promised Georgie I will be there. Any other time and I'd be dead keen, I love tenpin bowling. I've visited the bathroom numerous times to check and recheck my make-up and then again to remove and reapply it. I've styled and restyled my hair. I've curled it and then straightened it. I look at myself in the mirror and sigh. I try to curl it again with the styling brush but the brush gets tangled and I can't get the bloody thing out. After telling myself not to panic I go into panic mode as the smell of singeing hair wafts up my nose. What's the bloody point of having release buttons on the damn things when they don't bloody release? Seconds later I tug the thing out along with several tufts of hair. I let my head fall with a thud onto the dressing table and burst into tears. I hate Ben Garret. I hate him. How can he make me feel like this? What's wrong with me? He didn't design the sodding curling brush did he? But the least he could have done is to have pulled out of the evening. I angrily pull clothes out of the wardrobe. What am I doing? It's a bloody night at a bowling alley. I pull on my jeans and fumble through the drawers for a black vest and then don a flowery shirt over the top. I'm not out to impress am I, not Ben bloody Garret anyway. Who am I kidding? Of course I'm out to impress him, but the fact is he won't want anything to do with me. He must know by now that I am Amy Fisher. I'm just surprised he hasn't written a scathing piece about me for *Vanity*. He probably has but isn't publishing it until after the wedding. I imagine Georgie has asked him not to. God, I wish I could stop thinking so much. I'm driving myself insane. I grab a hairslide and twist my hair into it just as the flat buzzer sounds.

'I can't go,' I greet Rosie.

'Have you gone out of your mind? You can't let Georgie down. Have you forgotten how much you've let her down already?'

'It's impossible to forget with you constantly reminding me,' I say huffily.

'What's that burning smell?' she asks, sniffing the air.

'Oh shit.'

I'd only gone and left the damn styling brush on and now there's a bloody great singe mark in the carpet.

'Damn it,' I curse. 'Well I can't go now can I? I need to clear this up.'

'We're going,' she says decisively, 'even if your flat had burnt down. Now, come on.'

That's it then. I've got to face Ben Garret and that scornful look of his. Oh well, I guess it's what I deserve and best to get it over with.

'Jack's coming with us,' she says shyly as we head to a waiting cab. 'Georgie invited him.'

'I want to be on your team,' he grins. 'If I remember you were quite the champ at bowling.'

'Look on the bright side,' smiles Rosie, 'at least you can drink, and that must help.'

I really must buy that hip flask.

The party is in full flow when we arrive. Several of the girls I remembered from the hen do, rush up to us. Chardonnay and Gary are sitting at one of the balloon decorated tables with a bottle of white wine.

Georgie and Greg come over to greet us. Greg kisses me shyly on the cheek and Georgie hugs me warmly.

'We're still waiting for Patsy and a few others,' says Georgie.

'We thought we'd have a few drinks and sort out the teams,' says Greg.

'Babe,' yells Chardonnay on seeing me. Her warm hug does a lot to relax me.

'Lucy was telling us about the 'ole sheikh and the 'ava Nagila thing. What a scream,' she laughs.

'Oh, you've made it,' says Lucy, joining us. 'For a while there I thought you weren't coming.'

Lucy knows me too well.

'We've got a bottle of Prosecco on the go,' says Greg. 'Do you want a glass, or we've got wine.'

'Sweet and dry,' laughs Chardonnay.

At that moment I see Ben Garret enter and look around him and for a moment his eyes meet mine but then he quickly looks away.

'Prosecco,' I say, 'a large one.'

I link my arm through Chardonnay's and lead her back to the table. Greg hands me a large glass of Prosecco with a wide smile.

'So glad you're here. It all feels perfect somehow, and Georgie is so happy.'

Before I can reply he is called away by Georgie. The background crash of bowling balls scattering pins adds to the atmosphere and I help myself to some crisps.

'Gary's bleedin' useless at bowling ain't you Gal? So you'll have to be on our team,' says Chardonnay.

'Hello everyone,' yells a familiar voice. I turn to see Patsy. I haven't seen her since I told Georgie the truth and she looks at me cautiously.

'What are you having?' Greg asks her.

'White wine please,' she replies, looking at me.

'Hello Amy.'

'Hi Patsy, how are you?' I ask nervously.

'Let you out of prison then?'

'Patsy ...I ...' I stutter.

'Oh it's okay,' she says, before sipping her drink. 'If Greg and Georgie can forgive you then I suppose I can. Sorry for calling you a fat bitch though.'

'I probably deserved it. Anyway, you're going to make a fabulous maid of honour, let's just focus on that.'

She clinks her glass against mine and then says,

'Hi Ben, we're just toasting Greg and Georgie's perfect wedding.'

I spin round to face Ben and in the process spill the contents of my glass down the front of his shirt.

Chapter Sixty-Two

'I'll get a cloth,' says Patsy and rushes off.

'I've got wet wipes,' I say, fumbling in my bag and managing to pull out my make-up purse scattering topless lipsticks, dry mascara brushes and powdered blusher everywhere.

'Bugger,' I mumble. I bend to pick them up and unwittingly spray his shoe with a topless can of dry shampoo in the process. He dusts the white powder off without a word.

'I'm sorry,' I mutter.

I'd do anything for the floor to open up and eat me alive along with the contents of my make-up bag.

'Ooh, I love this one.'

I look up to see Sophie holding one of my lipsticks.

'Hi Sophie, you can have that if you like. A late birthday present, did you have a nice day?' I say, standing up and stepping on Ben's foot.

'I had a Minion cake,' she says, studying the lipstick. 'Is it okay?' she asks, turning to Ben and holding up the lipstick.

'I guess so,' he says without looking at me.

Patsy returns with a wet cloth. He takes it and dabs at his shirt.

'I'm so sorry,' I say again.

I wish he'd say something, even if it is only to tell me to go away.

'Ben, great you're here. Can I get you a glass of wine?' offers Greg.

'I've already had one,' Ben says, looking down at his shirt. There is no humour in his voice and my heart sinks.

'Hi Sophie, excited about the bowling?'

She nods and holds up the lipstick.

'Look what Amy gave me for a birthday present.'

'It's the perfect colour for you,' says Rosie, joining us. She looks at Ben.

'I don't think we've met, but I've heard lots about you. I'm Rosie, a friend of Amy's.'

He takes her hand and smiles for the first time.

'Nice to meet you and this is my niece Sophie, who loves bowling and lipstick, as you can see.'

'I want to be on the winning team,' squeals Sophie.

'Don't we all,' says one of Georgie's friends.

I scoop up a dried-up mascara brush and excuse myself to the ladies. I really am the sorriest person on earth. I've screwed up badly, really badly. I finally meet a man that is perfect for me. I think he's perfect anyway and I've totally buggered it. Right, well, crying won't put things right will it so I might as well go out there and win this bloody bowling match. If nothing else that might impress Ben Garret, although I think that where I'm concerned nothing will impress him.

'The fairest way is to pull names out of a hat,' says Patsy loudly as we change into our shoes.

'I want to be on Amy's team,' says Sophie, sidling up to me.

'Here we go,' calls Patsy, pulling a name from a glass. 'Ben Garret, team one.'

Sophie squeals with delight and squeezes my hand.

'Georgie, team two and Patsy ...'

I wait patiently for my name to be called and cross everything that can be crossed that I'm on team two.

'Sophie ...'

Sophie takes in a sharp breath.

'Team one, and Amy, team one.'

'Yey,' shouts Sophie.

I feel Ben's eyes on me and force myself to meet them.

'I'm really sorry,' I say quietly. 'I can swap with someone if you like.'

'Do I look that immature,' he snaps.

I hold back the tears that threaten to engulf me.

'This is great, we're going to be the best,' says Sophie, oblivious to the tension between me and her uncle. 'I'm so glad you're on our team,' she says hugging Rosie and Jack.

'This don't bode well for the 'appy couple,' smiles Chardonnay. 'Gary ain't never knocked a pin down in his life, 'ave you babe? Sorry Georgie.'

'We're going to do great,' says Georgie.

'Right, let's crack on,' smiles Greg. 'Choose your team names.'

'The Mighty Minions,' says Sophie before any of us have a chance.

'Good choice,' smiles Ben and my heart flutters unmercifully. If he keeps smiling like that my heart is likely to go into overdrive before I even start bowling.

'Vicious and Delicious,' suggests Patsy.

'Sounds good to me,' agrees Greg. 'Let's get this show on the road, and may be the best team win.'

It seems the more beer I drink the better my aim.

'Yes,' Ben yells, as the pins fall. He goes to hug me but controls the urge at the last minute. Our team are winning but Greg is determined to fight to the death.

'We're not having that,' he says, his mouth grim with determination.

'More beer?' laughs Ben, handing me another bottle. 'The more pissed you are the more of an expert you become.'

Our hands touch and we both pull away. I want to scream in frustration. Why doesn't he talk to me, why doesn't he ask me what really happened with the sheikh? I slide onto the bench next to Jack and Rosie who frankly are so besotted with one another I'm amazed they've been able to break apart long enough to throw a ball.

'I don't remember you being this good at bowling,' says Jack.

'Apparently it's the beer,' I say, wiping the perspiration from my forehead.

'We have to keep her tanked up,' grins Ben, opening another bottle.

'That's not the normal reason a man likes to get a girl wasted,' Rosie laughs.

I blush and Ben's shoulders twitch.

'Bleedin' 'ell Gal, even I knocked down free of the bloody pins,' groans Chardonnay as Gary's ball misses all ten.

There are cheers as Greg gets a strike.

'My go,' shouts Sophie.

I sip my beer and help myself to a handful of crisps. I don't want to be overweight again but this time I'm going to watch my weight for me and not for a man. There are shouts of encouragement as Lucy aims her ball down the alley and raucous laughter as she almost takes herself with it.

'Come on Rosie, your turn,' says Jack, pulling her up.

'Can I get another Sprite?' Sophie asks. Ben nods and we are left sitting at our table alone.

'Ben, I'm really sorry for everything,' I say, spurred on by the effects of the beer.

'I'm really not interested ...'

'Ben ...' I plead.

'I don't understand how you could have lied to us all. We talked about taking our friendship further. In the same conversation I ask you about Amy Fisher and you still didn't say anything. Would you have taken it further and not told me who you really were?'

'Of course not, it all got out of hand. I was up for telling Georgie, and then Greg had his accident and things got complicated ...'

'Things got complicated?' he says cynically.

'I hadn't bargained on having feelings for you.'

Maybe the beer is good for winning the bowling match but not so good for loosening my tongue.

'The more I tried to sort things out the more complicated they became, and then the sheikh blackmailed me and ...'

'Oh yes, how is His Majesty?' he says sarcastically.

'I wouldn't know he ...'

'Your turn Amy,' calls Georgie.

'This is it,' says Greg. 'It's all on you.'

'You can do it,' says Sophie.

'Need another beer?' asks Jack.

I throw back the remainder of my beer and then walk slowly to the alley. I've had so much to drink that I'm seeing twenty pins. This doesn't bode well.

'Come on Amy,' screams Sophie.

I look back at Ben who nods encouragingly.

'We're depending on you,' says Rosie.

I take a deep breath and line up the ball with the pins. At least I hope I'm aiming them at the pins. It's hard to know when you're seeing double. I take three steps, swing and release the ball with as much force as I can, almost taking myself with it. It seems like the whole bowling alley holds their breath as the ball rumbles down the centre of the lane. It hits the pins and the place erupts as all ten pins fall. Sophie throws herself into my arms and I swing her around.

'You're the best,' she says, kissing me. 'Isn't she Uncle Ben?'

He smiles but I notice he doesn't agree. Jack and Rosie high five me and Greg offers to buy the congratulatory drinks.

'Fanks for 'aving us,' says Chardonnay. 'It's been fun ain't it Gal?'

'Yeah,' says Gary.

'We'll finish up here and then go for a pizza,' says Georgie.

'I'll give it a miss if it's okay Gina. I need to get Sophie to bed,' says Ben.

'Oh, but Uncle Ben ...' complains Sophie.

'It will be a late night and ...' he argues.

'It won't be the same without you,' says Georgie.

She's quite right it won't be. It just won't be the same without his gorgeous face, his unique smell and warm eyes. In fact life won't ever be the same again without Ben Garret in it. I hide behind my beer glass and swallow the contents down with my tears. There's no more I can do. I've apologised ad nauseam. It's really time to stop and move on. I shall now put all my energy into Georgie and Greg's perfect wedding.

Chapter Sixty-Three

You are cordially Invited
to attend the perfect wedding of
Greg and Georgina
At
St Andrew's Church,
St John's Wood, NW8
2.30 p.m.
Reception to follow at
The Ivory Hotel

I take a final look at the wedding invitation and then study my reflection in the mirror. I'd gone for a slip dress in floral layered print. It's simple but elegant and I'm in no danger of overshadowing the bride, who I know is going to look spectacular in her Chanel wedding gown. I pick up the laced black shawl I had bought to accompany the dress and check the contents of my clutch bag. Finally, as happy as I can be with my reflection, I grab the folder marked 'Georgie and Greg' don my white satin shoes and pink hat and leave my flat for the waiting black cab.

It's mayhem at Georgie's parents' house. Patsy greets me with a hair full of rollers.

'Thank God you're here,' she says, 'Georgie's got cystitis. We've been overdosing her on Cranberry juice but the damn stuff is doing sod all.'

'She'll be fine, it's probably just nerves.'

'I thought you got that after the bloody honeymoon, not before it,' she sighs. 'Have you checked the weather, it's going to piss down later.'

'At about four o'clock,' I say confidently. 'Perfect timing, we'll have the photos done and everything and it can rain as much as it likes then, meanwhile it's lovely and sunny.'

'I wish I could be as positive as you.'

I find Georgie sitting in her under slip in her parents' bedroom. Her mum is clucking around her like a mother hen.

'She's got thrush,' complains Mum.

'I thought it was cystitis?' I say.

'It's neither, it's just the thong I'm wearing irritates but I want to wear it for Greg.'

Georgie's mum mutters something and leaves the room.

'She's driving me nuts,' Georgie groans.

'You're going to have the perfect wedding today, that's all you have to remember.'

She turns and hugs me.

'You look lovely Amy, and I have a present for you. I want you to wear it today.'

She takes a prettily wrapped package from the dressing table and hands it to me. I'm used to brides giving me gifts but a present from Georgie means so much more. I tear the paper from the package to reveal a pink box. I lift the lid. Inside is a gold bracelet with a single disc hanging from it.

'Oh Georgie, I really didn't expect anything.'

'Read it,' Georgie says eagerly. 'It's inscribed.'

I turn the disc over and read the words *Friends Forever G&A*.

'Oh Georgie ...' I begin, and then tears stop me saying more.

'I really thought about everything Amy, and I can understand your pain. That's love isn't it? Greg was wrong and he knows that. But you didn't try and steal Greg. You knew it was wrong and in the end you were doing everything to make sure I had my perfect wedding, even stopping me getting the tattoo ...'

'That was Ben,' I say.

'Only because you phoned him,' she reminds me. She clips the bracelet onto my wrist.

'Talking of Ben ...' she begins.

'I really don't think this is the time to talk about Ben,' I say firmly. 'You need to get ready and I need to get to the church and make sure everything is going to plan.'

'You should have told him.'

I nod.

'He's already been badly hurt and ...' she continues.

'Don't worry Georgie. There is no danger of me hurting Ben Garret. I'm the last person he's interested in.'

I look at the Chanel wedding gown hanging on the wardrobe door.

'Ben has good taste,' I smile.

She nods happily.

'You get that on and I'll see you at the church.'

I kiss her quickly on the cheek and make a hasty exit.

'What do we do about the cystitis,' yells Patsy as I reach the bottom of the stairs.

'Keep your voice down about it for a start, and it isn't cystitis.'

'It's a thong,' says Georgie's mum.

'A what?' asks her dad.

'I'll see you later,' I say, before things get too complicated. The cab driver takes one look at me and says,

'When you've been married as long as me, trust me the only tears you shed are those of regret.'

'Thanks for that. St Andrew's church please.'

And to face the best man, Ben Garret.

Chapter Sixty-Four

My senses are buzzing as I walk down the pathway to St Andrew's church. A string quartet waits at the church gate ready to play when the church bells stop ringing. The walk to the church is lined with flower pots bursting with blue and white tulips, Tottenham's team colours. A little touch that I know Greg will appreciate. I look ahead to the church door which is bordered with flowered hearts and the names, *Georgie* and *Greg* embedded in roses sits in the centre.

Ben stands at the entrance, greeting guests. I feel myself take a sharp intake of breath at the sight of him. He looks impressive in his grey tailcoat, white waistcoat and blue tie. He's adjusting someone's carnation as I approach, and the unique freshness of him wafts over me. My heart flutters as it always does whenever I am near him. He looks at me fleetingly and turns back to the guest.

'Enjoy,' he smiles, handing him an order of service before turning to me.

'Well, the day has come,' he says. 'They tell me you were here first thing this morning.'

'It's my job,' I say simply.

He gives an impressed nod.

'The church looks beautiful. I imagine the reception hall looks pretty impressive too.'

'Is this your way of complimenting me?' I smile.

'I like to give credit where credit's due,' he smiles. 'You've even controlled the weather, sunshine until four.'

'And then according to Patsy it is going to piss down with rain,' I laugh.

I take a deep breath and say,

'You look very smart.'

'And you look quite lovely,' he responds. 'Divine in fact, you may well give the bride a run for her money.'

'How was the stag do?' I ask, feeling the blush redden my cheeks.

'As out of control as we could make it, but sadly the groom stayed fairly sober, and talking of grooms,' he points.

A nervous looking Greg makes his way towards us and stops to look at the tulip pots.

'That's so great,' he grins.

Ben glances at his watch.

'I thought I'd best be early,' Greg says shakily.

'Come on mate,' says Ben leading him into the church.

'You look lovely, Amy,' Greg says, kissing me tenderly on the cheek.

'Thanks Greg.'

'You've got the rings haven't you Ben?' he asks anxiously.

I follow them in and pull my notes from my folder ticking things off against my checklist. Greg gasps as he enters the church.

'My God, this is amazing.'

'It is, isn't it?' says Ben before ushering guests to their seats.

The spring sunshine streaming through the stained glass windows gives everything a warm and colourful glow. Female guests are holding red roses with their blue and white embossed order of service. I'd arranged free-standing candle sconces around the church which were now lit with cream pillar candles. Two sweet pea flower arrangements stand at the altar in the colours of Georgie's bouquet.

'Amy,' squeals a little voice and Sophie runs towards me, skidding to a stop just in time. 'Do you like my make-up? Mummy said I could wear the lipstick just this once to come to the wedding with Uncle Ben.'

'You look very pretty,' I say, checking her snowdrop flower headband which looks beautiful.

'Not as pretty as you,' she says stroking my dress. 'Can I be your bridesmaid when you get married?'

'You can, but it may not be for a very long time. Are you still okay to scatter the rose petals?' I ask.

Sophie nods eagerly before skipping away.

'Bride or groom,' I hear one of the groomsmen say from behind me.

'We're neither mate, we're friends of the bride,' says Chardonnay.

I turn eagerly and her face lights up.

'Bleedin' 'ell girl, this is the business. You know 'ow to do a wedding awright. I can't wait for mine. It was nice of Georgie to invite us weren't it?'

'I'm thrilled she did,' I say hugging her.

I spot Lucy gesturing to me from the vestry.

'Everything is okay isn't it?'

'This came and I don't know what to do with it.' She hands me an envelope. It's addressed to Ben Garret.

'Give it to him of course,' I say, turning to walk away.

'It's from Prince Abdullah. His aide here in England took the dictation over the phone from Saudi Arabia and was asked to deliver it urgently to Ben Garret today.'

I feel my legs weaken.

'You should still give it to him.'

'But supposing he's causing trouble ...'

'That's for Ben to decide. Any other problems?'

She shakes her head.

'The bride should be here soon. I've checked the hall and the music is all in hand. I've gone through the checklist. I think we can relax and enjoy the ceremony.'

The vicar inclines his head towards me and I make my way to him.

'Wonderful job Amy, I think this has to be your most perfect wedding yet.'

'Thank you. I wanted it to be.'

I see Rosie and Jack arrive and hurry towards them.

'Sorry we're late,' Rosie apologises. 'It's looks amazing Amy. You really are 'Amazing Amy'.'

'You don't think its unhealthy then?' I joke.

'Okay, don't rub it in.'

We step to the side as the groomsmen light candles that have been set up at the end of the pews and then right on cue the bell ringers stop their peal and the string quartet begins to play the gentle sounds of *Pachelbel's Canon*. The bride has arrived. I move quietly to the entrance where Sophie waits with Patsy and the bridesmaids.

'Everything looks ...' Patsy says, tears filling her eyes.

I hand Sophie a basket of rose petals.

'You're going to be great,' I whisper into her ear.

She smiles proudly.

Ben and Greg take their places and I hold Lucy's arm.

'Come on,' I whisper. 'Let's get to our seats.'

'Amy,' she says quietly as I turn. 'You did the right thing. I always knew you would.'

Chapter Sixty-Five

A Midsummer Night's Dream wedding march begins and we all turn to watch Georgie float down the aisle on her father's arm. Sophie leads then in perfect step, scattering rose petals to make a crimson path for the bride. I give an approving nod as she passes.

Georgie looks stunning just as I knew she would. Patsy also looks terrific in her pale pink dress. Her hair is styled in a perfect bun and, without her glasses on, her full lashed eyes can be seen in all their beauty. She holds the train elegantly and manages a quick smile my way. The other bridesmaids follow at a perfect pace and I sigh with contentment. I so love weddings. Georgie reaches Greg and he looks at her in adoration. The music stops.

'Dear friends,' the vicar addresses the congregation. 'What a joyous day this is and what a pleasure to invite you all to our church, which is looking the most beautiful I have ever seen it to celebrate this momentous occasion with Georgina and Greg. Let us all join together in our first hymn before we proceed to the wedding ceremony of our lovely couple.'

When the vicar asks if any man can show any just cause or impediment why the couple may not be lawfully joined together, I feel sure eyes turn on me. But I could have imagined it.

The rest of the ceremony passes in a blur and I find myself spending most of it studying the back of Ben Garret's head and remembering the good times we had together. The string quartet comes into the church during the signing and plays softly in the background until the newly married couple are ready to depart. The vicar gives the signal and the quartet strike up *My Heart will Go On* and Greg and Georgie walk down the aisle arm in arm.

The photographer snaps with his camera and then they are outside having their official photos taken by the church doors. Greg points out the tulip pots to Georgie.

'That was a good move on your part,' says Ben from behind me.

'Thank you.'

'How did I do?' Sophie asks, rushing up to us.

'Brilliant,' smiles Ben. 'You've still got more to do as the flower girl. They'll be calling you for the photos soon.'

'This is so much fun,' she giggles.

We watch her run off and Ben gives a little nod and says,

'I'd better do best man duties, check my speech and all that.'

Before I can reply he has gone. I see Lucy approach him and hand him the envelope with the sheikh's letter inside. I push it from my mind and take my little box of confetti from my bag, and wait patiently for Greg and Georgie to pass.

Confetti falls through the air, sparkling in the spring sunshine. Georgie and Greg kiss under the deluge for the photographer to get a picture and then they head to a waiting Rolls-Royce.

'The reception awaits,' says Jack.

'Too right,' says Chardonnay. 'I need a bleedin' stiff drink after that lot. It really choked me up.'

'It were really nice,' says Gary. 'I ain't ever been to a wedding like that before.'

'Well you will when we 'ave ours,' laughs Chardonnay.

I look over to see Ben reading his letter. Lucy shrugs apologetically at me.

'Any of you guys want to share my cab to the hotel?' I say.

'Sounds great,' says Rosie.

'Yeah, thanks babe,' says Chardonnay.

We walk along the flower-lined path to where the cab waits. I feel an urge to glance back to see the expression on Ben's face, but I force myself not to, and climb into the cab. I've still got a perfect wedding to finish.

A pianist under a canopy in the hotel gardens plays *Nothing Could Be Finer than to be in Carolina* while waiters bustle around with canapés and trays of Bucks Fizz and champagne. Guests help themselves to cornets and tubs from an ice cream stall while the kids watch a Punch and Judy show. The sun is still shining but the clouds are beginning to gather. Georgie and Greg are having their official photos taken in the gardens of the hotel and I'm just about to check with the chef that everything is okay for the dinner when Georgie approaches me. Her cheeks flushed with happiness.

'I've been looking all over for you. Come on, we need you for the photos.'

'Oh no,' I protest. 'I shouldn't be in your wedding photos.'

'Oh yes you should,' says Rosie joining us. 'Come on.'

I'm pulled along by each arm. My plan to keep a low profile at this wedding is not working very well. Chardonnay, Gary, Ben and Jack are waiting for us.

'We need Sophie and Patsy in this one,' says Georgie. 'We want all our close friends. Where's Lucy?'

Lucy waves shyly from the side lines. She's pulled into the group and Rex, the photographer, orders us into our places. It's just my luck that he puts Ben at my side and Sophie in front of us.

'Okay, that looks brilliant. Move in closer Ben.'

Oh no.

Ben sidles closer to me and then I feel his arm around my waist. I cling onto Lucy's arm as a surge of desire for him shoots through me.

'Everyone say *pizza*,' laughs Chardonnay.

Rex clicks several times, and arranges us into different positions. Ben removes his arm from my waist without a word and moves next to Greg for another photo. As soon as it's over I grab a glass of Bucks Fizz from a waiter. It's usually my policy never to drink at weddings, the one's I organise that is. Believe me I drink pretty well at any other wedding. But this is a whole other ball game. I down the Bucks Fizz in one and then swipe another from a passing waiter. An announcement is made for dinner and everyone heads for the hotel entrance just as the first drops of rain begin to fall. I couldn't have timed it better. If only I could plan my love life as well as I plan other people's weddings.

You'd think as the wedding planner I would have remembered to change the seating plan. There had been so much to think of that I had completely forgotten to move myself to a different table. So, I find myself seated at the same one as Ben. It's the friend's table. And, as Patsy was seated with the other bridesmaids I was able to fit Chardonnay and Gary onto ours.

'We want you all to come to our wedding don't we Gal?' says Chardonnay, sipping her wine.

'Yeah,' agrees Gary.

'We 'ave to send out the invites soon don't we Amy?'

I nod.

'The 'all looks brill too, don't it Gal?'

'Yeah,' says Gary.

The hall does look good. It is exactly how I had imagined it would look for my own wedding to Greg. It's my own perfect wedding dream. Glass chandeliers hang from the ceiling and the walls are decorated with burning sconces, just as I had always imagined, and the crystal shimmers under their lights just as I knew they would. On every table is a single red rose in a tall crystal vase. This is my blissful reception. I move aside as a waiter places smoked salmon onto my plate and feel my arm brush Ben's, who sits beside me.

'Got your speech ready Ben?' Jack asks.

'Yup,' Ben nods.

'I remember I bloody lost mine,' laughs Jack. 'I was about to go back for it ...'

Rosie nudges him and he looks at me apologetically.

'It's okay,' I say.

'Shit, I'm sorry, Amy.'

'It's okay,' I say again, leaning across to a bottle of wine.

Ben reaches for the bottle and fills my glass.

'Thanks,' I say softly, not looking at him. I really don't know how I'm going to sit next to him for the next few hours without my body exploding from desire.

Heavy rain lashing against the French doors can be heard above the soft music from the live band. It seems for the first time in months everything is going right for Amy Perfect, or at least going right for Amy Perfect's Perfect Weddings business. I've decided to make lots of changes after this wedding. I'm going to go back to the Amy who gave up on love. After all, she was far happier than this one. Looking for love just makes you miserable if you want my opinion. I'll continue to plan other people's weddings, and by the way Jack and Rosie are glued to the hip at the moment, I can't see theirs being far off and then of course there's Chardonnay and Gary's, and a few more lined up on the calendar. Then maybe I'll go to Tibet and do yoga or something. Or is it India? Anyway, I'll go and meditate on those mantra things until I find myself again. Although how I managed to lose myself in the first place I'll never know. I'll come back all Zen like and happy. That's the plan anyway.

The MC raps on the microphone. Its speech time and Ben scrapes his chair back.

'Good afternoon ladies and gentlemen, boys and girls. For those of you that do not know me, my name is Ben Garret.

This is the first time I have been asked to carry out the best man duties, and I must confess to being extremely nervous. This must be the fifth time today I have left a warm seat with several pieces of paper in my hand. No, I'm only joking. Now I did read somewhere that a best man's speech should not take any longer than it takes the groom to make love. So, on that note ladies and gentlemen, and not wanting to disappoint, can I ask you all to raise your glasses as we toast the new Mr and Mrs Martin.'

There is much laughter as Greg stands up, his fists raised playfully.

'Only joking,' grins Ben. *'As with any wedding there is a list of people to say a few special words about and firstly I would like to thank you all on Georgie and Greg's behalf for making the journey here today to help celebrate this wonderful*

occasion. Thank you to the ushers, and a huge thank you to both sets of parents, Steven and Marilyn and Mitchell and Susan. Mitchell, I know you must have been the proudest father in the world today as you walked Gina down that aisle.

To the bridesmaids and flower girl, you all look absolutely amazing and have done a fantastic job today. I must say, I am looking forward to that first dance later tonight Patsy.'

Patsy blushes and lowers her head.

'And before I come to the most important couple I really must thank Miss Amy Perfect, sitting at the side of me.'

He looks down at me with a smile.

'Who planned every detail of this wedding from the invitations to the Tottenham style decorations at the church. I'm sure you will all agree that both the church and the hall are astounding in their beauty. Amy Perfect promised Greg and Georgina the perfect wedding and it can't be denied she gave it to them.'

There is loud applause and I blush profusely.

'And finally, I come to the bride and groom, Greg and Georgie. What more can I say other than Georgie, you look absolutely stunning, and Greg, I cannot thank you enough for giving me the chance to be your best man and sharing your special day.'

There are cheers from the guests.

'What can you say about a man who came from humble beginnings, a man who is now quickly working his way to the very top of his profession'

As a shipping clerk? Rosie and I glance at each other. Ben is generous, I'll give him that.

'A man who is beginning to distinguish himself at the highest and where nobody can say a bad word against him, so here's to your own import and export company Greg, and may it prosper.'

More cheers from the guests and wide eyes from me.

'Blimey,' whispers Rosie.

'Greg and I got to know each other properly when Greg met Gina. It didn't take long for me to realise that Greg's first love was football. He played football, watched football, talked football. I suppose you could say Greg lived football. After

many matches Greg would more often than not go home in a drunken state, some things don't change. We were only talking about this the other night, so I pointed out to Greg that you can base your marriage around football.

Ensure you are fully committed every week.

Try your best to score every Saturday.

No tackling from behind – especially on your wedding night.

When Greg asked me to be his best man I did have some questions. Who had dropped out? Was I really the best he could come up with? Having accepted the role, I'm pretty happy with how things have gone so far. Greg and Gina have been together for some time now, and seem to have found their soul mates in each other. In life, it's hard to imagine Romeo without Juliet, Posh without Becks, Angelina without Brad and Georgie without Greg. On a serious note though, Greg did set some initial ground rules regarding the best man speech. He asked me not to mention certain skeletons in his closet from the past which, fortunately for him I know very little about. There are some stories I could tell you about Greg though. There was the burger van and budgie story for example, or choosing the wrong card for his fiancée after proposing. Then there was our boozy night in Liverpool which frankly even I don't want to remember.

However, before I accepted to be best man and spill ALL the beans, Greg seemed pretty keen to strike up a deal with me. Ben he said, do me a favour, please go easy on me with the speech and I promise I'll let you be best man at my next wedding.'

Georgie gasps.

'Don't worry Gina, he was only joking.

For the next bit of my speech, I need a little assistance from you both. Gina, please can you put your hand flat on the table, and then Greg, place your hand on top of it. All will be revealed in a short time, but if you could leave your hands as they are I would appreciate it. Although I am not married myself, and I could bore you with that one but I won't, I thought it only fair that I offer you both a bit of advice for the future. Gina, the five key points you need to remember are:

A man will treat you right and always stand by your side.

A man will comfort you in times of trouble.

A man will shower you with gifts and compliments.

A man will please you and grant your every request.

But, most importantly and finally, make sure that each man does not know the other one's name.

Are those hands still together?

Greg, I now have a few things for you to consider.

Somebody once said marriage is a 50/50 partnership, but anybody who believes that knows nothing about women or fractions.

Never forget those three magical words ... 'You're right Georgie'.

The best way to remember your anniversary ... Forget it once.

But please, remember, Gina, don't keep him in the doghouse too long, he might give his bone to the woman next door.

After asking around today, it does appear that there is a lot of confusion over where they are going on their honeymoon. I thought, perhaps like many of you, that they were off somewhere warm and sunny like Jamaica. But now I am a little unsure. Having spoken to Greg before we went into church, I think they may be heading to North Wales. Well, that's what I assumed he meant when he said after the wedding he was going to Bangor for a week.

I'm sure you are all wondering why I asked Greg to place his hand on top of Gina's? I will now let you know. Greg ... As my final role as best man, it has been with great pleasure that I have been able to give you the last few minutes, in which you will have the upper hand over Gina in married life. I do hope you appreciate it mate.

On a serious note and joking apart, words cannot express how happy I am that you have finally tied the knot today. I know, and I am sure everybody else here would agree with me, Greg you could not have made a better choice in Gina.'

His eyes lower to mine and I look away quickly.

'For me, as I said earlier, it has been a great honour to be your best man today. I would just like to finish off with a quote

for all you romantics out there. 'Marriage is not about finding a person you can live with, it's about finding the person you can't live without.' In Gina, Greg has definitely found that person and vice versa.

So, ladies and gentlemen, it gives me immense pleasure, not to mention relief, to invite you all to stand one more time and raise your glasses, in a toast to Greg and Gina, the new Mr and Mrs Martin. We wish them well for the future and hope they enjoy a long and happy marriage.'

Everyone lifts their glasses.

'To Mr and Mrs Martin,' they chorus.

For some ridiculous reason that even I couldn't fathom, hearing the words Mr and Mrs Martin had me excusing myself to the loo. It suddenly occurred to me that I was never going to be Mrs anybody. I'd well and truly missed the boat.

Chapter Sixty-Six

My name is being called and I'm sitting on the loo with my knickers around my ankles and a toilet roll in my hand. I haven't got a single tear left in me. I'm overindulging in self-pity. Everyone has someone in their life. Rosie has Jack; Chardonnay has Gary; Georgina has Greg; Patsy has, well okay, maybe not everyone. All I've got to look forward to is Gerald. I might as well top myself right now.

'Amy, are you in there?' Lucy asks, tapping on the door.

'Why can't you leave me alone?'

'Because the bride is making her speech and she mentioned you and has something for you. Can you please come out?'

Bugger, talk about bad timing. I yank up my knickers, pull down my dress and open the loo door.

'Right,' sighs Lucy, 'scrub that face and let's go.'

I'm dragged from the ladies and led back into the hall where someone shouts,

'Here she is.'

Georgie goes to speak into the microphone but instead it lets out a high-pitched shriek. Someone fiddles with it and then Georgie says,

'Amy, we'd like to thank you for all your hard work and for giving us this wedding which is way beyond our dreams ...'

'But you'd buggered off to the loo,' laughs Greg.

I try to laugh with them but it's getting harder by the minute. Sophie comes forward in her pretty dress and dainty shoes and hands me a bouquet of flowers along with an envelope, and for one awful minute I think it is the same one the sheikh gave to Ben.

'It's a voucher for a day at the spa. You deserve it after this stress,' says Georgie, hugging me. Her wedding dress rustles under my hug.

'Thank you,' I whisper.

'A big hand for the lovely Amy,' shouts the MC.

There is applause and I go back to my seat, top up my wine glass and throw it back. The band strikes up and Greg and Georgie take to the dance floor for their first dance.

'Flowers, a voucher *and* you get paid. Can't be bad,' smiles Chardonnay.

'Indeed,' says Ben.

I turn to face him.

'What does that mean?' I demand.

'I was agreeing,' he shrugs.

'No you weren't. You were hinting that I charge too much and don't deserve the flowers and voucher as well.'

'I never said ...'

Before he can finish, the music stops and the MC shouts into the microphone,

'Okay, all you single ladies, line up.'

'Ooh, I want to catch this,' cries Patsy, jumping up.

'Come on,' says Rosie, pulling me from my seat. 'You've got to be in on this.'

I'm tugged to the queue of single ladies. Do we look desperate or what? Georgie smiles before turning her back to us.

'Okay ladies, I want a clean fight,' says the MC.

After a count of three, Georgie throws her sweet pea bouquet over her shoulder. There is a female rugby scrum for it. It glides through the air and there is no doubt where it is heading. Several girls fall over each other in their bid to catch it. There are screams of excitement as they leap up to reach it, but they don't stand a chance. Without taking a single step forward Rosie holds out her hands and the bouquet falls straight into them.

'Faaackinell,' shouts Chardonnay above the screams of the girls.

'Lucky cow,' Patsy yells, hugging her.

I kiss her on the cheek.

'Congratulations, future bride,' I smile.

I make my way back to the table to collect my clutch, the flowers and envelope. My head is thumping from the stress of the day and the tears I had just allowed myself to stupidly indulge in.

'You're not leaving are you?' says Rosie as I throw my shawl around my shoulders.

'I've got a thumping headache. I really don't think I could sit through a live band.'

'I can drive you home,' offers Jack.

'I'll call the cab. He was coming back for me anyway.'

I make my way over to Georgie and Greg who are jiving on the dance floor. The music jars through my head and I have to shout to get them to hear me.

'I'm making a move,' I yell above the music. 'I've got a splitting headache.'

'Oh no,' says Georgie sympathetically.

'I've had a wonderful day seeing you enjoy your perfect wedding.'

'Oh Amy,' says Georgie, hugging me. 'We'll see you when we get back from the honeymoon, won't we?'

'Of course you will.'

I somehow think they will be too busy. I hug Greg and find myself wondering what I ever saw in him and then phone the cab driver before hugging everyone else and heading out of the hall and down the stairs to the foyer. Through the revolving doors I can see the rain lashing down.

'Do you have a coat madam?' asks the doorman.

I shake my head and check my BlackBerry. There's a message from my cab driver.

'Traffic is bad. I'll be twenty minutes.'

I'm about to fumble in my clutch for some painkillers when I see Ben running down the stairs. Oh no, I'm really not up to a confrontation with him. My head is thumping unmercifully and I'm having difficulty holding back my tears. It's as though everything has crashed around me and I feel like I'm the only person in the world without any hope of happiness. Karma is punishing in the way that it should, and I'm not taking my punishment very well.

'Amy wait,' he calls.

What for him to have another go at me? No, I don't think so. I look through the revolving doors to see if the cab has arrived. Damn, there is no sign of it. I push my way through the doors and hope I don't do my usual party trick of swinging my way straight back and into Ben's arms.

But I don't. The rain is pelting down and within seconds I'm drenched. My slip dress clings to my thighs and my bouquet droops under the pressure of the downfall. The doors whirl behind me and I turn to see Ben.

'You're soaked,' he says.

'I'm fine,' I say stupidly.

I'm not really. Even Elnett supreme hold is struggling.

'It's just a bit of rain.'

That's an understatement. It's a sodding monsoon.

'Have you reached that point where you just can't get any wetter?' he smiles.

'This isn't a film,' I say.

Romantic films have happy endings don't they, but I'm far from the happy ending.

He steps towards me.

'Amy, there is so much to say. You can't just rush off like this.'

His jacket is drenched within seconds. We look like two well-dressed drowned rats.

'It wasn't until I made my speech that I realised ...'

'Realised what?' I ask before holding my breath.

'That I don't want to let you go. I've been an arrogant fool. It was wrong of you to lie about who you were, but you thought Greg was the love of your life and if you don't go to extremes for the love of your life then when will you?'

'But what I did was wrong,' I say, looking for the cab driver. 'I know that and I'm paying for it. I had no right to try and come between Georgie and Greg.'

'But you put it right Amy. You more than put it right and I was wrong to judge you without knowing the facts. The truth is I was jealous as hell of that prince bloke.'

He was?

'He sent you a letter,' I say. 'Was it to cause trouble?'

He laughs.

'I'd show you it but it won't stand a chance out here. But no, it wasn't to cause trouble. I think he wants to put things right.'

The cab heads down the driveway towards us.

'You should get out of the rain,' I say softly.

'The worst thing that can happen is I'll drown,' he smiles before adding, 'We could have chosen a better movie to re-enact don't you think. *Notting Hill* would have been a lot dryer.'

I can barely breathe. All I want to do is gaze at him but it's bloody difficult with torrents of rain falling on your head.

'I'm sorry I wasn't more supportive about the Prince. I couldn't see past my jealousy and my anger at you about Gina.'

'Sorry I'm late,' calls the cab driver. 'You're bleedin' drenched ain't ya?'

'I should go,' I say, while not moving at all. The truth is I can't get any wetter.

'If it's any consolation I don't think you charge enough. This wedding was priceless. You certainly didn't overcharge for this one.'

'Thank you,' I say, turning to the cab.

'Amy, can I ask you one question?'

I nod.

'When we've dried off, do you think you might like to spend some time with me? Take in a movie, have a drink, walk in the rain. Maybe not a Tsunami next time but ...'

I exhale. Is this really happening? Is Ben Garret asking me out?

'Well, I was thinking of going to Tibet to meditate, but I could put that on hold.'

'If it's not too much trouble?' he grins.

'It's no trouble at all,' I smile.

'You want the cab or what?' calls the driver.

Ben cups my face in his hands.

'I don't think we do, do we?'

I shake my head and then I am his arms, his warm lips on mine and I'm in heaven, and I really don't care if they have opened.

'You two are aware it's pissing down aren't ya?' asks the cabbie.

'Is it?' I smile. 'I hadn't noticed.'

And with that I return my lips to Ben's.

It Had to Be You

When 29-year-old Binki Grayson is offered a Christmas bonus by her boss at the office party she didn't imagine he meant a quickie over his desk. Things for Binki just go from bad to worse and by Christmas Day she is not only jobless but boyfriend-less, so when she discovers her late Aunt Vera has left her something in her will she thinks things can only get better. What  she doesn't realise is that her inheritance comes with a complication by the name of William Ellis.

A mishmash of misunderstandings, sex-shop escapades, high finance and a blooming romance make *It Had to Be You* another hilarious romantic comedy by the uproarious Lynda Renham.

Fifty Shades of Roxie Brown

Roxie Brown loves erotica and her friend, Sylvie, loves crime ... novels of course. On a girls' night out they meet The Great Zehilda, the tea leaf reader, and suddenly Roxie's Fifty Shades fantasies about her millionaire boss, Ark Morgan, look about to become a reality. But then she looks through the telescope and her life is turned upside down. Roxie and Sylvie, with help from Sylvie's flatmate, Felix, set out to crack the case. Can Ark Morgan save her or is he the man she should be running from? Then enter Sam Lockwood and her heart is shot with another arrow. Come with Roxie Brown on her hilarious crime-busting romantic adventure and discover if the love of her life is the man of her dreams or if the man she loves is her worst nightmare.